PRAISE FOR *TIED*

"Carian Cole did not hold back with this story. I dare you not to shed a tear."

—LJ Shen, *USA Today* and *Wall Street Journal*
bestselling author of *Vicious*

"Poignant, raw, and real. *Tied* will leave an indelible imprint on your heart."

—Meredith Wild, #1 *New York Times* bestselling author

"This book owned me. Soulmates tangled in a forbidden, twisted situation. Every word is painfully beautiful."

—Abbi Glines, #1 *New York Times* bestselling author

"Carian Cole is a master storyteller. Beautifully poetic, *Tied* is a journey of two damaged souls who find love and healing in each other." —Gemma James, *USA Today* bestselling author

ALSO BY CARIAN COLE

TIED

CARIAN COLE

FOREVER

NEW YORK   BOSTON

*For those who choose to hide in the shadows, away from
everything the light reveals . . . you're beautiful.
Yes, you.*

Forever
Hachette Book Group
1290 Avenue of the Americas, New York, NY 10104
read-forever.com

Originally published in ebook by Forever in July 2023
First trade paperback edition: April 2024

Forever is an imprint of Grand Central Publishing. The Forever name and logo
are registered trademarks of Hachette Book Group, Inc.

The publisher is not responsible for websites (or their content)
that are not owned by the publisher.

The Hachette Speakers Bureau provides a wide range of authors for
speaking events. To find out more, go to hachettespeakersbureau.com or
email HachetteSpeakers@hbgusa.com.

Forever books may be purchased in bulk for business, educational, or promotional
use. For information, please contact your local bookseller or the Hachette Book
Group Special Markets Department at special.markets@hbgusa.com.

Print book interior design by Emily Baker

Library of Congress Control Number: 2023950951

ISBNs: 9781538766002 (trade paperback); 9781538766019 (ebook)

Printed in the United States of America

LSC-C

Printing 1, 2024

PROLOGUE

Once upon a time...

I watch as the flames crawl across the pages of the pink-bound book, obliterating the tiny words until that very first sentence goes up in flames and smoke.

One by one, I toss all my childhood fairy-tale books into the fire and watch them get eaten by the orange flames. Tears spill down my hot cheeks, and strong arms embrace me from behind, pulling me back against his chest before I can fling myself into the fire to save my precious books. Those worn pages, and the stories they hold, once saved my life.

It's more than just the books, though. I want to feel the searing burn of flesh like he did. I want the smoke to seep into my lungs and suffocate me like it did to him.

"Let it all go." His warm lips brush against my ear as he pulls us backward, his arms tightening around me.

He always knows what I'm thinking, what I need to hear or feel from him—often before I do. He understands the aches of my heart and the memories that lurk and claw at my soul. He's the only one who knows how to chase it all away.

When the last page has burned, and there's nothing left but ash and memories, we turn away. He drapes his arm across my shoulder, presses his lips to the top of my head, and leads us from the fire as wisps of smoke trail after us like ghosts not wanting to be left behind.

This is where it ends.

Exactly where we began.

CHAPTER 1

Tyler

The stillness of daybreak has been my favorite time of day for as long as I can remember. That short span of time between dark and light, when the day is slowly awakening, has always felt surreal to me.

And quiet. So very quiet. With the exception of chirping birds and other woodland creatures. But I don't consider that noise.

Sunbeams peek through the trees. Morning dew glistens over the mossy forest trail beneath my boots as I walk through the woods, barely making a sound. I'm not an intruder here, among the lifting fog and the faint singing of birds—this is home. I've walked this path hundreds of times.

I *am* daybreak and dusk. I'm no longer light or dark, but some vague, messed-up place in the middle.

I'm the gray area.

Pausing, I tilt my head at the odd sound coming from my left, recognizing it as the same noise I heard out here yesterday but didn't have time to check out. I push the hood of my sweatshirt off my head, straining to hear the sound again, but all I hear is my own breath for a full minute.

Urgh! Urrgh!

At first, I think it's a deer huffing, but I've never heard one sound like that before. It seems to be making the sound too often, and too frantically. Veering off the trail, I make my way through the trees toward the sound. It could be the lost dog I've been trying to find for the past week, possibly hurt or caught in a trap. Dogs get lost up here in the woods all the time, usually with hikers who think their dogs would never run off chasing a squirrel and not come back when called.

So I, Tyler Grace, the alleged small-town psycho, lure and catch the lost dogs and bring them back to their owners. Actually, that's not true. I don't bring them back myself. I let someone much more sociable do that part. I let them play the hero. I just like the thrill of chasing and catching things. It satisfies my inner stalker.

Urgh!

The tortured, haunting sound makes my neck hairs stand on end, and an uneasy feeling settles deep in my gut. As I walk deeper into the woods, the noise grows louder until it sounds as if I'm practically right on top of it, but I see nothing.

Urgh!

Fuck. I *am* on top of it. The sound is coming from somewhere beneath me.

What the hell?

I kneel and run my hands through the layer of dead leaves covering the ground, confused and not sure what I'm looking for until my hand catches on something hard that feels like rusted metal. I brush more of the leaves aside, and a chill settles in my bones when I realize what it is.

Nestled into the dirt is a round wooden door. I grasp the rusty metal knob and slide a heavy wooden door to the side to reveal what may have been a well or shelter at one time. I blink and stare down into the dark hole, thinking the scene in front of me is going to disappear, but it doesn't.

There's a teenage girl down there, staring back up at me

with sheer terror in her huge eyes, rocking back and forth. She's huddled against the earth wall clutching a small white dog, and it makes that horrible sound I now recognize as the sound of a dog with its vocal cords severed. A child's purple backpack is on the ground next to her, torn and dirty, and it reminds me of one my little sister had when she was young. It's cool out here in the woods, especially during early fall in this part of New Hampshire, so she must be chilled to the bone down in that hole.

I yank my cell phone from the back pocket of my jeans and dial 911, relieved that, by some miracle, I have service up here in the middle of the woods.

"Nine-one-one. What is your emergency?"

I need help! my brain screams. *I found a girl. In a hole. In the woods.*

"Hello? May I help you? Are you there?"

Just send someone. She's a mess.

"Are you hurt? If you're there, please try to speak. I'm right here to help you, but I need to know where you are."

"Try to speak," she says. I almost laugh. I can't even remember the last time words came out of my mouth. And now that I have to, I can't seem to get the words to come down from my head and past my lips.

The girl with the tangled wild hair and her little dog continue to stare at me as I swallow hard and force my brain and mouth to get their shit together.

It's like riding a bike, Ty. You don't forget how to talk.

"A girl...in the woods," I rasp. "A hole." My voice is strained and unnatural, too loud or maybe too soft, much like the dog's strangled bark.

"There's a girl in the woods? Is that what you're saying?"

"Yes."

"Is she hurt?"

"Maybe."

"Are you hurt?"

"No."

"Are you with her?"

"Yes."

"Are you in the hole with her?"

"No."

"Do you know her name?"

"No." I cough into the phone. My throat is dry and raw, and I'm already exhausted from this interrogation. How hard is it to just get help?

"What is your name, sir?"

"I'm going to get her."

"Can you tell me your location?"

My throat catches again with the struggle to make more words. "Five miles off Rock Road. Old hiking trail. On the left. Not far from the river."

Ending the call, I peer back down into the hole. It's about four feet in diameter and maybe ten feet deep. I reach behind me and grab the eight-foot dog leash that's hanging off my belt, wrap some of it around my wrist, and toss the other end into the hole.

I nod at her, hoping she'll understand my plan, but she gives me a leery glare and moves backward like the leash is going to bite her.

Talk to her. "Grab it. I'll pull you out."

Her mouth parts slightly, and she pulls the dog closer, protectively, against her chest, and I realize she's afraid I expect her to leave the dog down there.

"Hold the dog. Grab the leash. I'll pull you both out."

She stands painstakingly slowly, picks up her tattered backpack, loops her arm through it, then shuffles hesitantly toward the dangling leash. Her feet are bare, poking out from a pair of threadbare sweatpants that look about four sizes too big for her. A very thin once-white T-shirt is barely visible beneath her tangled waist-length blond hair and the furry dog she's got in a bear hug.

"It's okay. I'm going to help you," I say when her eyes dart from me to the leash, then back to me again. Her teeth clamp down on her bottom lip as she grasps the leash.

"Hold on tight," my voice growls. "Don't let go. I can pull you up."

Pulling her out of the hole is easy, and it's not because I work out a lot. The truth is she weighs next to nothing. The words *starving, malnourished,* and *anorexic* spring to the forefront of my mind. I'd be surprised if she weighs ninety pounds, including the dog and whatever she's got in that backpack. With both hands, she hangs on to the leash with the dog against her chest, his paws over her shoulder as if he somehow knows he should be hanging on. Her body scrapes and bounces along the rough dirt side of the hole as I pull her up, but she doesn't let go, not even when I pull her onto the ground next to me.

"It's okay," I repeat as softly as I can, but my voice isn't very comforting with its fucked-up, hoarse, raspy tone that I can't change.

She leans against me as I kneel next to her, one of her hands gripping my shirt, the other holding the dog at her side, her forehead pressed against my shoulder. I can actually feel her heartbeat, beating wildly in her chest like a hummingbird.

"Shhh... You're going to be okay now. I promise."

I can't ignore what I see. Scars, some old and some new, mark her arms and the tops of her feet and, no doubt, places I can't see. But when our eyes meet, the damage and torment I see there is far worse. *Just like me.* My heartbeat skips when she stares up at me, at my face, and she doesn't recoil at what she sees. She looks right in my eyes, unwavering, and she sees *me*. She lets out a deep, shuddering breath that sounds like it's been bottled up inside her for a very long time.

But the moment quickly passes, and I tense up when her entire body begins to tremble, her arms wrapping tighter around her little dog as her pale blue-gray eyes slowly slide away from mine and shift to something behind me, widening with new fear.

I realize we're not alone.

I turn to see a man coming toward us, his lips set in a grim line, fists clenched at his sides.

"No...no...no," the girl whispers frantically behind me as I rise to my feet. "The bad man is coming."

He quickly closes the space between us and throws a punch at me before I have a chance to block him. His fist crashes into the side of my face. I shake my head, then throw my body against his and take him down hard to the ground. Suddenly, he's clutching an eight-inch blade in his hand that he must have pulled from a hiding place on his body before I took him down.

He came prepared.

His eyes are dark, blank pits, and if the saying that the eyes are the window to the soul is true, this man definitely has no soul. I can almost feel the evil radiating off him, and his determination to win this fight. I wrestle him for the knife as he tries to sink it into my gut, knowing without a doubt that he'll definitely kill me if I don't get it out of his grip.

Fighting to twist the knife out of his hand, I get on top of him, my knees pinning his shoulders down. Suddenly the girl appears, holding a large rock in her shaking hands. A scream erupts from her as she brings the rock down hard on his head. He lets out a surprised grunt, his eyes rolling back into his head, and slowly goes limp. He drops the knife, which she grabs and throws a few feet away. She's panting and shaking from the effort, but her eyes meet mine for a second. There's determination and strength there as she stares back at me. There is silent agreement.

The little dog makes those pitiful sounds, its whole body wriggling and wanting to attack, but it stays near its master: the girl. When I hear low moaning, I look back down at her captor. At a face I've never seen before with eyes that don't deserve to see the light of day. Amazingly, the hit to the head doesn't faze him for long, and I don't even see any blood oozing from him. Once again, he focuses his venomous eyes on me. A strange sense of déjà vu comes over me as I grab his throat with both hands and squeeze.

It's going to be him or me. I knew that the moment I saw him coming for the girl. He isn't going to allow her to leave him, and he isn't going to be caught.

I make a choice.

I commit to it.

I execute it.

There's no going back. No second thought. No momentary hesitation.

I squeeze his throat harder as he struggles beneath me, grabbing my hands with his own, kicking his legs up. But he grows weak and I grow strong, and I win.

The girl sobs on the ground behind me, and the dog lets out its pitiful howl, which sends a chill down my spine as years of anguish break free from the cage of my heart. It swirls up inside me like a tornado and unleashes its destruction as I choke him to death.

I witness his last breath, hear his last gurgle, and feel him go lifeless beneath me.

And fuck…it feels good.

♥ ♥ ♥

I stand and slowly back away from the well-dressed body of the man I just killed. I try to catch my breath, my heart racing from the rush of adrenaline and this sick shock coursing through me like lightning.

I just killed someone with my hands. A total stranger. He could be anyone—her father, her boyfriend, a kidnapper. I have no idea, and the fact that I don't care is both surprising and concerning. Regardless, he tried to hurt me and I stopped him, and it's given me a euphoric high that hasn't subsided yet.

I flex my sore fingers, continuing to eye him to make sure he doesn't get up.

The sound of scurrying behind me forces me to tear my gaze off the body to find the girl running farther into the woods after the dog, which has suddenly bolted.

"Get him!" the girl yells.

I take off after them, afraid they're both going to get themselves lost out here in the woods. The girl's bare feet must be getting torn to shreds as she runs over rocks and dried leaves, but it doesn't stop her from chasing after the small white dog.

"Stop chasing him," I yell, but I'm not sure she hears me or can make out my hoarse, choppy words. Chasing a running dog only makes it run more. If she would stop chasing him and just sit and wait, he'd most likely stop and come back to look for her.

"Freeze!"

The deep voice booms through the forest behind me and for a moment, I think it's the man I just strangled—not dead, after all. I stop in my tracks, then glance back and realize it's not him.

"Get him!" the girl shrieks.

"Put your hands up and don't move." Three cops have guns

aimed at me as they inch closer. Their eyes are locked on me, waiting for me to either run off or pull out a weapon of my own.

Oh shit. They think she's telling them to get *me*.

I don't resist. I don't try to say anything at all. I do exactly what they tell me to do, their guns still pointed at me and each officer waiting for me to make the wrong move. I slowly put my hands over my head as two of the officers come after me and the other goes after the girl.

I had completely forgotten about the 911 call and, honestly, I'm surprised they were able to find us. But I now notice that the whole scene is suddenly crawling with people.

Confusion shrouds my brain as I'm put in handcuffs. It hits me how this appears as I look around, at everyone's hard glares and the accusations on their faces. I barely listen to the officer reading me my rights. They march me past the hole and the dead body that's being covered, toward the dirt road where several police cars and an ambulance are waiting with strobing lights. Panic has caused my voice to retreat to its hiding place, where it's only heard in my own head.

Let me go.

I didn't hurt her.

I saved her.

Hands push me roughly into the back seat of the police car, and the door is slammed in my face before the officer walks away to talk to someone else. The girl is being carried—crying, arms and legs flailing—into the back of the ambulance by a male and a female officer. We lock eyes before the doors of the ambulance are closed.

I only wanted to save you.

Tell them I saved you.

Tell them I'm not crazy.

CHAPTER 2

Holly

When I close my eyes, I replay the moment he found me.

I was frozen with fear and fascination as he strangled the bad man. I watched as the man who had kept me for years struggled to breathe, his eyes bulging from his head. As much as I wanted him dead, a twinge of guilt twisted up like a vine around my emotions as I witnessed his death. He was, after all, the hand that fed me. He was the only person I had seen or had any interaction with for years.

The man choking him was an animal with long, messy blond hair and wild eyes, his muscular arms and hands covered with brightly colored tattoos. His voice was rough and raw, but it was the most beautiful sound I'd ever heard. He killed my captor with zero hesitation. Once he gained control, that was it. The powerful fierceness that poured from him was controlled. Owned. Unstoppable. He had no fear.

He was beautiful. Exquisite. My captivation quickly shifted from the man who took me to the man who now mesmerized me with every fiber of his existence. He was, in every way, the man I knew would save me.

♥ ♥ ♥

Too much is happening at once. There are too many people, too many sounds, too many smells, too much brightness. Too much everything. I need my books. I need Poppy.

And where is the prince?

I know these people are doctors and police officers because I've seen them on television. Not these exact ones, but similar ones. I lie motionless on a hospital bed as they poke at me, hoping if I don't move maybe they'll get bored and go away. Or maybe some crisis will happen, and they'll all run from my room and forget me to go witness a fight or a proposal. That's what usually happens on TV.

I'm free. The realization suddenly hits me.

"Can you tell me your name, sweetheart?" asks a gray-haired nurse. She has a friendly, sincere smile that makes me want to smile back. Earlier, she gently helped me into a thin robe that feels scratchy against my skin. She keeps trying to hold my hand, but I pull it away and shove it under my body to hide it from her. I don't mind the smiles, but I don't want touching.

My name, my name. What is my name?

Hollipop, Hollipop, you're my little Hollipop...

The song Mommy used to sing to me floats through my head. Her voice is as clear as it was way back then, but that's not my name.

Is it?

I'm given a glass of orange juice and cookies on a tray next to the bed, and my stomach twists at the sight of them. Cold juice! I want the treats so bad my hands tremble and my mouth waters, but I'm afraid to touch them and bring them to my lips. Nice things mean something bad will happen, and I don't want any more bad things to happen today. I resist the urge to throw them at her.

"You must be thirsty and hungry," the nurse coaxes, and I want so badly to trust her, but I've heard those words before. "Do you want something different, honey? I can get you soda, or water, or apple juice. I have crackers, or I can get you a bowl of chicken soup?"

I want every single thing she listed.

Instead, I shake my head defiantly. No, I'm not willing to trade today. I can still stand. I can still lift my head. I can still see clearly. I am not yet sick or weak enough to give in to trading.

Disappointment and concern shadow her face. "You can talk to me. You're safe now. The doctor will be in soon, and she's going to have a nice talk with you and the police officer, so we can find your family and get you home."

My heart jumps to my throat, and air rushes up my lungs. Home? I can go home? Mommy and Daddy will finally come get me?

He told me I'd never see my family again and I'd never be going home again. Not ever. He said they didn't want me anymore and had replaced me with a new little girl who was better than me. Is it possible they're really coming for me?

My head falls back onto the pillows, my eyelids growing heavy. I remember beds and pillows now, how soft and warm they are. I don't ever want to lift my head from this softness again.

Clutching my backpack close to me, I let the wave of exhaustion take hold of me so I can dream of my prince with his bright blue eyes. I always knew he would come save me.

Strangers wake me up and smile unfamiliar smiles at me as they talk and whisper among themselves in the corner of the room and in the hallway outside my door. I have no idea how long I've been here, or how long I've been asleep. There's a clock on the wall, but I forgot how to tell time long ago. The sun shining through the blinds is startling, and I want to go to the window and stare outside. I want to feel the warmth on my face.

I don't know who these people in my room are, but they're wearing uniforms so they must be important.

"Where is Poppy?" I finally ask to no one in particular.

"Who is Poppy?" the nearest woman asks, taking a step closer. The others turn, waiting for my reply.

No one has talked back to me in so long that I'm surprised whenever these new people respond to me. I'm used to watching people talk on television, and sometimes I talked to them, but they never actually talked back or asked me questions.

"My friend," I answer.

She smiles encouragingly. "Was someone else being held with you in the woods?"

"Yes, Poppy."

"Is Poppy a boy or a girl?"

"A boy."

"What happened to Poppy?"

"Poppy ran away. We have to find him. The bad man might get him and hurt him." Fear, confusion, and sadness wash over me in a wave. Poppy and I need each other. He must be just as scared as I am right now.

The woman steps closer to the bed and holds up a photograph. "Is this the bad man?" she asks, her voice low, almost soothing. "Or is this Poppy?"

I shake my head, my eyes locked onto the photo. "No. That's the prince. He came to save us."

She nods slowly. "I see. Can you tell me your name?"

I stare back at her, only wanting to take the picture from her so I can keep it. I have been asked my name so many times but...

"Hollipop," I whisper.

The woman smiles again, nodding vigorously. "Yes, that's *very* good. It's Holly," she says. "Holly Daniels."

Her words make my breath catch, and those two words repeat over and over like an echo: *HollyDanielsHollyDanielsHollyDaniels-HollyDaniels...*

I pull my backpack closer and lift it onto my lap. On the back, across the top, are faint letters written in black magic marker. Mommy wrote them so I would know it was mine.

The woman leans closer, following my finger as I run it slowly over the faded letters, which are just barely visible. "This is you," she says softly. "You're Holly Daniels. You were kidnapped when you were five years old. Do you remember, Holly?"

Yes. I remember the bad man pulling up to my friend Sammi and me on the sidewalk while we were walking home from school. He grabbed my arm so hard I screamed. My friend screamed, too, and I watched her run away. I watched her leave me alone. I remember being yanked into the back seat of a dark car and a big hand being held over my mouth. I remember the taste of blood when I bit him.

"You've been gone for eleven years, Holly," she tells me very gently. "You're safe now, and your family is on their way here right now."

My hands grip the tattered backpack filled with my books. Eleven years...that can't be true...It just can't. I know how to add—I practiced with rocks and my books—and eleven years is so many. Eleven years is a big pile of little rocks.

All the questions made me remember my time with the man, especially the beginning. At first, I cried nonstop and begged to go home. When that didn't happen, I prayed for someone to come get me. When that didn't happen, I tried to find a way out of the room I was trapped in. When there was no way out, I read my books, over and over and over, losing myself in the stories until I became a part of them. That's how I found out the prince would come save me. It was in all the books, clear as day. So I waited as patiently as I could for him to come.

Even after the bad man gave me a television, I continued to read the books every day. They were my lifeline and the only thing I had that was mine, from before the bad man. Mommy always told me I was very smart for my age. I could read things my friends couldn't. She said I was special and gifted. I slept with my head on my backpack, using it as a pillow, and the words from the books inside seeped into my dreams, saving me little by little, telling me not to give up hope. Sometimes the man would take me out of the basement, cover my head with something dark and smelly, and carry me to a hole in the woods. He'd leave me there, to make me appreciate him more. I have no idea how long he kept me in the hole each time, but it felt like forever. And he was right. I was always glad to see him when he came back and pulled me out. Even he was better than total darkness and silence.

I didn't realize it had taken the prince eleven years to finally come, but he did, and that's all that mattered. I wonder when he'll be coming back for me, to take me to the happily-ever-after part.

I hope it will be soon.

As much as I kick, scream, and play dead, people continue to fuss over me, making me feel very uncomfortable. They wash me and brush my hair, and I scream the entire time until they finally leave, allowing me to breathe a sigh of relief. I wish I could change the channel and see something else now. I don't like this show anymore.

I pick at the food they gave me, leery of its hidden agenda, odd textures, and flavors. I yank it all apart with my fingers and nibble on tiny pieces, my tongue searching for a hint of acrid flavor that will make me feel tired and sick. After my meal, I huddle on the bed, pulling the thin white sheet against me, wondering what's going to happen next. My question is answered instantly when a group of people burst into the room and close the door behind them.

Trapped in a moment I once begged and cried for, I feel numb, both mentally and in my heart. They stare at me, and I stare back. At first I don't recognize them, but slowly their faces merge with my memories and small flickers of recognition speed up my pulse.

My parents look older, with slightly graying hair, but they still look like they do in my very dim memories. My mother looks a lot like I remember her, still with shoulder-length blond hair, the same color as mine. She's beautiful, like a movie star. My older brother is a handsome man now, not a teenage boy who used to give me rides on his shoulders and push me on a swing in our backyard. My father looks like an older version of my brother, with the same light brown hair, although my father has gray streaks through his. They have the same brown eyes. Both of them are big, strong, and athletic.

I shift my attention back to the TV on the wall, unease rippling through me at the way they're looking at me. Like they're waiting for me to do something that I don't know how to do, or expecting me to say words that will take away the pain and confusion in their eyes.

I'm in a cloud of surrealness, and I feel nothing but curiosity about these people as they stare at me. As the seconds tick by, I become more and more uncomfortable under their intense expressions and sobs, and I wish they would go away. I want Poppy. I want my prince. They don't look at me this way.

My parents suddenly come forward and try to hug me, and my body stiffens from the unwelcome, foreign touch. I should know them, and feel safe with them, but I don't. They're just as much strangers to me as the nurses and doctors who have been coming and going.

Instinctively, my hand rises in self-defense when my mother reaches out to touch my face, and she starts to cry so hard my father has to console her and guide her away from me. I let my mind drift back to my stories, where it's safe and comfortable.

Once upon a time, there was a beautiful girl...

"Holly? Are you listening?" My brother, Zac, has pulled a chair next to my bed and lightly touches my arm. "Holly?"

"Huh?" I shake my head and blink at him. I didn't realize he was talking to me. I forgot Holly is me.

"You're going to be okay," he says hesitantly. He smiles, but when I don't return it, it falters. "I always knew someday you would come home. I missed you. We all did. We just can't believe you're really here."

I nod and hug my backpack tighter. He reaches a hand toward me again, but I shrink back. He blinks at me with a look of surprise and hurt at my reaction and then pulls his hand away.

"Whatever happened, it doesn't matter. It's all behind you now." He pauses, his expression sincere and almost hopeful as he leans forward. "All that matters now is that you're home where you belong, and you're safe."

I listen, but my eyes are on my parents, who are now out in the hallway talking to doctors and police people. And a cute little blond girl is holding my mother's hand.

"Who's that?" I ask, my voice barely a whisper.

Zac's eyes follow mine questioningly before he turns back to me. "That's Lizzie," he says carefully. "Our little sister. She just turned six."

My teeth clench as I scan her from head to toe. Lizzie looks almost exactly like I did before the bad man came and took me away. A perfect, happy little girl with braided hair and clean clothes, hanging on to Mommy's hand. She glances around nervously at the people walking by, and Mommy pulls her closer to her, protectively.

The bad man hadn't been lying about a replacement.

Zac's mouth is set in a thin line as he watches me for a few long moments. "Mom didn't think you'd be ready to meet her yet," he says, his tone flat. "They didn't want you to feel overwhelmed."

Overwhelmed isn't what I'm feeling at all.

I'm feeling like this is a show I never want to watch again.

CHAPTER 3

Tyler

I'm not sure how the news traveled so fast, but somehow what happened in the woods has spread like wildfire in this small town. By the time the cops bring me to the station, a crowd of crazy, pissed-off people is waiting in the parking lot, yelling names and accusations at me as the cops try to maneuver me through them to get to the door:

Kidnapper!

You're a monster!

Pedophile!

You'll burn in hell, you freak!

Murderer!

Rot in prison!

Lock the psycho up!

I use my shoulder to wipe someone's spit off the side of my face and keep my head down. I became an outcast in this town when I was seventeen years old, so I'm used to people staring at me and treating me like a sideshow freak. But I still can't believe these idiots think I could actually hurt a young girl. I'm the one who found her and saved her from that psychopath. Doesn't that make me the hero? *Fucking morons.*

🖤 🖤 🖤

"What were you doing out in the woods so early in the morning?"

I stare at the wall behind their heads, craving a cigarette really bad and getting edgier by the minute. The bright light of the room is bothering my eyes, and the walls are closing in on me.

For hours the detectives have had me holed up in this tiny, stale room at the station, asking me the same questions, which I don't try to answer. After the display in the parking lot, I don't trust anyone. Especially when they're all trying to pin kidnapping and murder charges on me.

"We know you can talk, Tyler, so cut the shit," Britton says. The haggard-looking older detective doesn't hide his disgust for me. He checks his watch for the hundredth time, then glares at me. "We're tired. Answer the fucking questions so we can all get out of here."

Taking a deep breath, I close my eyes and thrum my fingers on the table between us. Nobody understands how hard it is to make myself talk, how much my own ears hate hearing my voice, or how difficult it is to just get the words out of my head, especially when I'm stressed out. I'm not stupid—I know part of it is psychological and part of it is physical, but that doesn't make a rat's ass bit of difference to me.

Britton leans forward, his small eyes narrowing even more. "One more time. What were you doing out there?"

When I don't answer, the younger detective—Nelson, I think his name is—impatiently pushes a pen and a pad of paper across the table to me. "Just write down your answers, then. We can't sit here all day."

I grab the pen and write quickly:

I live up there. I walk every morning.

They exhale simultaneously and exchange glances.

"And you just happened to stumble upon a girl in a hidden hole in the ground?" Britton's voice is dripping with sarcasm.

I nod but write:

Yes. I heard a noise. It was the dog.

"What dog?" Nelson asks, frowning.

The girl's dog.

The detectives glance at each other. "We didn't find any dog," Nelson states firmly.

It ran off. It was there. It was making a strange noise. It was debarked.

"Debarked?" Nelson reads my words out loud, confusion on his face.

I shift in my chair and scribble some more.

It's when a dog's vocal cords are severed so it can't bark.

Nelson raises a suspicious eyebrow. "And you know this... how?"

I read a lot.

The detective tilts his head to the side and smirks at me. "Maybe you're the one who took the girl. Maybe the guy who's dead is the one who was trying to save her. That's what everyone is thinking."

A demonic laugh comes out of me, and while not deliberate, it's fitting.

Stop fucking with me. I didn't do anything.

"We don't like you, Tyler," Britton states coldly. "We don't like your creepy ass living in the woods, and we don't like your fucked-up face riding that piece-of-shit motorcycle through town in the middle of the night and annoying the good people of this nice, quiet town."

I lean back and chew the inside of my cheek, then grab the pen again.

There's no law against being ugly, living in the woods, or riding a motorcycle at night.

Nelson scoffs. "There *is* a law against murdering people, though."

It was self-defense. He pulled a knife on me. He had that girl in a hole. Ask her. Check the evidence. You guys know how to do that, right?

"Well, that's the funny thing," Nelson drawls. "Maybe what you have is contagious because the girl won't talk."

I don't blame her. Most conversations aren't worth having.

Maybe she doesn't want to talk to two assholes.

Nelson looks up from my writing and glares at me. "Watch yourself, buddy. Why were you chasing her when the officers found you? Why was she screaming 'get him'? Care to explain that?"

I wasn't chasing her. We were chasing her dog that was running away.

"Nobody saw a dog," Britton says, his voice rising. "What we have is a dead man who left a widow and two kids, a junkie who strangled him with his bare hands, and a scared shitless girl running through the woods that was supposedly found in a hole in the ground after being missing for eleven years."

Fuck off. I'm clean. I want a lawyer.

I snap the pen in half and throw it at them. I'm done with this bullshit.

It's then that I recognize Nelson as a guy I went to high school with. The years haven't been so good to him, taking most of his hair and the muscular build he had when we were on the lacrosse team together. He hauls me up out of my chair, and the next thing I know, I'm thrown in a cell, where I pace like an animal until my older brother, Toren, can get a lawyer to come fix this mess for me. As I walk the perimeter of the small cell, my thoughts wander back to the girl in the woods. The terrified look in her eyes and the way she held on to that dog will haunt me for the rest of my life.

I can't shake this eerie feeling in my gut that I've seen those eyes before.

CHAPTER 4

Holly

My parents are picking me up from the hospital today, after two weeks of being questioned, stuck with needles, examined endlessly, bathed, and given IV fluids, medications, supplements, and food several times per day. It's been exhausting and frightening. I went from living a life where I would go weeks at a time with no human interaction at all to having people practically on top of me all day long. Several times I've found myself wishing I was back in the dark, cold room with Poppy, my books, and the television. My time there was easier.

Most of the time, that is. When I was alone.

It feels strange wearing the jeans, sweater, and shoes that Mommy brought for me a few days ago. The clothes I had on when the man took me were all I had until they no longer fit and became too thin, torn, and dirty to wear anymore. After that, I was given an old white shirt to wear and a pair of his sweatpants. Nothing else. Now I'm hyperaware of the texture of the denim against my legs, the boots squeezing my feet, and the tag of the sweater scratching the back of my neck. I wish I could take it all off.

I nod and awkwardly shake hands with the hospital staff and police officers who have all come to say goodbye and wish me well. I try to smile at them and parrot back what I know they expect me to say in response. I've learned a lot from watching them these past couple weeks. They mean well, but I know I'm just a project to most of them and an object of curiosity for the rest. Everything has felt stressful and surreal. Like being wheeled out of the hospital right now in a wheelchair, which the doctor insisted on. *Is this real?* I glance around when the hospital lobby doors magically open, and a whole new world is revealed to me like a huge television screen. So much is here. Colors, sounds, smells. All of it rushes back to me as if screaming, *Remember me?* My eyes catch on everything: cars, buildings, more people, and movement everywhere I look. Fear and panic grip me with each moment, but I allow my father to push me—he and my mother unaware of the silent scream inside me.

Nearing the car, my parents try to take my backpack away. I get out of the wheelchair and stomp my feet and cry until they back away from me and agree to let me keep it. They smile awkwardly at people staring at us in the parking lot. I'll never let my backpack and my books go. Why can't they understand I need the books, and I have to read them every day to stay safe? Besides, it's the only way I can see the prince until he comes back again. I've told them this many times, but they refuse to listen and just shake their heads at me and tell me to calm down. I don't care if they say my backpack and my books are old and dirty. They're mine.

When Daddy opens the car door, I climb into the back seat and settle in the middle. I don't ask where Zac and my new little sister are. In fact, I haven't seen them since that first day at the hospital.

"Will Poppy be there?" I ask my parents from the back seat. *Buckled in*, as Mom put it.

I catch them exchanging an uneasy look that I can't read as we pull out of the hospital parking lot.

"What's wrong?" I ask, alarmed. "Is Poppy okay?" I was told

Poppy wasn't allowed in the hospital, so I'm sure he must be waiting at home for me.

My mother turns in the passenger seat to face me. Her blond hair is swept up in an intricate knot at the back of her head, and her eyes study me for a moment. She always pauses before she speaks to me. "Holly, Poppy's gone to live with another family for a while. He's safe, and he's happy, and he's being very well taken care of. I promise."

I blink several times and gulp over the lump in my throat. "What? Why? Why isn't Poppy coming home with me at my house?"

My father jumps in before Mom can answer. "We spent a lot of time talking to your doctors about everything that's happened to you. You're not going home yet, Holly." He glances at me in the rearview mirror. "You will soon, but just not yet. You're not ready."

"Can I go live with Poppy, then?" His new home sounds really nice. But somehow, I'm not sure Poppy really *is* safe and happy. Something about my mother's voice didn't sound honest to me.

My heart sinks as Mommy firmly states, "No, Holly. That's not possible—"

"But why? Wh-where am I going?"

Back in the hole. Until you can be a good girl.

My mother touches my father's shoulder, stopping him from answering me. "You're going to be staying at a very nice place for a little while," she says, not meeting my eyes. She gives me a quick, strained smile. One of many I have seen. From everyone. "It's different, kind of like a hospital but not like the hospital you were just in. It's also like a school, and there are small apartments, too. It will be like your own safe little world. It has everything you need. There are really nice doctors and teachers that will help with more...life things that you need to learn."

I crinkle my nose. "Life things?"

"Yes. Like math, and reading, and social skills, coping, and behavior. Cooking and laundry. You'll be around other people your age who have been through similar...experiences. And once you get better, you'll even have your own little apartment and a roommate. A girl close to your age." Again, my parents exchange a look, but this one I read perfectly; it's one of discomfort. "A special doctor will talk to you about the things that... happened...to you, so you can feel safe and normal."

Safe and normal? I'm not sure any amount of talking is ever going to make me feel safe and normal. "I don't even know what that's supposed to feel like, so how will I even know if I feel it or not?"

"Honey, you will," she says, slightly exasperated. "That's what the doctor is going to help you with. It's what they specialize in. Don't you worry."

The familiar feeling of panic and helplessness starts to creep up again. "I don't want any help," I say emphatically. "I just want to go home and be with Poppy. Please..."

My begging is ignored. *As usual.*

"We know, and we want you to come home soon, but your father and I think it's best that we take it slow." My mother hesitates and shakes her head slightly. "We both have extremely busy jobs. We can't be home during the day to be with you. Zac has his own condo with his girlfriend, and Lizzie has piano practice and gymnastics." She rubs her hand across her forehead. "We just have to figure it all out. But it's not far from where we live at all. Just across town, actually. We'll visit you, I promise."

Defeated, I pull my backpack across the seat and onto my lap, ignoring my mother's look of disapproval. I might not know a lot of "life things," as they said, but I've seen this on TV many times.

They don't have time for me. They've all moved on and built their lives around each other, and I'm just the oddball in the way now.

"I don't need a babysitter," I protest, but it comes out weak and immature, which I am well aware is something I need to work on to fit in. "I can find things to be busy at just like everyone else."

"We know you can, Holly," my mother says. She sounds almost too confident. Another quick, strained smile follows. "And you will. It's just going to take some time."

"And what about the prince?" I ask, worried that it might take him another eleven years to find me again now that they're moving me. "Are you going to let him know where I am?"

"Yes," she says with an eye roll. "Now, please, stop getting yourself all worked up over silly things. Look out the window, it's a beautiful day."

She turns back around in her seat, and both my parents stare out the windshield as if I'm not even there, leaving me confused and forgotten.

Abandoned.

Beautiful day or not, I'm going from one prison to another. For so long I wanted to go home and be with my family again, and now that I can, it's all gone. Time has taken everything away from me.

CHAPTER 5

Holly

Two years later

I feel numb as I'm once again sitting in the back seat of my father's latest BMW, watching all the houses go by as we enter the outskirts of town for my first visit home. I vaguely wonder if I'll recognize my childhood home when I see it or if it, like everything else, will be different. There were many promises of me coming home for the holidays and weekends over the past almost two years, but there was always an excuse at the last minute as to why it wasn't a good time or it couldn't happen. After a while, I just accepted it and stopped looking forward to it. I got used to feeling disappointed. To be honest, I'm not even excited about the weekend visit I've suddenly been granted by my parents. I have my own schedule now, just like everyone else.

At least, being at Merryfield, I've watched less television. In fact, everything there was very regulated at first. My exposure to televised news, newspapers, and other outside influences was limited. The focus was learning and coping. And talking. Talking and talking and talking. I learned to cook, do laundry, and plant flowers and vegetables in a garden. I caught up on my education and found out that I was actually still very smart. Sometimes the bad man would bring me schoolbooks during his visits, and he would teach me math, reading, and spelling. He would even quiz me randomly. I learned the hard way that he did not like bad grades.

At Merryfield, I learned to share my feelings with a group, and I learned that, later, most of that group would whisper about me behind my back. They called me the Girl in the Hole. Thankfully, my roommate, who had named herself Feather, didn't say bad things about me. She became my first, and only, friend.

The prince hasn't come for me yet, but I know he will. I dream of him and his sky-blue eyes all the time, and each dream is more vivid than the last, with a little house in the forest, friendly bunnies, garden faeries, and singing birds. In my mind, Poppy is also there with his broken bark. It's all there, the things that matter to me most, waiting for me.

"Here we are," my mother announces in a singsong voice.

I snap out of my daze, my mind having gone blank the whole ride here. I often lose my sense of time still, and hours, days, and months merge together. For eleven years I had no idea what day it was, or even what time of day it was. For me, time was segmented by what was on TV.

Gazing out the car window, I finally notice my surroundings. The artistic New England neighborhood, the perfectly manicured lawns, the big fancy houses. On TV, everything is perfect. Like what I see around me right now. In the TV shows, problems are always easily fixed, and doubt is merely a momentary inconvenience, quickly smoothed over and forgotten until it can be conveniently brought up again to create drama, only to be forgotten again. I've learned that real life isn't like that at all. But sometimes I wish some of the fake world I immersed myself in daily was actually real. Then I would know what to expect. Nothing is predictable to me outside of Merryfield, and that's one of the things I need to learn to cope with.

Wordlessly, I step out of the car as soon as it's parked in the driveway and gaze up at the two-story brick house. It looks somewhat familiar to me, but I don't remember all the brightly colored flowers in a perfect circle around the tree in the center of the front lawn or the stone walkway leading to the front door.

The warm fall sun beats down on me, and I'm sweating slightly despite the cool early afternoon breeze. I wipe my sweaty palms on my new mom-purchased clothes—a blue ribbed sweater, dark gray skirt, and black knee-high boots—while gazing up at the house. A few old memories emerge. They are hazy at first, then crystal clear. I'm bombarded with new sights and sounds, like the first day I left the safety of the hospital. I am, once again, a stranger in a strange land.

My father takes my small suitcase from the back seat, and I immediately take it from his hands. "I can carry it myself," I say quickly, afraid they will take it away from me as soon as we get inside. He frowns, nods, and moves away after he slams the car door shut. He never seems to know what to say to me, so he simply doesn't say much at all. I don't know what to say to him either, so I guess it's all fine and this is just how things will be. At least for now. I hold on tightly to the handle of my suitcase and keep it close to my body as I tentatively walk forward.

My mother showed up three days ago with several new outfits for me to wear for my weekend visit home. I thought this was extremely strange as I already have new clothes, but she informed me I should always have lots of new *clean, fashionable* clothes for visits outside of Merryfield and she would take me shopping for more. Personally, I like my jeans, which Feather showed me how to distress and put little holes in, and my cozy sweaters and sweatshirts.

I've learned my mother is seriously focused on clothes. So much, in fact, that maybe she needs a week or two at Merryfield to discuss her worries about shirts and pants and the potential perils they could cause. I suggested this during our last family therapy session, and the idea was not well received.

My doctor says I need to learn to filter my thoughts and not just say everything I'm thinking. In the same breath, she also told me not to keep all my thoughts bottled up inside. I don't like all the contradictory and confusing rules of social behavior. I just want to be me. In some ways, I think my parents expect me to be all trained up as a normal young woman, with no defects at all from a deranged past, after my almost-two-year stint at Merryfield. I wish it could be that easy, but I'm still a work in progress, learning new things every day.

"Do you remember living here?" my mother asks as we walk toward the front door.

"A little . . . ," I say, frowning and glancing around again, "but I don't remember the flowers. And I thought the big front window was different."

She smiles, and I know I've said the right words. I almost expect a little pat on the head for remembering correctly. "You're right," she says brightly. "We didn't have flowers like this back then. We have a landscaper now who does all that. There's also a pool in the backyard now. And all the windows were replaced a few years ago, so you're right about that, too."

When I follow her through the front door, I'm welcomed by a sprawling WELCOME HOME banner stretched across the foyer, and Zac, his girlfriend Anna, and Lizzie take turns hugging me hello. I count to ten in my head until the touching is over. I reward each hug with a smile and a "thank you." My brother usually comes to Merryfield twice a month to visit me. Sometimes Anna comes with him. I don't mind because she's always nice to me and brings me chocolate, magazines, and books. She seems to have a keen sense of what I like and takes the time to learn about me by asking me questions with real interest. Lizzie has never visited—not even for the required family therapy sessions that happen every month.

"I'll show you to your room; then we can have dinner and maybe watch a movie if you'd like that?" my mother asks, leading the way out of the living room.

I nod. "That sounds really nice." The others remain behind, offering smiles of encouragement. I follow her upstairs, and memories of living here start to filter through my mind. I stop at the second door in the upstairs hallway, my emotions bubbling up. Strong emotions I don't usually feel. "This is my room?" I say excitedly, peering inside. My excitement quickly dissipates. Everything is different. My pink comforter is gone, along with my bookcase full of books, my unicorn posters, and all of my stuffed animals, which used to sit on my bed.

Now everything is yellow, and there aren't any books or stuffed animals. There's a dollhouse and a tiny table in front of the window with little dolls sitting on the chairs, drinking imaginary tea. I hate dolls and their creepy eyes. What are they doing in my room and what have they done with my teddy bear?

"No, honey, this is Lizzie's room now." My mother takes my hand and leads me away from the door. "You'll be staying in Zac's room when you visit. He cleaned it up and painted it just for you, and Daddy and I helped decorate it with things we thought you would like. And it has its own bathroom."

"B-but I w-want my room. Th-that's *my* room," I stammer, choking back tears and trying to pull my hand from hers. The need to be in my own room is overwhelming, almost crippling. I need something that's mine here. I want to be home, in my own bed, with my own things. I don't want any more new things. Mom stops walking and smiles sympathetically at me.

"Holly, I know this is very hard for you," she says slowly and with mild frustration in her voice. "It is for us, too. We're all doing the best we can. You'll love your new bedroom. It's very grown up. You don't want a little girl's room anymore. Come see, okay?"

But I do. I want the little girl's room. I want to be the little girl again and have my life back.

Reluctantly, I allow her to lead me to the other end of the hall to Zac's room. Or to what used to be my brother's room and is now mine *for visits*. She finally lets go of my hand as I enter. New paint, pretty colored throw rugs over the polished hardwood floor, a dark purple comforter and matching drapes—and *presto!*—new bedroom for the lost daughter. A huge flat-screen television is mounted on the wall across from the bed, and beautiful watercolor paintings of butterflies and flowers hang on the other walls. On the nightstand is one of those iPad things that Zac taught me how to use during one of his visits. This one is bigger than the one I have at my apartment, so I assume it's a newer model. In one corner is a chair next to a small table that has a stack of paperback books waiting to be read. I smile, knowing they were put there by Anna. She promised to buy me new books after she and Zac caught me reading my old childhood storybooks at Merryfield. I don't think they understood that I wasn't reading them because I had no other books. I read them because their familiarity always makes me feel grounded when nothing else does. They're still my anchor.

"It's beautiful...thank you," I finally say as politely as I can, remembering my new social etiquette. And the room *is* pretty and so incredibly luxurious. After years of sleeping on an old bean bag chair without a blanket or a pillow, with a cold concrete floor under me, this room is amazing. My small bedroom at my tiny apartment in Merryfield is nice, but nothing compared to this.

"I knew you would love it," my mother gushes.

I step farther into the room and set my suitcase on the floor in front of the bed. "I do. It's perfect."

It's not perfect, though. And it's not that I'm ungrateful that they've made this beautiful bedroom for me. It's just not my room. There's nothing of me here, no sign that Holly Daniels grew up here. No photographs, no favorite toys from childhood sitting in the corner. No scratches in the paint or scuffs on the floor from me growing up in this room. It's clean and sterile.

Unlike me.

Maybe a part of me was hoping my childhood toys would be in this room. Or at least some of them. I thought for sure my favorite teddy bear that I slept with every night would be waiting here for me. Or maybe one of my favorite posters framed and hung on the wall. Something that said, *This is your home. You grew up here, for a little while, and we remember.*

Thankfully, my faded purple backpack and my books are hidden in my suitcase, despite my mother's continued insistence that I get rid of them because they are filthy reminders.

Filthy reminders for her, not for me.

"If these items give her comfort, let her keep them," Dr. Reynolds said to my mother during one of our recent therapy sessions. *"She'll let them go when she's ready."*

Standing here in this room that isn't mine at all, I'm not sure I'm ever going to be ready.

Later that night, after a home-cooked dinner of spaghetti and meatballs with my family and watching a cute comedy with them in the living room, Zac and Anna go home to their own apartment, almost as if they can't leave fast enough. I get the feeling family time doesn't happen often.

I catch Lizzie staring at me as our parents clean up the popcorn and soda from the living room. "Do you want to help me set up my new dollhouse?" she asks shyly. "I just got a couch, a fireplace that lights up, and a cat in a bed to put in it."

Before I can answer, my mother has practically warped herself into the room with lightning speed. "Lizzie, Holly must be exhausted with it being her first day home. Maybe another time she can play with you. I'm sure she just wants to go to her room and relax." She clears her throat. "Besides, it's late and Grandma is coming tomorrow, so you should be getting to bed soon yourself."

I stand. "Mom's right," I say, even though the last thing I want to do is go to my room and be alone. I haven't spent the night alone in a dark room since I was in the bad place. Feather, who sleeps in the bedroom next to mine at Merryfield, is quiet like me, but she's still good company.

Our mother visibly relaxes, like she just dodged a bullet, and I smile weakly. I wonder if she notices my smile rarely reaches my eyes. Most likely not—she never looks at me long enough to notice. I turn and give Lizzie a real smile, because she's young and innocent in this whole mess.

"I think I'll go to bed," I tell Lizzie gently. "But I'd love to spend some time playing with you tomorrow if you want." From the corner of my eye, I watch my mother's face and, just as I suspected, she grimaces slightly at my last comment. At first, I thought I was imagining that she's been purposely keeping Lizzie away from me, but now it's too obvious to ignore. For some reason, she's doing her best to keep the replacement from getting too close to the defective daughter.

The sun shining in my face awakens me, and I squint toward the window, spotting tiny flecks of dust floating in the beam of light, like microscopic faeries in flight.

Sometimes I wish I were a faery that could just fly away.

Mornings are still confusing to me, even two years after returning to society. When I was held captive, I wasn't quite sure when I went to bed. I just slept whenever I felt tired or bored. I think I usually took a few naps during the day, but I never slept for long periods. The ritual of people going to bed at night, staying asleep, and then getting up in the morning to start a new day is still a bit hard for me to get used to.

Waking up in my dedicated weekend-visit bedroom at my parents' house is no exception. Funny, I thought sleeping and waking here would feel different, since it's where I slept for the first five years of my life. It's the only place I felt safe and had a routine. I thought a certain degree of contentment would return to me, but it hasn't. The room feels uncomfortable. The paint is too new, the bedsheets and comforter too stiff. Maybe if I had been in my old room, where Lizzie now gets to sleep and feel safe, I would feel like I was really home.

But this isn't home, not anymore, and it scares me inside to realize that I really don't belong anywhere. I'm still lost and alone, living an illusion, a ghost haunting my own past.

I rise from the bed, stretch, and go to the window to look at the tree-lined street of huge houses that all look mostly the same. I wonder if the prince lives in a house like that, but I quickly decide he wouldn't. He would live in a castle on a hill that touches the clouds or in a cottage deep in the forest.

Please come get me soon, I silently beg, hoping he will somehow hear me, wherever he is.

A knock on the bedroom door distracts me from my wishful thinking. "Holly?" Mom's voice is muffled through the door.

"Yes?"

The door opens and she walks in, smiling at first, but her expression immediately changes to disgust when she sees me at the window.

"Holly! Get away from that window. You're barely even dressed!" she yells.

Startled, I back away from the window and look down at myself, confused. I'm wearing a long, dark blue cotton nightshirt that hangs to just above my knees. Feather sleeps in the same thing, and so do some of the girls I see on television.

I cross my arms over my chest and cower slightly. The bad posture the therapist at Merryfield tried for months to get me to change returns in an instant. "I just woke up. This is what I slept in."

She shakes her head and raises her hand to her mouth. "You cannot walk around like that. You're a young woman and shouldn't be half naked. Didn't they teach you that?"

I blink at her, completely confused.

"How many times, little girl, have I told you not to stand unless I tell you to?"

"Um . . . I don't remember anyone telling me what to sleep in . . . It was in the pajama section of the store, though. Feather got one, too."

"I don't care what Feather does. I'm going to buy you some proper nightclothes." She crosses the room to pull the curtains over the window. "Please don't stand like that by the window. You don't want the neighbors to see you, do you? It's bad enough they know what . . . what happened to you," she stammers. "We don't need to feed the gossip hounds."

"I'm sorry. I only wanted to see outside." Windows are still something I consider a luxury, along with everything that comes with them. Like the sun, and the clouds, and birds, and the sky. And air.

The usual forced smile crosses her face. "It's fine, honey. You don't know any better. Daddy just went to pick up Grandma. She's so excited to see you." She goes to the closet and pulls out another gray wool skirt, black leggings to wear underneath, and a black turtleneck.

"Wear this. You'll look lovely."

I try not to let the cringe I feel on the inside show on my face. "I don't like those kinds of neck shirts," I protest. "I feel like I'm strangling."

His hand tightened around my neck, cutting off my air, suffocating me. "I can kill you now if I want to..."

"Don't be ridiculous. It's very soft."

I wish she would listen to me and try to understand that I'm not being ridiculous. I just want to get through my days without some kind of reminder of something bad happening to me. I don't remember my mother being like this when I was little, before I was taken. Or maybe she was, and I forgot over the years that passed. In therapy, we talked about how sometimes we romanticize people in our own heads, make them better than they actually are, to make ourselves feel better and to justify liking them and missing them.

"You should get dressed, put a little makeup on, and come downstairs. I can't help both you and Lizzie get ready. I have things to do before your father gets back with Grandma."

Apparently, my mother thinks I need supervision. Does she think I don't get up and dress myself every morning? I may have been held against my will by a sick man for years, but I would have gotten dressed in new clothes every day if I'd had a choice. Even at five years old, I knew I was supposed to get dressed every morning.

"I'll be down as soon as I can," I reply. "I'll brush my hair and my teeth, too."

She nods and leaves the room, closing the door behind her, oblivious to my mild sarcasm. Dr. Reynolds tells Feather and me we shouldn't make sarcastic comments, but sometimes it just comes out, and it kinda feels good.

When I'm sure my mother won't be returning to my room, I tiptoe back to my window and pull the curtains open.

"Oh my, look at you, my sweet baby! Come here." My grand-mother comes directly to me as soon as she enters the living room, where I'm sitting on the couch wondering how mad my mother will get if I take these uncomfortable shoes off. I stand, and Grandma immediately pulls me into a hug. At first I stiffen, but then my body relaxes and I let her embrace me. I can almost feel the love pouring from her as she clings to me, rubbing my back. I put my arms around her, too, gently, as she's shorter than me and feels very frail, like a little bird, and I'm afraid I may hurt her.

"My sweet Holly. I missed you so much," she says with a sob. "Every day I prayed for you." She pulls back to look at me, tears in her eyes, her mouth quivering. Her hands lightly touch my hair, then my cheeks, before finally resting on my shoulders. This woman loves me. I barely remember her, and I wasn't allowed to see her until today, but her love for me is overpowering, in her touch and in her eyes. She honestly, truly missed me.

"You're so beautiful," she says softly, and all I want to do is let her hug me again. Now I understand the comfort of a person's arms around you. "So grown up, but so much the same. I'm so glad you found your way home while I'm still alive. I would have died with a broken heart if you hadn't come back."

"Mom, can we save the morbid talk, please?" My father shakes his head as he walks past us and goes into the adjoining kitchen.

"I'm sorry, Grandma." I have no idea what else to say. I don't want to break anyone's heart or make anyone sad.

She grips my hand in her thin, bony one. "Don't you dare apologize. Come sit with me. I have something for you." She holds on to my hand as she sits on the couch, and I sit next to her, captivated by the rings on her hands, all diamonds and colored gems. I remember these rings. When I was little, I used to call them stars because they sparkled and shone.

"You still wear the stars on your hands," I murmur, and her entire face lights up at hearing those words.

"You remember...I was so afraid you would forget me." She squeezes my hand even tighter, and I decide it's okay to let her believe I didn't forget a moment with her. Deep down, I wish I actually did remember more of her because I can feel in my heart that we were close. I haven't felt like this with anyone else. This pull of remembrance, of belonging and feeling loved.

"Lizzie...bring me my bag that's over by the front door," Grandma says, and Lizzie gets up from where she's been playing quietly on the floor to retrieve a large shopping bag that Grandma dropped when she saw me.

"Do you have a present for me, Grammy?" Lizzie asks, peering into the bag.

"Not today, sweetheart. Today I have a special gift for Holly because she hasn't gotten any in a very long time."

Lizzie nods absently and goes back to her game, and Grandma

reaches into the bag, pulls out a wrapped, rectangular box, and hands it to me.

"But it's not my birthday or anything," I say, placing the box on my lap.

"That's okay, this is just a special gift."

Intrigued, I tear off the wrapping paper to find a dark burgundy photograph album with the word *Memories* embossed in fancy script on the front. I glance at my grandmother, and she gives me a warm, encouraging smile as I flip the book open. The first page is filled with photographs of me as a newborn, and I don't even have to ask if it's me because Grandma has added a little strip of colorful paper beneath each photo with my name and the date and place in pretty writing. A lump forms in my throat as I slowly turn each page, watching myself grow older, playing with my brother, blowing out birthday candles, at the beach with my father holding me at the edge of the water.

Suddenly the photos of me stop, but the pages continue with pictures of Zac, my parents at parties and holiday dinners, and photos of my grandparents. Seeing the photos of my grandfather brings back vague memories of him, but I don't ask where he is. I'm afraid to hear that answer. I turn a few pages and there are photos of baby Lizzie, and she looks just like I did earlier in the album, with wispy blond hair, bright eyes, and a big smile. I see Zac's prom photo, and I'm delighted to see Anna standing next to him in a pretty dress when they were both so young, then Zac graduating from high school, then college, Lizzie's first day of school, and so much more. Every photo has been labeled by my grandmother. My hands shake as I flip through the pages of memories that should have been mine, in my head and not here in photographs, but I am so very grateful she made this for me.

"I don't know how to thank you for this." My words catch

in my throat, and I turn to hug her. "I love this so much, and I needed this."

"You don't have to thank me. This is your life. All of this belongs to you."

"I'm still not sure seeing all that is good for her recovery." My mother entered the room while I was hugging my grandmother. "You should have let me talk to her doctor first."

"That's nonsense," Grandma says. "She has every right to have these photographs and see herself, and her own family. None of this is a secret. And I won't be kept from my granddaughter any longer, Cynthia." She continues to talk over my mother, who attempts to interrupt her. "I'm eighty years old. I'm not going to live forever, and I want to see my granddaughter while I still can. I've respected your wishes long enough."

My mother purses her lips, and her hand grips her wineglass tighter.

"All right, if that's what you would like," Mom says. "We only wanted Holly to have time to reintegrate into society first and recover mentally and physically. She was quite a mess when she first came back. It would have upset you, and that's not good for your heart."

"I was a mess?" I ask, surprised by this news. I don't remember being a mess exactly.

"You weren't yourself. It would have upset Grandma immensely to see you that way."

"That's bullshit." Grandma once again holds my hand, and I try not to laugh at her swearing right to my mother's face. "It upset me *not* to see her. Now, let us talk. Go stir something in the kitchen."

When my mother is out of earshot, Grandma says, "I never should have let her keep me away from you."

"It's all right," I assure her, feeling terrible that my mother wouldn't let her visit me if she wanted to. "I can see you whenever I want to. I'm at residential status at Merryfield now. That means I can have visitors anytime, and I'm allowed to come and go as long as I sign in and out."

My grandmother looks both happy and a bit sad to hear this news, which I don't quite understand. "Well, I don't live far away at all, so we will definitely be visiting each other from now on. Would you like that?" she asks.

I nod enthusiastically. "Yes. I would like that very much."

By the middle of my grandmother's visit, I've decided she's one of my favorite people, right up there with Zac, Anna, and Feather. Later, when she's getting ready for my father to drive her back home, I promise her I'll visit her as soon as I'm able to. I don't have a driver's license or my own car yet, but it's something I plan on working on right away. Until then, I plan to call her on the telephone.

Dr. Reynolds told me to make a list of goals since I transitioned to residential status last month, and right now my goals are to get a part-time job, learn to drive, get a car, visit my grandmother, and get my hair highlighted while I continue to wait for the prince.

Lizzie and I stand next to each other at the front door and wave to Grandma as our father drives her away, and that momentary feeling of dizzying panic I often get suddenly strikes me. Placing my hand on the doorframe for balance, I slowly do my breathing exercise and count to ten.

One, two, three, four . . .

Thinking of the goals has overwhelmed me. One minute I feel so normal, and the next—bam! Everything closes in around me, and I want to hide. The what-ifs penetrate my thoughts, taunting me. What if I can't get a job? What if I never learn to drive?

What if I can't get a car? What if my parents never relax and just learn to love me? What if I never see the prince again? What if I never feel... *real* again? What if I never stop feeling lost—and never really feel found?

I take a gulp of air. *One, two, three...*

"Holly, are you okay?" Lizzie asks from beside me, concern all over her young face. "You're not dying again, are you? I'll go get Mommy..."

Grabbing her hand to stop her, I smile through my shallow breaths. "I'm fine. Just a little tired." She nods, content with my canned answer, and leaves me there at the door while she goes to help Mom fill the dishwasher. I am still continually surprised at how people out here accept words as truth. Even though I said I was fine, I'm not. Inside, I'm scared, and screaming, and crying. Inside, I'm still in that dark, lonely room, waiting for the bad man to show up again, not knowing if it'll be a good day, where he just talks to me, or a bad day, where he will touch me and say nasty things. Why can no one see, from the outside, that I'm not fine?

And how have I slipped into the habit of lying about how I really feel, constantly covering up my feelings?

It's not until later that night, after watching a movie with my parents and Lizzie, when I'm lying in bed in Zac's converted room, that I realize Lizzie asked me if I was dying *again*. I have no idea why she would ask such an odd question. I drift off to sleep wondering, and I jolt awake some time later, drenched in sweat, after having a nightmare. I was in a dark hole, being buried alive with dirt and worms being shoveled over me. I tried to scream, but no one heard me—no one came. *"I'm alive!"* I screamed silently in the dream. *"I'm not dead."* And then I saw it was my mother with the shovel. *"You're not yourself,"* she kept saying as she shoveled more dirt over me.

I feel a tremor, and waves of nausea and dizziness hit me as I stare at the ceiling, until I stand on wobbly legs and go to the bathroom to splash cold water on my face and sip water from my hand. After a few minutes, the sick feeling subsides, taking most of the horrible visions of the nightmare with it. I make my way back to my bed in the dark, stopping at my suitcase in the corner first. As quietly as I can, I unzip the suitcase, pull out my backpack, and take it to bed with me.

CHAPTER 6

Holly

"I think a day out will be good for both of us." Feather glances at me in the passenger seat of the car her father gave her a few weeks ago. "I love the mall. It has everything we could possibly need in one place. You've always wanted to get your hair and nails done. No better time than the present, right?"

I nod in vague agreement. I think the real reason she wants to go is because while I was away for the weekend, she tried to cut her own bangs and give herself layers. Now her shoulder-length black hair is only shoulder length in some places, and her bangs are on a wicked slant.

Hair trauma aside, Dr. Reynolds *is* always telling us to live in the present—the gift of life. Not the past or the future. So today seems like a good day for me to finally have my first salon experience.

Early last night, my father dropped me off at Merryfield after my first weekend visit at their home. Other than seeing my grandmother, the weekend was disappointing. Stupidly, I had daydreamed about my parents telling me all about the past eleven years of their lives and sharing cute, happy childhood stories about me in an effort to bring my memories back and help us bond. Instead, they were polite and friendly, but distant. When my father announced after dinner that it was time to drive me back to my apartment in the confines of Merryfield, I felt relieved. I couldn't help noticing they seemed equally relieved.

At least I have the photo album from Grandma, which Feather and I stayed up late looking at together. Feather said hardly anyone has real printed photos anymore and that my grandmother must be amazing to have printed them all out like she did and label them.

On the way to the mall, Feather takes me to my first drive-through to get us each a Starbucks latte (also a first for me), explaining that she recently read in a popular magazine that every morning should start with a good coffee or else we're doomed to have a craptastic day. I don't think the person who wrote that article has any idea what a truly craptastic day would even entail, and I'm sure if Feather or I wrote in and shared our past craptasticness with her, she'd rethink her belief that a coffee with the perfect amount of froth could make a person's day better.

That being said, as I sip the vanilla latte Feather ordered for me, the warm, sweet creaminess is actually very pleasing.

"Don't forget your father gave you a gold card and said you can spend as much as you want," Feather reminds me on our way into the shopping center after spending half an hour looking for the closest parking spot possible. "I think he's got the major guilts just like my dad does and thinks buying us stuff will make it all better. I don't think there's anything wrong with us taking them up on that and buying a few things, right?"

"Right," I say, because I know that's what she wants to hear. Feather was sexually abused by her stepfather when she was younger. Her biological father didn't come into the picture until Feather developed a drug addiction a few years ago, at age sixteen, and went into a severe depression. Her stepfather went to jail, and her mother moved away. Feather was already in the therapy program at Merryfield when I arrived, and we both transitioned to residential status at the same time.

During our stay at Merryfield, Feather and I occasionally went shopping with a few of the other girls. This was part of our treatment program—getting out into the world. Those outings were nothing like my current experience with Feather, who takes it upon herself to bring me to all her favorite stores and pick out outfits for me. Apparently, Feather used to shop a lot before she became a patient at Merryfield.

I let her drag me into each store and choose clothes for me because it seems to make her happy. And she's good at it. Everything she picks out fits me perfectly. When our hands are filled with shopping bags, she brings me to a salon at the far end of the mall for us to get manicures. Then she talks me into getting my hair dyed a lighter color blond, then cut and styled while she gets her hair fixed. Even though I feel completely overwhelmed and anxious to get back home, I go along with all of it, hoping to feel excited about girl things because it feels like it's something I *should* like, and I want to fit in.

"You look gorgeous, Holly," Feather says when the stylist finishes with me. I smile at her reflection in the mirror of the stylist's station and lift my hand to touch my hair, which feels incredibly soft and silky. I never knew hair could feel so soft. As I stare at myself in the mirror, I realize I look like a young version of my mother. I actually look pretty; the hair highlights bring out the color of my eyes in a way I didn't know was even possible. I look so...normal. Just like the pretty girls on TV. I know that, out here in the real world, the outside of people seems to matter more than the inside. I quickly learned that the illusion of appearance will always outweigh the truth of what's really inside.

"Thank you," I reply automatically. "It feels so different. I love it."

"It was like straw before. You seriously look amazing." Feather unzips her purse, rummages around, and triumphantly pulls out a small silver tube. "Let's just give you a little bit of color to polish you off."

I freeze as she comes at me with the lipstick, the waxy tip bright bloodred. *"Be a pretty, bad little girl for me..."*

"No...," I whimper. I pull back and swat her hand, sending the lipstick flying. It lands on the floor and rolls underneath the sinks. "No!" I scream, bursting into tears. "I don't want to do that anymore!"

Feather and the stylist look at each other and then at me, forced awkward smiles on their faces.

"Holly, what's wrong?" my roommate asks, glancing around the salon at the other women staring at us.

"No more lipstick," I whisper, my body shaking. "I don't want to be a bad girl anymore."

"Jesus Christ," Feather mutters, taking a deep breath and tossing her newly styled hair over her shoulder. "Another trigger? I'm so sorry. What the fuck kind of shit did he do to you?"

The stylist hovers behind us, her hand at her throat. "Is everything okay? Can I get you some water?"

"She's fine, Marcel." Feather flashes her a friendly smile. "She just had a flashback. Just give her a sec, and we'll be out of your way."

Marcel gapes, her eyes wide. "Oh! I thought you looked familiar..." Her tone is hushed but still loud enough for everyone nearby to hear. I feel my cheeks flush with warmth. "You're the one who was taken years ago, right? My goodness, I'm just remembering all the media coverage from the day you were found...I hadn't realized...that bastard deserved to die."

Trigger. Taken. Flashbacks.

I fill my lungs with air and count to ten, avoiding my own reflection in the mirror. When I think about the bad man, I feel conflicted and sick to my stomach. As much as he hurt me, he was the only person to show me any kind of attention or care for eleven long years. He was all I had, other than Poppy and the TV. Of course, I know now that his actions weren't caring at all and I was merely a toy that he kept alive to play with. But at the time, he was all I knew. I was only a child and needed *someone*. I'd learned to wish for his presence, to stave off the darkness and the never-ending silence while stuck in that dark basement. While my young mind knew he had taken everything away from me, I also knew that he was the only one who could give me anything. It spawned a very confusing love-hate conflict in me that only grew over the years.

When I think of the other *him*, my prince, I feel a sense of calm and safety inside, like I felt that day when he pulled me out of the hole and held me. He was the first person to make me feel something new, feelings so completely different than anything I'd ever felt. Sometimes, if I close my eyes, I can almost feel his strong arms around me, protecting me, saving me. I can still remember the way the blue of his eyes took my breath away, and how his unique ragged voice soothed me. He still infiltrates my dreams and haunts me in my waking hours. I haven't forgotten him, not for a moment, and I'm still waiting for him.

I'll never stop waiting and hoping for him.

I often wonder if he even remembers me, and if he ever thinks about me.

He does. I know he does. We just have to wait for the right time.

Feather pats my shoulder, which should be comforting but is not. Not when I'm wishing for *him* right now. "Yes," she says to Marcel, a bit sharply because neither of us wants to be remembered as the victims we once were. "But she's fine now. I just scared her by accident." She squeezes my shoulder, trying to comfort me and sending me a hint to please not embarrass us again. Her eyes meet mine in the mirror. "You're totally cool now—right, Holly?"

I nod and force my lips into a smile. It's a mask I have a feeling I'll be wearing for most of my life. "I'm fine. I'm so sorry. Red just isn't my color." I shake my new bouncy hair like she did a few moments ago and boost myself out of the chair. "I'm a total klutz. I'm ready to go."

Feather and Marcel share a relieved smile that radiates to the other women in the salon, who all go back to talking and texting and burning color onto their hair and flesh. The crisis is over. Nobody had to confront the bad thing in the room.

My heart is still racing as Feather and I walk past the lipstick on the floor and head to the front lobby, where she grabs a few bright pink bottles off a glass shelf. "Let's get some really nice shampoo and conditioner. We can share it at home. We deserve to have the best after the evil shit we went through," she says casually. Like nice shampoo and conditioner will somehow remove the "evil shit" that was done to us. Buying things seems to comfort her, but it leaves me a little befuddled. I don't think any of these people will ever understand me, maybe not even Feather. Dr. Reynolds has told me to accept that and to not hold it against people. It's just how the world is—people don't want to get personally involved. They cover things up, bury them, and mask them.

I'm not sure I can live that way. Or if I even *want* to.

I wince at Feather's words and smile awkwardly at the questioning glance the girl behind the counter flashes at me. She averts her gaze back to her register.

"That would be great," I reply, using my go-to phrase. It makes everyone happy, puts them at ease even if my delivery is less than *great.* Finally, we leave the salon, and I let Feather take the lead so I can take a break from faking smiles. My face is starting to hurt from forcing myself to look happy when all I want to do is get home and hide in my room for the rest of the night. I can only venture out for so long before I start to feel stressed, and my *no more of this* meter is teetering on level ten right now.

On our way back to the mall exit, Feather pulls me into a boutique that sells jewelry, clothes, and home decor made by local craftspeople. I'm in awe of all the beautiful things to choose from, and she helps me pick out a few scarves and a bracelet and necklace made of hand-blown glass beads. I'm so taken by all the pretty things that it almost erases the salon fiasco from my memory.

Her phone rings and she raises her finger to me as she answers it, signaling that she'll be back in a few minutes. Nodding, I continue to wander around the store until a collection of small, black-framed photographs on the wall catches my eye. There are four, all taken of a lone fir tree in the snow-covered woods, decorated with Christmas ornaments. In one photo, a small red fox is sitting a few feet away, staring into the camera as snow falls around him. I was born on Christmas Day, and when I was little, I was fascinated with all things Christmas. Those are memories I never forgot. The one thing I looked forward to while in captivity was watching all the holiday movies and cartoons on my television. Of course, I never knew when they would be on, so it always came as a surprise when Christmas commercials and movies finally started playing. I was never given any gifts by the bad man, but I was grateful for the fantasy world the TV let me live in.

"Aren't they beautiful?" A salesgirl has come up next to me as I gaze at the photographs, and I silently pray she doesn't recognize me.

I reach out and touch a frame, as if in some way it will connect me to the photo more intimately, bringing me into its scene and letting me stay there. "They are," I say, my voice low with awe. "I love them." And I mean it. I'm in love with these photos, and I have no idea why.

"It's a cool legend." She nods at the photos.

"Legend? What do you mean?"

She tilts her head at me and smiles, no recognition in her eyes. "You must not be from around here. It's a cute children's legend in this town—the Forest Santa."

"Forest Santa?" I'm instantly intrigued.

She nods, smiling at me. "Yeah, for the past...maybe twenty-something years...someone decorates random trees way up in the woods, in the middle of nowhere, around Christmastime. Hikers usually find the trees, and photographers are always hunting for them, which is how we got lucky enough to have these photographs. Nobody knows who actually decorates them, so at some point, he or she was given the nickname Forest Santa. There's a myth that woodland animals can speak on Christmas Eve, so part of the legend is that Forest Santa decorates the trees with them and they celebrate Christmas together. The little kids love the story."

"I would like to buy them, please," I say, not taking my eyes off the photographs. I'm captivated by the magical feeling of the photos and the legend behind them, and now I can't bear the thought of not being able to look at them whenever I want.

The salesgirl stares at me; then she eyes the four pictures. "They're quite expensive, two hundred dollars each—"

"That's fine," Feather interrupts, suddenly appearing next to me with a big smile. "She'll take all four. Can you wrap them up for her?"

"Of course!" the salesgirl says, responding instantly to Feather's confident demeanor, which I know is an act that she plays very well. "I'll meet you at the register with them." The salesgirl carefully takes them down from the wall.

Nerves rattle my stomach. Money is not a concept I'm at all comfortable with, and I don't feel like I have a right to spend someone else's money. Especially my father's. He barely speaks to me.

"Feather... that's a lot of money, and I don't need them. I didn't know—"

My friend puts her hand up to shush me. "Holly, stop. You're allowed to have things. I know you probably don't know this, but your dad makes a lot of money. He took me aside last night, when you were putting your suitcase in your room, and told me to make sure you bought anything you wanted after I told him we were going shopping."

I bite my lip. "Are you sure? I'm not used to buying things."

"I know—that's what I'm here for. I'm a pro." She grins and loops her arm through mine. "Come on, I'll let you slide the card. It's totally addicting."

It's nearly eight o'clock by the time Feather and I are on our way home to Merryfield. It's dark outside but even darker inside her car due to the tinted windows. I squint, my gaze wandering around the interior of the car. The darkness reminds me of being in that hole, the dirt in my nostrils, the sounds of the woods at night frightening me. I could hear things walking around at night, and I never knew if it was my captor or a wild animal. I always tried to hush Poppy by gently putting my hand over his mouth, afraid he would make the bad man mad or bring a wild animal to eat us.

"Did you scream for help while you were in the hole in the woods?"
the female officer asked.

"No . . . never," I answer.

"Why not?"

"I guess I forgot someone would ever help me."

I thought we were only going shopping, but Feather surprised me by also taking me to her favorite restaurant for dinner, and now we're finally on our way home. I look at her uneasily as her manicured fingertips tap out a text message on her phone with one hand as she steers the car with the other. I don't have a cell phone, and the insane appeal of them is lost on me. What can be so interesting on a little phone?

"Sorry . . . Steve is telling me about his day," she says, referring to her sort-of boyfriend, a guy she's known since she was very young, who is mostly a friend but is slowly turning into more. She puts her phone in the console between our seats, and I can breathe a little easier knowing she actually has her eyes on the road and the traffic around us. "Are you feeling okay now? I'm sorry about the lipstick thing . . ."

"It's okay. You had no way of knowing. I just feel bad I embarrassed you."

"The guy . . . he made you wear lipstick?" She's the only person who ever asks for any details whatsoever about what happened to me, and I usually don't mind telling her.

I chew my lip, torn between wanting to tell her and not wanting to remember any of it. "Yeah," I finally admit, feeling ashamed, even though the logical side of me knows it's not my fault. "Bright red lipstick. He'd put it on me before he . . . touched me."

She grimaces. "God, that's fucking sick. That's like the shit you see in movies. I'm so glad my mom's husband didn't do weird shit like that with me. He just liked to get drunk and grope the hell out of me."

Just thinking *red* and *lipstick* starts to make me panic, and I break out in a cold sweat. I clamp down on that sensation, force the images and feelings of fear away. I don't want to freak out again, or Feather may not want to take me out in public again. I use the breathing and visualization exercises Dr. Reynolds taught me to do when I feel overwhelmed with emotions.

Counting to ten, I squeeze my eyes shut. I bite on my lower lip and try to clear my mind. I force my thoughts away from those memories and into less dangerous territory. I think about Poppy, in his new home, happy and loved. I think about my prince, his words promising me I'll be okay. I think about my books and the stories that always give me comfort. I think about my grandmother's hugs. I think about my new Christmas photographs. Soon I feel better. Less out of control.

According to Dr. Reynolds, I suffer from what's called posttraumatic stress disorder, and I'll likely have to deal with it for the rest of my life. Her focus was on teaching me how to understand the triggers I'll face and how to calmly deal with them, especially in public. Which I guess I kinda failed at today. Talking about how to deal with triggers in the safety of her office is a lot different from experiencing it in real life, and now I'm completely exhausted from this day.

I open my eyes and glance over at Feather discreetly. She doesn't seem to notice my anxiety; her attention is on the road and the radio. That small bit of information about my past seems to have satisfied her, so I don't offer any further details. We're almost home, and I'm looking forward to being alone and forgetting about the bad parts of the day.

Feather seems to have recovered from her abuse better than I have, and I'm a bit jealous. When we first met, she was quiet, depressed, and withdrawn. Now she's much happier, like a lot of weight has been lifted from her. I often wonder how she feels about me as a friend. Does she feel sorry for me? Disgusted by me? Her head is bobbing slightly to the music coming from the car stereo, oblivious to me watching her. I wish I could be as carefree as she appears to be lately.

We stop at a traffic light, and Feather picks up her phone again and types wildly on the tiny keyboard illuminating the interior of the car. I hope she's not telling Steve about me and the red lipstick incident.

The thundering roar of a motorcycle pulling up next to us startles me, and I peer out the window at the rider. It's early October, but even with a chill in the air, all he's wearing is a black shirt with the sleeves pushed up, revealing muscular, tattooed arms. A black knit hat covers his head in lieu of a helmet. Long blond hair sprouts from the hem and just touches his collar. He must feel my gaze because he turns sideways toward me.

I gasp—

The lower half of his face is covered by a mask that looks like a portion of a bloody skull. His eyes are hidden behind dark glasses. He grabs the burning cigarette dangling from a hole cut in the mask and blows a puff of gray smoke in my direction before carelessly flicking the cigarette onto the street between us.

But that's not what's got me nearly crawling out of my seat and jumping out into the road. I sit forward slightly and lean closer to the dark-tinted window, not sure he can even see me.

"Did you see that creeper throw his cigarette at my car?" Feather shoves her phone back into the console. "I should run that asshole off the road."

My heart gallops in my chest, and I lean even closer to the

window, my breath puffing against the cold glass, my eyes riveted to his tattooed hand wrapped around the handlebar grip.

The last time I saw that tattooed hand, it was squeezing the throat of the man who had kept me prisoner for years.

My eyes widen, poring over him. The way his powerful legs wrap around the rumbling motorcycle, the broadness of his shoulders, his arm muscles flexing, the colorful ink covering the exposed parts of his forearms, the stray wisps of hair blowing in the breeze. An indescribable ache sears through me, a longing like nothing I have ever felt before.

Look at me, look at me!

I want to scream it. I want him to see me. I *need* him to recognize me.

I'm right here!

But his gaze doesn't linger. His head turns away, and he guns his engine.

No! He's going to leave me again. I'm going to lose him again. There he is, just six feet away from me—the man who saved me. My beautiful, strong prince. My breath catches as he kicks the bike into gear with a scuffed black boot, then speeds off down the dark road, disappearing within moments.

I wish I could have stopped him.

I wish I could thank him and tell him I'm sorry for what he went through for me.

But most of all, I want to tell him how I waited for him.

Hoped for him and dreamt of him for so long.

How I'm *still* waiting.

Is it possible to wish someone right out of your heart into existence?

Yes. Yes, it is.

Now we just have to find each other again.

CHAPTER 7

Holly

"Do you know what you want?" Zac asks. I peer up at the cafe menu written on a huge chalkboard, completely overwhelmed by all the choices. I don't even know what half the stuff is. Like biscotti.

It's been over a week since my outing with Feather and seeing my prince at the traffic light. I find myself peering around the cafe and out into the street, hoping to see him again. I have no way of knowing how to find him, but this town is very small—I can only assume he must live here. I wonder how close we have been to each other all this time.

For the past two years, I've asked my parents if they know where he lives, so maybe I can write to him, but their answer is always the same: "Leave it alone" or "That's not acceptable." I asked them when I first moved to Merryfield and even asked Dr. Reynolds if there was a way for me to contact him, but they were all adamant that it was best for me to leave him alone, as he was "mentally unstable." For now, I push those thoughts away so I can focus on my outing with my older brother.

Next to me, Zac orders a bagel and coffee, then turns to me. "Well?" he prods, gently breaking into my thoughts.

He came down this weekend just to see me. I appreciate his effort. I know it's a hassle for him to visit me since he lives in the

city, but it breaks the monotony of my days. Usually he takes me
out of Merryfield and Anna joins us and, for a few hours, I feel
like a normal person and less of a freak. Zac always tries hard to
treat me like I'm just his sister and not some kind of victim. He's
never condescending, never full of pity, and he never acts like he's
in a rush to get away from me. He was even nice enough to hang
my Christmas tree photographs on the wall next to my bed this
morning so I can look at them every day.

"Um…" I look at him for help while the young guy behind
the counter waits with a bored expression on his face. Behind
us, the line is getting restless. The pressure becomes even more
unbearable, but Zac seems unconcerned, and I'm grateful for his
patience. Decisions aren't easy for me. For years, all I was given
was bread, water, dry cereal, Fruit Roll-Ups, little boxes of juice,
trail mix, and an occasional apple, cookie, or cupcake used as a
bribe.

*"Do you want the cupcake? Be a good girl, then. Bend over and don't
scream or fight and I'll let you have the cupcake."*

I'm ashamed to admit that, some days, I wanted that cupcake
so bad that I bent over and bit my tongue until it bled to keep
from screaming as he touched me. I always regretted it later,
when the sweet icing was burning in my stomach, the appeal of
the treat long gone.

"Holly?"

I shake my head and force out a breath. Those memories
always sicken me, but no one needs to hear them. No one needs
to know how they continue to torment me. The bad man is dead,
and I have my prince to thank—if I can ever find him.

"I'm sorry," I say. I apologize a lot because it makes everything
feel better, like saying everything is "great." I recite what Feather
always gets for me. "A blueberry muffin and a vanilla latte with

skim milk." I have no idea if I like anything else, and I'm embarrassed to ask him to describe everything on the menu to me.

"Okay." Zac grins, his left dimple making an appearance. "Why don't you go grab us a table, and I'll bring it over."

Nodding, I head for a small table by the windows, avoiding eye contact with the other customers, and settle into one of the wooden chairs to wait for Zac.

"You should talk to someone about that," a female voice says, and I turn to see a girl at the next table pointing at my arm. "I used to cut and burn, too. You can get help. Self-harm isn't the answer."

My cheeks burn with embarrassment as I pull my sweater sleeves down to my palms and push my hair back over my shoulder. "Thank you," I say as politely as I can. "But I didn't do it to myself."

With wide eyes, she shakes her head, sending her short, black bob bouncing around her shoulders. "Girl, that's even worse. Don't let some asshole hurt you. I been there, too."

Zac sets the tray of food in front of me, looking from me to the girl as if he's waiting for an introduction.

"Did *he* do that to you?" The girl shoots him a look that could melt ice.

"Do what?" Zac asks, his brow creasing.

"Put them cigarette burn marks all over her arms. That's what."

The look of surprise and hurt on his handsome face makes my chest hurt, and I struggle to breathe. I want to run to the car, to my backpack in the back seat of Zac's car. He always lets me bring it if he takes me somewhere as long as I leave it in the car.

"No," I reply. "He's my brother. He would never hurt me."

"What's going on?" Zac demands, his defenses rising.

"Nothing, Zac." I glance back at the girl, wishing she would just go away and mind her own business. "Thank you for your concern, but I'm fine."

Her eyebrow rises. "You sure about that?"

The couple at the table next to us lean close to each other, their eyes darting over at us as they whisper. About me, most likely.

"Yes, I'm positive. Thank you." I force my millionth fake smile.

Suddenly her face changes, going from suspicion to shock to pity. "Holy shit." She lowers her voice to an excited whisper. "You're that girl who was found in the hole out in the woods, aren't you? You're little Holly Daniels. I read about you."

I meet her eyes and put on my best look of defiant confidence. "No. I have no idea what you're talking about." *There. I did it. I deflected her. I don't owe anyone anything.* I focus all my attention on removing the paper from my muffin as she gets up and walks away, mumbling to herself about assholes and denial.

"What was that all about?" Zac still looks confused.

I shrug, wanting to move on and not make this outing any more uncomfortable than it already is. Since I was found, my family has had to deal with this kind of attention from random, nosy people in both public and private ways. I was mostly shielded from it, being at Merryfield, and I wonder if that's part of the reason my parents sent me there. Not just for the therapy, but to also hide me away.

"She saw the burn scars on my arms and thought I was hurting myself or had a boyfriend that was hurting me, I guess." I sigh. "Then she recognized me."

"Jesus." He shakes his head. "People just don't know boundaries sometimes."

"It's okay. I forgot to pull my sleeves down."

He dumps a packet of sugar into his coffee, his jaw clench-ing. "You shouldn't have to wear long-sleeved shirts all the time. People should just shut the hell up and be respectful of others." He's angry for me, and I hate to see him this way. He's a very calm, soft-spoken guy most of the time, and it bothers me that being around me makes him mad.

I reach over and touch his hand, which is stirring his coffee with a fierce briskness. He stops and glances up at me with a look of surprise on his face. I never initiate touching, and I pull away quickly. Reaching out to him felt like an impulse, almost an invol-untary reflex. Maybe it means I'm starting to trust.

"It's okay, Zac," I say softly. I rub my hand against my thigh, still feeling slightly awkward about touching his hand. I'm brim-ming with so much I want to say, but it's like there's this cork inside me that keeps me from letting it all out. I want to tell him how scared I am that I'll never feel normal. That I'll never feel like part of the family. That I may never have a relationship. That people will always look at me like I'm damaged and dirty. I want to tell him I'm sorry he has to deal with the questions and the stares sometimes, too. "I really don't want to talk about it but... people recognize me, they ask questions. I have to get used to it."

"I don't know how you don't scream at these rude-ass people." Zac busies himself spreading butter from a tiny plastic cup onto his bagel.

You screamed. You know what that means. You scream, you get burned. You pull away? The dog gets burned. Get it through your head.

I shake my head, momentarily afraid to speak.

"So, how was your visit with Mom and Dad?" he asks.

I focus on my brother's face and wait for the memory to fade back into the dark hole it seeped out of. "Good. The same." I take the lid off my latte, peer inside, and put the lid back on. "Thank

you for letting me stay in your room. It really came out pretty."
He nods, and I continue. "Mom and Dad were nice...but they
didn't talk to me much at all. It felt like they were only seeing me
because they *had* to, not because they *wanted* to."

He nods again, and I pull a blueberry from the soft, yellow fluff
to examine it. "I don't know, I'm still just trying to fit in. Feather
has taken me shopping and out to eat a few times, but she usually
spends most of the time we're together typing on her phone. I
tried to spend some time with Lizzie during the visit, but Mom
acts a little crazy about it, like she doesn't want me near her."

He chews his bagel and swallows. "That's because she told
Lizzie a few years ago that you were an angel in heaven. Lizzie
thought you were dead, and now here you are, alive and well." He
says it matter-of-factly, without easing into it.

"What?" My muffin sticks in my throat, and I sip some of my
latte to try to force it down. It's so sugary sweet, it gives me a
momentary jolt. "Mom told her I was dead?"

"Yeah." He looks like he can't believe it himself.

"You're dead, little girl. Dead, dead, dead. You don't even exist."

"But...why? Did they have any reason to think I was dead?" I
ask. It never even occurred to me while I was gone that my family would assume I was dead. I always believed they would keep
looking for me until they found me.

Zac shakes his head. "No...there was nothing that ever hinted
at that. No evidence at all. Your friend ran home and told her
mother what happened, and she called nine-one-one. Everything
happened so fast. But you disappeared without a trace. In her
panic, Sammi didn't notice what the guy looked like, or his car.
She's always felt really guilty about that...We've talked a few
times over the years. You should maybe contact her. She would
probably love to hear from you."

I had never even thought to contact my childhood friend who had run off while the man dragged me into the car, and I've never wondered how she felt about it. "Unfortunately, no one saw anything, even though you two were right in our neighborhood. The leads dried up pretty quickly. It just seemed hopeless. And so I think, for Mom, it was easier to say you had died than to tell Lizzie you were kidnapped and missing. That's scary for a little girl to hear."

"I lived it, Zac. It was scary for *me*."

"Holly, *I* know that." He leans forward. "But Mom is just...in denial about a lot of things. She always has been. She can't deal with reality."

I push the other half of my muffin across my plate, my appetite gone. "No wonder Lizzie stares at me all the time."

My brother takes an uneasy pause. "Mom's very overprotective of her. She had a total meltdown after you were taken. For months, all she did was lie in bed and eat Valium. When she wasn't sleeping, she was pacing all over the house or walking up and down the street. She didn't start to act normal again until she got pregnant and Lizzie came. Lizzie totally distracted her from everything and, in some ways, that was good—but bad in a lot of ways, too. She put herself in denial about what happened to you, and projected all her love and happiness onto Lizzie. She barely lets her out of her sight." He lets me absorb that for a few minutes before continuing. "And Dad just thrust himself into his work. Our whole family fell apart. Nothing has ever been the same."

I shouldn't feel jealous that my mother is trying to protect Lizzie from something bad happening to her, like what happened to me. But I do. A mix of envy, jealousy, and anger simmers deep in my stomach. "I don't even know what to say," I finally tell him, not wanting my emotions to come vaulting out of my mouth in the middle of this quiet cafe.

"They feel guilty, Holly. They blamed themselves for a long time. Still do. What parent wouldn't?"

Does blame and guilt make you wish your child was dead instead of missing? Was that actually easier for them to cope with? My bottom lip quivers. "I think they wish I never came back. Maybe me being dead would have been better for them. For all of you..."

Zac's eyes turn a darker shade of brown. "Holly, don't even say that. We're all glad you're back, safe and alive. We love you."

Counting to ten, then fifteen, I breathe deeply, feeling overwhelmed. Emotional. Feelings I'm not used to. "It doesn't always feel that way. And I don't mean you... you've been so nice to me since I came back. You've never acted weird around me. I always look forward to seeing you. And I really like Anna. But I feel like an outsider around everyone else. It all feels... awkward. I feel like I don't belong."

There. I finally said it. A tiny weight lifts from my shoulders.

He listens intently, leaning on the table, exactly like when we were younger. "I know, Holly. Listen," he says. "I've been wanting to talk to you about something. Next summer, Anna and I are moving to New York. My friend John has a business out there. Do you remember John?"

I search my memory, trying to remember a John. "John from next door?" I ask as the image of a skinny, sandy-haired boy with hazel eyes comes to mind.

"That's him. We've been best friends since we were kids. He's offered me a great job. A partnership, actually. The money is good, and the business is doing great," he says, his eyes lighting up. "I don't think it's an opportunity I can pass up."

I almost drop my coffee at what he's implying. My brother and his girlfriend are the only ones I feel even remotely close to, other than Grandma, and now they're going to move away?

"You're leaving?" My voice wavers on the words.

"Yeah, that's the plan. I haven't even told Mom and Dad yet. The thing is, we wanted to ask if you want to come with us. We can get an apartment that has enough room for you, and you could kind of...start over. You could go to school, or maybe look for a job—something easy just to get your feet wet. We'll help you." He rubs his hand across the short beard he's grown recently. "I think a change of scenery might be good for you."

I'm shocked speechless at his offer and take a few moments to catch my breath as well as my thoughts. "Really? You mean that?"

"I do. I wouldn't joke about something like this." He takes a bite of his bagel. "I love our parents, but they're not exactly easy to get along with. I think you figured that out." I nod over the edge of my cup. "I've seen how they act like you're a visitor, and I can see how much it hurts you, how much you're struggling. Anna has noticed it, too. And honestly? We think it sucks for you. Maybe living with me and Anna will be less stress on you emotionally. You can just take your time to figure stuff out with people who are a little more easygoing, who love and support you. It's a clean slate."

"Am I allowed to move? Where is New York?"

He lets out a small laugh. "Holly, you're going to be nineteen in two months. You're an adult. You can do whatever you want. New York is about four or five hours away by car. It's where the Statue of Liberty is."

"Mom and Dad say I'm not ready to have a job, or make decisions, or meet too many people. They think it's best I stay at Merryfield...maybe for another year or two." Maybe they're right and I'm not ready for any of those things. Just the thought of getting a job and having to see new people every day scares me. While Merryfield is a therapeutic facility, living there as an outpatient resident has been a nice transition for me. I've learned a lot during my time there, and it's been a good way for me to learn independence with a safety net. But I do have to admit, the few times I've ventured out of the safe confines of Merryfield have been a bit of a shock.

"Dr. Reynolds seemed to feel the same as I do every time I was at the meetings with you. She wants you to get out there, make some friends, find some hobbies, figure out who you are. Maybe do some friendly dating. Your entire childhood was spent locked in a room with some lunatic telling you what to do. You don't want to spend the rest of your life hiding, avoiding new things, and having Mom and Dad tell you what you can and can't do, do you?"

I shrug slightly. "Part of me does, and part of me doesn't."

"I think that's normal, Hol. But as your big brother, I want better than that for you. If I can help you, then I'm going to. You're beautiful, sweet, and smart. Don't let what that guy did ruin the rest of your life. If I can, I'm not going to let that happen."

I'm shaken by his words, which are so new to me. His care and concern for me haven't changed at all over the years. He's still the same protective big brother I had as a little girl.

Pulling my sleeves down to my palms again, I stare out the window at all the people walking by, wondering if I can blend in with them, or if I'm always going to be the Girl in the Hole. Almost everyone in this small town knows what happened to me. Moving to a new place would give me a chance to start over and, hopefully, put everything behind me.

"You have a lot of time to think it over. You don't have to

decide today," he says. "I just wanted you to have an option. You need to have choices, Holly. I think it's important. If you want to move with me and Anna, we'd love to have you. And if it doesn't work out, you can always come back here."

I give him a weak but grateful smile. "I'm going to think about it. Seriously. I honestly never even thought I could go somewhere else."

My first real adult decision has been put in front of me, and it's terrifying. Sometimes I wish the bad man were still telling me what to do, forcing me to do things, and putting clear choices in front of me that don't involve a lot of thinking. I can't tell anyone that, though, without them thinking I'm crazy.

CHAPTER 8

Tyler

Age seventeen

She's hovering by the door, looking at the floor, out the window, at her hands. She's looking everywhere but at me, and she's sticking by the door like she's going to bail any second. All I want is for her to come closer. I need to see her smile and feel her hand in mine. I need just one thing to feel normal right now. I've waited days for her to visit me and assumed she was waiting until my family and friends weren't piling into the room so we could be alone.

"Come here." I try to hold my hand out to her, but the IV in my wrist and the bandages covering most of my hand make it hard to move.

She continues to look downward, peeking up at me from beneath her long bangs for a moment before looking down again.

"Please?" Weak is not a role I play well.

She crosses the room painstakingly slow and stops next to the bed. She doesn't touch my waiting hand. For the past year, her hand has been intertwined with mine whenever possible—until now.

"I'm sorry," she whispers.

I try to force a smile, but the pull of skin and muscle on the left side of my face makes me grimace in pain. Everyone who's come to visit me has said they're sorry—an offer of pointless consolation. "It's okay. I'm pretty fucked up, but the doctor says it'll get better. I don't think I'll be taking you to the prom, though, unless I wear a mask." My teasing tone reeks of desperation in the tense space between us.

"I can't see you anymore." She's whispering toward the floor, but I hear her perfectly. My body lurches in an attempt to sit up, but the pain that sears through my body immobilizes me. The edge of my vision hazes, but I fight it. I'm not going to pass out like a wuss.

"Wendy..."

She sniffles and rubs her nose with the back of her hand. "I'm so sorry, Tyler. I just can't look at you...like this."

My heart plummets like a rock into the pit of my stomach, and I feel like I might throw up. "It'll get better. I talked to the doctor today. It's not as bad as it looks right now. I can have surgery."

A tear falls off her cheek as she shakes her head violently enough to rattle her brain. "I just can't. I can't do this. I'm sorry. I know I'm a shitty person..."

I grind my teeth through the pain, which has doubled in intensity since she started talking. She's supposed to be making me feel better, not worse. Isn't that what you do for the people you love?

"Wendy, you're not. I know this is hard for you, too. Just give it time. It's only been a fucking week."

She turns away, and I want to grab her face and force her to look at me. To see me, still in here under the ugly burned flesh.

"I have to go. My mom is waiting for me. I'll miss you, please believe that. I just can't deal with all of this." Her long auburn hair flies behind her as she bolts from the room, taking her broken promises with her. I'm a friggin' idiot for believing she loved me enough to stay with me through this.

"Fuck you, Wendy!" I roar after her. My lungs burn, my eyes sting, and white-hot pain shoots through my skull like a dagger, but I don't care. Nothing fucking matters anymore. I rapidly jam my thumb into the patient-managed painkiller button, begging for another shot of magical

liquid to be shot into my vein. It will never reach the pain that's now got its grips on my heart. Pain of the flesh is one thing, but pain of the heart, that's an entirely different animal, which is now going to ravage my life. Wendy just took the last shred of hope I had out the door with her.

A week ago I had everything. Straight As. Popularity. Great friends. Dating the prettiest girl in my class. On my way to getting a lacrosse scholarship. My life was great and only getting better.

And now I'm a charbroiled mess lying in a hospital bed, watching it all slip away as I melt into a morphine-induced haze.

CHAPTER 9

Holly

Every morning, for the rest of October and November, the first thing I do when I wake up is stare at the pictures of the Christmas trees hanging on the wall next to my bed. Something about them makes me feel happy inside, and that's a new feeling for me. I decide I'm going to leave them up when the holiday season is over.

Boredom has been settling in for the past few weeks, making me restless. Even though I clean the apartment every day, including Feather's room, take walks on the Merryfield property, work in the garden, and visit with one of my counselors, I still feel like there's a gaping hole in my life. Since Feather and I became roommates not long ago, I've watched her get a part-time job, start a relationship with a guy, and get a car. I can see progress with her. But with me? Not so much. My life still feels very much like it did when I was captured: each day the same and going nowhere.

Last week, I asked my parents again if there was any way I could get my driver's license and learn to drive a car, but they were adamant I should wait until summer and give myself *more time*. I'm not sure what that means exactly, but I do know I'm tired of more of my life ticking away, so I've taken to going for longer walks every day, beyond the perimeter of the Merryfield property.

When I told my mother over the phone a few days ago that I've been walking farther each day, she became very agitated, and while I can understand why she's nervous, I'm making this decision for myself. My father, luckily, jumped on the phone and sided with me, agreeing walks might be good for me, but I think it was just his way of appeasing me since he won't agree to my getting a car.

I know my parents worry about me but, as Zac said, I'm going to be nineteen in a few weeks. I'm an adult. I'm determined to do *something* on my own, even if it's just walking. I need to test my boundaries.

At first, I only walked down the street and back to Merryfield. I had to force myself for a few days, until I felt comfortable, and I gave myself pep talks to walk a block, then another, and another.

My sense of adventure increased quickly. Being free was addicting. Each day I walked a little farther, blocks turning into miles. This morning I walked to a small park a few miles away, and I realized it was the exact place I had been taken, halfway between the school and my parents' house.

Wow. This town really *is* small.

I freeze to the spot on the sidewalk with the deep zigzag crack that I always avoided stepping on as a little girl. I had been stepping over it when the man had grabbed me, my pink sneaker in midair. The crack is wider now, with moss growing between its edges, weathered from time. My head swims and I sway slightly in the wind as my stomach clenches and threatens to empty here on the sidewalk. I swallow hard and step over the crack.

I make it to the other side, and I grab the hand of the little girl in my memory and pull her with me where she belongs.

My eyes scan the area, my heart pounding. It looks harmless. Like a typical park, with benches, swings, and paths. It's empty at the moment, except for some birds hopping around on the ground. The only thing that's different from that day is the season. Today, the leaves have already changed colors, the grass has turned brown, and the sky is dark with the promise of icy rain. I huddle inside my fall jacket as a breeze whistles down the street behind me. That day, the sun had been out and white fluffy clouds had filled the sky. Monsters don't come out in the daylight, right in front of butterflies and blue jays, in a tiny town where everyone knows everyone.

But, in fact, they do.

I sit on a bench nearby and stare at that place on the sidewalk for a long time. My memory of being taken is both fuzzy and clear. The feelings are more vivid than the actual events. I can still feel how hard my heart pounded in my chest, how his fingers dug into my arm when he grabbed me. I can't remember what my best friend, Sammi, and I were chatting about. Nor can I remember what the man was wearing, what color the car was, or if anyone else was around.

I shrieked. Sammi screamed. I was yanked backward. Sammi ran. A hand covered my mouth. The car door slammed. A man laughed.

It happened so fast.

In a matter of mere seconds, I was taken. Stolen from my own life.

And it was *easy*.

I've never been told the details of my case or the technicalities of all the crimes committed. All of that was kept from me by my parents and various psychologists and therapists. Feather says I could probably find out most of it by searching the internet, but I don't want to know. I lived it. I know enough.

There are only two things I want to know in relation to my

past. The first is to find out where Poppy is. The second is to find my prince. I already know his real name, as I overheard one of the detectives talking about him when I was being questioned. *Tyler Grace*. Feather says she could find him in about two seconds, but I've told her no. In the books, the princess doesn't go hunting for the prince. He finds her. Or they find each other. I'm afraid if I do it wrong, I'll ruin the story.

I'll ruin *our* story.

And if I do that, the happily-ever-after may not happen, and that's something I cannot begin to accept. That's the only thing that kept me going for all those years I was alone in that dark room. The mere idea of it not happening is unthinkable.

Each day I walk a little farther, always feeling triumphant as I walk past the spot by the park. I make it downtown, walking by stores and cafes, then turn and walk back to my apartment. I learned at Merryfield that I could *move*. Being locked in a small room for years, with no option to go anywhere else, created an invisible spatial barrier in my mind. It took months for me to get used to the idea of going to other rooms, of being able to go out-side, walk around, and return to where I started. The expectation of a wall popping up and stopping me, trapping me, continues to linger.

I still expect him to sneak into my space, even though I watched him die. Death doesn't erase fear or memories. The monsters that live inside us are much harder to get rid of.

I'm getting better at battling them, though.

One morning, I decide I'm going to be extra adventurous and take a taxi to a street near the part of the woods where the photos of the Christmas trees were taken. I'm going to hunt for a Forest

Santa tree and see it with my very own eyes. It's another huge step for me—doing something on my own without direction or permission.

I know that going into the woods to look for trees might sound crazy. And it probably is. But I don't let that deter me. I feel like this is something I *have* to do. I'm not going to tell anyone because I don't want any negativity ruining my mood.

A while back Zac gave me his old iPad, making me promise I would only use it to read books, find out about potential jobs, or other safe activities. He made me promise I wouldn't go looking at news sites, join social media sites, or search for information about my past. I agreed, feeling no desire to do any of those things anyway.

Yesterday, I kept my search simple, safe, and specific. I found the website of the tree photographer. Two emails later, he told me where he had found the trees, off an almost-hidden trail that branches off the main path people use to get to a small waterfall in that area. Of course, this doesn't mean there will be any decorated trees in the same place this year, but after some mental coaching, I decide to trek up there and look.

Dr. Reynolds keeps suggesting I take on some projects and goals, so why not this? At least I'll have something exciting to tell her when we meet next month.

Getting a taxi is a lot easier than I thought it would be. Just a simple phone call from the landline and, within the hour, she's pulling into the lot in front of the apartment. I make sure I have keys and my wallet, with a credit card and some cash, in my backpack—just as my mom insisted I should do every time I leave my apartment. I dash outside, practically run to the taxi, and climb into the back seat. The female driver asks me for directions with a rather bored attitude and, next thing I know, I'm off. Free. Doing what I want.

I watch the scenery pass by, trees and houses blending into a blur. I get more anxious with every passing mile, and the woods loom ahead. When we arrive at the destination, the girl driving the car asks me for an extra fifty dollars to wait for me while I walk around the woods, and I give it to her just to make sure she won't leave me stranded here. Thankfully, my father sends me money every week, which I rarely spend.

Having donned boots, gloves, a scarf, and a hat, with my backpack over my shoulder, I start up the trail. Even though it's the first week of December in New England, it hasn't snowed yet, so I only have cold air to deal with. I'm well aware I should probably be scared to go walking around in the woods alone, but my desire to find a decorated tree far outweighs my fears. And what are the odds I would be abducted twice?

The research I did on the magical little iPad provided very few clues about Forest Santa. One short article I read on a local Wiki page, though I'm not entirely sure what a "Wiki" even is, stated that the trees have been found decorated as early as the beginning of December and as late as Valentine's Day. I wonder if the mysterious Santa goes back to the trees and *un*decorates them. I decide that he must—otherwise decorated trees from the year before would still be around and, according to my research, they're not.

As I walk away from the taxi, logic once again reminds me I should be terrified of being alone in the woods—where the bad man kept me—but I practice my breathing techniques to help me rationalize. It's not the woods I should be afraid of, but a person. The woods never hurt me—a person hurt me. I imagine my prince protecting me, like a guardian angel and, with each step, my worry fades. As part of my initial therapy, Dr. Reynolds would take me outside, sometimes in the sun. This was new for me since I hadn't been outside at all during my captivity—other than when the bad man moved me, with a cover over my head, to the hole—and I had no window to view the outside world. Other times Dr. Reynolds would take me outside in the dark. Then I slowly graduated to talking to people. Part of my rehabilitation was to not fear the world or hide from it now that I was living in it. Going outside was terrifying at first, but with help and practice, I overcame it and soon started to enjoy it.

I try to pay close attention to my surroundings as I walk, keeping an eye on my watch to make sure I don't lose track of time and end up walking for hours in a daze. I space out a lot. Or maybe it's daydreaming. I'm not really sure what the technical term is, but Dr. Reynolds says it's because I was alone for so long and had no one to interact with other than Poppy and TV.

And him.

After I've walked for more than an hour, disappointment at seeing nothing but squirrels makes me turn back toward the road, where I hope my driver is still waiting for me. Something sparkly captures my attention out of the corner of my eye and there, about twenty feet to the right, is a small fir tree draped in gold garland, with colored balls hanging from the limbs, the tip of the tree topped with a glistening silver star. Various boxes wrapped in bright red paper with white bows are beneath it, and I wonder if they're empty or if they hold real gifts. The mysterious boxes pull me like a magnet, but I resist the urge to open one.

A smile touches my lips. I can't believe I actually found one of the trees, and it's just as beautiful and magical as the photographs. As I step off the path and walk slowly through the heavily wooded area to the tree, a man appears in the distance, on the other side of the Christmas tree. Startled, I hide behind the trunk of a large oak tree as he comes closer, singing an eerie version of "Jingle

Bells," his voice hoarse, strange—but oddly familiar, though I can't quite place it.

"Jingle bells, jingle bells, jingle all the fucking way. Oh what fun it is to ride in a one-horse fucking sleigh..."

Curious as to who is desecrating one of my favorite holiday songs, I peer from behind the tree to catch a glimpse of who I can only assume is the notorious Forest Santa. He's too far away for me to see his face, but he's wearing a big floppy red stocking hat with a tattered white pouf and a bell on the end. He's in faded blue jeans and a gray flannel shirt but no jacket.

"Ho, ho, fuckity ho," he mumbles, then lights up a cigarette as he stands back and looks over his beautiful tree. Seemingly satisfied with his creation, he turns in the other direction and whistles.

I lean forward, my mouth falling open when a small, white dog comes running from the forest and falls into step beside the man, tail wagging happily.

Poppy!

There's no doubt in my mind it's Poppy. I cling to the tree trunk and watch them walk away while my mind races wildly and my chest heaves in panicked breaths.

After a quick debate in my mind, I decide I can't just let Poppy walk away and lose him again, so I follow the direction the man and my dog disappeared, hoping I can find him and not get myself lost. For the first time, I wish I had a cell phone to call for help if I needed to. Oh well. I lived eleven years without being able to call anyone for help. I'm sure I can get through a walk in the woods. But when I glance around, the man's disappeared, and so has Poppy.

Suddenly, a body drops right in front of me. *From the sky.* I have no idea how, but he somehow came from above me and landed on his feet with a solid thud. It's clear he didn't fall, meaning he must have *jumped* from a tree.

I stumble backward, almost falling.

He's not wearing a Santa hat. *No.* This man has a black bag over his head, tied with a frayed rope around his neck. Harsh, crooked holes are cut out over his nose and mouth. The forest falls deathly silent—the only sound is our breathing. Mine is ragged; his is steady and even.

We stare at each other, or at least I think we do. His eyes are shadowed beneath the dark material over his head, but I assume he's staring back at me because I can feel it right down to my bones, and it freezes me with fear.

"I can smell your fear. It's so perfect, so raw and innocent. The more scared you are, the more I like you."

My voice is almost less than a whisper. "I wanted to see the tree. That's all." I'm back in the dark, dirty room with an even darker and dirtier man, bowing to his insane demands, trying to avoid further confrontation.

"Tell me what you were thinking right before I came in here. Tell me what you miss the most."

His head tilts slowly to the side, his silence menacing as he studies me.

Sometimes, silence roars. I've heard it.

Newly acquired common sense tells me to run. But I ran in the past, and I was caught and punished. An innocent person who tried to help was hurt, too. *Because of me.* Backing up slowly, I keep my eyes leveled on his masked face. "I'm going to leave now," I say softly, continuing to back up. When he doesn't move, I turn and walk back in the direction I came, silently praying he lets me walk away. I take twenty steps, with my heart pounding, before I turn to check behind me.

He's gone.

Turning in a circle, I frantically search my surroundings, dizzying myself, but he's nowhere to be seen.

Monsters are everywhere. You can't escape them. They will always, always find you.

I walk as fast as I possibly can back to the road, my eyes darting through the woods, hoping to see Poppy while also being petrified the strange man will jump out at me again. Did that even happen? I push my hair out of my face and press my fingers to my temples, not sure if I imagined it all.

Miraculously, I find the road, relief that I didn't get lost overpowering me. When I reach the driver waiting for me at the side of the road, I'm out of breath and covered in a cold sweat.

"You okay?" she asks as I slam the car door behind me.

"Yes," I reply, heart still racing. I press my face nearly into the window, looking out into the woods. "Did you see anyone?"

"Who?" she asks, confusion in her voice.

"Anyone," I answer impatiently. "Did you see anyone walking around? Or a little white dog?"

She shakes her head and starts the car. "You trippin'? I didn't see anyone at all. Or a dog. Sorry."

As scared and worried as I am, I tell myself Poppy looked happy. His tail was wagging. He went willingly with the man with the Santa hat, so he must be a good person. Poppy would never wag his tail if he was scared. But even with that small amount of comfort, I know I can't just forget him and hope he's okay forever. I need to make sure he's safe, and maybe, just maybe, I can bring him home. Having Poppy living with me would definitely make me happy.

When the taxi driver drops me off at Merryfield, she gives me her business card so I can contact her again when I need to be taken someplace. I shove it in my pocket, already knowing I'm going to be calling her tomorrow.

For once, I'm glad Feather is engrossed in a deep phone conversation when I get home. I'm way too rattled to talk to her right now, and I definitely don't want her to see me this way. She'll start hammering me with questions I'm just not ready to answer. I'm not even sure if what happened today really happened. There's a possibility I made it all up in my head.

I take a long, hot shower—one of the few things in life that calms me. I didn't have a shower when I was taken, only an old, dirty bathtub with no hot water, which still makes me shiver just thinking about it.

Before I climb into bed, I do my nightly ritual of looking out my window at the moon and stars, which are bright like city lights tonight.

"I miss the sky and the sun and the moon and the stars. I miss knowing if it's day or night out."

"Day or night, it's all the same for you, little girl."

A tiny spark of light draws my attention away from the sky. Out in the yard, near one of the storage sheds, I can barely make out the shadowy figure of a man smoking a cigarette in the dark. Frowning, I pull the window blind down and step away. It's probably one of the other patients, even though smoking is not allowed here.

As odd as today was, I'm grateful for two things. First, I set out to achieve the goal of finding one of the decorated trees, and I found one. And second, I learned that Poppy is alive and well, and he appears to be living with the legendary Forest Santa. I'm sure I didn't imagine that part of what happened today. It was real.

I'm not going to let the bizarre man in the scary mask stop me from going back to find my dog, even though my mind is spinning with questions. Is he the Forest Santa? Why would he try to scare me? Isn't Santa supposed to be happy? Or was it someone else entirely? I was so stricken with fear when the man jumped out of the tree, I didn't notice if he was wearing the same clothes as the man with the Santa hat. All I could see was that eerie mask.

The next morning is almost an exact replica of the one before it. The driver takes me to the same place she did yesterday, and I walk up the same dirt road to the path, only this time with the added fear of running into the man with a plastic garbage bag tied around his head.

The scent of burning wood floats through the air, getting stronger with each step I take on the frost-covered trail. This time, I turn left at the fork in the path. Soon, I spy a tiny house with smoke curling out of the chimney. The house is small and well hidden among the trees and looks almost exactly like the tiny cottages in my fairy-tale books. The small windows have white shutters and flower boxes, waiting for spring flowers. A vine, gray from the cold, creeps up the house on a trellis, all the way up to a tiny stained glass window on the second floor. A stone walkway begins not far from where I'm standing, runs to the front door, and branches off to a matching detached garage. Various birdhouses, all painted in bright colors, hang from the trees and sit atop wooden posts. It's simply the most magical place I've ever seen in real life.

My excited breath is a cloud of mist as I approach the house. I'm so busy huffing out more puffs of my own personal clouds that I almost miss the man perched, still as a statue, on a huge rock between the house and the small garage. He doesn't look in my direction, even though my boots are crunching rather loudly in the dead leaves. Poppy, however, comes running to me like a white tornado as soon as he sees me. His odd bark makes me smile, and I'm relieved to see that he *is* real and not a figment of my imagination. I kneel down in the dirt and leaves and gather him up into my lap, his little body wiggling with happiness in unison with his tail.

"I missed you so much. So much," I whisper, kissing his head as tears of happiness fall down my cheeks and onto his fur. "Did you miss me, too?" He responds by licking my face and making happy whimpering noises. He must have been bathed because he's much whiter and softer than I remember him and he smells fresh and clean. Feather would be impressed that even Poppy's "evil shit" has been washed away.

I lift my head and finally lock eyes with the guy on the rock, and my heart does a leap into my throat. *It's him.* I almost didn't recognize him. Now it all makes sense. Yesterday he was wearing a hat, and his long-sleeved flannel shirt covered his tattoos. But today, his shaggy hair is visible, and the sleeves of his sweatshirt are pushed up. There's no denying those tattoos are the same ones I've seen twice before. I can't believe he's had my dog all this time. That *he's* been here this whole time. Surely my parents and my doctor knew he lived right here in the same tiny town, knew I could have run into him, but still refused to let me write to him.

He appears normal to me—not mentally deranged, as I was told—other than defiling a holiday song, decorating a tree in the middle of nowhere, and not wearing a jacket in the cold.

He continues to stare at me, totally expressionless.

Tyler Grace. In my head, he's always been the prince. Silly, I know. But that's who he is to me. I stand, holding Poppy in my arms, and slowly walk toward him, stopping about ten feet away. Not because I'm afraid of him, but because he seems to require a lot of personal space.

"Hi." I quickly swipe the damp tears from my cheeks with my fingers. He looks away from me, and I frown at the back of his head. This is not the reunion I was expecting. I take one more step closer. "You're Tyler, right?"

His mouth opens, but instead of answering me, he yawns. Yawns!

For so long, I believed that he would return to me one day, and instead, I've returned to him. I tell myself it must be fate. And instead of sharing in my excitement, he yawns.

"Do you remember me?" I ask, undaunted.

Nothing. As irritating and rude as it is, his ability to completely ignore me is impressive.

Hesitantly, I take two steps closer to him. The unique tattoo on his hand is visible, as is the strange, ragged, discolored skin of his other hand. I remember how those hands squeezed the throat of my captor after I dropped the rock onto his head to make him release the knife he was swinging. That knife and I were very familiar, and I have the scars to prove it. The paralyzing fear I felt in that moment, before I let the rock fall on his head, was intense. I made the choice of who would live or die that day.

"I'm the Girl in the Hole." For all the times I hated being called that, here I am using it to introduce myself.

He nods slowly but still refuses to turn to face me or speak. I understand his silence, the fear of speaking words. Or hearing them. I felt that way for months after I was found.

"You don't have to talk. I just wanted to say thank you. You saved my life. And you kept Poppy. I never thought I would see him again." I hug my dog tighter, and he nuzzles his face into my neck just like he used to. "I had no idea what happened to him. I've missed him more than I can even say."

Finally, he glances over at me and, wow, his eyes are a startling bright blue.

"You're the Forest Santa?" I half ask and half state. "I love how you decorate the trees. My birthday is on Christmas Day, so I sorta have a thing for anything Christmassy. My parents even named me Holly." My babbling is becoming embarrassing. "Don't worry, I won't tell anyone that it's you. I'm good at keeping secrets."

A faint smirk crosses his lips. It's small, and not really a smile, but I saw it before it disappeared, and it's enough to make me want to see a genuine smile from him. I have a feeling it would be the most beautiful smile I've ever seen.

I shift nervously on my feet. "I should probably go. I have a driver waiting for me. Not like a chauffeur. I just don't have a car. Or a license. I don't even know how to drive." One of his eyebrows rises, and I can tell he thinks I'm an idiot. "Can...can I take Poppy home with me? I really miss him. He's my family."

He shrugs and pulls a pack of cigarettes out of the back pocket of his jeans and lights one up. I'm not sure exactly what happened to him, but I remember the detective who questioned me in the hospital telling me Tyler was in a fire when he was younger. They asked me to describe his scars, but I didn't remember them at all until the detective mentioned them. All I could remember were his eyes and how I wished I could walk right into them, like an ocean. He didn't frighten me the day he saved me. Not even a little. I was transfixed by him, grateful to him. Curious about him. And I still am. It's odd to me that he would want to put a small stick of smoke and fire into his mouth after going through such a horrific accident.

I wait for him to do or say something—anything—but he just

stares off into the distance, as if he hopes I'll just go away if he ignores me long enough. A tactic I tried many times with my captor. I may be new to interacting with people, but I can definitely take a hint.

"Okay," I say awkwardly. "Thank you again for everything. Take care."

Still holding Poppy, I turn and head back in the direction I came, expecting him to stop me and demand I leave the dog with him—or want to talk to me after all—but after I've walked for at least five minutes, it's clear he's not going to do anything of the sort. My heart sinks like an anchor that may never surface again.

For months, I've daydreamed many different scenarios in which I saw him again, and not one of them was even close to what just happened. He was completely uninterested and borderline rude. How hard is it to say hello? Or you're welcome? Or how are you? Or hey, take your dog and just go. *Something.* Disappointment seeps into the places in my heart that shut down a long time ago, and a dull ache sits in my chest as I walk back to the waiting car. For years, before the television was given to me, I sat on the dirty floor with my fairy-tale books, daydreaming of walking into a beautiful sunset with the man who would eventually come to save me. That's where the happiness is supposed to happen. It's in the books. The prince saves the princess, and they live happily ever after.

The bad man would step on my books, leaving his smudged shoe prints on the white pages that I loved so much. He'd pick them up and hold them behind his back, taunting me until I knelt and obeyed. And I did. I choked, and I cried, and I begged until it was over and my books were given back to me.

"Fairy tales don't come true, little girl," he'd say, zipping his pants. *"No matter how many times you read them."*

"It's not true, Poppy," I whisper, shivering against the cold breeze.

Dead people should stay dead, especially the bad ones. But they don't. They keep living in our heads and come out whenever they want to keep hurting us. I know Tyler tried, but he didn't kill the bad man. He's still here, torturing me, even from the grave. I won't let him win. And I won't give up on Tyler.

The secret to fairy tales is believing in them. That's what makes them come true.

"Where did you get a dog from?" the taxi driver asks sharply, peering over her shoulder when I climb into the back seat.

"It's my dog. A friend was watching him for me." I settle Poppy on my lap. "Is it okay for him to be in the car?"

"Usually I'd rather not, but I guess it's okay." She frowns. "He seems well behaved, and he's tiny. I wouldn't want some huge-ass dog back there."

"He's very well behaved. Is there a pet store we could stop at on the way back to my apartment? I need to get him a few things. It won't take long, I promise."

She shrugs. "Sure thing, honey." I wonder if she thinks I'm crazy. She knows the place she picks me up and drops me off at is a recovery facility, and with this being such a small town, I'm sure everyone knows what kind of people live at Merryfield.

When Poppy and I lived in the basement, all he had was a food and water dish, which is about the same as I had. He never had any toys, bones, or doggy beds to sleep on. He went potty on the floor, and I would have to clean it up with paper towels and put it in a bucket until the man came and threw it away. Sometimes the smell would be horrible, but I loved the company of the dog so much I didn't mind.

I pet his head absently as I stare out the window, making a mental list of things I will need to buy at the pet store. Finally, the money my father sends me is going to some use. "Get yourself something nice," his card always says. I hope dog supplies fall into that category.

After a quick stop at the local pet store, the taxi driver expertly navigates through the afternoon traffic and pulls in front of my apartment unit at Merryfield.

Poppy whines in my arms and licks my chin as I grab my bags, thank and pay the driver, and walk up the small walkway to my and Feather's apartment. Because we're considered residents now, we have a private apartment with a separate doorway that leads outside. When I was just a patient here, I had a much smaller shared space in the main building, like a hospital room, with a door opening into the main hallway so the staff could monitor us.

Feather is draped across the couch, engrossed in a phone call, when I walk in. She does a double take when she sees me, bolts up, and tells the person on the phone that she'll call them back.

"You got a dog?" she asks incredulously.

"No...I found *my* dog. This is Poppy. Remember I told you about him?" I ask excitedly.

She eyes me suspiciously. "Okay...how exactly did you find your dog? I thought you went for your usual walk?" Her tone is laced with disbelief—like she thinks I've possibly lost my mind.

"I was looking for the Forest Santa, and I found him in the woods. The man who saved me had him. I couldn't believe it when I saw him! Poppy, I mean. And the Forest Santa! He's the guy, Feather, my prince! He didn't talk to me, but seeing him again was so unbelievable."

Her eyes get bigger, and she shakes her head really fast.

"Wait...what? Slow down a little, because I'm lost. You were looking for *what*?"

Sighing with impatience, I put Poppy down on the floor, and he runs over to sniff Feather's feet. She leans down to pet him, and he licks her hand, making me smile. Even after everything he's been through, he's still a friendly dog.

"The girl at the store where I bought the Christmas tree photos said there's a legend that a person they call Forest Santa decorates them."

She nods. "Okay, yeah. I think I've heard of that before, when I was little."

"Well, I wanted to see if I could find one of the trees, so I emailed the photographer, and he told me where he found them. So I decided to get a taxi and go there."

"Holy shit, Holly, are you crazy? You shouldn't be traipsing around in the woods alone! Why didn't you ask me to go with you?"

I shrug and clasp my hands together. "I don't know," I admit, and I really don't, other than I'm used to doing everything alone. "I didn't even think about it. I just kinda went."

Her face takes on a disapproving look, much like my mother's. "You have to be careful."

"I was very careful." I decide not to tell her about the masked man jumping out of the tree. "Anyway, I walked for a little while on the path, and I found a tree, and it was beautifully decorated and magical, just like I knew it would be!"

She raises her eyebrows at me, and I can tell she will never appreciate my love of Christmas trees.

"And then there was a man by the tree, with a Santa hat on, singing Christmas songs."

"Singing? In the woods? With a Santa hat on? Holly..." Her head tilts. "Are you sure about all this?"

"Yes," I insist. "Then Poppy came running, and he went right up to the guy with the hat, and they walked away together. I was literally just stunned."

"I know the feeling," she says, falling back onto the couch. "You do realize this sounds crazy? Like I legit think you may have hit your head and just stolen someone's dog."

"I did not. I'm totally serious." My eyes burn with tears of frustration. I need her to believe me and not think I'm crazy.

She puts her hands up. "All right, don't get upset. I'm sorry. It just sounds like a crazy coincidence, that's all. Tell me what else happened."

"Well..." I try to recall where I was in the story, and I wish she hadn't interrupted me when she knows sometimes it's hard for me to remember things when I'm talking. "Then I walked some more. And I found a little house in the woods, and Poppy was there—and so was the prince."

"Holly, you have to stop calling him that. This is real life now."

"But he's *real*."

She scratches her head and thinks for a moment. "Do you mean Tyler Grace?" she finally asks. "The guy who found you in the woods and killed that douchebag loser pedophile?"

"Yes. I think he's had Poppy ever since."

"Just...wow," she says as I sit on the floor to play with Poppy. "I can't believe you actually just...stumbled across him. And he's the Forest Santa? That's a lot of what-the-fuck going on with him."

My guard rises. "Feather, he's not what-the-fuck. He's just very...special, I think."

"That's one way of putting it." She checks her phone real quick and then puts it back down. "What else happened? Was he surprised to see you? Because I'm pretty sure he was thinking 'what the fuck' when he saw you."

"He didn't say a word," I say quietly. I wish he had talked to me—acknowledged me in some way other than yawning and shrugging. He hurt my heart, and he probably doesn't even know it.

"Did he see you?"

I roll a tennis ball across the floor and watch Poppy chase it happily, then plop down with it in his mouth. "Yes...I talked to him. He just didn't talk back."

Sensing my sadness, Feather's face softens a little and she doesn't shoot another sarcastic comment at me. "So what are you going to do now?" she asks.

I look up from Poppy. "What do you mean?"

"You can't keep him, Holly. There's a no-pet policy here."

My heart slams in my chest, and the tug toy I'm holding falls from my hand. "No-pet policy? What's that?"

"It means we can't have any cats or dogs. We can have fish tanks, but that's it."

"No," I say, my hands shaking. "They have to let me keep him. This is my home, so it's his home, too."

"I don't think so, Holly. Rules are rules. Hang on, I'll be right back."

I pull Poppy into my arms while she goes into her bedroom. I stroke his head, not remembering anyone ever saying we couldn't have pets here. I've never seen any of the other patients or residents with a pet, but maybe it's just because no one has one. That doesn't mean I can't keep Poppy, though.

"I won't lose you again," I whisper. "I won't. I love you. It's going to be okay."

Feather returns with a small booklet in her hand. "It says right here, pets are not allowed to live on the premises. Patients and residents are permitted to have one ten-gallon fish tank. Certified therapy pets are permitted only on a special case-by-case basis."

"Can't Poppy be a therapy pet?"

"No...they have to go through special training. You can't just say he's a therapy dog, even though I think—in a lot of ways, for you—he *is* a therapy dog." She puts the pamphlet on the coffee table. "I'm sorry, Holly. I know how much he means to you."

I blink my eyes hard, a dull pain throbbing in my forehead.

"There must be something I can do...Help me think, please?"

Feather kneels next to me. "Okay. Don't get upset. Take a few deep breaths. Do you want me to get one of your pills?"

A sedative is the last thing I want right now. I don't want to sleep—I want to be able to think.

"No, please. Just help me think. I'm not good at ideas, Feather. But you are." I search her eyes, pleading for her to come up with an answer for me because I have none. I don't know enough, haven't learned enough yet to come up with plans.

She combs her fingers through her hair. "Let's see..." She chews on her lip and stares across the room. "What about your parents? Could they keep Poppy for a while? Until you're ready to leave here?"

A momentary burst of hope surges through me but is quickly extinguished when I remember we're talking about my parents, who have never shown any kind of compassion for me regarding Poppy. Every time I've brought him up, they've dismissed me. They led me to believe he was happily living with a family. So either they never knew where he was and didn't even care, or they knew he was with Tyler all this time and didn't tell me.

"I don't think they'd take him," I reply. "They don't seem to like dogs."

Or me.

She sits back on her heels and meets my eyes. "Holly, I think you have to bring him back. He seems happy and clean." Her hand gently caresses Poppy's back. "It looks like he's being taken care of, right?"

I nod, the tight lump in my throat plugging back my words.

"I'm sure he would let you visit him, and you can go back and get him when you're ready to have your own place. I'll bet he would agree to that. He's obviously not a bad person."

"You can't trust anyone, little girl. Evil can hide in anyone. You brought out the evil in me."

"I guess you're right. I just really wanted to keep him." I hold Poppy closer, not wanting to let him go again. He's the only friend I had for so long. The only one who loved me. Without him, I think I would have totally forgotten what any kind of good feelings for another living thing felt like. Without him, my entire world would have consisted only of fear, contempt, and survival.

"I can drive you there now, okay?" Feather offers softly. "I really think it's for the best. You don't want to get in trouble here or do anything to set back your therapy. You're doing so good."

Some days, I *do* feel like I'm doing good. I feel strong and brave. Other days, I feel lost and unsure. "You're right." I let her help me rise to my feet. Usually, I enjoy her snarky side, but tonight I'm grateful to have this nicer, more caring side of her. My instinct has been to keep people at a distance, but maybe Dr. Reynolds was right when she said I needed to form friendships with people to help me heal and move forward.

"Let me just get my keys and send a text to let Steve know I'll be a little late. We're going to dinner tonight."

I gather up the bag of pet supplies and my backpack while I wait for her to return, and when she does, I notice she changed her clothes for her dinner tonight, and she looks beautiful. Instead of her usual baggy hoodie, she's wearing a V-neck sweater that shows off her thin waist and a small glimpse of the curve of her chest. The mere idea of a boyfriend still scares both of us, but at least she's trying. Once a man has touched you in an inappropriate way, it's hard to ever imagine enjoying touches or kisses.

"You ready?" She puts her arm around my shoulder, and I let her lead me outside.

Poppy's tail wags nervously as we get into Feather's car, and I'm pretty sure he knows things aren't going well for me tonight. He's always been able to sense my emotions.

Feather turns the radio up, and we don't talk much after I tell her where to drive. Instead of staring out the window at all the trees, as I usually do, I spend the ride whispering to Poppy, telling him how much I've missed him, how much I love him, and that I'll come back for him as soon as I can. I tell him to be the very best boy, as I know he always has been. His huge dark eyes stay solemnly on mine as if he understands every word, and I wouldn't be surprised if he did. After all, I spent years talking to him as if he were a person, and I even talked for him, in a voice with a slight made-up accent, so we could have pretend conversations.

When Feather pulls over by the dirt road that leads to the path in the woods, she tells me she'll wait in the car if I promise to be careful, but she also asks me to try not to be too long since Steve is waiting for her. The sparkle in her eye when she mentions his name makes me wish there were someone, somewhere, waiting and wanting to see me, but there's no one.

"You're my favorite toy. I count the days until I can get away and come play with you."

Shivering, I kneel down and clasp the new blue collar and leash on Poppy before we start up the trail, so he can walk with me like a real dog with a real girl in a real life that we never had.

"You look so handsome." I smile down at him, prancing next to me, and he wags his tail happily at me as we walk quickly through the woods.

Luckily, I find the small house again without getting lost, but he's no longer sitting outside, so I have no choice but to go up to the house, lightly knock on the front door, and wait for him to answer. When he does, he looks startled and nervous, shaking his head so his long blond hair falls over half his face. Continuing with his silence, he takes the leash from my outstretched hand, not inviting me in.

"I'm sorry." My voice wavers with a mix of restrained tears and anxiety. "The place I live...we can't have dogs. I didn't know." I hand him the bag of dog supplies, and he takes it from me, our fingers lightly brushing against each other during the exchange, sending a shiver up my arm, through my chest, and right into my heart. He inhales quickly with a faint hiss, making me wonder if he felt it, too. "I bought Poppy some things. Toys and dishes and food and a bed. You probably already have those things, but maybe you could still let him have them? From me?"

He nods and sets the bag on the floor just inside the doorway.

Taking a deep breath, I gaze up into his bluest of all blue eyes. "Can you take care of him for just a little while longer? I'm moving with my brother in a few months. If he says it's okay, can I come back and get him then?"

The words come out of me without conscious thought, and I wonder if that's how life decisions are usually made. *Just like that.* All of a sudden, it just felt like starting over, somewhere new, with my brother and Anna would be best, and my choice was made.

He glances down at Poppy, then back to me and winks at me.

The small gesture is unexpectedly affectionate, and in that fleeting moment, I see the ghost of who I am sure was young Tyler Grace. Playful. Incredibly handsome. Confident. *Free*.

A euphoric dizziness spreads through me. My knees weaken, and my empty stomach ripples with an odd, jittering sensation that has nothing to do with hunger for food. *Wow*. So being near the man of your dreams feels like a panic attack…only you never want it to end.

"Is that a yes?" I ask softly, still caught up in the dazed feeling.

He nods again, then holds up his hand, the one with the brightly colored tattoos all over it, with one finger pointed up. Confused, I wait as he disappears inside. He comes back a moment later and hands me a small piece of ripped, cream-colored paper.

This is his home as long as needed, says the note in blocky writing similar to what I've seen in comic books.

I look up to meet his eyes, hoping I don't faint right here on his doorstep from this overload of strange feelings. "Thank you."

He motions for me to turn the note over.

I remember you.

Written or typed words on paper have such an intense impact on me. Maybe because I lost myself in books for so long. Or maybe because we can keep them, read them again and again, and see the words whenever we need them. They can become new again, or be an old, familiar, faded memory. While I long to hear Tyler's voice, this little three-word written note is something I'll cherish forever and probably read a thousand times.

This time, I'm the one who nods, and an unspoken acceptance of sorts passes between us as his gaze stays on mine. He doesn't breathe for a few moments, and then slowly lets out a steady breath.

I realize he expects me to look away with discomfort, and

when I don't—when I stare right back with what I can only guess is a mirror of his own expression of hesitance and pleading—a flicker of relief flashes in his eyes. His tongue slowly moves across his bottom lip, and I wonder if he's going to say something, but he remains quiet. His eyes, however, continue to burn into mine with a myriad of emotions that I can feel but am unable to begin to describe.

Once again, my insides flip, and it reminds me of the excitement I felt the first time I had ice cream again. I wanted to gobble it all at once but forced myself to eat it slowly, savoring its deliciousness.

That's how Tyler makes me feel.

"I better go," I say, wrenching my eyes from his. "My friend is waiting at the road, and it's getting dark. She has a date to get to..."

He looks off behind me and up at the darkening sky; then he hands Poppy's leash back to me as he steps outside, closing his front door behind him. I look at him questioningly, and he points to the trail leading back to the road and nods.

Wordlessly, he walks me back to the end of the dirt road as the sun begins to set, the sky turning a dazzling reddish orange behind us. I turn several times to see the sky change color, and he watches me with amused interest.

He's not rude, I decide. Plagued with a bad attitude? Yes. Guarded? Definitely. But enough of a gentleman to walk me back to the car so I don't have to walk alone. On television, that's what the nice guys do when they like a girl.

"Thank you, Tyler." I hand the leash to him after crouching to give Poppy a kiss and a pet goodbye. I hope Tyler doesn't notice my hand shaking. "For saving me, and for taking care of Poppy for me. I know 'thank you' isn't enough..."

He stares down at his feet for a few seconds, and it almost seems like he's struggling, maybe wanting to say something, but when he raises his head, he just nods and then walks back up the trail. I remain rooted where I'm standing and watch them walk away. Right before they disappear from view, Poppy turns to see if I'm still there, and of course I am.

For reasons I can't understand, I long to go with them, back to the little house in the woods.

"It's about time," Feather says when I get into her car, pulling me back into reality. "I was starting to get really worried."

"I'm sorry, I went as fast as I could."

"So, what did he say?"

"Nothing. He doesn't talk."

"Still? Is that like a permanent problem? Did you see his face? What the hell happened to him?" She puts the car in drive and burns rubber back onto the road.

I don't answer her because all I see when I look at him are eyes the color of a sky I ached to see but was kept hidden from me for almost twelve years.

CHAPTER 10

Tyler

If not for her misty, blue-gray eyes, I never would have recognized the beautiful woman in front of me as the same girl I pulled out of a dirt hole. It seems like a lifetime ago.

Back then, I thought she was much younger. I guess not being able to eat or get outside in the sun and air robs a person of being able to grow properly. She's still thin and pale, but her genes obviously refused to be denied, and now her natural beauty has surpassed dirt and malnourishment. Unfortunately for her, not much can erase tragedy and heartache from forever lingering in her eyes.

I'm reminded of that little fact myself every morning when I look in the mirror.

She's still holding the note I gave her when I leave her standing by the side of the road. As I walk away, I want to turn back to see if she's still there watching me, but I don't let myself. Her dog looks back, though, and I can tell she's still there just by the amount of time it takes him to face forward again. The endless, unconditional love and loyalty of a dog are serious goals.

Call me a bastard, but I'm glad she brought him back because I would've missed this little white fucker. Sure, I still have the fuzzy red lunatic to keep me company, but the dog on the end of this new blue leash weaseled his way into my heart a year ago. We're kindred spirits, me and him.

Both debarked.

Both scarred.

Both lost.

Both worried about her.

Both still thinking about her.

As soon as I get back home, I climb into the loft to lie down but I don't fall asleep as fast as I normally do. It's been an unusual couple of days, and they keep playing over in my head. I never get visitors or people traipsing into my yard unless it's a lost hiker.

If I had known it was her, I wouldn't have tried to scare her with the mask. The thing is, though, she didn't run back toward the road screaming her head off like most people do when I play let's-scare-people-out-of-my-domain. She took control of the situation and calmly got herself away from me. She handled it like she was well trained in dealing with someone unhinged.

It made me admire her strength even more. Later, I rode into town after dark, parked down the street from where she lives, and walked to her apartment, my dark clothes blending into the shadows. I found out a while ago that she still lives in this place with the ironic name. I've checked up on her whereabouts a few times since I found her that day last year, although, if you asked me why, I wouldn't have a good answer. I just needed to know. I stood outside the facility she lives in and watched her window like the creeper I am. I needed to see her again, even from afar, just to make sure she hadn't been a figment of my imagination. And she wasn't. I'm pretty sure she saw me standing there as she peered down from her window, and I wondered if she realized it was me or if she had completely forgotten about me.

I wanted her to know it was me.

I wanted her to know I was watching her.

I wanted a small shiver of apprehension to creep up her spine.

I wanted to be responsible for igniting a feeling in a soul just as lonely and broken as my own.

On my ride back home under the moonlight, I'd been determined to put her out of my head, because nothing good can come from me obsessing over a woman. But twice today she showed up, surprising me both times with her hypnotic chatter despite my ignoring her.

Why the hell she'd be walking through the woods completely alone, after what happened to her in those same woods, I don't know. It's totally fucked up. Does she have no fear? Harboring a death wish maybe?

I can relate to that.

I felt bad toward the end, and that's why I wrote her the note. Her puffy eyes, tearstained cheeks, and the heaviness of the defeat in her voice got to me bad. It bothered me that she wasn't living at home with her family, and she couldn't keep her own damn dog.

Years ago, before my accidents, I would be at my mom's animal shelter when the lost dogs were reunited with their families. The owners were always so happy to get them back. They would hold on to the dog extra tight and cry with relief. Second chances make people more grateful and make them pour more love and care into what they thought they'd lost forever.

It makes me sick that a little stolen girl doesn't seem to be getting that same kind of love.

Three weeks after the girl brought the dog back to me, I'm in my garage fabricating new metal rings and belt buckles to sell at my brother's bike shop. Suddenly, a whiff of vanilla and lavender tickles my senses.

I glance up from my work, my vision focusing on the gap

where the side door is open a few inches, and there she is—walking toward the front door of my house with a paper bag in her hand and a backpack over her shoulder.

Squinting, I realize it's the same backpack she had the day I found her.

Strange.

When I don't answer the door, her head turns, the wind blowing her long blond hair across her face. She scans the yard with a slightly worried look, notices the side door of the garage ajar, and heads this way.

"Shit," I mutter, quickly untying my hair from its ponytail holder and letting it fall over the messed-up side of my face.

I'm wiping my dirty hands on my jeans just as she pokes her head around the door, and I wish I had closed it and locked it so she would have just gone away. Usually I don't have to worry about anyone springing an unwelcome visit on me, but this chick obviously hasn't picked up on my antisocial rules yet.

She steps inside but stays right by the door, peering around at her surroundings. Her eyes flash with curiosity and a hint of fear as they rove over my massive collection of horror masks decorating one wall.

Finally, her eyes land on me. I suppose, compared to the masks, I might seem less scary. At least a little.

I hope.

"Hi." Her shy, soft voice is so out of place in this space of dirt, noise, and horror. Like white lace being dragged through a puddle of sludge.

I say nothing.

"I hope you don't mind...I bought some gifts for Poppy." She holds up the paper bag as evidence. "For Christmas."

I *do* mind. She's not supposed to keep coming back here. Does she think I agreed to some kind of shared custody situation with the dog?

"I could never give him things before," she continues. A strand of golden hair blown loose by the wind is stuck to her mouth, and I have an incredible urge to brush it away. "And...I was wondering, did you find him after he ran off...that day? Did my parents know you had him?"

I tear my eyes from the alluring and perfect heart shape of her lips and blink at her. She shouldn't be here, with her bag of dog gifts, her expressive eyes, her perfume, and her pin-up girl lips. I can't remember the last time a girl spoke to me like a regular person, without cringing or staring, and I don't want or need reminders of the finer things in life I'm missing out on.

She's looking at me today the same way she did the day I found her. Like she only sees *me*, not the ugly scars that are like a map imprinted on my flesh. It's rattling. Back then, in the craziness of those moments, I didn't attempt to cover my face or keep my head down like I usually do when I meet new people, and I'm surprised she didn't scream when she saw me, going from one monster to another. Instead, she looked at me like I was some kind of hero or knight in shining armor. And the way she looked at me a few weeks ago when she brought the dog back reminded me of how the girls used to look at me in high school. I remember how they used to stare at me, smile, and giggle. All I had to do was flash my infamous smile at them, and they'd be blushing and slipping me their phone number. I reveled in the feeling of being wanted, accepted, and liked.

I steer my brain back to her question.

After the police let me go, I searched for her dog night and day—for a week, actually. Then one day he just strolled right into my yard. Much like she keeps doing. I fed and bathed him, took him to the vet who takes care of the dogs at the shelter to have him checked out, and hunted down Holly's parents so I could return him. Instead of taking him from me as I stood in the dark on their doorstep, they sneered at me like I was yesterday's trash, threw a few hundred dollars at me, and told me never to come back. They had no fucking idea how hard it was for me to go to their house and put myself in that position. To show up in the rich side of town in my old rusted truck, with my ripped jeans and dirty boots, scarred to hell, leaving myself wide open to judgment. So I shredded their cash, put it in a box with a fresh pile of the dog's shit, and mailed it back to them.

Mature? No. Immensely satisfying? Hell fuckin' yes.

She bites her bottom lip and looks down when I nod in response, sparing her the details of that day. "I thought so," she mumbles softly, then pushes the stray hair behind her ear. When her gaze rises again, there's a glimmer of defiance and hope battling the disappointment. "Can I see him?" she asks. "Just for a few minutes?"

This girl is getting on my nerves because, seriously, how the hell can I say no? She's a major block to my usual assholism.

I let out a sigh to let her know exactly how much she's bothering me and push roughly by her through the doorway on the way to the house. She doesn't follow me, so I let Poppy out, and he runs directly to her in my workshop like he already knew she was there with his doggy radar.

Ignoring her while she sits with the dog on my garage floor, I go back to my workbench, hoping she'll just play with the dog for a few minutes and then leave so I can go back to my day in peace. She talks absently to the dog and occasionally to me, but I stay focused on my work, throwing her glances every now and then from behind the curtain of my hair, wondering when she's going to figure out that I don't do conversation.

"Is this what you do for work? You make this stuff?" she asks, pointing to the finished rings, bracelets, and belt buckles lined up on one of the workbenches.

I nod, not moving my hair out of my face, afraid she'll finally come to her senses and see the ugliness that is me and run for the hills.

She stands and takes a closer look at the items. "I really like them. The skulls are a little scary, though."

When I don't respond, she resumes her one-sided conversation.

"Last week I started working part-time at that frozen yogurt and ice cream place in town. It's one of the few places close enough for me to walk to. It's my first job, and even though it's only two days a week, it's kind of scary." Her eyes squint a little like it hurts her to think about it, to have to feel it. "I guess I'm just not used to being around people yet. I love the bubble tea, though. I drink one every day when I walk back home after work. The lady that owns the shop lets me have one for free."

My head snaps up. "What the fuck is bubble tea?"

She jumps at the sound of my voice, and I'm equally surprised because usually I have to force words out of my mouth. This time, they just slipped out without any effort.

Her eyes twinkle. "Wow, is that really going to be the first thing you say to me?" she asks.

I wait for her expression to change to one of disgust, fear, or nosy curiosity about the oddness of my voice, but it doesn't. Instead, a smile crosses her lips, and now my ability to speak has been whisked away by how incredibly beautiful she is when her demons loosen their grip on her. When was the last time a woman genuinely smiled at me? *Years.*

"Bubble tea is a creamy, cold, sweet drink that has these little things called tapioca bubbles at the bottom of the cup, and you chew on them. They're squishy. Some are different, and they pop. It's one of the best things I've had since I . . ." Her voice trails off uneasily. "Since I got back home."

Strange shit like bubble tea and lattes with fucked-up words for sizes makes me believe hiding away is actually a good choice. What happened to root beer floats and a coffee with extra cream and sugar? And why the hell is she walking to and from town every day? If my memory's right, that's how she got kidnapped in the first place.

"Sounds weird," I reply, but even stranger is how relaxed my throat muscles feel. The words are flowing out naturally, without effort, like they used to before my life went to hell.

"It is," she agrees. "But it's such a good weird." A wistful look settles on her face as she stares off, thinking about her favorite drink. It's sweet and sad, how something so simple makes her happy, and it almost makes me feel guilty for being drawn to such a bittersweet smile.

I give her ten more minutes, and then I light up a smoke and point to the door.

"What?" She looks back at the door behind her. "You want me to leave?"

I flick off the lights, and she practically runs outside with the dog at her heels, stopping a few feet away to turn back as I lock the door behind us. I didn't mean to scare her, but at least it got her out.

"Okay." Her voice is laced with disappointment. "I'll go. Thank you for letting me see Poppy again."

I chuckle a little. Before she started dropping by, I was calling him Buddy. *I was close.* I take a drag on my cigarette and whistle for the dog to follow me into the house. He hesitates halfway between us—looking from her to me, his loyalty torn—then runs back to her.

Little traitor.

She picks him up and carries him to me, her eyes brimming with tears as she places him gently in my arms like a baby, her perfume invading my personal space. She smells of everything soft, feminine, and delicious, but the dark mascara-stained tears tracking down her cheeks tell a far different story. *Fuck.* The allure of tainted beauty is not a delicacy I can indulge in. No matter how tempting it is.

I used to like to break things and put them back together again, to see how they worked inside. Toys. Engines. Myself. No way am I adding a woman to that list. Especially one who's already trying to figure out where her bent and twisted pieces are supposed to go.

"Merry Christmas," she murmurs before she turns away, reminding me that Christmas is just a few days away.

"Happy birthday," I call after her.

Of course I remembered. It's my dad's birthday, too.

CHAPTER 11

Holly

A swarm of people have piled into the tiny ice cream shop. I count four adults and at least ten little kids. They're excited, running around. Tipping chairs over and shrieking.

The other girl who usually works with me is out sick today, and the owner doesn't come by until after four, so I'm here by myself. We thought it would be slow today since it's two days before Christmas, but we were wrong.

"Can you make the cones faster?" the man on the other side of the counter asks. "Some of the kids are finished with theirs already, and others haven't even gotten any yet. That's why they're screaming."

I smile weakly, my hand shaking as I pull the handle on the vanilla soft-serve machine. My head spins, and my thin shirt sticks to my arms and torso. I hand the man the cone and grab another one. "I'm sorry, did you say vanilla?"

"Chocolate. And I need that one in a dish," he says impatiently. "You should really be writing this down."

As I reach for a paper dish, my shirt sleeve catches and knocks the entire teetering stack of cones off the counter. The customer huffs behind me. Overwhelmed with all the noise and rushing, I pick one up and start to fill it with ice cream.

"Excuse me," a female customer says in a nasty tone, leaning over the counter. "You just picked that up off the floor, and now you're filling it with ice cream? Are you serious right now?"

Shaking my head, I throw it in the trash and grab a new one from a stack of smaller sizes. "I'm s-so s-sorry," I stammer, on the verge of tears. "You're r-right."

"Do you people even clean this place?" the man continues, his tone getting angrier. "Where is the manager?"

I look over my right shoulder at him. "She's not here right now," I answer, my voice hoarse.

He shakes his head like maybe he thinks I'm lying. "I want to speak to the manager. You could have just given one of our kids ice cream in a dish that was on the floor."

"You want to eat, little girl? Get on your knees and eat it off the floor."

I try to fill the cone with ice cream, but the man's voice stops me from doing anything. My ears start to ring, my face burns, and the room feels like it's suddenly a thousand degrees. The screaming kids are getting louder. The other adults waiting shoot me dirty looks.

"I'm sorry. It was an accident…" My voice trembles uncontrollably. My mind goes blank. I can't remember what he wants or what I'm doing here. *Where am I?* Terror seizes me like a vise.

Once upon a time, there was a beautiful princess…

My eyes clamp shut, the memorized words playing out in my mind, soothing me, taking me back. *Yes. Please take me away from here. To the castle, or the cottage in the forest with butterflies and singing birds, blue skies, and fluffy clouds.*

I try to focus, clear my mind of all the noise—out here and in my head—but I can't remember my breathing exercises.

"What the hell is wrong with you? Are you on drugs? Hey!" he shouts. "Are you even listening to me?"

I can't move. The edge of my vision grows dark, and the

voices of the children and the adults yelling become distant and distorted.

I fall—deep into the only place I feel safe—once again.

A bright light shines in my face. I think I'm dead. I must have died in the ice cream shop. Maybe that angry man killed me.

"Holly?"

I turn toward the voice to see my brother's girlfriend. "Anna? What happened? Where am I? Are we dead?"

Her face looms over mine. "No, silly, we're not dead." She gives me a quick smile meant to be comforting. "You're in the emergency room. You passed out at work, and one of the customers called an ambulance. You had a really bad panic attack on the way here, so they gave you a sedative. You've been asleep for a little while but you're fine."

"Oh." The memories of lying on the floor with the ice cream dishes and the ride in the ambulance rush back to me. "I knocked over the dishes. Everyone was so mad."

Worry stamps Anna's face as she sits on the edge of the hospital bed and touches my hand. People always seem to be touching me, and while it still makes me uncomfortable, I've learned to tolerate it. Anna must have come from work because she's wearing beige dress pants, high heels, and a silk blouse. Her dark hair is in a sleek ponytail. I'm not sure where she works, but it's definitely not in an ice cream shop.

"It's okay, Holly. It was just a bad day, that's all." Her voice is reassuring, but her eyes betray her with their deepening concern. "Do you feel all right? I can call one of the nurses back."

My chest heaves and my throat constricts as the memory of what happened in the ice cream shop comes back to me. I know I didn't just faint. I had a meltdown and blacked out. It's happened before—in the basement with the man, and at Merryfield during my first month. "I feel fine...but it's really not okay, Anna. I freaked out, I think." I shake my head, recalling the kids and the screaming and being alone in the shop with no help. And the angry man who wouldn't stop yelling at me. "Too much was happening, the man was getting mad at me and I—"

"Slow down. Take a deep breath." She takes one with me, breathing in and out. "It's not your fault. You really shouldn't have been alone there. It would be a lot for anyone to handle."

"Am I in trouble?" I ask.

"No, not at all...but I did speak to the manager, and she thinks it's best that you not come back." She squeezes my hand tighter between both of hers and leans closer to me like she's going to tell me a secret. "It's probably for the best. I'm not sure that was the ideal job for you. I think something quieter would be better." She looks at me hopefully. "If you come to New York with Zac and me, I'll help you find a job that will be good for you. Like maybe in a small, cozy bookstore. You love books, right?"

I let that sink in, and I actually do like the sound of that. "Yes... I would like that," I say slowly. "I liked the ice cream shop, but I'm just not used to so many people and everyone talking at once."

"That's understandable, Holly. You're going to need time, that's all. Customer service is one of the hardest jobs out there." I can see why Zac likes her, with her soft voice and caring eyes. "I give you credit for working in a place like that to begin with. If I did, I'd gain fifty pounds in the first week from eating everything in sight."

"I really loved the bubble tea," I tell her, remembering Tyler's first words to me, and how it felt like getting a surprise gift to hear him talk. Earlier today, before the disaster, I had the idea of bringing him a tea to use as an excuse to see Poppy again. *And him.* "Is my mother here?" I sit up to look around. I realize I'm not in a room at all, but a corner of a much larger room sectioned off with dividers and curtains. I can hear other patients just on the other side of the curtains.

"No, but she's on her way," Anna says after a slight hesitation. "They called her first, but she was in a meeting, so she called Zac. He's in the city today, so he called me."

I'm slightly saddened by the fact that it took a chain of phone calls to get to someone who could come see if my brain was leaking out of my head.

"I'm so sorry, Anna. You can go back to work. I'll be fine here," I tell her. I don't want her to think I'm going to be too much trouble, or else she may not let me move with them.

"You're no bother at all. You're my family now." She glances at the clock on the wall. "The nurse was in here right before you woke up. She said a doctor would be in soon and they'll probably want to do a CT scan." She must notice the look of fear on my face because she quickly reassures me. "That's just a simple X-ray. It won't hurt at all, and they mostly just do them as a precaution. You're totally fine, and I'm sure you'll be out of here in a few hours."

"Really?" I ask, dubious and a little wary. The last time I was brought here, I didn't get out for weeks, and then I was sent to Merryfield.

"*Really,*" she emphasizes. "I promise."

A nurse comes to take my vitals; then a doctor arrives and examines me for all of two minutes before sending me for the X-ray. When the nurse brings me back to my area in the ER, Anna is gone but my mother is there in her place, and she immediately starts to question the nurse. I sit on the bed and wait, feeling like I am the cause of a lot of stress for everyone.

"What happened?" my mother finally asks me when the nurse leaves. I give her a shortened version of my day, leaving out how the man yelled at me and how I blacked out. Instead, I tell her I felt dizzy and fainted.

She smooths down my hair. "You poor thing. I told you I thought it wasn't a good idea for you to get a job yet. It's too much. You need to rest and let your mind and body heal from all the abuse. If you need money, Daddy and I can give you whatever you need."

Sighing, I wish we could go just one day without her bringing up what happened to me in some way. As much as she says we all need to forget it, she is always the one bringing it back up. "Mom, I need to do *something*."

"Well...maybe just start with a hobby," she suggests.

"Like what?" I ask.

"I don't know, Holly. Maybe photography? You love those pictures you bought." She pulls back the privacy curtain and stares around. "Where the hell is that doctor? I need to get back to work. I have meetings all day long today, and I have a ton of baking to do for Christmas. It's just two days away."

"I'm sorry."

"Don't be sorry." She looks at me apologetically. "It's just a very busy time of year, that's all. Do you know how to bake?"

I stare at the woman who should know everything about me and knows absolutely nothing. "Yes," I answer softly. "They let us bake at Merryfield. We're allowed near ovens."

"Good," she says, clearly not catching my newfound dry sarcasm. "You can start baking the cookies when I take you home. I think it's best I take you right to the house from here and not back to your apartment until after the holiday. I want to keep an eye on you." She pulls her phone out of her purse and starts to read her emails. "Maybe you could take up cake decorating or cupcakes. Lots of young women do that." She doesn't look up from her phone as she makes these suggestions. "Then after the holidays, we'll think about online college classes. Your father and I are discussing what's best for you so we can help you have a good future. That's all we want for you, so you can put the past behind you and try to live some kind of a normal life someday."

Some kind of a normal life? Someday? She says it like it's almost an impossible feat. Like there's a huge mountain of insurmountable obstacles in front of me. Like I'm so severely backward and damaged that I'm doomed to a life of...what? Living in a supervised facility? Living with my parents? Not being able to do something worthwhile and important? Not able to get married and have a family someday? Her insinuation hits me harder than anything that anyone else has said to me since I've been freed. I lost my childhood and the opportunity to form friendships and relationships. I missed out on a lot of my life. I was mentally and physically abused. But I'm not stupid. I'm not afraid to live and learn. I *want* to. Determination sprouts and grows in me as her words resonate through me. I'll prove her wrong.

I'll prove everyone wrong.

Soon, the doctor comes in to discharge me and advises me to rest for a few days before resuming daily activity. I almost laugh at that. If I spend any more time resting and sitting still, I'm going to lose my mind. I can't do it anymore.

CHAPTER 12

Tyler

Nineteen years old

This party is boring as hell, but I didn't come here to socialize. I came here for my three favorite things: oxy, weed, and speed. Oxy to kill the pain, weed to chill me out, and speed to wake my ass up.

I wouldn't mind a side of coke and a blowjob to top it off, but neither one of those seems to be an option for me tonight, judging from this crowd.

My old high school friend Jimmy invites me to all his college parties, even though I haven't had any sort of academic goals or socialized with friends since I was pushed into a bonfire two years ago and came out looking like a side of beef jerky.

By the time I had gone through countless burn treatments, skin grafts, and other horrific shit I'd rather not think about, school was no longer a priority for me. My chance of getting an athletic scholarship was gone. Most of my so-called friends had gone MIA, one of them taking my girlfriend with him.

Good riddance, assholes and bitches.

Friends were overrated anyway, once morphine became the love of my life.

Pre-fire, I worked out five days a week and ran every morning. I ate lean and clean. I meditated and did yoga. I had a few beers and got stoned maybe once or twice a month with friends to unwind. My body and my mind were my ticket to everything I wanted in my future: athletic success, inspiring others, and an equally beautiful and healthy partner to share life with.

At seventeen, I had a clearly defined path mapped out for myself, and I wasn't going to let anything get in my way. I had watched my father struggle to pay bills and work his ass off seven days a week at the motorcycle shop he'd owned for twenty years. Pop had a lot of biker friends, and if they needed something, he was there. That included fixing their bikes for free because that's what bikers do. It's one big family. That shit didn't pay the bills, though, and I refused to follow in his footsteps. I'd let my brothers do that. Me? I was getting out of this town, population of twelve hundred.

Raising the bottle of whiskey to my lips, I welcome the burn as it seeps down my chest and into my gut, recalling, with equal bitterness, how I left the hospital with a flicker of hope and a handful of prescriptions. Hope soon took a back seat to an addiction that had crept up on me slowly, obliterating my plans.

My physical scars were easy to see, splayed out across my flesh for people to stare at, back away from, and question endlessly. The scars on the inside, though, managed to go unnoticed as they snaked through me like poison.

A tall, lanky kid approaches me where I'm perched on a fence post thirty feet away from the crowd of college kids drinking, dancing, and making out. He wouldn't be coming over here in the dark unless he had good reason, so I know he's the one I've been waiting for.

"You Ty?" he asks nervously, his eyes scanning the area like he expects the police to jump out of the shadows.

"Well, I ain't Mickey Mouse."

He pushes his silver-rimmed glasses up his nose. "Jimmy sent me to hook you up."

I take a pull off my drink. "Yay for Jimmy," I say sarcastically. "Whaddya got, Waldo?"

He reaches into his jacket pocket and produces a clear plastic bag filled with weed, pills, and a small vial of coke.

"How much?"

"Eight hundred."

Without much regret, I pull out a wad of cash. Some worked for, some stolen. "Guess I won't be eating for a while," I say, handing almost all of it over to him.

He double-checks my count. "Or you could just not do drugs."

Laughing, I snatch the bag from him and cram it down the front of my jeans. "Not exactly good advice coming from a dealer. Don't they teach you marketing in college?"

"I only sell it. I don't do it."

I jump off the fence and give him a friendly smack on the back. "Do yourself a favor and don't do either."

Too tired to find a girl drunk enough to go down on me, I ditch the party and head for my car, parked on a dark, dead-end street. On my way, I spot a lone girl leaning against a car in front of Jimmy's house, her face in her hands, crying. As I get closer, I realize it's Wendy.

Lighting up a cigarette, I saunter over to her. "Whatsa matter, Wendy? Karma biting your ass?" I slur.

"Fuck off, Tyler," she lashes out, wiping away the snot that's running from her nose. Two years ago, I thought she was one of the prettiest girls in school. Somewhere along the line she lost her glow, and a dull version of my first crush stands sniveling in her place.

Cradling her chin in my palm, I lift her face toward the

streetlight to see the purple and blue discoloration on her cheek and the beginnings of a black eye.

"Don't touch me." She jerks her face out of my hand and looks down at the ground between us. "Get away from me."

"You still can't look at me, can you, Wendy?" I ask, leaning closer to her, my body inches from hers. "Do I make you that sick?"

She lifts her head, and her cold gaze flits from my eyes to the mottled flesh that runs across half my forehead and down the side of my face. Gulping, she closes her eyes and turns her head away.

"You're drunk and probably high, Ty. *That* makes me sick."

"Then look at me." I rest one hand on the car door next to her. "Look at me like you used to."

Still looking away, she tries to melt into the car door in an effort to put more distance between us. "I can't, okay?" she says defiantly. "It skeeves me out. Are you happy now?"

I take a long drag off my cigarette and blow the smoke in her face. "Yeah, Wendy, I am. 'Cause it looks like you're getting exactly what you fucking deserve."

I leave her standing there, wondering what kind of future she thinks she's going to have when, at nineteen years old, she's decided that a good-looking guy who hits her is more appealing than one who's scarred but treated her like gold.

My emotions are broiling when I get behind the wheel of my old pickup truck. Two years after the accident, and Wendy still has the ability to twist the knife—reminding me that, even after seeing her every single day for three hundred and eighty-six days—I never realized her shitty-ass version of teen love came with a condition, and that condition was *looks*. Everything I did for her was forgotten in an instant once I wasn't good-looking enough for her anymore.

Back then, I'd never pinned her for the shallow type. I was wrong. Just like I was wrong about a lot of things and a lot of people. I was served a crash course in reality after I was pushed into that fire, and it still eats at me like acid because this isn't supposed to be my life and I don't know how the hell to change it.

I shouldn't be driving, drunk, and underage with a bag of drugs in my pants, but I drive home in a rage anyway, not giving two fucks if I get pulled over and thrown in jail.

By the time I get home, it's after 2:00 a.m., and my father is in the dark living room, dozing on the couch with a horror movie playing on the television. My parents always go to bed together, so I can only assume he stayed up to wait for me. I creep by him on my way to my room, but I trip over a dog toy in the middle of the floor and then bang into the coffee table, which I could've sworn was two feet to the right.

"Shit," I mutter, rubbing my shin.

My father stirs and sits up, squinting in my direction against the glare of the television. "Ty? That you?"

"Go to bed," I reply, swaying.

Instead, he stands and flicks on the lamp next to the couch, narrowing his eyes at me.

"You look like shit."

"Thanks, Pop."

"I can smell the alcohol on you from here. You been drinking again?"

Obviously. I lean against the wall to keep from falling on my ass. "Don't start, okay? I've had enough shit for one day."

He steps closer and grabs my shoulder, pulling me off the wall. His six-foot-four muscular frame looms over me. My father was a badass back in the day, and he's still tough enough to kick my ass if he wanted to.

"Stand up like a man, Tyler," he says. "You drove home like this?"

My vision blurs, and I see two of him in front of me. "Yeah..."

"You tryin' to get killed? Or kill someone else?"

I blow out a breath and shove my hand through my long, tangled hair. All I want to do is lie down before the nausea rippling through me makes a messy appearance. "No...just blowin' off some steam."

He rubs his forehead in frustration. "This shit is gonna stop. *Today*. Your mother and I aren't going to sit back and watch you throw your life away—"

"What life, Pop?" I scoff. "What fucking life do I have?"

"Any life you want."

"Like this? Looking like this?"

"Scars don't define you, Tyler. What you do—and how you treat others—does. You're hurting. You're mad at the world. I get it. More than you know." A hint of sadness and regret deepens his tone. "But people live with far worse problems than what you're dealing with. Stop letting this ruin you. You're better than this."

No one seems able to grasp that, to me, I *am* ruined. Broken and wrecked and wandering around lost without a compass. "Well, sorry I'm such a big disappointment to you. Thank God you got five other kids to be proud of."

His eyes soften, my words hitting him like a punch. "That never even crossed my mind. I've always been proud of you. You've always been special. But you need some help getting out of this fucking hole you're in. You think I'm just going to let you get drunk and high every day?"

"I'm nineteen. I can do whatever the hell I want."

"Not under my roof you won't. And not in my business. This bullshit of coming to the shop stoned every day is gonna stop, too. It's time to grow up. I want you in rehab tomorrow."

No way am I going to rehab to sit around with a bunch of drunks and addicts sharing my feelings and listening to theirs. I'm not like them at all, and I'd rather gouge out my own eyes and ears than put myself through that.

"Fuck that." I push past him, but then I turn back. "And ya know what? Fuck all this. I'm outta here." I fish my keys out of my pocket. "I'll just get out of your house and your shop for good."

His shoulders drop as he sighs. "Tyler...just go upstairs and sleep it off. We'll go together tomorrow. In a few weeks, you'll be clean with a much better outlook on your life. Trust me."

An obnoxious laugh erupts from me. "I seriously doubt that."

Ignoring him as he continues to talk to my back, pleading with me not to leave, I stumble out of the house and jump on my bike, with him chasing after me in his bare feet. I glance back to see him stop halfway down the driveway—waving his hands at me, probably cursing me out—as I tear down the street.

Music blasting from my earphones quells my mood slightly as I ride up to the mountains, the only place I feel at peace, away from everyone. My bike tears up the dark, twisty mountain road, heading to a lookout point where I can pull over, roll a joint, and stare at the stars until this never-ending pain deep in my chest subsides. Tomorrow I'll figure out what the hell I'm going to do next, but I definitely won't be going to rehab or facing my parents. The last thing I need is more hospitals, doctors, and counselors telling me I'm going to be okay. None of them understand how not okay I really am.

And probably never will be.

It's pitch-black when I pull over to the remote dirt area that overlooks the towns below, but the glow of my phone gives me just enough light to find the old fallen tree I sit on every time I come up here. I watch the tiny car lights in the distance as I smoke the joint I just rolled, my only company the occasional breeze and an owl hooting off in the distance. Despite my peaceful surroundings, Wendy's words continue to echo in my ears.

It skeeves me out.

Yeah, she was probably a bit drunk, and obviously in the midst of a fight, but she meant what she said. There's a lot of truth in the words of angry people. There was a time when I thought I loved her, but I felt nothing but pity and disgust when I saw the bruises on her face. If I had ever really, truly loved her, it would have enraged me. I would have hunted that douchebag down and beaten him to a pulp, even if she wasn't mine anymore. Maybe we never really did love each other. I reach into my pants, pull out the bag of drugs, and swallow two pills dry. I wait for the bitter pills to drag slowly down to my stomach before I grab my phone and press the speed dial for my older brother, who picks up on the fourth ring.

"Yeah?" his deep, groggy voice bellows from the tiny phone speaker.

"Tor...it's me." I clear my throat of the burn. "Can I stay at your place for a while?"

"Ty? What the fuck? Do you know what time it is?"

"Around four...maybe. I think. Not sure."

"Are you drunk?"

"Sorta. Among other things." Hey, at least I'm an honest junkie.

His exasperated sigh travels through the phone. "Where are you?"

"Up at the lookout smokin' a few."

"Tell me you didn't drive up there."

"Nope." I exhale smoke and watch it drift away into the dark. "I took the bike."

"Seriously, Ty?" His voice grows louder as anger wakes him. "What the hell is wrong with you? Are you out of your fucked-up mind?"

"Skip the lecture, I've had enough for one night. Can I just stay at your place for a few days? I'm going through a rough time…"

The sound of sheets rustling sifts through the background. "No. I'm going back to bed. And I'm going to wring your neck the next time I see you."

Click.

"Asshole." Standing, I snuff out the joint and put the roach in my pocket for later. He could have easily said yes, especially since his band is going on tour and his place is going to be empty. What's the big deal if I stay there? He can fuck off, too, along with everyone else.

I start up my bike and ride into the brisk mountain air. It's just me, the road, and nature, and maybe that's the way it's supposed to be. My body relaxes, my mind eases, and I sink into the numbing, welcoming haze.

It was dark, and there was light.

Flashing, burning.

There was warmth, and there was ice.

Melting, oozing.

I was flying, but I had no wings.

Floating, drifting.

Until there was nothing at all.

The silence screamed the loudest, crying to be heard.

"Tyler?" My brother's voice booms through the fog. "Just nod if you can hear me. Stop trying to move."

Tor is singing Pink Floyd songs. Why?

I nod, not wanting him to sense my confusion. The familiar sterile, bleachy smell and the faint beeping in the background bring me to the slow realization that I'm back in a hospital.

"I convinced your doctor to let me tell you what's going on, but he's right outside the door and he's going to come in after I leave. Are you okay with that?"

I nod again, niggling fear mounting when I realize I can't move or talk. And my brother is acting weird, talking to me almost like I'm a child.

"You're going to hate me for a while, Ty. And that's okay, because I hate you right now, too, because I need you, and you're a mess. I'm gonna make this short and sweet because I can't be in six places at once." He coughs into his hand. "You crashed your motorcycle into someone's house. You went right through their living room wall of floor-to-ceiling windows."

Fuck.

"No surprise—the doctors found alcohol and drugs in your system, and in your pocket, so I'm having a hard time feeling sorry for you right now." He slowly shakes his head, disappointment emanating from him. "I love you, bro, but you did this to yourself. You can only dance with the devil for so long."

I nod, the weight in my chest growing heavier, like a rhinoceros sitting on me.

"You're pretty shredded up from the glass. To put it mildly? Your scars now have scars. Everywhere. You've got a few broken bones, but you're lucky to be fucking alive, and you're damn lucky those people were in bed, or you probably would have killed them while they were sitting in their living room watching TV."

He avoids my eyes as I stare up at him from the hospital bed, silently begging him to just stop talking. I can't hear any more of this or bear any more of the suffocating pressure in my chest.

His eyes finally sink into mine, and they're darker than I've ever seen, like something has sucked the color and life from him. "I want you to listen to me, Ty, because I'm not going to have the strength to repeat this. You got that?"

I blink and nod, an icy chill scattering through my veins.

"A shard of glass pierced your neck and, by some miracle, didn't hit your jugular, but it *did* damage part of your vocal cords. The doctor said it went in at just the perfect angle." He steps away and stares out the window, watching the rain fall outside. "You're going to need surgery, and you're not going to be able to talk for a while, if ever. I'll let the doctor explain after I leave. It's probably best if you don't try to speak."

My heart pounds harder, a deep bass of fear and remorse, and when he turns back around, I'm sure the devastation on his face mirrors my own.

I can't talk. I might never speak again.

There's even more scars. Scars that will never heal.

You skeeve me out.

I could have killed someone.

I wish I had killed myself.

"I know you're scared...but there's more." He takes a shaky breath before continuing. "Pop's gone." My brother's baritone voice cracks and wavers. "He had a heart attack last night, and he died before they could get him to the hospital."

I stop breathing. Everything around me stills. The sounds and smells tunnel backward. I silently will this moment to stop, to change, to not ever exist. I refuse to breathe, because I don't want to move to the next moment: a time where my father no longer lives.

Tor covers his face with his hands for a moment and then slowly drops them. "I wish I could stay with you, but I can't.

Mom's not dealing well with all this...none of them are...and I need to go make the arrangements." He rocks on his heels, his hands stuffed into his front pockets as he stares down at me, his exhausted, bloodshot eyes staying on mine, watching me absorb the worst news of my life. "I don't have it in me to make this better for you, Ty, and I hope someday you can forgive me for that. If it's any consolation to you, my life is ruined now, too. I can't leave Mom and the rest of you alone. I can kiss the tour and the band goodbye."

I blink, and a tear slips down my scarred cheek. Silent sobs rack my body long after he leaves me alone in the cold hospital room. I cry for my father, who I'll never get to make things right with or apologize to. I cry for my mother, who lost her best friend and the love of her life. I cry for my brothers and my sister for losing an amazing father. I cry for Tor, for coming so close to his dreams, only to have them ripped away.

The faint voice that's been whispering to me for the past two years, telling me how ugly I am and what a mess I am, finally finds its voice and screams through my soul.

This is all your fault.

I've never been a man afraid to cry, but right now I'm afraid I'm never going to stop.

CHAPTER 13

Holly

"Holly! Wake up!" Lizzie bursts into my room, still wearing her red pajamas. "It's Christmas. You have to come downstairs for presents."

Turning my head on the pillow, I glance at the clock next to my bed. It's barely 6:00 a.m., but my little sister is wide awake and hyperexcited. Sitting up, I cover my mouth as I yawn. I have yet to get a full night's sleep since I was freed. Nightmares jolt me awake several times per night, and then I have a hard time falling asleep again.

"Sleep is an earned privilege, little girl. Not a right."

"Come on," Lizzie urges.

I smile at her, remembering the excitement of my own childhood Christmas mornings before there weren't any ever again. Until today.

Today I get to have a Christmas and a birthday with my family again. I'm here for a four-day visit this time, the longest I've ever stayed at my parents'.

"Okay, okay," I say teasingly, throwing my blanket off. "I'll be down in a few minutes."

She races down the hallway, her small feet thumping down the stairs to the living room. Stretching, I gaze out the window and smile when I see snowflakes slowly falling. Snow on Christmas! I run to the window to see the ground covered in a velvety blanket of white. After breakfast, I'm going outside to walk in it, make footprints, and catch snowflakes on my tongue. As I cross the room to grab the robe draped over my chair, I spot something strange on one of the other windows in my room. Frowning, I approach it slowly, knowing it wasn't there last night, and it's on the *outside* of the window.

My eyes focus on the red envelope taped to the glass. Cautiously, I peek around the edge of the curtain, not seeing any footprints in the fresh snow or on the sloped porch roof under the window. Quickly, I unlatch the lock, push up the window, and grab the card. I close the window just as fast and make sure I lock it immediately.

"If you run away, I will find you. I'll take you again. And again, and again, and again."

Someone, somehow, got up to my second-story window. While I was sleeping.

Goose bumps sprout up on my flesh as I turn the card in my hands.

"Holly!" my mother calls from downstairs, making me jump nearly out of my skin. "We're waiting for you."

"I'll be right there!"

With shaking hands, I rip the envelope open and pull out a white greeting card. There's a tiny penguin on the front, balancing a wrapped Christmas present on its head. It doesn't appear threatening at all. Slowly opening it, I see the printed words *Merry Christmas* and below that, in blocky handwriting, *and Happy Birthday*. A photo has fallen out of the card and fluttered to the floor at my feet. My heart lurches when I pick it up and turn it over.

It's a photo of the decorated tree, deep in the woods, with Poppy posing next to it with a Santa hat on, a happy doggy grin on his face. Tears of happiness spring to my eyes. Only Tyler could have left this card here for me. But why? And more importantly, how? Did he actually climb up the house in the middle of the night? And how did he know I was here, and which room was mine?

How bizarre.

How stalkery.

How romantic.

A new shiver courses through me, this one warm and tingly and unlike any sensation I've ever felt. After what I went through, things like this should scare me. Someone watching me should be a huge red flag. I'm intelligent enough, and I've watched enough TV, to know that. If it was anyone else, I would be terrified. But it's Tyler, and he's an exception. He's special, and he doesn't scare me. I hold the photo and the card over my heart for a moment before putting them in my nightstand for safekeeping.

Christmas morning is a whirlwind of exchanging gifts, listening to holiday music, and eating an unimaginable amount of food. Zac and Anna join us, which seems to be the norm from what I can tell. My parents cook pancakes, waffles, eggs, and bacon together and appear happier than I've ever seen them as they tease each other in the kitchen. After breakfast, they surprise me by singing "Happy Birthday" and piling more presents in front of me. Being the center of attention is awkward for me, and poor Lizzie can't understand why I'm getting extra presents and she isn't.

I rise from my seat on the couch and put my arm around her, which she always loves. "I'm going to put some clothes on and go walk in the snow. Do you want to come with me?" I ask her, hoping it will cheer her up.

Her face lights up. "Yes! Maybe we can make snow angels!"

"Awesome. Go get dressed, okay? You can't go outside in your jammies."

"Lizzie," Mom says from the kitchen. "Maybe you can go outside later. Daddy is going to get Grandma soon. Go put your nice new dress on."

My little sister pouts and stomps her foot. "But I want to go out in the snow with Holly. We're going to make angels like Holly used to be."

I open my mouth to respond, but Mom gives us both a warning look before shoving a casserole dish into the oven and turning back to us. "Lizzie, it's Christmas. Don't be difficult."

The happiness I felt a moment ago is replaced by growing anger as I watch my sister stomp off to her room. My mother refuses to look at me as I stare at her.

"I'd love to take a walk," Anna offers, sensing the tension. "If you don't mind me going with you?"

"Not at all." I force a smile onto my face, resuming the mask. "I'll be back in a few minutes."

I take my presents upstairs and change into jeans, a sweater, and boots. As I'm leaving my room, the sound of my mother in her bedroom across the hall catches my attention. Mustering up courage, I nervously run my fingers through my hair and cross the hall to knock on her bedroom door.

"Come in."

Her face is full of surprise when I enter the room and close the door behind me. I watch her as she lays outfits out on her bed for evaluation. "Holly . . . do you like the presents we got you? You're so hard to buy for. We can exchange anything you don't like."

"I loved everything. Thank you." I now have more clothes than I ever thought possible. Zac and Anna gave me two new books, a candle, and a coffee mug that changes color with temperature, which I thought was fascinating. I've never seen anything like it and can't wait to use it.

"Mom...," I say hesitantly. "Did I do something wrong?"

She looks up from the four outfits on her bedspread with a distracted frown. "What? Why on earth would you ask that?"

I lean against her dresser and clasp my hands in front of me. "It's just...every time I try to spend time with Lizzie, you jump in and stop it. It's been going on for months. It confuses her. And to be honest, it's confusing for me, too. She's my sister. I'm trying to get to know her."

Her lips close into a thin line, and silent admission is all over her face.

"Why?" I urge. "I'm not contagious."

"Holly, don't be ridiculous. Lizzie is just a little girl...and she doesn't really know you. She's very vulnerable and innocent." Her chin lifts slightly. "I don't want her to know any details about your past. I've tried very hard to protect her from all of it. She'd be petrified if she knew the truth."

I remember being petrified. I remember it very well. And I was also just a little innocent girl. "Details?" I repeat coldly. "Do you think I'm going to tell my little sister I was starved and raped, Mom? Do you think I'm going to tell her how I was kept locked in an old dirty room for most of my life?"

Her hand goes to her neck, fingering the gold cross necklace she wears every day. "Keep your voice down, please," she says, but there's a manic edge to her voice. "Everyone is right downstairs. They don't need to hear such awful things."

"I would never tell her those things. But she *is* my little sister, and she *is* curious. Eventually, she's going to ask questions. What am I supposed to say? I wasn't on vacation." I swallow hard over the anger that's slowly building up in me. "You told her I was dead. Do you want her thinking dead people come back to life? That's just as scary as what really *did* happen to me."

She looks away, still fingering her cross necklace. Maybe she's praying for this topic to end. "Honestly, I don't know what to tell her," she says, her voice harsh. "I have no idea how to explain this to a child. Nobody should ever have to have such conversations."

I take a moment and stare at the woman who gave birth to me nineteen years ago today. Her jaw is tight, and she holds her body rigid, almost defensively. From me? My words? What? I wish I understood her. I wish she'd *talk* to me like a real person and not like I'm some kind of stranger who just happens to stay in her home occasionally.

"She should have been at the family therapy sessions," I say as calmly as I can. "That's what those were for, to help us become a family again. Because it wasn't just me that needed therapy, Mom. It was all of us. Just because Lizzie came into your life after I was gone doesn't mean I'm not part of her family."

"You're right." She walks to her dresser and randomly opens and closes drawers, not taking anything out. "It's just a very difficult situation, and it was all very unexpected, devastating, and confusing for everyone."

"Because you never expected me to come back. I feel like I..." I grapple for the right words, sensing my mother is becoming more and more uncomfortable. "I feel like me coming back was a disruption, especially for you. Like I ruined your perfect life you put together. I feel like I ruined it by being taken, and then I ruined it again coming back."

Her mouth falls open, and I feel bad for making her feel cornered. I really do. But I don't know how to live in this awkward space. All I want is to get out of it.

"That is not true." She licks her lips nervously. "And I'm very hurt you would even think that."

I take a deep breath, arming myself emotionally for what I'm going to ask her. "Did you know where Poppy's been for the past two years? Because I know he's with Tyler Grace." Her face lights with surprise and then annoyance at the mention of his name. She fingers a blouse on the bed. "I found him, Mom. Entirely by accident and coincidence, but I found him. Or should I say *them*, since you knew I was looking for both of them."

She doesn't say a word. She just stares at me, this stranger who is my mother. I held hard to the memories I had of her while I was gone, not wanting to ever forget her. I could remember her hugging me, singing to me, rocking me to sleep when I was sick, and setting me on the stool in the kitchen so I could stir cookie batter. I was a mommy's girl, and I loved every moment with her. When did she become so mean and uncaring? Did my disappearance do this? Or my reappearance?

"You have no idea how much that dog meant to me and what I had to do to keep him safe…" Tears slide down my cheeks, the memories assaulting me, but she either doesn't notice or doesn't care. "I can't believe you kept him from me."

"And that is exactly why, Holly. He's a reminder of what you went through, and you need to put all that ugliness behind you." Her voice starts to waver with emotion beneath the anger. "That evil man gave you that dog to manipulate you. The dog was a pawn, not a pet. Do you not see that?"

"I don't care why he was given to me," I protest. "All I care about is I love him and he's the only friend or family I had. Did you know Tyler has had him the whole time? Did you lie to me about Poppy living with a family? Just to shut me up?"

Her face is stoic and unreadable. "The dog was the least of

my worries, Holly. I was trying to deal with a daughter who had been kidnapped and horribly abused in every way imaginable. I just wanted you to focus on getting better, and not clinging to a mangy dog and a filthy bag of books. I didn't know that savage had him."

I cringe at her choice of words. "He's not a savage. And it's not okay to tell lies."

"You're right," she finally says softly. "I shouldn't have lied to you. I thought I was doing the right thing. You have to understand I'm new at this, too, Holly. I've never been through anything like this. I know I haven't handled any of this in a good way. Not back then, and not now. I...I just can't think about it or talk about it. I want it all just gone."

"For it all to be gone, *I* would have to be gone," I whisper, pain clenching my heart like a tight fist. "Is that what you want?"

Her chest heaves up and down beneath her robe and, for a second, she looks like she's going to faint, but she recovers quickly. "Please, Holly. It's Christmas Day, and it's your birthday. Now is not the day to be talking about such horrible things and getting upset. I promise we can talk about all of this on another day. I promise I'll be better. Everything will get better, you'll see. I don't want you gone. That's a terrible thing to say. I love you. I just need time to sort it out in my head." Although she smiles hopefully, her eyes are begging me to drop this conversation.

As Feather would say, my mom can't deal. It's taken me a long time to build up the courage to confront her. I would rather just continue to talk about it now, but I suppose she's right that now is not the best time.

"All right," I agree reluctantly.

Relieved, she steps closer and pulls me in for a quick hug. "I'm sorry this is all so confusing for everyone. I really am. I know I haven't been the best mother to you. We'll work on fixing it, okay? We just need time. That's all. We have to get to know each other again." She holds me at arm's length and looks into my eyes. "I want you to be happy, please believe that."

Returning the smile, I slowly disengage from her embrace, not quite knowing what to believe. She and my father are so distant, barely part of my life at all. I can't help but wonder how much of it is from being busy with their lives and jobs and how much of it is because I just make them too uncomfortable.

The quiet of my bedroom is a welcome haven that night, even if it's in a house that feels not at all like home to me. My mind is filled with so many different emotions from the day that I'm not even sure what I'm feeling, other than purely exhausted, mentally and physically. Spending time with my grandmother earlier cheered me up after the talk with my mother, but I still feel an odd emptiness inside, like something big is missing but I have no idea what it is. Before changing into the clothes I sleep in, I peer out the window, searching for any new footprints or signs of Tyler, still curious as to how he got to my window and secretly hoping he'll come back.

After I climb into bed, I reach into my nightstand and pull out the card and photo. I wish Tyler was in this photo, kneeling in the snow next to Poppy. I try to imagine him there, with his long hair that almost matches the color of mine, his strong, colorful arms, and those bright blue eyes that mesmerize me. He's far too beautiful to not smile, I decide, and I set a new goal for myself: Make Tyler smile. A *real* smile.

CHAPTER 14

Holly

Two days after Christmas, my family has gone back to their normal busy routine, my mother has dodged any further in-depth conversation, and I've been driven back to Merryfield. I decide the best thing for me to do is put my Make Tyler Smile plan into action. I need something to feel good about.

On the way out of town, I ask my usual taxi driver to stop at the ice cream shop. My worries about going in there again after I was let go were for nothing because when I place my order, the new girl working there doesn't know I'm the Girl in the Hole Who Passed Out in the Soft Serve.

The driver laughs at me when I get back into her car carrying two large purple drinks with fluorescent-green straws. Before I'd gone in, I'd offered to get her something, and even offered to pay for it, but she declined.

"I'm not drinking them both," I inform her. "One is for my friend."

"Hey, I don't judge. People bring all sorts of weird things into the car."

My stomach twists into knots as we get closer to the edge of the woods leading to Tyler's house. What if he doesn't want to see me again or refuses to talk? Obviously, he *can* talk but chooses not to. His voice is hoarse and different but, to my ears, it doesn't

sound so bad that he should be ashamed or afraid to speak. I actually like the way it sounds and the way it makes my insides flitter
around like I swallowed a butterfly. Unless, perhaps, it causes him
physical pain to talk. Or emotional pain, which in some ways can
be worse.

The driver has brought some paperbacks with her and agrees
to wait for me once again. She doesn't seem to mind waiting as
long as she's getting paid, and sitting here reading is probably better than driving random strangers around all day. I really need
to talk to my parents about getting my driver's license and a car,
because this is becoming expensive. I think I'm more than ready
and able to drive a car.

Carrying the two teas, with my backpack over my shoulder, I
make my way down the path. It has a light dusting of snow over
it, and I'm curious whether anyone else lives out here or if his
house is the only one. He certainly has gone out of his way to
put himself as far away from other people as possible, and I can't
help but wonder why. Whatever that reason may be, it led him to
saving my life that day.

As soon as I enter his yard, via a short dirt road that's overrun
with weeds, Poppy comes running to me from out of nowhere,
with another dog chasing after him.

"Hi, Poppy!" I say, not able to pet him with my hands full of
drinks. "You have a friend today."

The small reddish-brown dog starts to run circles around my
feet, round and round and round, making a strange squealing
noise, while Poppy stands to the side and watches with his tail
wagging, looking very amused.

"Wow, you're very excited," I say to the red dog, who has
turned and is now running counterclockwise around my ankles,

in a blur, preventing me from walking. I have never seen such an
odd dog, and he's making me very dizzy.

A whistle suddenly pierces the air, and the dog stops cycloning
around me and runs to the source of the whistle: Tyler.

He's standing at the open door to his garage, with mirrored
sunglasses hiding those beautiful eyes and a cigarette hanging
from his lips. He must not feel the cold since he never wears a
jacket—just jeans, boots, and a thick flannel shirt with the sleeves
pushed up. The dog bolts to him, its massive tail flying behind
him like a fluffy flag, and that's when I realize it's not a dog at
all—it's the red fox that's in the Christmas tree photographs I
bought. Poppy and I approach Tyler and his fox together, and an
odd sensation of comfort encompasses me, like the four of us are
old friends or family.

Dare I say, a feeling of belonging?

"You have a fox," I say excitedly, watching the animal play with
Poppy. He's beautiful—hyper and goofy—unlike Poppy, who's
much calmer. They seem like best friends as they frolic around
the yard, and it warms my heart to see Poppy in what looks like
a very happy home. Tyler nods and snuffs out his cigarette, then
throws it in a small garbage can next to the door he's leaning
against.

"Is he a pet?" I ask. I've never heard of anyone having a fox
for a pet, but my life knowledge is still pretty limited. Merryfield
taught me nothing of exotic pets and wildlife.

He nods again while taking the sunglasses off and placing them
on top of his head. His eyes settle on me, slowly looking me up
and down, but not in a creepy way. More like he's just...taking
me in. Getting used to me being in front of him.

I hold one of the drinks out to him and smile. "I bought you a bubble tea. This one has the bubbles that pop. They're not the squishy tapioca ones. It's my favorite."

He takes the drink from me and examines the clear plastic cup, watching the bubbles swirl around. "It's purple," he states, and that dry, hoarse voice of his shoots through me like a laser, bringing a mix of guilt, unease, and excitement. I never knew little things about a person could make my body feel such boggling sensations. His eyes, his voice, the width of his arms—even his handwriting has a baffling effect on me. These feelings are totally alien to me, and experiencing them with a man brings on small waves of uncertainty. Are these feelings normal? Are they safe?

The words of Dr. Reynolds echo through my memory. *Not all men are bad. Be cautious, but also be open to enjoying what a healthy relationship can feel like, physically and mentally.*

I exhale while my mind and body struggle. "It's called taro," I finally say, enjoying his skeptical face as he inspects the straw.

"Bubbles are fucked up enough, but purple, too?" He shakes his head and holds the drink up again.

"Try it." I take a sip of mine, my eyes still peeking up at him. "It's good. Trust me."

A small, crooked grin touches his lips, making him look like a little boy who's up to no good. It's not a smile, though, so it doesn't count toward my goal.

"You sure this is safe?" he asks.

"I promise."

I watch him take a sip and suck one of the bubbles up through the wide straw. Out here, in the daylight, I can see the jagged, leathery scars that run along the side of his face, disappearing beneath his hair, and a scar in the shape of a jagged X at his throat. *Something happened to him. Something bad.* More scars are visible on the back of his hand and his fingers wrapped around the plastic cup, the skin rippled and rough-looking. A gust of wind blows his hair away from his face, and he quickly looks down and to the side so his hair falls back over his scars. Then slowly, he raises his head back into the wind, letting his curtain of hair fan away from his scarred forehead, cheek, and neck. His eyes meet mine as he sucks the tea up the straw, waiting for my reaction. He's letting me see him. I breathe slowly, watching him, seeing him clearly for the first time. He's more beautiful than I originally thought, and it makes my heart actually swell and ache.

"Well?" I ask when he pulls the straw from his lips, a quarter of the drink gone.

"It's a good weird." He mimics my words, winks at me, and pops one of the bubbles in his mouth.

A big smile curves my lips. "I'm glad you like it. I don't work there anymore." He raises a questioning eyebrow at me, and I continue. "I had an ... episode and they let me go."

"Episode?"

Sighing, I watch a small windmill at the edge of his yard spin in the wind. "It's stupid, really. I was working alone, and a bunch of people came in all at once. I got stressed, knocked some dishes over, had an anxiety attack, and passed out. They called an ambulance."

"That happen often?"

If I tell him the truth, will he think badly of me? Will he think I'm a mess?

"I guess I feel overwhelmed sometimes. I'm not used to ... people. Or doing things. Or much of anything, honestly, but I'm trying. I don't pass out much, though. That was only like the second time in the past year."

"You shouldn't be walking around the woods alone. It's not safe. You do know that, right?"

I think about it, sipping my drink. He's right, but the difference is that with Tyler here with me, it feels like a different place. To me, these aren't the same woods that haunt my dreams, where my nightmares, both in reality and in sleep, took place. Here, with Tyler, this is the forest I read about in books and daydreamed about for so long. These trees, this soil, this *everything*, is part of my happily-ever-after. I can feel it. I'm not going to tell him that, though.

"No, not really," I finally say.

He doesn't blink; his sky-blue eyes never leave me.

"Believe it or not, I'm not scared here, even though I know you found me not far from here, and I was kept in a dirty basement just a few miles from here. Hearing the birds chirping, seeing the clouds through the trees, even the breeze here is...comforting. It almost feels like home. I feel safer here than I do anywhere else."

Slowly, he nods. "I hear ya."

He lights up another cigarette, and I have to fight myself to not ask him why he smokes so much and tell him how unhealthy it is. It's possible he fell asleep while smoking...maybe lit his bed on fire and woke up in a fiery inferno. I shudder.

"Why do you keep coming back here?" he suddenly asks, and I get the feeling it's been on his mind.

Because you're my prince. You just don't know it yet.

There's no annoyance or accusation in his voice, but embarrassment still flushes my cheeks. "I miss Poppy. He was all I had for years. Just me and him." We both look over at Poppy, lying in the sunlight next to the fox, who's lying on his back, looking at us upside down, small fangs peeking from his lips.

"I really don't have anywhere else to go," I admit. "I don't have any friends, well, except for my roommate." I pause under the intensity of his stare. "I'm not sure what I'm supposed to be doing, like I missed that part in life where you decide what you're going to do." I pull my sweater sleeves farther down over my palms. "I meant what I said, as crazy as it might sound. I like it here in the woods. With you. I like hearing you talk. When you do. I like looking at your arms. I like how blue your eyes are. I like how it feels when you look at me. And I wanted to see if you would smile."

He flicks ashes onto the ground. "You always so honest?"

I shrug awkwardly. "Yeah. I try to be."

"It's good," he says, staring at the ground, his voice a bit raspier. "Don't change it."

He turns and goes back into his workshop, and I follow hesitantly, not sure if I've been dismissed or invited. "Like I said, I'm pretty sure I'm moving to New York with my brother in a few months, and I'd like to take Poppy with me. Until then... I thought maybe I could come here to see him," I repeat, since I never got an answer the first time I asked. "I won't get in your way, I promise."

He places some metal into a vise on his workbench and turns it, not looking at me. I realize I sound desperate, and I hate it. I don't want him to feel sorry for me.

"I could maybe help you with whatever it is you do?" I offer, trying to sound hopeful.

I notice his lip curve up slightly at that, like it's an absurd idea that I could help.

"Or maybe we could just be friends?" I suggest.

He looks up at me, his expression blank. "Friends?" The word comes out a little softer, less hoarse.

I can see him thinking about it and it spurs me on. "Yeah... we can be the kind of friends that don't have to talk a lot, or even see each other every day, but we always just kinda know we're not alone."

He pins me with his bright eyes, then blinks and shakes his head. "We *are* alone," he says, hurling his hammer into his tool-box, where it lands with a loud clang of metal.

"But we wouldn't have to be," I add, losing some of my earlier bravado, "if we had each other to talk to . . ."

His hooded eyes close for a moment, and he lets out an irritated huff of breath before he looks at me. "Let me think about it."

I swallow nervously. "Okay."

Resuming his stance of ignoring me, he goes back to his work, and since I have no idea if he expects me to leave, I plop my backpack down on the floor and settle next to it. Poppy and the fox immediately come over and take turns rolling over for belly rubs and trying to squeeze onto my lap. Tyler seems agitated by my offer of friendship and slips back into mute mode, only nodding or shrugging as I throw occasional questions and commentary at him from my spot on the floor. I try to remain smiling and hopeful but, on the inside, sadness is brewing. Earlier, I thought we were making progress as friends. But now I feel like we've taken a big step backward.

The more interaction I have with people, the more confused I get. I wonder if I am just as confusing to others. Perhaps it's a human epidemic of sorts, to keep us all in a state of what-the-heck-is-going-on-ness.

When I see the sun fading outside, I stand and announce that I should probably get going.

"Fine," he replies reluctantly. "Come back tomorrow. I wasn't ready for friends today."

My heartbeat speeds up. "Really? I can come back?" I ask excitedly.

"At noon," he grumbles.

"Okay. Noon is good." I wait for him to look up from something he's soldering, but he doesn't. "I'll see you tomorrow."

Still nothing.

I say my goodbyes to Poppy and the fox, pick up my backpack, and slowly leave, closing the door to the garage behind me so the pets can't chase after me. As I walk back to the road, I'm so lost in my thoughts about Tyler and his odd mood swings that it takes me a few seconds to process the fact that my driver is gone.

My head snaps to the left, then to the right, my eyes searching the desolate road, hoping the car will appear. The minutes tick by as I stand at the side of the road waiting. The sky grows darker. The air turns colder. The ache in the pit of my stomach deepens. She's obviously not coming back.

Gripping the strap of my backpack tighter, I realize I have two options. I can turn around and go back to Tyler's house, or I can walk home. Glancing behind me, toward his house, I recall how he didn't even say goodbye to me. Instead, he seemed relieved I was leaving. If I show up unexpectedly again, he will probably be even more annoyed. The drive here isn't very long, so walking can't take too much longer. I'm sure I can make it back to Merry-field before dark.

Pleased with my decision, I begin walking, crossing my arms over my chest against the freezing wind and wishing I had worn a warmer jacket. Not long ago I didn't have any jacket or sweater to wear, and I shivered almost nonstop all winter long for years. A short walk home in the cold should be easy for me if I refocus my mind like I used to.

As I walk, the sun disappears completely, and the sky becomes darker and darker, and I haven't even reached the town yet, proving that my ability to judge time and distance are still incredibly skewed. I honestly don't have a clue how far away I am from Merry-field, or Tyler's house, or the small town. There are very few streetlights and houses on this road, and they're quite a distance apart, and that's not easing my worries. I refocus that fear to anger, which is an easier emotion for me to deal with.

Why couldn't my parents let me have a mobile phone?

Why couldn't my parents be open to the idea of me driving and having a car?

Instead, I'm now walking around in the dark, with no idea how far away I am from my own apartment, with no way to call for a ride.

I always seem to be finding myself trapped and alone in some way or another, and I can't help wondering if it's part of my destiny or some cruel stroke of recurring bad luck that's going to plague me for my entire life.

The sound of an engine approaching from behind me fills the silence, and headlights illuminate the road. I'm not sure if I should hide in the trees on the side of the road or try to get their attention and ask for a ride. Can I trust a random stranger to drive me home?

No. It could be another bad man.

Tucking my head down, I continue to walk, but as the engine gets closer, I realize it's a motorcycle and not a car. It passes me with a loud rumble, then pulls over to the side of the road a few feet ahead of me. I stop walking when the engine turns off and the red brake light goes with it. The rider kicks the kickstand down and swings his leg over the bike. Even though he's nothing but a large shadowy figure in the dark, I know it's Tyler Grace. I can *feel* his vibe. He walks toward me, the metal buckles on his boots making a faint clink with each step.

"I keep finding women," he muses, stopping about two feet in front of me, close enough for me to see he's wearing the half-skull mask that I saw him wearing that day at the traffic light. "What do you think that means?" he asks.

"I'm not sure," I reply, wondering who else he's found and why he wears the scary masks when he rides.

"Well, at least you didn't run."

"Why would I run from you?"

His eyes stay on mine as he pulls the mask off, then removes his leather jacket. "You blind? Can't see my fucked-up face? Or the psycho mask? Take your pick."

His words both shock and hurt me. Obviously, he's much bolder with his thoughts in the dark.

"You don't—"

He thrusts the jacket toward me. "Put this on."

"Why?"

" 'Cause you'll freeze your ass off on the bike."

I squeak at the mere idea of getting on the back of that motorcycle with him, being forced to be so close to him, to have to put my hands on him to keep from falling off. *Oh my God.* I think I'd rather keep walking.

He steps closer, and I'm still so lost in the anxiety of either getting on the bike with him or walking for who knows how long that I let him take my backpack out of my hand, and I slip my arms through the sleeves of his jacket. It easily fits over my own, the sleeves hanging inches past my fingertips. Heat, tobacco, and pine linger in the worn leather, encapsulating me in his raw masculinity as if I've stepped inside him. Slowly, he drags the front zipper up, sending comforting warmth through my veins. His fingers shake—maybe from the cold—and linger at the pulse of my throat, at the end of the zipper trail. I feel like a little girl again—safe, protected, taken care of.

Innocent.

"Won't you be cold now?" I ask, my voice quivering. "Without your jacket?"

"I'll be fine. Let's go."

I follow him to his bike, my legs weak and wobbly with growing apprehension. I've never been on a motorcycle before. I haven't even been on a bicycle since I was a little girl. Even scarier than that is how close I'll be to him. The seat is small, with no backrest and nothing to hold on to. Except him.

"You gonna pass out?" he asks, eyeing me as I shift my weight from one foot to the other.

"I might," I admit.

"I'll go slow," he says. Then, "But you never know...you might like it fast, too."

I smile weakly, wondering why my heart has suddenly started to beat faster and my cheeks are flushing with heat even though I'm cold. Something about his voice...his words...

He throws his leg over the bike, settles onto the seat, and kicks the kickstand up in one smooth, natural motion, as if the bike is an extension of his body. His head tilts toward me as he pulls out a pack of cigarettes, taps one out, and lights it up with the same silver lighter he always seems to have in his pocket. "All aboard, sugar."

The act of jumping behind him and parting my thighs around the back of his body is making me feel woozy in a strange, electrifying way.

"When I tell you to spread, you spread. I'll break your fucking legs."

I rub the back of my neck nervously.

Get out of my head. Please. You're dead...

He exhales smoke tendrils from his nostrils like a mystical dragon. "Tell me what you're scared of."

Being lost forever.

Never feeling normal.

I stare down at the ground, fighting the fears in my head until he reaches toward me and hooks his pinky finger into mine, tugging gently. "I could walk you home," he suggests in his soft, scratchy way. Our voices are intimate in the quiet of the chilly night air, as if we're the only two people who exist.

My head snaps up, and tears instantly pool in my eyes when I see the depth of sincerity in his. He's not kidding. He'll leave his bike right here on the side of the road and walk me home, in the cold and the dark, just so I won't be alone.

"No . . . that would be silly," I reply.

"Not if it's what you want." His finger tightens around mine, connecting us in the tiniest, sweetest way possible, somehow knowing anything more would be too much for me.

"I appreciate that . . . very much." Hesitantly, I curl my finger around his, returning the gesture and the silent understanding attached to it.

His fingers press against his lips as he takes a drag from his cigarette. I realize I'm way too captivated with his mannerisms, his habits, his voice . . .

"Focus on where you are," he says. I'm fascinated with how he talks, with the smoke still in his lungs, making his voice deeper and huskier. "And who you're with." Turning his head, he blows three small circles of smoke into the air. "It's just a ride home." He turns back to me and gives my finger another reassuring tug, stealing my attention from the floating hoops. "You trust me?"

He saved my life. He killed for me.

He's holding my pinky finger in his.

I shift my gaze to meet his. "I think you're the only person I trust."

Releasing my finger, he cocks his head to the back of the bike, to the tiny square of leather behind him. "Show me."

I throw my backpack strap over my shoulder. He lifts the mask over his face. Shoving all anxiety aside, I put my hand on his shoulder for balance and climb onto the seat behind him, resting my feet on the bullet-shaped foot pegs. I stiffen when he reaches behind him, grabs my hands in his, and places them on his waist. His palms press against the backs of my hands, holding me until I relax and curl my fingers into the fabric of his shirt.

The feeling of exhilaration and freedom is empowering as we cruise down the dark road, and he was right—I want to go faster, feel freer, let the wind and the road detox me of all the poison. His hair whips into my face as I lean over his shoulder and breathe one word into his ear: *faster.* Laughing, he grabs one of my hands, pulls it around his waist, and places it over his belt buckle. Fear flashes through me, but I swallow it, force it away before the voice comes. *I will not freak out. I will not pull away. I'm allowed to have a few minutes of fun. I'm allowed to be close to a man.*

I'm allowed to be free.

Clamping my eyes shut, I wrap my other arm around him and hold on to him tight. It doesn't matter that I'm on the back of a motorcycle with a guy wearing a scary skull mask over his face. All that matters to me right now is I feel free, safe, and brave.

I'm with my prince.

Sadness washes over me when he pulls the bike into the parking lot of Merryfield. I'm not ready to step back into life yet and would rather stay in the fantasy world the ride on the motorcycle created—even if only for a few more minutes.

Or forever.

Just as I'm about to point out my apartment in the row of buildings, he heads right for it and parks the bike not far away, in a guest parking spot, the one farthest from the light. *He knows where I live.* He touches my leg lightly as he turns the engine off, then lightly taps me, letting me know it's okay to jump off now.

"I liked that way more than I thought I would."

He pulls the mask down to reveal a crooked grin as he gets off the bike and stands next to it. "Good to know."

I'm not sure what to do or say now. Do I just thank him for the ride and go inside? Do I invite him in? Or does that send a bad message? We never talked about this kind of thing in my therapy sessions. I glance up at him, and he's staring off toward the road, looking just as confused as I feel, which is almost comforting.

"I got your card and the picture. On Christmas Day," I say finally, smiling shyly. "I loved it. It really made me happy."

He studies my face, not reacting or responding. I can't stop staring into his eyes or letting my gaze linger on other parts of his beautiful face, the angle of his jaw, the slight stubble on his cheeks and chin. I think he could have been a model, before what happened. He angles his head down toward me. For a second, I think...oh my...he's going to kiss me, and my pulse goes into crazy rapid beats, and I pray I don't faint. But all he does is lift his hand to pull a dead leaf out of my long hair, and I feel a slight tug as he gently pulls out whatever other bits are tangled in the strands. He flicks the pieces away just like he does with his cigarettes. I wonder how long I had a leaf on my head, and how silly I must have looked. Hopefully, it got stuck in there during the bike ride and not earlier. How embarrassing.

He doesn't move away after he removes the leaf; instead, he stands there smelling of smoke, pine trees, and leather—just like his jacket, which I'm still engulfed in—and the scent transports me back to when he pulled me out of the hole and I fell against him. He smelled the same then, and it was frightening and inviting at the same time, just like it is now. Standing this close, with barely three inches of space between us, I feel his body heat, and it makes my insides quiver.

I have to force my brain to think, calm down, and not be so obviously affected by him, to not let him invade all of my senses. With the bad man, I had to hide my feelings to avoid a reaction from him. But Dr. Reynolds said I have to learn to let people see my feelings, and I have to let them have their own feelings. She said most people are good and genuine, not menacing or manipulative. Trying to retrain myself to believe that is difficult and confusing. Trusting people is hard.

"How did you get up there, onto the second floor of my parents' house?"

"I'm good at climbing."

Hmm.

"How did you know I would be there? Or which window was mine?"

His head tilts slightly to the side. "Maybe just a lucky guess?" His voice has a slight teasing tone.

I wait, then realize he's not going to say anything else about the matter. I blink up at him. "Oh. Okay...well, if you do it again... climb up to my windows...be careful."

His eyes flash with a darker emotional intensity. "Afraid I might fall?" he asks, and, again, his words seem like they might be hinting at something else entirely.

"Yes," I whisper.

"Me too." The rasp is deeper now, raw and scratchier. It reaches my heart and drips down to my thighs. I feel like melted butter. I feel like I'm dreaming.

Are we talking about windows anymore?

I blink at him.

"You got a phone?" he asks, his voice still low.

The question throws me. "No. I have no one to call. My parents don't want me to have things like that."

He scoffs and leans closer to me again, tilting his head down toward my ear. "Don't be a prisoner anymore, Holly," he says softly. His breath makes me shiver, and my hands itch to reach up, to touch his arms or clutch his shirt, but I fist them at my sides, not wanting to do anything to break the spell we seem to be caught under.

"I'm trying," I whisper back, although I'm not exactly sure what he means.

We pull back at the same time, and our faces are still so close I can almost feel his skin graze against mine. I shiver all over again, head to toe, everywhere.

"I think I should go inside." I unzip his jacket and slowly pull it off. "Thank you for the ride."

"Tomorrow. Noon." His eyes lower, his chest rising and falling as he shoves his arms into the leather jacket and lifts his hair out from beneath the collar.

"Okay." I wonder what happened to my taxi girl and why she left me. Surely she must have had a good reason. I'll call her in the morning and give her a chance to explain before I find a new driver, which is something I'd rather not have to do.

"Thanks for the good weirdness, Holly." Straightening, he gives me a smile, which has a glint of wickedness in its curve, and gets back on his bike.

He said my name. And he smiled. *At me.* I feel the way those girls look on the TV shows I spent so much time watching, when the guy they like finally pays attention to them. I feel giddy and nauseous, scared and happy and glowy. For the first time ever, I feel like a real girl. Nothing has ever felt better.

CHAPTER 15

Holly

The anticipation of seeing Tyler again today, as friends, kept me awake for most of the night. I kept peeking out my window after he dropped me off, wondering if he was still out there. I wouldn't mind if he was, to be honest. I liked his attention, fleeting as it was.

Earlier, while I waited for Feather to get out of the shower, I called Maria, the taxi driver. She apologized frantically, telling me she had gotten a call that her two-year-old son was sick and she'd had to leave quickly. She had no way of calling me, so she had no choice but to leave. She told me she worried about me all night, wondering how I would get home. I could actually hear the relief in her voice when I told her I was fine and would like another ride today.

"I'm going shopping. Want to come?" Feather asks, coming into our small kitchen where I'm drinking a cup of tea and eating a blueberry muffin.

"I can't...I'm going to see Poppy today. The driver will be here in about an hour."

"You mean you're going to see Tyler," she comments with a grin, grabbing her car keys off the heart-shaped key rack on the wall. The hook next to hers is empty, mocking me and my car-less life.

I shift uncomfortably at the small wooden table. "Of course he'll be there, too."

"I saw him drop you off last night. I can't believe you got on that bike with him." She leans against the doorframe, her long hair flowing down her shoulder and over her chest.

"You were watching me?"

"You can hear his motorcycle a mile away, Holly. I heard it in the lot and looked out the window, and there you were, all googly-eyed, staring up at him while he played with your hair. He's actually pretty hot from a distance. The arms on him... damn, girl." She pops the gum in her mouth and flashes a teasing smile at me. "I can see the appeal."

"Feather..." I shake my head at her and tuck my hair behind my ear. "He wasn't playing with my hair. There was a leaf stuck in it. I was embarrassed having foliage on my head. I wasn't googly-eyed."

Or was I? I certainly felt all googly and woogly.

"It's okay to like him. You don't have to get all embarrassed and nervous. I'm not sure he's the best guy for you to be crushing on, but he'll do as a stepping stone."

"Stepping stone?" I repeat. "What's that?"

She lifts her hand to inspect one of her chipped nails. "Someone you see while you're waiting for the next one to come along. Like training wheels for dating."

My mouth falls open. What a horrible way to treat someone. "He is *not* a stepping stone." Rising, I grab my dishes and bring them over to the sink to wash later. "Is that what Steve is for you?"

She actually stares off, contemplating her answer. I'll be disappointed in her if she says yes, and I'll feel sorry for Steve, who seems to really care about her.

"No," she finally replies. "I really like Steve. I always have. We have a history, and we started as friends. I suppose, in a way, I wanted him to be a stepping stone, but he turned out to be a lot more."

"I have a history with Tyler," I say with slight defensiveness. I get to have a past with people, too, even if it's not quite perfect and only started two years ago. It's still *my* history.

"Pulling you out of a hole isn't quite the kind of history that's going to lead to everlasting love, Holly." She turns before I have a chance to reply. "I'll see you tonight. Have fun but be careful," she calls out just before she closes the front door behind her.

I file our conversation into the messy back room of my mind, with the other things I don't want to think about, and take a quick shower with what's left of our hot water. I should know better than to let Feather shower first if I don't want to end up with luke-warm water. As I'm toweling off, I slowly inch the towel away to reveal my reflection in the full-length mirror on the back of the bathroom door as the fog slowly dissipates.

I'm not used to looking at my body. I had one tiny, compact mirror while being held by the bad man, so I was only able to see two circular inches of my body at a time. He only gave it to me so I could put the awful red lipstick on, but sometimes I stared into it when I was alone and watched my lips talk to myself. Other times, I could angle it just the right way to see the cigarette burns he'd branded into my skin and the thin red slash marks the knife had made when he threatened me.

Once, I used it to look at the letters carved across my stomach, even though the reflection made the word backward. That was the first and last time I used the compact to look at the ugly letters on me.

Feather has told me numerous times how pretty I am, how she wishes she had a body like mine. *Rockin' curves* were the words she used. At the time I laughed nervously and told her to shut up, not believing her, or even caring. I didn't need or want to be pretty.

But lately, I've been wondering if I really am pretty. More specifically, I wonder if Tyler thinks I'm pretty. As the fog fades from the mirror, I wrap the white towel around my body to cover it all up. Even if he does think I'm pretty, he'll change his mind damn fast if he ever sees what I look like under my clothes. The pretty girls on TV don't have scars and words carved into them.

💜 💜 💜

This time, when I get out of the taxi, he's sitting on the ground waiting for me, his back leaning against a tree, staring up at the sky with a small twig in his mouth. Poppy and the fox are sitting with him, and it's obvious by the way they stick by his side that they're very attached to him. I think that's a good sign because animals don't like bad people. His subtle acts of chivalry might seem small, but to me they are huge. It's a hint that he cares, maybe even likes me.

Or is it a sense of responsibility? I wonder what it feels like knowing you saved someone's life. Do you feel forever responsible for them? Like feeding a stray cat that keeps coming back and you're not sure what to do with? So you just keep feeding it out of a sense of pity and obligation?

God, don't let me be a stray cat.

He stands as I approach and brushes debris off the back of his jeans. "They wait for you?" he asks, nodding toward the taxi.

"Yeah."

"Tell her to go."

"But how will I—"

He interrupts me. "I'll get you home."

I hesitate, leaning down to pet Poppy, not sure if I should trust Tyler so completely yet. Last night was nice, but not enough to gauge who he really is. If I tell the driver to leave, I'll be stuck here—on the edge of town, on a back road near the woods—with a man I barely even know.

Alone.

Trapped.

"You can trust me," he says. "I'm a good weird."

Smiling at our inside joke, I walk back to the car to tell the driver she doesn't have to wait for me today. She eyes Tyler suspiciously, doing nothing to hide her obvious distrust of leaving me here with him. It was clear from our conversation on the phone this morning that she feels some sort of concern for me, but she finally relents after I insist that I'll be fine. Apprehension simmers through me as I watch her drive away. This is another big step for me, letting part of my safety net go voluntarily.

Without a word, he turns and heads down the dirt road, and I walk briskly to catch up to him, as do Poppy and the fox. "How did you come to have a fox for a pet?" I ask. "Are they common as pets?"

"No, they don't make good pets at all. They're destructive and hyper and almost impossible to train." He coughs. "I found him as a kit, stuck in a trap. He had a broken leg."

"Oh...that's so sad."

"Yeah. I tried to release him back into the woods after it healed, but he kept showing up at my door, scratching and crying. He didn't want to go. So I let him stay."

Oh no. He does have stray cat obligation tendencies.

"He's in one of the Christmas tree pictures I bought at the boutique. I look at his adorable little face every morning. He almost looks like he's grinning. What's his name?"

"Boomer. Well, Boomerang. Since he kept coming back."

Yikes. Just like me.

He's a magnet, I convince myself. That's why the fox and I keep coming back. It's not because we're desperate. It's something about *him*.

When we get to his yard, he points to an old wrought-iron bench that sits in what will be a flower and rock garden when the winter season has ended, and we sit on it together. Without thinking, I put about two feet of distance between us.

He reaches into the inside pocket of his black leather jacket, pulls out a mobile phone, and holds it out to me. "For you," he says softly.

I stare at it, my brow furrowing, not sure what he means. "I'm sorry?"

"I got it for you."

"Oh!" I exclaim. "Wow…" I hold the silver phone in my hand, not sure what to do with it or how to even say thank you for such an unexpected gift.

"I had my brother pick it up for me. I don't do stores."

"I…I don't know how to use it," I stammer. "And I don't really have any calls to make…"

Ignoring my protests, he reaches over and presses the power button, and when his scarred fingers brush across mine, an electric tingle runs up my arm. I wonder if that feeling will ever stop. If he were to touch me every day, for the rest of my life, would I still feel it? And is it crazy if I want to find out? I don't believe what Feather said this morning, that everlasting love can't happen with him. My heart knows better.

"You should have one," he says. "For emergencies."

Statements like that always make me want to burst out into insane hysterics. I had many emergencies over the past twelve years that I managed to live through, yet people like Feather freak out if she's half an hour late to meet Steve, and then she makes ten phone calls to let him know, like some terrible tragedy is happening, when it's actually just that she can't find the perfect shirt or can't find her black eyeliner.

I run my finger along the smooth edge of the rectangular phone. *My first phone.* Does this mean he might call me?

As if reading my mind, he says, "It's easier to talk. With texts. For me."

Ohhh. I had forgotten about texting. Like Feather and Steve do all the time, with little smiley faces and three-letter codes that I don't understand. I'll have to ask Feather for a cheat sheet.

"If you want to," he adds quickly. Behind the shaggy hair covering half his face, he slowly lifts his eyes to meet mine, and it feels like a visual caress, the way they change color from turquoise to sapphire and back again like a kaleidoscope. Long ago I learned how to read the eyes of a man, to use them as a meter to gauge mood and intention.

In Tyler's eyes, I see the man behind the scars and the mask, the man he was before life tore him apart and drove him to hide in the woods. Before some tragedy made him a man who could strangle someone to death. Just like me, there's a person hiding in there who had their very soul stolen from them, and I see him, trying to let me in.

I see him trying to get out.

"I want to." My voice shakes, and so does my hand holding the phone. "Very much."

He spends the next half hour showing me how to use the phone to make calls and how to text back and forth. He adds himself to my contacts and shows me how to use the camera. He takes a photo of Boomer and adds it as the photo for "Tyler" in the contact profile. I want to use a picture of him, but he refuses, agitation instantly evident in his eyes and body language at the mention of capturing him with a photograph. He does, however, take a photo of me holding Poppy and uses that for my profile in *his* phone.

Slowly, our walls are deteriorating.

"Let me give you some money for the phone," I say, reaching for my backpack, where my wallet is hidden.

"No."

"I'm sure it was expensive. I have money my father gives me."

He grabs my hand, stopping me before I reach my wallet, and for a moment, I freeze as old demons rise to the surface. Sensing my reaction, he immediately lets go.

"Sorry. The phone's a gift." He coughs into his hand. "For you."

I've noticed after he talks for a while, his voice becomes wheezy, cracking over certain words and shifting in odd places. Matching his mood and intention to his tone of voice must be difficult, and maybe that's why he'd rather not talk. Thankfully for me, his eyes are very expressive of his feelings, and I'm sure once I get to know him better, words won't even be necessary for me to know what he's thinking.

"Thank you." I put the phone in my backpack along with my wallet. "Does it hurt?" I ask softly, treading lightly because I know all too well how much a simple question can offend. "When you talk?"

His lip twitches. "Not really. Just dry. Fatigued. It's fucked up."

I don't ask how it happened, and he doesn't tell me. I hope maybe someday our friendship will be in a place where we can share our pasts, but I have no problem waiting. Time and patience are two things I can offer in abundance.

"Will drinking help?" I ask.

"Quit drinking years ago."

"Um...I meant water. Or tea." I bet honey would help soothe his throat, and I make a mental note to read up on that.

He lets out a gruff laugh. "Water helps a little." He stands up from the bench and tilts his head at me. "Want to do something with me?"

My mind spins with excitement and nervousness. *Yes. No. What?*

"Sure," I answer, rising to my feet with him.

I follow him inside the large garage, where he walks to a corner filled with workout equipment and weights, and returns with a large plastic storage box. Lifting the lid, he reveals what's inside. Christmas ornaments...garland...and wrapped presents with big bows.

Excitement bubbles up inside me. "We're going to decorate a tree?" I ask, almost hopping up and down with happiness. His lips turn up into a handsome yet slightly snarky grin. "Yeah. This one is late." I wonder what that means as he pulls a Santa hat out of the box and puts it on his head. "No laughing," he warns. "I have to wear it." I can't help smiling, but I don't laugh. There must be a story here, with the trees and the hat, and I'm not about to do anything to make him not want to tell me all about it someday.

Poppy and Boomer accompany us as we quietly walk up into the woods, farther than I've walked before.

"You pick," he says.

I glance up at him. "I get to pick the tree?"

When he nods, I start to scope out all the trees in the area, trying to find the perfect shape and fullness, but it's an imperfect tree that catches my eye, set apart from the others, almost like it's the outcast. It's short, its branches aren't as full, and it has a few dead spots, but once the decorations are on, it'll be beautiful.

"This one," I announce.

Tyler sets the box down on the ground and silently starts to decorate it. I watch him for a few minutes, admiring how meticulous and thoughtful he is about placing the decorations, and then I help him. When the last red globe has been hung, he places six wrapped boxes under the tree, just like in my photographs and the tree I saw in the woods the day I saw him and Poppy.

"This is the last tree," he says. "Until next year."

"How many do you decorate?" I ask.

"Six."

Six. I wonder if it's a coincidence that there are also six wrapped presents.

"I'd love to hear how you started doing this," I say. "The girl in the store where I bought the photos said it's like a legend out here. She said the little kids love to hear about it, and people hunt for the trees."

He nods, the white pouf on the hat bouncing, the small bell jingling. "My father started it. When I was little, he brought me up here to look for a tree to cut to bring home." He pauses and clears his throat. "I was like, why can't we just decorate it here? For the animals? Why cut it and drag it out of its home?" He smiles at the memory, and I smile, too, picturing a young Tyler in my mind, same shaggy blond hair and blue eyes. "The next day we came back. We both wore the hats. We sang. We decorated the tree. I was all excited." He takes a deep breath. "Dad said, 'We're going to do this every year and make it our own tradition, just me and you.' Christmas Day was my dad's birthday. He wanted to do something special with me. I'm one of six kids, and he tried to make each one of us feel special. This was our thing."

"Ty...you should have told me it was your father's birthday, too," I say, but he shakes his head.

"We don't celebrate it anymore. Other than doing this." He stares off to a faraway place I can't see, his face shadowed.

"Why six trees?" I ask softly, hoping to bring him back.

He takes out his pack of cigarettes, pulls one out with this mouth, and lights it.

"One for me and one for each of my brothers and sister. It was my idea, when I was little, to decorate one for each of them even though they never actually saw the trees."

Poppy and Boomer frolic around the tree, the fox especially interested in the present boxes, sniffing them and nudging them with his charcoal-black nose.

"It means a lot to me that you told me. I've been fascinated with the story since I heard about it, and it's even more special to me now."

He moves a few ornaments to different branches as I talk, not meeting my eyes.

"Your dad sounds like a really nice man."

"Yeah. He was."

Was. Past tense. Meaning he's gone. He must be heartbroken missing him, and that must be where his sadness is stemming from.

"Thank you for letting me share this with you," I say. "I'm not part of any of my family's traditions. I'm not even sure if they have any or ever did. To be honest, they barely even talk to me. You're lucky."

He kneels and puts the lid back on the box. "I *was* lucky, Holly. Now I'm just a mess."

He ends the conversation by picking up the box, whistling for Poppy and Boomer, and walking back in the direction of his house. All I can do is follow him in silence.

♥ ♥ ♥

I'm not sure how I never noticed it before, but he has an old pickup truck parked on the other side of the garage. It's tan and rusty with oversized tires, the leather bench seat ripped from age. It suits him perfectly, though. He drives me home in it, and it's loud and bouncy, the tires rumbling over the road like an animal. Neither the radio nor the heat works, but I'm not bothered by it. I'm on a high from spending half the day with him, Poppy, and Boomer.

When he parks in the small lot in front of my apartment unit to let me out, I'm not sure how to say goodbye, and the awkwardness reminds me how socially behind I still am. I put my hand on the door handle, my other hand clutching my backpack, wondering if and when I'll see him again or if today was just a one-time thing. He doesn't look at me as I hesitate; he just stares out the windshield, deep in thought once again.

"Thank you again for the phone," I say. "And for today." Is it appropriate to thank a guy for sharing part of his life with you? Or am I hammering more nails into my own coffin of social inadequacy?

He nods at me again and I tell myself it's because he talked a lot today and his voice grew hoarser and hoarser as the day went on, so he's probably tired. Taking a breath, I try to pull the inside handle of the truck door, but it's stuck, not budging under my grip.

"I can't—"

He reaches across the bench seat, his arm stretching across my body, and yanks the door handle. It opens with a loud creak, and I worry it might break right off its hinges. His face is so close to mine his hair brushes across my cheek, soft and wispy like a

feather. Leaning back into his space behind the wheel, he takes
his sunglasses off the rearview mirror and puts them on, hiding
his eyes from me just when I want to see them the most. Does
he feel like I do when we're close to each other? Does he feel that
odd shimmy shiver?

"Talk soon," he says. "Slam the door shut."

I jump out of the truck and gingerly push the door shut, still
nervous it might crumble into a pile of rust, and he immediately
drives away. One thing I've quickly figured out is Tyler is really
bad at hellos and goodbyes. I feel a small amount of consolation
that he's even worse at it than I am, so maybe he doesn't notice
how much I struggle.

Later that night, when I'm lying in bed reading one of the books
Zac and Anna gave me for Christmas, I hear a strange noise in my
room. Putting the book down on my comforter, I glance around
the room in confusion, and I hear it again.

The sound of a tiny bell, coming from my leather trunk.

I crawl out of bed, pull my backpack from the trunk, and fish
inside it for the cell phone. Its screen is lit up, and the text message
indicator is on.

My heart speeds up to an unnatural and frightening pace. My
first text message. Holding the phone close to me, I get back in
bed and pull the blanket over myself before sliding my finger
across the tiny screen to read the message, which is, of course,
from Tyler Grace.

Tyler

:-)

A tiny yellow smiley face.
I type one back, just like he showed me.

:-)

Tyler

I frown at the screen. Is this what texting is?
The phone dings again.

Tyler
You asked me two questions today. About my voice and
the trees. Now it's my turn.

Okay. That's fair.

Tyler
Tell me about the backpack. You had it that day I found you.
You always have it.

He went from smiley faces to something so deeply personal
and hard to talk about that I don't even know how to begin to
explain. I suppose I did the same to him, though, asking about his
voice and the decorated trees, and he answered me.

My favorite books are in it. I read them every day
when I was little, before I was kidnapped. I had it with
me the day he took me. He let me keep it, and I kept
reading them every day. I had nothing else. Maybe
it's silly but the books made me feel safe. I made
myself believe I was part of the stories.

A few seconds go by, and he replies.

Tyler

> That's not silly. Not at all. We all need something to help us escape.

> They still make me feel safe. I feel unsettled without them with me all the time.

I read the text back to myself, and I'm afraid I sound like a weirdo.

> It's hard to explain.

Tyler

> You explained it perfectly. Now I understand.

I let out a small breath of relief.

Tyler

> I get another question.

> Okay.

I brace myself for what could be next. I had no idea texting could be so stressful.

Tyler

> Do you want to see Poppy tomorrow?

Smiling, I type back quickly:

> Does Poppy want to see me?

Tyler

> You can't answer a question with a question.
> It's in the texting rulebook.

Ah, he has a sense of humor.

> I would like to see Poppy.

Tyler

> He says to be ready at noon. That a good time?

> Yes

Tyler

> We'll pick you up :-)

Still smiling, I keep my eyes on the screen, waiting to see if he sends something else. How do people end texts? Am I supposed to say goodbye? Send another smiley face? Send a different face? I fall asleep with the phone in my hand and dream of sky-blue eyes.

CHAPTER 16

Tyler

This lost girl with the stormy eyes has become my caffeine, my morphine, my new drug of choice. I can no longer get through a day without a shot of her, whether it be seeing her or just a simple text message. And like any addiction, as much as I enjoy it, I know it's something that I can't do forever, and I'll eventually have to quit it and forget it.

For the past month we've texted and had random conversations in the garage while I work, and she's become the closest thing to a real friend I've had in a long time. With each day that's passed, I've noticed little changes in her. Her confidence has grown. She smiles and laughs more. She's developed her own style. She reminds me of how Boomer was when I first found him, so scared and timid at first, afraid of me getting too close to him. Slowly, over time, he learned to trust me and grew attached to me. I realize that was a mistake on my part because it prevented him from going out and living a normal fox life.

I can almost feel the same thing happening with Holly, because as much as I want to see her go off on her own, move to New York, and do amazing things with her life, I'm going to miss the hell out of her.

I'm selfish as fuck. I want to keep her all to myself.

Finders, keepers . . .

Right now she's burning the shit out of my clutch and giving me whiplash while I try to teach her how to drive my old pickup. I can't even be mad because she looks so cute and serious in the driver's seat, barely able to reach the pedals or see over the steering wheel.

"Aren't there easier cars?" she asks as she stalls it again on the dirt road and both our heads slam forward. My inner mechanic groans.

"Yeah, an automatic, but I don't have one."

"Maybe having other people drive me around wasn't so bad after all," she says, trying to start the truck again.

"You're doing great." I try to make my voice sound reassuring. "You're going to pass that test."

I hate this shit of her parents not letting her have a car or wanting her to have a phone. I can't wrap my head around what they think they're accomplishing. Making her walk or take a taxi everywhere is in no way safer than driving, and if they think it is, they're out of their damn minds. The more she tells me about them, the more I don't like or understand them. It's almost like they *want* her to continue to be secluded.

She doesn't know it, but I already have a car for her, waiting in the parking lot of my brother's motorcycle shop. It's just a little all-wheel-drive SUV with about ninety thousand miles on it, but it's clean and dent-free, and it runs well. If she's moving to New York, she won't need a car anyway, from what I gather, but at least while she's here, she'll be able to get around like the adult that she is. In the meantime, I don't want to think about her moving to New York because it makes me feel ragey.

"I think without this clutch thing I might be okay," she says, almost sideswiping the corner of the garage with the side mirror as she parks. I nod and rub the back of my neck, which is starting to ache from the constant jerking of the truck. Seeing her smile and learn something new makes it worth it, though. It reminds me of when my father taught me how to drive his old truck. This same truck, actually.

I jump out and walk around to the driver's-side door, open it, and help her out. She touches my shoulder lightly as she jumps down but quickly pulls it away as soon as she's on her feet. That old familiar burn of rejection manifests in my chest.

What I wouldn't do to feel her hands on me. Just once, even for sixty seconds. Fuck, I'd settle for ten seconds.

A gust of wind blows, and she hugs herself against it as we walk around the garage to the side door and step inside, but I don't go to my workbench like I normally do. Usually, she likes to sit on a mat on the floor and play with Poppy and Boomer, or she sits on a stool and watches me work, but today I don't have much work to do, and I'd rather be inside with the fire going, just chilling. I'm getting sick of spending all my time with her in my workshop-slash-garage, surrounded by tools, weights, lawn equipment, and my collection of horror masks. The thing is, she's never been inside my house because she's afraid of small spaces after being kept in a room for eleven years. My house is tiny, just three hundred square feet, with only one way in and one way out. A claustrophobic's worst nightmare.

"You feelin' good today?" I ask her casually, leaning against my workbench.

She smiles. "Yeah, I'm happy."

"I want to go in the house," I say.

She stares up at me, and as usual, my eyes take a sweep of her, wearing jeans with tattered holes in the knees, black boots, a soft sweater, and a leather jacket that's more stylish than warm. I'm struck by how incredibly beautiful and normal she looks, like any other girl hanging out with her friends, and it makes me believe she's going to be okay out in the world. Her damage is easier to hide than mine. It's not until the long sleeves are gone, and the sun sets, that glimpses of her reality come to light.

"Oh," she says. "I can go home, then. I can call a taxi…"

"No…I want you to come with me." Her eyes narrow on me as she absorbs the words she's never heard from me before. I wonder if she's been hoping for them or dreading them.

She looks out the window toward the house, worry creasing her brow.

"Holly…it's okay if you don't want to. I'll take you home. But there's a fireplace in my house, it's warm, you can sit on the couch and be comfortable—instead of on the ground. I'm a little tired of you sitting in the dirt every time you're here."

Torment flashes all over her face, the fight-or-flight instinct kicking in. Her teeth clamp on her bottom lip, her pink lipstick smudging along her perfect white teeth. It only makes me want to kiss her and smudge it even more. She has no idea she makes me feel this way, and it's real innocence, not that fake clueless act some women put on in an effort to flirt.

"How about this," I say as softly as I can force my voice to be without it fading to inaudible hisses. "You go inside first. I'll wait here. Look around. Leave the front door open. You won't feel trapped. See how you feel. If you don't like it, just come back out."

"Really? I can do that?" she asks.

I nod.

She takes a few deep breaths. "Okay. I'm going to try it," she finally says. "You'll stay right here? You won't move? You promise?"

"Promise."

She takes two steps and turns back to me. "Is anyone in there?"

"Nobody. I live alone."

I watch from the garage window as she walks toward my house with the dog and fox following her, opens my front door, stands on the threshold for a few minutes, looks back toward the garage, and disappears inside.

She's braver than I am, confronting her fears. Unlike me, hiding from the world like a pussy.

A few seconds later my phone rings, and I pull it out of my pocket to see Holly's number on the screen.

"You okay?"

"Yes," she says. "Your house is so cute and cozy. But...where is the rest of it?"

I laugh into the phone. "What?"

"The other rooms? How do I get to them?"

"There aren't any more rooms. Just the bedroom loft upstairs. Use the stairs to go up there and look around. It's one room with a bed, some drawers under the bed, and a small window. Nothing else."

"I don't think I want to go up there."

"Then you don't have to."

"Where is the basement?"

"Don't have one."

There's a long silence as she contemplates whether this could be true.

"You're sure?" she asks suspiciously. "There's no rooms under the house?"

"No lie. Cross my heart."

Another long silence, except for the sound of her breathing.

"I think I'm okay. You can come in now."

"You sure? You can have more time."

"No. I'm okay."

I end the call with a grin on my face that comes partly from being proud of her, and partly from finally having her in my house and being able to smell her perfume in my personal space.

When I go inside, I find her sitting in the small leather chair right by the door with Poppy on her lap.

"I'm sorry, Ty," she says, looking down at the dog.

"For?"

Her shoulder lifts in a slight shrug. "Being difficult."

I take off my leather jacket and hang it on a metal skull hook by the door. "You're not. I'm trying to help you, that's all." I hold my hand out to her. "Take your jacket off. I'll hang it up with mine."

"Are you stray-catting me?" she asks, pulling off her jacket. "Is that why you asked me to come inside?" She chooses to shove her jacket behind her on the chair rather than give it to me, and I know that's because she feels safer having it with her, in case she has to run. I'd guess she probably lifted one of my kitchen knives, too, and has it hidden on her someplace.

Shaking my head, I go to the small kitchenette and put some water in a teapot to boil. About a week ago, she told me her stray cat obligation theory, and how she's worried I'm only hanging out with her because I feel sorry for her because no one else wants to. In true me fashion, I shot back that maybe she's only hanging out with me because I saved her life, and now she has white-knight syndrome.

Insecurity eats at both of us.

"Don't fish," I say.

"Fish?" Her nose crinkles with confusion, something she does that pisses me off with its cuteness. There are so many little things about her that just get to me lately. Things that make me smile when I don't want to, that make me fight to focus on what she's talking about rather than getting lost in the shape of her lips. Even the way she talks nonstop sometimes, like a song in my head that, even though I've heard it a hundred times, still puts me in a good mood.

"Fishing for validation." I pull two mugs from the cabinet and put tea bags in them. "Do you like milk and sugar in your tea?" I turn to face her, and she's staring at me like she has no idea who I am.

"Holly?" I hope she's not going to have a meltdown and pass out in the middle of my tiny living room. There's really no way she can fall without banging her head on something on the way down.

"You're making tea?" Her voice is laced with surprise.

"Is that okay?" Maybe tea is a trigger, something she was poisoned with in the past. One night, during our texts, she told me all about how that asshole would put something in her water to make her fall asleep. It put me in such a rage I couldn't sleep for two days. My inner demons were begging to get high or drunk—anything to numb the feelings battling inside me.

Instead, I drove to the city, to a dirty warehouse I've spent a lot of my time in since my second accident. Underground street fighting, my favorite stress and violence outlet. My brothers used to fight, too, to make extra money to help support Mom and the bike shop after Pop died. They quit fighting a few years back, but I've secretly kept going about once a month. I don't do it for the money, though. I do it mostly for the self-punishment. I let my opponent beat the fuck out of me until the very end, and then I take him down. Ninety percent of the time, I win. Every opponent becomes the face of karma to me first, giving me what I deserve for destroying my family, and then my opponent morphs into the asshole who kidnapped and hurt Holly, and I get to beat the hell out of him all over again. This last time I didn't have to worry about explaining cuts and bruises all over my face when I saw Holly the next day because I chose to not even let the guy get a punch in. I just pummeled him right from the start and walked out with two grand in dirty cash that reeked of weed.

I guess the thing about Holly that makes me the craziest is how being around her is like being on an emotional train, and every stop brings something new and unexpected. Happiness, fear, anger, care, desire. Unfortunately, the train doesn't let me get off. I've got a one-way ticket to places I never wanted to visit again.

Or even thought I *could* visit.

"Tea is good. I like milk, sugar, and honey. You should have honey, too," she adds. "I just didn't know you made tea. It's so... nice." She says it with a hint of disbelief. "And validation of what?"

I've been so lost in my thoughts I have to back the conversation up in my mind to remember what we were talking about.

"Validation that I like being with you."

"I wasn't fishing," she protests, pouting a little.

She was definitely fishing, but I don't mind giving her reassurance when she needs it. Grinning, I hand her a mug and sit on the couch across the tiny room. Boomer is asleep in his favorite spot, crammed under the small stairway that leads to the loft, which is good because when he's awake, he likes to tear around the house and knock things over. He also likes to pull socks and shoes off people and run and hide with them.

Holly gazes around the inside of my house with genuine interest, studying the nature photographs on my walls—which I took myself. She takes in the miniature inset lights, the incense holders on the mantel, the bookshelf filled with my collection of books by Stephen King, Madeleine L'Engle, Anne Rice, and Marquis de Sade, and the statues of foxes, wolves, angels, and grim reapers that Tor's friend-turned-girlfriend leaves for me by the dog-feeding stations that they set up in the woods when we think there's a lost dog in this area. I check the stations at night and early morning, and I'm hoping maybe someday Holly will go with me like Kenzi does with Tor.

Holly's eyes rove over the full-size fireplace, which is the focal point of the house, with its gray stone chimney reaching all the way up to the second-floor loft and its thick stone mantel.

"You built all this?" she asks.

"Me and my brother Tanner. There was a house here before, but we knocked it down. The garage was here, so I just fixed that up."

"It's beautiful. I've never seen anything like it."

"Thanks. Tiny houses are kind of a fad, but that's not why I live in one. I only wanted what I needed." I take a sip of my tea. She's the only woman who's ever been in here, other than my mother and my sister, and that was a long time ago, before I told them I never wanted them to come back. I couldn't stand seeing the sadness in their eyes or the way my mother constantly touched her wedding band, rubbing her finger over the white gold like it was a genie's lamp, missing my father with every breath she took. I couldn't take seeing the damage I'd caused the people I loved.

Holly's sweet voice floats across the room, sucking me back from the edge. "It's so cozy and warm. I thought I would be scared or feel cramped, but I'm not and I don't. I feel like I'd never want to leave."

Then don't.

"Isn't that what a home should be? A place you'd never want to leave?"

"I hope so," she agrees. "I don't feel like that at my apartment, though. Or at my parents'."

"Because home is more than a bunch of walls and floors."

With a faraway look, she nods and wraps her hands around her mug. I wonder if anyone ever hugs her, or if she has to constantly comfort herself. I want to pull her into my arms, show her what it's like to let someone else make her feel better and not hurt her.

"That's true, Tyler," she says softly.

"Someday, you'll have your home. A real home that you'll never want to leave."

She smiles weakly. "I'm hoping when I move to New York I'll feel that way with Zac and Anna."

I clear my throat, not trusting my voice to reply to that. I'm going to need a better truck if I plan on road-tripping out to New York to visit her. My old rust-bucket truck isn't gonna make it there in one piece.

"My parents gave my old room to my little sister. She was born after I was taken." She stares into her tea. She hasn't talked about her family much, and I haven't pried, so I'm surprised she's bringing them up.

"How does that make you feel?"

"Replaced." My heart wrenches for her. "And jealous."

"Totally understandable feelings." Sometimes I'm her friend. Other times I'm her therapist. She takes on those same roles with me.

I want more than that with her, though. I want to taste her lips, stare into her eyes, wrap my hands around her tiny waist...

"They told my little sister I was dead," she continues. "And now that I'm not dead, they're all awkward when I visit. It's like they don't want me there. I can feel it. I make them uncomfortable. I think they think I'm dirty. They barely even talk to me or look at me."

"People can be assholes when they have no idea how to deal with their feelings. It's not you. It's them." *Yes, listen to the poster child of how not to deal with your fucked-up feelings.*

She grips her mug tighter and gazes out the window. "You're the only one who seems to understand. My doctor listens...but she's paid to. And Feather—she understands, but her situation is different. Nobody really knows what happened to her. It wasn't made public like what happened to me. Her outsides are normal. She's beautiful. People only know what happened to her if she tells them." She licks her lips nervously. "I kinda envy that about her."

"You're beautiful on the outside *and* the inside, Holly." Honestly, she's not just beautiful—she's fucking breathtaking, adorable, and sexy. If we weren't two majorly fucked-up people, full of scars and rampant dysfunction, I'd be going out of my mind trying to get her to go out with me.

Her cheeks flush at my compliment, and her eyes shift back down to her teacup. "I feel like I'm made out of glass and everyone can see...everything. Like I'm a big gaping window. They know...what that man did to me. I want to just forget it. But it's hard when people look at me a certain way, and then bring it all up, like they have the right to ask me questions."

"Just remember *you* didn't do those things. Those things were done *to* you."

"I know, but..."

"I know it's hard. People can fucking suck. They do it to me, too. They think my scars will jump onto their own skin and make them ugly. They cringe when they hear me talk. They call me a murderer, a monster, a freak."

Her eyes squint closed as if each word I say hurts her. "Oh my God. You're not any of those things! How do you deal with that?" Compassion strains her voice.

"I fuckin' don't anymore. Everything I need is right here. Everyone can fuck off."

"But…what if you want to go out…like shopping or to dinner?"

"I'm a vegetarian. I don't go out to eat. I make my own food."

"So you really don't go out at all?" she asks, her mystical eyes widening.

"Nope." I shrug. "Unless it's dark out and I don't have to interact with judgmental douchebags. I'm over it. Most things I need I can have delivered, or one of my brothers will bring it to me. I ride my bike at night, that's my escape outta here if I feel stir-crazy. But I like it here in my little fucking bubble."

She nods in slow agreement. "I've never told anyone this," she whispers. "But sometimes…I feel like being locked away was easier. I didn't have to make decisions or try to fit in. I knew what I was dealing with, if that makes sense?"

I nod and take another sip of my tea.

"Out here in the world, I have no idea what people want, how they're going to act, what they want from me. Being free is a lot harder than I thought it would be."

I clear my throat. "I get what you're saying, sugar. You just have to find your groove."

"What about you? Is this your groove, or are you still trying to find yours, too?"

I love how she's not afraid to ask me questions. And I love how she listens to me so intently, absorbing everything I say like a sponge.

I let out a sigh, lean back in the couch, and put my foot up on my coffee table. "I think this is mostly my groove. Most days, I'm content. I can live with the choices I've made. That's what I need the most—peace of mind."

"But are you happy? Because you don't seem very happy to me."

Me? Happy? "I kinda forgot about being happy and just wanted to find peace. But…I'm happy when you're here with me. You wanted to make me smile, and you do. That's not an easy feat." I wink at her from behind my cup, because I like the way it makes her eyes twinkle. She's a hard one to read—sometimes she trembles and her eyes go dark with terror if I stand too close or touch her in a casual way, and other times she looks at me like she's totally ga-ga over me. Without knowing it, she twists me all up, oblivious to the way her fear knocks on the door of my hidden desires, and her sweetness melts the ice around my heart and lulls the voices in my head.

Not for the first time, I wonder if I do the same for her.

"I like when you smile," she says softly.

Today, she's ga-ga.

"Where's your television?" she suddenly asks, looking around the room.

"Don't have one."

This fascinates her; her eyes are big like an owl's as she stares at me. "Really? You don't?"

"I'd rather read or go for a walk."

"I had a TV . . ." She squirms in the chair nervously. "Back then. I watched it almost nonstop. It got to the point where I almost thought those people in the TV were my family. I didn't have a calendar, or a clock, or a window to see if it was day or night, so it was hard for me to figure out when my favorite shows were going to be on, so I would just sit and watch and wait."

"That sucks." I can't even imagine living with time deprivation like that. What a severe mind-fuck.

"Without the TV, though, I wouldn't have had any company before Poppy was given to me. It's how I learned a lot of things. By watching TV."

Warped is the only word that describes a child being raised by a television. How she isn't completely fucked up is a miracle in itself. Yeah, she's innocent and naïve in a lot of ways, but she's got a good idea of what's right and wrong, and she knows what she wants. The more I learn about her, the more I admire her.

And the more I want her.

"What is this?"

I rip my stare from the fireplace, which often mesmerizes me with unwanted memories of flames and burning flesh, to find her fingering a throw blanket draped over the chair she's sitting in.

"It's just a blanket."

She lifts it and rubs it across her cheek, her eyes falling closed as she revels in the sensation, an act so intimate—almost sensual—that it makes my cock jump to a rock-hard state almost instantly.

What the fuck.

"It's so soft!" She continues to torture me by rubbing it across the other side of her face, the fabric sliding across her lips. "It's softer than anything I've ever felt in my life."

"It's plush or something," I mumble, my brain short-circuiting as I watch her basically face-fuck a blanket my mother gave me.

"I love it."

I stand uncomfortably and walk the few steps to the sink and put my mug in it, trying to distract myself from thoughts I shouldn't be having about someone who is my only friend and I'd like to not lose or fuck up.

"I never had a blanket," she says, her voice quavering with emotion. "I never had anything soft like this. I used my backpack as a pillow, and I had an old thin sheet. I didn't know things like this...so incredibly soft and comforting...existed. I don't even have anything like this at my apartment, or at my parents'..."

I'm so glad I killed that douchebag.

And now I wish I was a blanket, my every fiber being slid over her body, taking in her warmth and curves, comforting her...

By the time I turn around, tears are falling down her cheeks and her hands are trembling, and it fucking guts me and fills me with guilt. I walk over and kneel in front of her and coax the dog out of her lap, and he immediately curls up at her feet. I grab the throw blanket, shake it open, and gently lay it over her.

"No crying here," I say softly, reaching up to wipe her cheeks with the back of my hand. *Not the badly scarred one. I won't touch her beautiful face with my ugly flesh.* I take her hand in mine and slowly slide it across the plush fabric of the blanket covering her leg. "Feel the fabric. They say texture helps ground you if you're having an anxiety attack."

Her eyes track our hands moving along the blanket, and she sniffs back her tears. "It does feel so good and soft," she whispers.

"This house...this is my only happy place," I confess. "And it can be yours now, too."

Nodding sleepily, she pulls the blanket up to her chin and leans her head back against the chair. "I need a happy place so bad, Ty. I love how soft and warm this is...It's like magic." Her eyes drift closed. "It makes me feel like you do...safe and weirdly good."

She falls asleep snuggled up under the blanket, and I sit on the couch with her dog in my lap and try to pretend that having her in my house isn't making me question my life of solitude.

I want her to be part of my groove.

She jolts awake when I open the door to let Boomer and Poppy outside, and stares around in wide-eyed, open-mouthed confusion for a few seconds until she remembers where she is.

"Sorry," I say when her eyes focus on me, still standing at the door waiting for the pets to return. "Had to let them out."

Sitting up straighter, she runs her hand through her hair. "I can't believe I fell asleep. I'm so sorry. This blanket made me feel all woozy." She rubs her eyes, looking so innocent and alluring that I just want to kiss her until our lips are numb. "I'm still trying to get used to only sleeping at night. Before...I slept whenever. My doctor says my inner clock might be confused for a while."

My inner everything is confused. "You were comfy and sleepy. It's okay to nap. Rest is good for mind and body, nothing to be ashamed of."

"Isn't it rude?" she asks. "To do it in someone else's house?"

"Not at all. I want you to feel comfortable here."

"I do. More than I do anywhere else. It really is my happy place."

She may have been comfortable physically, but the way she twitched and whimpered during her nap made it clear she wasn't comfortable mentally. Dreams were torturing her—maybe from her past, maybe from her present. I was equally tortured wondering how she would've reacted if I had carried her to the couch and let her nap in my arms, under the blanket together.

I'm afraid to find out. I'd rather stay in this comfortable limbo we're in forever than risk losing her or seeing rejection in her eyes.

She folds the blanket, drapes it back over the chair, and then glances at her watch. "Can you take me home?"

I look at the wall clock. "Now? It's only two." Usually I take her home around four or five.

"I'm going out to dinner with Zac and Anna tonight, and their friend John. Zac said he had something exciting to share with me."

My jaw twitches. "Then I'll drive you home." I was hoping she'd stay longer today and have dinner with me for the first time. I have no right to be upset, though, since that wish only lived in my head and I never actually asked her to stay.

Maybe next time.

♥ ♥ ♥

While we drive back to her apartment, she watches the trees go by for a few miles, before she turns to me. "I'm nervous about dinner," she blurts out.

"Why?"

"Because of what I mentioned earlier...People recognize me sometimes. They stare at me and ask questions."

"I get the same. Ignore them." *Oh, like you do, Ty? Hypocrite.*

"It's hard to."

"I know."

"I wish you could come, too," she says wistfully. "I feel better when we're together."

My heart jumps in the air, grabs her words, and runs back to the darkness to savor them. "Trust me, they'll stare more if I'm there." The people of this small town would go nuts if they saw Holly and me together. The murderer and the Girl in the Hole to some, the hero and the victim to others. Both the scarred-up freaks in one place for them to stare at and spread rumors about.

No fucking thanks.

"Can I text you later? When I get home?" she asks when I pull over at the usual place in front of her apartment. I always stay parked there, watching her, until I see her go inside, safe and sound. Sometimes I still watch her window, late at night, just so I know she's still okay, and so I can be close to her. Is it stalking if you're trying to take care of someone from afar? Does that, in fact, put me in that feeding-the-stray-cat category?

Fuck it if it does.

I'll love someone however the fuck I want to.

Like them. I meant *like* them.

"Tyler?"

Shit. "Sure." I clear my throat. "Text me. Take a picture of your dinner and text it."

She looks at me like I'm crazy. "I can't do that...It's food."

"Everyone does. It's weird if you don't."

Throwing her backpack over her shoulder, she laughs. "Okay, then. I'll try."

🤍 🤍 🤍

After I watch her close her front door behind her, I continue to drive into town, turning down a side street to drive past the pet shelter my mom runs. I eye her car as I do a U-turn and head back to the main road. Then I drive past my family's motorcycle shop, noting all my brothers' cars out in the parking lot. *Where mine should be, too.* A new sign is hanging on the outside of the building, much larger, bolder, and brighter than the one that was there before. I hope that means business is going good for them. Tor used to send me text updates about how the shop was doing. He'd text me pictures of bikes that were scheduled for custom work, trying to entice me to come back to work my magic. I ignored his messages for months until he gave up. Now he just deposits money from the business into my bank account every month. Money I get because my last name is on the sign, not because I deserve it.

I donate most of it anonymously to my mother's pet shelter.

I miss my family, but they're better off without me there reminding them of all the heartache I caused them.

CHAPTER 17

Holly

The restaurant is dim with jazz music playing in the background. The tablecloths are bright white, the tables, chairs, and booths black wood. The floor is so shiny it's like a mirror, and I don't like walking on it. Everything feels expensive, and I feel cheap and out of place. Anna looks beautiful in her maroon wraparound dress, her dark hair falling in big, soft waves. I should have changed my clothes, but I didn't because I didn't know this was a dress-up type of night.

Apparently, everyone else knew, though, because even Zac and his friend John are wearing dark pants, light shirts, and jackets. Not jeans like I am. I'm seated across from my brother and his girlfriend, and John is next to me, on my right. To my left is the wall of the booth and a window. My eyes continue to shift to the window, trying to discreetly find the latch, but there isn't one that I can see. Does the window not open?

Count to ten, Holly. You're not trapped. It's only dinner.

My hand strokes my purse as they chitchat; inside is my phone with photos of every page of all my fairy tales. Oh, it's not quite the same as having the actual books with me, but it's close enough to make me feel less afraid without them.

John's leg accidentally brushes against mine, and I scoot farther to the left. A small person could fit between us now, but he still feels too close.

"We have news to share with you," Zac announces, and Anna smiles shyly. "We wanted to tell you two first."

I wonder how I became part of this special group, and while I like being included, I worry I can't live up to such an expectation. John is Zac's lifelong best friend. I'm a sister he barely knows. I begin to worry if I'll react to the news appropriately. Silently, I pray I don't hyperventilate and pass out. I wish Ty were here, sitting next to me, holding my pinky finger in his.

"Well, don't keep us waiting," John urges. "Tell us."

"I'm pregnant," Anna says happily. "We found out last month but wanted to wait to share."

"Holy shit!" John exclaims. "Congratulations."

I'm filled with all sorts of emotions and questions. I'm going to be an aunt. Will they still be moving to New York? Will they still want me to go with them? Will they let me near the baby? Or will they keep her away, like my mother does with Lizzie, afraid I might taint her?

I force my brain to be quiet, and I smile at my brother and his girlfriend. "That's terrific. I'm so happy for you both."

They clasp hands on the table. "We're really excited," Zac says. "Surprised, but excited."

"How far along are you?" John asks. He knows the right questions to ask. I don't.

"About twelve weeks."

"This doesn't change the plan, right?" John asks. "You're still coming to New York to work with me?"

"Definitely," Zac answers. "We'll just look for a bigger place, that's all. And Anna wants to look for a position that will allow telecommuting so she can work from home with the baby." His eyes travel over to me, and he smiles. "I hope you'll still come with us, Holly. You can help with the baby."

Anna jumps in. "Only if you want to, of course. I'm not going to force you to be a babysitter if you live with us." She playfully slaps Zac's arm. "Don't scare her off."

"I'd love to," I say quickly. "I've never babysat before, obviously…"

The waitress comes to the table and takes our order. As usual, I have no idea what I like, so I get the same as Anna orders because it's easier than reading the entire menu and asking people to explain what everything is.

"I'm glad you're coming to New York, too," John says to me after the waitress leaves. "We'll all have fun together."

"Thank you," I say, because I'm not sure how else to respond. "I'm looking forward to it," I add for politeness. I'm a parrot. Repeating words I don't even know if I feel.

Zac smiles at me across the table, and I get the nagging feeling that this was more than just a dinner with his sister and his best friend. I want to run to the ladies' room and be alone for a few minutes, but I don't want to ask John to move. That seems like it would be annoying, and that's the last thing I want to be, so I stay there and keep counting to ten over and over in my head until it aches.

Their voices sound like they're coming down a tunnel, and I know I've disconnected but I can't help it. I smile when they do, but I don't speak. Thankfully, they're so involved in their conversation that I don't think anyone notices, and I'm relieved.

Later—when Zac is driving us home, and I'm sitting in the back seat again with John—he leans closer to me. *Too close.*

"Can I get your number? Maybe we can talk sometime or grab a bite to eat."

I stare forward, at the back of my brother's head, dumbfounded. *Do I want to give him my number? Talk? Eat?*

"I...Me?" I stammer.

He smiles. "You don't have be nervous, Holly. I've been your brother's best friend since kindergarten." His voice and his eyes are soft, sincere. Trustworthy. "I know what happened to you, and I'm so sorry. I helped look for you, in the search party."

I look down at my hands in my lap, wishing he hadn't brought that up. This is the first I've heard mention of a search party, which is actually a very ironic term. I wonder how much he knows, and if he would understand that his knowing about me makes me even more nervous.

"Thank you..."

"I'd love to get to know you better, take you to some of my favorite places. Get you out a little more."

My hands shake, and my palms dampen. I'm not ready for this. I'm not sure I want to be known better by John. Or anyone. And I don't want to get out any more than I already am. My smile is shaky and awkward. "I think I'd like to think about it. If that's okay?"

"Sure it is." He reaches behind him, pulls out his wallet, and takes a business card out of it. "Here's my card. You can call or text anytime if you'd like to talk or go out. No strings or expectations, I promise."

I take the card from him and slide it into my small purse, having no plans of adding him to my phone. I don't want his number on my phone next to Ty's. That feels wrong to me.

After Zac drops John off at his apartment, I breathe a sigh of relief and open the window a few inches to let some air into the car. I feel so suffocated I want to hang my head out the window like a dog.

"Holly...," Zac says, looking at me in the rearview mirror. "Don't be scared. John's a really good guy. I trust him with my life. He thinks you're sweet."

I gulp.

"Who's my sweet little girl?"

"He really is a nice guy," Anna adds. "A real gentleman. And so handsome. I think he would be good for you to spend time with. Take it slow, one day at a time. He's very understanding. Who knows what could happen."

John might be nice, but his eyes are hazel, not blue.

He doesn't wear soft faded jeans with holes at the knees with torn edges. Or leather jackets that smell like smoke and woods.

He doesn't have pictures in his skin, a storybook for me to someday read.

And he doesn't make my heart flutter.

He probably doesn't even own a soft blanket.

He's not prince material, and he never will be.

Everyone knows there can only be one prince, and I've already found mine.

CHAPTER 18

Tyler

> Hey :-) You forget my picture, sugar?

A few minutes pass while I wait for her to reply, and I debate getting out of bed to go outside for a smoke to chill my nerves.

Holly

> I couldn't do it. It was a really nice place, and I didn't see anyone else taking pictures of their food.

> That's okay. I was just teasing you.
> Did you have a nice time?

Holly

> I guess so.

I frown at the phone, sensing a change.

> Everything okay?

Holly

> It was uncomfortable. My brother and his girlfriend are having a baby. I'm excited about that.

> That's good news.

Holly

It is. I've never been around a baby.

I'm sure you'll love it. Is that what
made you uncomfortable?

Holly

No. My brother's friend wants to know me better.
He wants to talk or go out and eat. He gave
me his card of phone numbers.

My jaw clenches. I saw this coming a mile away. I remember
Zac Daniels and John Parker. I went to high school with them.
They were both jocks, just like me. They're both nice guys,
not assholes. If Holly were my sister, I'd be trying to set her up
with a nice guy, too, because that's the kind of guy she needs.
Someone with a career, and a future who can give her stability,
maybe even a family. Not someone living in dysfunction junction
like me.

It's good for you to have more friends.

Holly

I have you and Feather and Anna and
Poppy and Boomer.

I can't help myself, so...

Do you like him?

There's another long pause, and the screen taunts me, my question just hanging there. The more I stare at it, the more desperate
and immature it makes me feel. *Do you like him?* What the fuck

am I, fourteen again? Of course she likes him. He didn't get beat
with the ugly stick like I did.

Holly
> He reminds me of the bad man. They dress the
> same. They have the same hair.

My heart sinks for her and rallies for me. It's hard to run from
bad memories. I try to say the right thing, because it's the right
thing to do, as the friend that I am. And above all else, I want
Holly to be safe and cared about.

> Give it time. Not everyone's the same,
> even if they look like they might be.
> We both know looks are deceiving.

Look at me, being nice. It's almost sickening.

Holly
> Can I see Poppy tomorrow?

She makes me smile. That's been our little way of avoiding
actually saying we want to see each other, but I long for a day
when we both say what we mean, and don't hide behind hints.

> Not tomorrow. The day after.
> I'll pick you up at noon.

I want to give her a day to think. About me, hopefully. But also
about John, because she deserves to have space to think and sort
her thoughts out.

I toss my phone on my nightstand and lace my hands behind my head, staring up at my ceiling. I try to imagine us together. I picture us on a date together, her so beautiful and soft spoken and me a mess of flesh and scars, growling like an animal trying to speak. What if people stare at my face or back away from my voice like they always do? Would she feel embarrassed? Would it just add to her own anguish? Would she ever be happy hiding from the world here with me, in the sanctuary I've created for myself? Or would she eventually resent me for putting her in another trap?

♥ ♥ ♥

"Sir...you can't touch those." The woman practically pulls the blanket from my hands. I glance across the aisle at another customer, clearly fondling bedsheets, her fingers wedged under the plastic wrapping around the sheets.

I never should have done this to myself. It took me two hours to force myself to get in my truck and drive across town to this bed and bath store, and I was right to think it was a mistake.

"Just trying to find a soft one," I say.

She cringes at the sound of my voice. "Well, you can't stand here and touch them all. It's completely unsanitary."

I point a skull-adorned finger at the other customer, who's trying desperately to ignore me. "She's fucking touching them," I growl, not giving a shit how I sound now.

The saleswoman gasps. "Excuse me, but you can't speak to me that way. I'll call security and have you thrown out."

"For what? Molesting blankets?"

Her eyes flit across the scars on my face, then down to my throat, my arm, and my hand. I should have put my leather jacket on, but I left it in the car because the stress of coming in here was making me hot and sweaty.

Another salesgirl comes rushing over, this one younger, with an apologetic smile. Her hair is dyed jet black, and a small silver hoop hangs from her nose. "Why don't you go work the register, Helen. I'll help this customer find what he needs."

Helen glares at me and walks away, taking the blanket I was holding with her like she just saved it from a life of misery.

The new girl makes a pained face. "I'm so sorry about that. She's just a rude old bitch," she says under her breath. "Can I help you with anything? Are you looking for a certain size, color, or fabric?"

Why does everything have to be so difficult and come with so many choices? "It has to be the softest," I answer. "It's a gift for someone special."

"Everyone touches them," she whispers, glancing at her bitchy coworker, who's still looking at me as if I'm Satan himself, sent here from hell to corrupt all the angelic blankets. "I've touched most of these myself. These over here are the softest... We have chenille, fleece, flannel, down." I follow her down the aisle as she points to each one, and she waits patiently while I feel each of them, trying to pick the one Holly will love the most. I debate just buying one of each so I can get out of here faster.

"You're Tanner's brother, right?" Her brown eyes squint at me, tiny wrinkles forming in the corners and across the bridge of her nose.

"One of them."

"I went to school with him. You're the one who saved that girl in the woods."

I nod uncomfortably and put two blankets off to the side. Chenille mink seems to be the winner.

"He was my uncle," she whispers.

I throw her a quizzical look.

"The man you killed."

I knew this day would come eventually. That pig had a wife and kids who, best as I know, still live here. And, apparently, a niece. I can't walk across this town without tripping over someone who either knows me, knows what happened to me, or knows what I did.

I finger a blindingly white down comforter. "I'm not gonna apologize."

"I don't expect you to," she replies quickly. "You did the world a huge favor."

I don't want to know if this girl helping me pick out blankets is another of his victims, or maybe someone he groped at family parties or exposed himself to, or who the hell knows what other kind of sick shit he did. The less I know about the man I killed, the better off I'll be.

I grab two of the softest throw blankets in the biggest sizes. "I did what I had to do," I say gruffly. "Thanks for your help."

An hour later I've got Holly in the passenger seat of my truck, two of the softest and most expensive blankets the store had are hidden behind my seat in a huge plastic bag, and we're on our way to my house.

Almost every day, we go straight to my workshop. I have no idea why she likes watching me work, but she does. She loves to clean and polish everything: the rings and buckles I make, and my hammers, screwdrivers, and wrenches. I must have the shiniest, cleanest tools in the world. Today I ask her to come inside the house for a few minutes before heading to the workshop.

At first, she hesitates at my request, which isn't unusual, and then she follows me into the house.

"Close your eyes," I say when we get inside. Instead, her complexion pales, and her eyes dart skittishly to the door.

"Ty...why..."

"Shit," I say. "I'm sorry." I gently touch her arm. "Don't be scared...I just wanted to surprise you." I don't know all her triggers yet—I have to learn them as I step on them, which causes a lot of moments just like this one. I hold the bag out to her. "This is for you."

She takes the bag from me, her hand shaking slightly, and it sucks that this girl can't even be given a gift without worrying it's something that's going to hurt her. I vow to change that.

"What is it?" she asks.

"Look inside. I promise you'll like it."

Nervously, she opens the bag and pulls out the two throw blankets in their plastic zippered cases. Her small, skeptical smile turns into a huge, excited one.

"You got me magic blankets?" she squeals, pulling one out of its plastic and holding it against her body, feeling its softness. "Oh my God," she practically moans. "It's so soft."

"One for here, and one for you to take home."

She yanks out the other and hugs them both to her, sparking my jealous streak. *What do I have to do to be hugged like that?* "They're so soft. I love them. Did you...did you go out and buy these?"

I nod. "Yeah."

"Wow." Realization sinks into her expression. *She gets me. Without question.*

"Yeah."

She looks up into my eyes. "Thank you so much," she says softly, and before I realize what she's doing, her hand is on my arm, and she's going up on her tiptoes, and she kisses my cheek. Not the pretty half that's not hiding behind my long hair. *No.* She presses her soft, perfect lips right over my scarred cheek and then hovers there for a moment.

Lavender vanilla perfume fills the air around me.

The room spins.

Our eyes meet and hold as she slowly settles back down on the flats of her feet. I want to kiss her, but I don't. I think she finally wants me to, but I still don't. I take a deep breath, bracing myself for rejection. "It's warmer today." I swallow, hoping it will clear the rasp a bit, but it never does. "Maybe we could take a walk out back, sit in the leaves, and talk. We'll bring the fuzzy beasts with us."

Her silvery eyes blink rapidly, like pages flipping through a book. Confusion, excitement, and a tinge of alluring fear and anticipation reveal themselves with every sweep of her lids. I can feel myself tumbling into an abyss filled with long kisses, breathless sighs, rose petals, and primal thrusts.

"Can we bring the blanket?" she asks.

Not at all what I was expecting. But everything I was hoping for. *Thank you, powers that fucking be.*

"We can bring anything that'll make you happy." Anything but the purple backpack. My gut tells me she's gotta let that go. Soon.

"Just you, Poppy, Boomer, and this blanket will make me happy." Our eyes lock, unfaltering, hypnotizing each other, planting subtle hints and suggestions in just the right places in our minds and hearts. I can almost believe this girl could love me, scars, damage, ugliness and all.

And oh, how ferociously I would love her back if given the chance.

It's unseasonably warm, and all traces of the snowstorm we had a few weeks ago have vanished. As we walk along the path stemming from what is mostly my backyard, I take a chance and reach for her hand, and hers slides into mine willingly, our fingers interlocking perfectly. Poppy and Boomer race ahead of us, come back to check on us, and race back down the path again. Holly laughs as Boomer jumps over Poppy's back, letting out his crazy happy squeal in midair before he lands in a pile of old leaves and burrows his face into it, peeking out at us.

"He's so funny," she says. "Was he like that as a baby, too?"

"Yes. He always makes me laugh. I guess I kinda need it."

"How long have you had him?"

"About four years."

"Poppy seems to really like him. I'm not sure if Poppy has ever been around another animal, or why he sounds funny. I don't know where the bad man got him from."

She always refers to him as "the bad man," and I wonder if she knows that his real name was Donald J. Loughlin, that he was a forty-two-year-old middle school teacher who drove a four-door Toyota, that he had a wife, two kids, and a beagle. He had no criminal record and no history of drug or alcohol use, but he had quite the hidden collection of porn featuring little girls and anime dolls.

I know exactly where Poppy came from, thanks to the microchip he has. Ten-year-old Poppy once belonged to a local elderly woman who had him debarked because he barked too much. When she passed away, her daughter brought him to my mother's animal shelter and two months later, Donald J. Loughlin, pedophile extraordinaire, came in and adopted him, apparently extremely intrigued by the fact he couldn't bark. Later we found out he told the volunteer at the shelter who processed the paperwork that he suffered from migraines, so the dog would be perfect. After Holly's parents basically told me to shove the dog up my ass, I decided to keep him.

I'm not going to tell Holly any of this, though.

"They got along right away," I assure her. "Boomer didn't really give him a choice. He decided they were gonna be best buds, and Poppy didn't really have a say." I wink at her, and she squeezes my hand tighter, so tight that I hate to tell her we've reached the place I had planned on us sitting because I don't want her to let go.

"Let's sit here." I reluctantly release her hand and spread an old, frayed blanket I brought with us on the ground next to a large rock. The rock is almost the size of half my truck and about twenty feet from the river, which has thawed and is slowly flowing downhill. We both take off our jackets, the walk here having warmed us up enough that sweaters are just enough to be comfortable, and we settle down on the blanket.

This is one of my favorite places to come and relax. I used to come here to smoke a joint every day, but since I've quit that, now I just come here to chill out and get my head together.

Knowing she feels uncomfortable with too much silence, I pull up my favorite playlist on my phone and set it off to the side on low volume, so we have background noise in addition to the sound of the river behind us.

"You remember everything," she says softly, pulling her new blanket into her lap.

"I try to."

She lies down flat on her back, pulling the blanket over her, and stares up at the sky. "I love watching the clouds. I think I could stare at the clouds and the stars every day for the rest of my life and never get bored of it."

"You'd love my loft bedroom. I have a skylight right over the bed."

She squints up at me. "What's a skylight?"

"It's a window in the ceiling, so you can see the sky."

The way her mouth falls open in awe is priceless and adorable. "Are you serious? There's ceiling windows?"

"Yup."

"I had no idea."

"You're welcome to check mine out any time you want. I'll stay downstairs."

She turns her attention back to the sky, but her mind has drifted as far away from me as those clouds. I can't tell if giving her distance makes her feel safe or unwanted. We have so many fucked-up gray areas between us we're practically a black-and-white movie.

"Can I lie down next to you?"

There's that flicker of uncertainty in her eyes, that moment when I can see her breath catch in her throat. Most likely a thousand bad memories are rampaging through her mind—and it sucks that I'm always the cause of it, constantly having to scare her to move forward with her.

I don't know why I'm even trying to move forward when I know damn well one or both of us will end up getting hurt or left behind. I have to admit, even in pain, there's a degree of pleasure, and I can't stop myself from wanting my own little shred of that.

"Okay," she finally replies, and I lie next to her, leaving half a foot of safe space between us, and she gently spreads the blanket over me.

"Does it make you feel safe, too?" Her soft voice has taken on a nervous lilt, and it makes my heart pound harder.

"Yeah. It does."

Poppy and Boomer join us, curling up at the end of the blanket for a nap after their game of chase and leaf stalking.

"I love being here with you and them...hearing the river... watching the clouds...having a soft blanket...I feel so free, like I can breathe." She turns to me, her blond hair cascading around her head against the flannel blanket. "Is that strange?"

"Not at all, sugar. You were forced to live in a state of defense for a long time. I think your brain and your body are just finally learning to relax."

"I like how you put that." She looks up at the clouds again. "I want to live in a place just like this. Do you think New York is like this?"

"Not if it's the city, but there are parts of upstate New York like this." I've always loved living here in this remote corner of the woods I've carved out for myself, but having her here lately has made it complete. She's like the star on top of the Christmas tree—that final glittering touch that brings it all together.

"I hope I can relax there, like this."

"I'm sure you will. Every day, you're getting stronger. I can see it."

"So are you."

"Me?" I ask. "How so?"

"You smile more. You don't seem as mad. You don't hide your face from me anymore. And you talk now."

"That's because you're like Boomer. I didn't have much of a choice with any of it." I say it teasingly, but it's all true. She's changing me.

I don't know how to admit it, or say it, but I don't want her to go. I prop my head up on my arm and turn to face her, the blanket falling to our waists. Her sweater has shifted, the scoop neck exposing the curve of her neck and shoulder, enticing me to caress or kiss...

Her gaze moves to my arm, which is bent between us. "Can I touch your tattoos?" she asks.

Hiding under most of my ink is bumpy, scarred flesh that a blind person could probably interpret into some strange language. No woman is going to want to feel that.

TIED   209

But I can't deny her anything.

"Sure." I force the word out, confident this will be the first and last time she'll ever touch me.

Her hand slowly moves along my forearm, her fingers trailing over the art, and she pushes my sleeve up farther so she can see— and touch—my shoulder. When her small hand closes around my bicep, I can't help but close my eyes and enjoy her touch for more than what it is.

"Your arm is so big and hard." Of course, she has no idea what she's saying—sexual innuendo isn't something she understands— but that doesn't change my body's reaction to her soft-porn commentary as she squeezes my arm.

"Mmm . . ." is all I can manage to mumble.

"What do the designs mean?" Down to my wrist her hand moves, slowly tantalizing me.

"They're mostly how my fucked-up brain felt at the time . . . abstract flowers, monsters, and words."

"It's all beautiful. Like a book, only better."

"I was pretty high when I picked most of those designs out. The ink on my back is a better representation of me straight and sober."

Her hand stills. "You do drugs?"

"Not anymore, but I had a wicked bad habit. That's how I crashed through a glass wall and almost sliced my own head off."

"Oh."

Hello, surprise and horror. I knew you'd show up and take away that sweet voice of hers.

"I'm totally clean now, Holly. I have been for years."

"Is that what happened to . . ." She halts herself, afraid to ask.

"To my voice?" I finish for her. "Yeah. A piece of glass severed part of my vocal cords."

"I'm so sorry."

"Don't be. I deserved a lot worse."

"Ty...how can you say that?"

I stare at her across the blanket, our faces just inches apart. Being this close to her lying down in the forest is much different than being this close to her standing up in my workshop or in my kitchen. Resting in the same space, our bodies under the same blanket, spins an entirely new intimacy level between us.

"Because it's true."

Her eyes are wet with the start of tears, and the heavy feeling in my chest returns. I don't want to talk about my past right now, or see her upset. All I want is to lie in my favorite spot with her, beneath her magic blanket, and for her to keep touching me and looking at me without pulling away.

"You don't deserve anything bad."

"No, I really, actually do. I was a junkie. I stole money from my family to buy drugs. I treated them like shit. The night of my crash I had a fight with my dad." I clear my throat, which is choking me. "He wanted me to go to rehab. I refused. I left the house in the middle of the night, high and drunk, on my bike." I swallow hard. "He chased me down the driveway and had a heart attack. That was the night he died. Because of *me*. My mother found him in the fucking driveway. I choked someone to death without a second thought. Once a month I go to private fight rings and let people punch the crap out of me; then I beat them to a pulp and walk out with a pile of cash I don't even want. I ride around with masks on and stare at people at red lights. I hide in the woods and scare the shit out of hikers. I'm a fucked-up freak."

And let's not forget how I used to fuck the crazy fans in the alley after the fights, with my rubber horror mask on, blood from my battered face leaking out from beneath it and running down my neck and chest.

How the fear in their eyes, and my blood smeared on their ripped clothes fueled all the fires of hate and dysfunction in my drugged-out mind as a nameless and faceless fetish fuck.

Her body trembles as she listens to my tirade. "You saved my life. You make beautiful jewelry. You help save lost animals. You decorate Christmas trees, and created a myth for little kids to love..."

All of that should make me feel better, but it doesn't. Not when the reflection of my father chasing me in the mirror of my bike is branded into my brain along with hazy memories of being a deviant pig.

"So the fuck what?" My self-hatred has joined our little get-together on the blanket and has no problem rearing its ugly head.

"Maybe you did some bad things, but you've done a lot of good things, too."

So many bad and ugly things. Things that would make her never want to look at me again.

"That doesn't change the shit I did. Nothing can change that. Ever. Good doesn't erase bad."

"No, but you don't have to punish yourself. You're a good person. You saved and kept Poppy. You took care of Boomer and kept him. You taught me how to drive. You gave me a phone and soft blankets. You're my best friend. Every day you take care of me, you let me see Poppy, you make sure I'm safe, you make me feel special."

"Maybe that doesn't make me a good person, Holly. Maybe that makes me a person who's just obsessed with the first person to give me any amount of attention. Or maybe I just like to collect things as messed up as I am."

Her face falls, and I immediately want to eat my obnoxious words, which couldn't be more untrue. Hurting her, this one little gem in my life, is unacceptable.

My psychiatrist's words echo through my mind. *Fear of trust. Fear of intimacy. Fear of giving and accepting love. Social and familial avoidance. Extreme self-loathing. Low self-worth. Unnatural focus on physical appearance. Drug addict. Severely depressed. Repressed memories. Deviant sexual behavior. Self-harm risk. Possible danger to others.*

She tries to sit up, and I put my arm around her waist and hold her down, ignoring the terrified stare she pins on me.

"No. I'm not letting you run off." I lower my voice and loosen my grip on her waist. "I didn't mean what I said." She turns her head away from me, a tear sliding down her cheek, and she stares blankly off into the distance. I can see her shutting down, running to the safe space in her head where she can slam everything out. Including me.

Fuck.

"Holly . . . I'm sorry. It's hard for me to talk about my father and my past. It makes me want to just hurt myself and anyone around me. It fucks my head up, but I'm trying to be better."

Silence.

"I care about you. And not for any other reason than you're beautiful and sweet and captivating and every day is better with you in it." I touch the side of her head and gently turn her to face me. "You make me feel a little bit less messed up, and you make me want to *be* less messed up."

"Really?" she squeaks.

"Really. You make me smile every day. Even when you're not here."

If I wasn't lying so close to her, I never would have heard her next words. "You make me feel that way, too."

She sniffles, her eyes showing a glimmer of a sparkle, and all I want is to see her smile at me again. I brush my thumb across her cheek to wipe her tear away. The intimate touch causes a tiny gasp to escape her. My barriers snap, and I lean down and cover her lips with mine, my hand moving to cradle the back of her neck, my fingers sliding through her hair, like it has in my dreams a thousand times. My tongue sweeps over her lips, and when they part in surprise, I slip inside, tasting her, coaxing her to open up to me. Her hand tightens on my shoulder, her nails digging slightly into my flesh. Taking that as a sign of passion, I roll my body closer to hers, half covering her, and grip the back of her neck, kissing her deeper.

I'm lost in our kiss, the delicious taste of her lips, her soft curves fitting perfectly against my body, shaking...

Shaking.

My eyes snap open to find hers staring back at me, wide with shock and panic, which only makes my cock throb harder in tune to my pounding heart. My fingers tighten in her hair, the locks laced through my fingers like silk ribbons. I can't let go. I lean down, craving more of her, needing her lips on mine again, wanting to feel her racing heartbeat against my chest 'til it nearly explodes and then calms to a soft, lulling beat. I want to feel it all.

Her hand releases its grip on my arm and falls to the ground beside her with a faint thud, and her head turns to the side again, but not before I see the emotionless, disconnected canvas of her stare.

Reality shatters the moment, which wasn't the moment I thought it was at all, and I slowly pull away from her. My ring catches on her hair, and I quickly untangle it while she lies there, completely detached.

"Sorry..." My voice growls with repressed desire. "I thought..." What did I think?

She rises slowly, pulling her knees up against her chest, and pulls the blanket up over her. Sensing her mood, Poppy crawls to her side and nudges his head under her hand.

In a matter of seconds, I fucked everything all up. I scared her. Tore her safety net from beneath her. Repulsed her.

I'm not equipped to be what she needs, because my own needs are too much, too fast, too soon, too hard, too raw. The thirst to taste fear, lust, love, trust, and ecstasy is a beautifully mixed cocktail for me, and sure poison for her.

I stand and offer my hand to help her up. "I'll take you home."

What could have been a perfect day took a U-turn into a day ending with an absolutely dead-silent drive back to her apartment. Sweet smiles and handholding have gone out the window. When I pull my truck in front of her building, she stares down at the blanket in her lap, fingering the soft fabric.

"Thank you for the blanket," she murmurs softly. "I love it."

I try to speak, but all that comes out is a faint choking sound. Frustrated, I wave my hand at her, and she opens the door, now a master of its handle, and slams it behind her—probably not on purpose, but because it's the only way it'll close.

The slam still fits the moment, though.

Rejection and disappointment have caused my voice to retreat back to its cave, which is fine because I think the only person I ever want to talk to is walking out of my life right now, as I sit in my truck and watch her unlock her door. I should go after her and fix this, but I don't know what I can say or do. Instead, I suck smoke out of a cigarette while I wait for her to turn and wave to me as she always does, but that doesn't happen. She just disappears behind the door.

CHAPTER 19

Holly

I turn into a crying mess the minute I close the door behind me and lean back against it, fearful my knees are going to buckle beneath me. Feather jumps up off the couch and runs over to me.

"What happened? Are you okay?" She puts her hands on my shoulders and forces me to look at her. "Did someone hurt you?"

"He k-kissed me," I sputter.

"What? Who?"

"Ty."

She takes a deep breath and smooths my hair back away from my face. "Did that nutjob force himself on you? I'll bash the other side of his face in with a bat if he hurt you."

"No..." I gulp back tears and start to count in my head. *One, two, three, four...*

Feather pulls me up to my feet and over to our faded couch, where she thrusts a box of tissues into my lap and sits sideways facing me.

"Now," she says. "Let's calm down and find our Zen." I stare at her and wipe my eyes. "Like we learned in therapy," she continues. "Take a deep breath and count."

"I *am* counting."

"Good. Now tell me what happened." She grabs the blanket I'm still holding. "Where did you get this? Is this rabbit fur?"

I tug it out of her hand. "No, it's not rabbit. He gave it to me."

Her brow furrows with confusion. "The dude gave you a blanket?"

"Yes...It's a magic blanket."

Her shoulders fall, and her head tilts at me. "Holly, please. No more Santa stories or Christmas trees or princes and magic blankets. You have to let go of this fairy-tale stuff. It doesn't exist."

"It does, Feather," I insist between sobs. "It really does. *You* just don't believe in it."

"I don't because I live in this cool place called reality."

Anger eases into my tears. "If you're going to be mean, I'm not going to talk to you."

"All right, all right. We'll let that go for now. Just tell me what happened and why you're so upset."

Taking a deep, shaky breath, I try to put my scrambled thoughts in order. Everything feels like an overamplified jumble in my head. What *did* happen? I look out the window, hoping to see Ty's truck still in the parking lot, waiting for me. "I'm so confused. I'm not even sure why I'm upset, or what happened. I just don't know how to be with people at all."

"That's not true. You can be with people just fine. You're just a little overwhelmed."

He didn't say goodbye. He just waved me away like an annoying bug. "He bought me this amazing blanket because he had one at his house that I loved. He actually went to a store and bought it for me, and I can't believe he did that, just for me."

Her eyebrows rise. "And that's amazing why?"

His hand shook when he handed me the bag with the blankets. It was a big step for him...and for us.

"Because he doesn't go out in public. Because of his scars. So for him, it's a big deal. We went for a walk in the woods, to sit by the river and listen to music and talk. And somehow we got to talking about his father, about how they had a fight the night he died, and he thinks it's his fault."

"Is it?"

"No!" I shout. "How could you ask such a thing?"

"Well he thinks it, why can't I?"

"He had a heart attack. I think it was just a horrible coincidence. Can a fight actually kill someone?"

"Only if one of the people actually does something to kill the other, Holly. Like stab them, shoot them, slam their head on something. Strangle them..."

That last comment was unnecessary, and I'm starting to question why I'm even talking to her, because she's not making me feel any better. Maybe I should have just put in a call to my therapist instead of having this conversation with my roommate.

"I tried to tell him that he's a good guy. He saved me and Poppy, right? And then he said something like maybe he's not good, and he just likes to collect messed-up stuff."

Feather slams her hand down on the couch. "Oh hell no. Who the hell does he think he is? He's the messed-up, fucked-up one, riding around with masks on."

"Can you please stop?" I yell back, an ache growing in my stomach. "You don't know him. He's...special. He's thoughtful and caring. He's just had a rough time."

"So have you! And so have I! I'm trying to believe he's a nice guy, but I don't like him hurting your feelings."

"He didn't do it on purpose. Anyway, suddenly he just kissed me. Like a movie kiss, with his whole mouth, and his hand on the back of my neck, and he licked my lips, and I couldn't stop shivering. I felt like he was going to swallow me, and I had no idea what to do with my own mouth, or my hands, and I just...froze." I chew my lip nervously. "It was horrible."

My friend stares at me, unblinking, with a smile on her face that seems very misplaced at the moment.

"Feather? Why are you looking at me like that?"

"Steve kisses me that way," she says dreamily. "Those are the best kisses. Trust me. That's some passion right there."

It wasn't horrible at all. *I* was horrible. I look down at my hands, embarrassed at what I have to tell her. "I've never been kissed before," I admit.

She sucks in a breath. "Oh, Holly...I had no idea. The guy who kidnapped you never..."

I shake my head. "No! Not ever. Why would he? And I would never want him to. That's disgusting."

"You're right," she agrees quickly. "Ty probably didn't know either, though. He might have just assumed..."

Acid rises to the back of my throat. Why would anyone assume that monster would kiss me? Kissing is for dating and loving. "I don't want to think or talk about that."

"We don't have to. But I think Tyler didn't realize it was your first kiss. And seriously a kiss like he laid on you would be scary for anyone's first kiss. Most first kisses are by thirteen-year-old boys who just peck at your lips and try to grope your tits."

If things had been different, I should have had my first kiss years ago. And if I had, I wouldn't have been terrified when the man I'm falling in love with finally kissed me.

I've missed everything I should have experienced growing up—every one of my firsts, every awkward and exciting moment that *should* have happened, shouldn't be happening now. The bad man didn't just take *me*—he took all the little parts of my life that were supposed to help me grow into the me I'm supposed to be today.

Feather's eyes are on me expectantly, waiting for me to react.

"That doesn't sound good," I say.

"It's not. Tell me what happened after he kissed you?"

I escaped to my safe place, back to the pages of my storybooks, away from everything scary.

I chew on my tattered fingernail. "I just...froze. I think I did the play dead thing. Like I used to."

She reaches across the couch and touches my arm. "Holly, it's all right. It was new and scary. You weren't ready. Remember in therapy we talked about how we should make our partners aware? Steve and I talked about what happened to me for hours and hours before anything happened between us. We took things really slow. Maybe you guys should have talked about this before-hand. I didn't realize you were more than friends."

"Neither did I. Not until today." Is that true? Lately, I've been wishing to be more than friends, and I've daydreamed about him holding my hand, hugging me with his beautiful arms, and—yes—even kissing me, but I had no idea kissing would feel so... intense and consuming. How was I to know it would leave me breathless and powerless—feelings I had only ever associated with pain and fear? I didn't know those feelings could also be so deliciously good. Feather's right, I wasn't ready, and he didn't know, and I ruined our first kiss.

Possibly our last kiss.

"I think I need to go call him," I say. "We didn't exactly end the day on a good note."

"Are you sure you want to talk to him? Maybe you need to step away for a while, give yourself more time before you get involved with him."

"I already *am* involved." I stand and grab my backpack and my blanket. "Thank you for talking with me. I feel better now."

"I'm here if you need to talk more. I'll be home all night."

Once in my room, I close the door softly behind me, change into sweatpants and an oversized sweatshirt, and call Ty's phone from mine. It rings four times and goes to his voice mail, which is nothing but a beep, not his voice, which I want to hear so badly right now.

That's odd. He always answers when I call him, unless he's on the bike. I send him a text message:

> Hi...I tried to call you

Tyler
> I didn't answer. I'm having trouble talking.

> Oh no :-(Why?

Tyler
> Just stress shit. Don't worry about it.

No little smiley faces accompany his words, a clear sign that he's angry or upset.

> Can we talk on here for a few minutes?

Tyler
> Ok. If you want to.

> I'm sorry. About earlier.

Tyler
> Don't be. It's forgotten.

My chest aches.

> Don't say that.

Tyler
> You're not the first girl to reject me.
> Won't be the last, either.

I stare at the small screen with tears in my eyes. This is not my prince talking.

> That's not it at all. I was just scared. I couldn't breathe.

Tyler
It's all good. Let's just forget it.

How can I possibly forget it? And how can he?

Tyler
Snuggle in your magic blanket and go to sleep.
Tomorrow will be better. Going to bed now.
Talk to you in a few days.

I toss and turn all night, finally falling asleep sometime after 2:00 a.m., only to wake with a jolt after dreaming I was wandering through the woods, alone and naked. I screamed for help, but no one came. I walked in circles, seeing the same trees and rocks over and over and over again, never finding my way out. All the while, a black bird followed me overhead, his large wings whooshing above me ominously.

I wake with tears on my cheeks and a pounding headache, and it takes me several minutes to drag my mind out of the dream and convince myself I am safe.

The scent of Ty's cologne lingers on the blanket, and I snuggle deeper under it, burrowing my face in it. I let the memory of his kiss surface. I let myself relive how it made me feel. I sift through the negative feelings, push them to the side, and focus on the good that's left, like I was taught.

The feel of his lips on mine was exhilarating.

His hand in my hair, cradling my head, made me feel wanted.

The fiery passion I saw in his eyes made me feel beautiful.

His hard body leaning into mine, his leg over mine, made me feel protected.

The way he wiped my tears away made me feel cared for.

All of it together made me jittery, light-headed, and nervous, but I wanted more.

But, oh God. How had I made him feel while he was giving me all these wonderful new feelings? Unwanted and rejected.

How do I undo that?

I sit up, rubbing my throbbing forehead and wondering if Feather will drive me to see my grandmother today, since Grandma has a knack for cheering me up. I kick off my blankets and check my phone, hoping for a text from Ty, but there aren't any. I hold the phone, debating whether I should send him a text, but I have no idea what to even say. I put the phone back down on my night table, and that's when I notice it...

My heartbeat speeds up. I rush over to my window, where a beautiful dream catcher is taped to the outside of the glass with a small envelope taped next to it. When does he do this stuff?

I don't care!

I yank the window open and gently untape them from the glass, then carry them over to the bed. The dream catcher is beautiful, made with white and silver webbing, white feathers, and pastel-colored beads. I rip open the envelope and pull out a note card:

I made this for you, I hope it helps with your bad dreams. Hang it over your bed.

PS—Poppy says he wants to see you tomorrow. He's sending me to pick you up at noon.

Smiling, I pull a tack off the little corkboard above my desk and hang the dream catcher over my bed. I put the note in my nightstand with the one he left for me on Christmas. I hope the gift and the note mean he's not upset or mad anymore. I can't bear the thought of not seeing his smile.

CHAPTER 20

Tyler

The first thing I do when I get inside the hotel room is turn off all the lights. I turn the TV on so the only light is the glow of the screen. I wait in the dark, trying like hell to ignore the swirl of guilt and anxiety eating at me.

Guilt is misplaced here. No matter how much I want Holly, no matter how much I live just to see her smile . . . she's not mine, and she's never going to be, even though I want nothing more than for her to be mine and to play out all my fantasies and dreams with her. Unfortunately, that's just not a safe place for her to be.

I'm not the prince. I'm the thing that goes bump in the night and sends shivers up her spine.

The electric lock clicks, and I don't look over as the door swings open and she does the high-heel strut directly to the thick envelope waiting for her on the table near the door. Her thumb feathers over the hundred-dollar bills, and I can sense her smile as she shoves the envelope into her bag. Her instructions were clear in the confirmation email: payment first. My instructions were just as clear: don't expect me to talk. No lights. No kissing. No screaming.

She falls onto the couch next to me, and her perfume permeates the space. It's flowery and feminine, but it's not the lavender vanilla scent that somehow calms me and drives me wild at the same time.

My breath is hot against my face behind the mask. This one is a favorite, with its bloody, oozing gashes and grotesque twisted lips.

Her hand rests on my leg, and for a second I'm pissed that she's distracting me from thinking about Holly and her perfume. That's the only place my mind and my heart really want to be. And so does my cock, which is exactly why I'm sitting here next to a two-thousand-dollar escort. For distraction.

I grab her wrist, seconds away from twisting it behind her neck and pinning her down on the couch. Or maybe just leaving.

"I like the dark, moody types," she coos in my ear.

Jesus Christ.

I know that voice. My hair stands on end. My blood goes ice cold. I release my grip on her and jump off the couch like it's on fire. *No pun intended.*

I rip the mask off my face. *"Tesla?"* I can't believe this. I want to turn on the light to see if it's really her but, holy shit, I can't. I refuse to see her sitting there.

"Tyler?" she asks, the shock in her voice rivaling mine. "Oh my God."

"Get the fuck out of here," I seethe, running my hand through my hair. This can't be fucking happening.

She stands and tries to grab my arm in the dark. "Tyler, please—"

I point to the door. "Get the fuck away from me, Tessie. *Now.*"

Instead, she flicks on the light, and we stand there staring at each other, both of us speechless, shocked, and humiliated. Her eyes shift to the mask on the floor, then slowly back to my face.

"Get out," I growl again. "Keep the fucking money if you need it bad enough to do this."

"No." Her voice shakes with emotion. "No way. I'm not leaving until we talk about this. And I'm not going to sit in the dark with my own brother."

"There's nothing to talk about. You're a whore, and I'm an ugly psycho. The end."

She slaps my face, hard, and I grin at her for having the balls to do it. Being raised with five big brothers made my little sister tough as nails.

"I'm not a whore, Tyler."

I cock my head at her and run my hand along my scarred, stinging cheek. "From where I'm standing, you are. Last I heard you were a hairdresser. When did sucking dick for money become part of that job description?"

"Fuck you. Don't you dare judge me. It's not as disgusting as you think. I don't stand on street corners. You went through the interview process to get me here in this room with you. You know firsthand it's all discreet and professional."

"Wow. That makes it much better." My voice drips with sarcasm. "You can get the fuck out now. Unless you want to wait here for your next customer?"

I barely recognize the girl shaking her head at me with hurt in her eyes. I haven't seen her in probably three or four years, and now she's a gorgeous woman. Not the cute teen I remember. And not the girl who screamed when she saw my face for the first time after the fire and ran to hide in her room.

She kicks off her black high heels and plops back down on the couch, pulling a pillow onto her lap.

"The fuck are you doing?"

She shrugs. "I'm not leaving. I haven't seen you in years. Since we're both here, let's talk."

My sister apparently has the crazy gene, too. "I don't talk."

"Well, maybe you should start. Your voice sounds good, by the way. A lot better than it did the last time I saw you."

I sit on the arm of the couch because I can't sit next to her when she's wearing a low-cut blouse and a tight skirt and I just gave her a pile of cash. "Yeah, I've been practicing." I don't try to curb the sarcasm.

Her eyes hang on me for a long time. "Believe it or not, a lot of my clients don't even come to me for sex. They just need a friend. Someone to listen. Most of them are just lonely. You can talk to me."

I let out a laugh. "Seriously? Men pay you two grand just to talk? C'mon."

An offended frown turns the corners of her mouth. "I'm totally serious. Obviously, something made you come here tonight."

"Yeah, to fuck someone who's not my sister."

"Jesus, Ty, can you just drop the attitude? You don't have to be an asshole all the time, ya know." She looks down at the pillow she's holding. "You used to be such a happy, sweet guy. That's how I remember you."

"Really? Because I remember you running from me screaming in terror."

Tears glisten in her eyes when she looks back up at me. "For God's sake. I was just a little girl. You can't hold that against me forever. I've apologized for that more times than I can count."

If only apologies had the magic to take pain away. What a better place the world would be.

I take off the guy-who's-not-getting-laid hat and put on the concerned-big-brother hat. "Why are you doing this, Tess? Do you need money? Because if you do, I'll give you money to keep your clothes on."

"No, it's not about money at all." She fingers the silver hoop hanging from her ear. "I just can't get into relationships and commitment. I'm not like you guys. But I like sex, and I like feeling like I'm making people feel better, whether it's physical or emotional. And the guys treat me really good. They buy me gifts; they take me on vacation. For now, it works. It's giving me what I need. I'm kinda thinking about becoming a sex therapist someday. I'm learning a lot."

A burn sears through my stomach. If Pop knew his little girl had turned to this kind of life, it would kill him. *Just like I killed him with my attitude and addictions...* I chew on the inside of my cheek, wishing I could light up a cigarette. "You shouldn't be doing this. You're so young."

"That's part of the appeal for most."

No surprise there.

"Is this even safe? Aren't you scared? There's better ways of doing research, Tess." *Does she know what kind of sick monsters are out there?*

Monsters like me.

"In every way. I use protection, I'm tested, I have a can of mace and a knife in my purse. Last year I took a self-defense class. I'm totally fine. You don't have to worry about me."

How can I not worry about my sister getting paid for sex? "Does anyone know?"

"No, so please keep your mouth shut. Mom would never understand, and the guys would have me locked up in a nunnery someplace."

I'm having a hard time accepting my little sister is getting banged by a bunch of rich guys, but I promise her I won't tell anyone. She's an adult, and it's none of my business what she does with her time and her body. I don't think our other brothers would feel that way, and they would probably flip the fuck out, but I'm staying out of it. Especially since there's no way for me to tell them without admitting how I found out.

"If you tell anyone about this, I'll break into your apartment and shave your head while you're sleeping," I warn her.

"Wow, Ty. Dramatic much?"

"Let's just keep this epic disaster between us."

"Fine."

Thank fuck she spoke before we actually touched. I'd slit my own throat if I accidentally touched my sister. My skin crawls thinking about it.

"Are you okay?" she asks. "We miss you. You don't have to be alone and live like you do. You have a family that loves you and wants you around."

"I like being alone." Except when Holly's around; then I never want to be alone again.

She stares at me in frustration. "I'm sorry about tonight; I really had no idea. I know you're embarrassed...but I can set you up with one of the other girls. Someone nice—"

"No," I snap. "I don't want someone nice."

A sly smile crosses her lips. "Okay, then I'll set you up with someone dirty. Someone else who's into what you want."

Dirty sounds perfect. I need physical and emotional freedom to just go wild on someone without worrying about whether I'm hurting them or taking them for a walk down fucked-up-memory lane.

"Just stop, Tessie. Fuck this whole thing."

"Your choice. I'm not going to force you. But for the record, I don't think you have to pay for sex. Even kinky sex. You're not ugly."

I laugh. "Trust me. Nobody wants to be with me."

"I think that's bullshit in your own head. Look at you. You have a great body, your tattoos are awesome, and girls love that messy hair. And you ride a loud bike, that's another turn-on for a lot of women." She tilts her head. "If Mickey Rourke and Kurt Cobain had a baby, he'd probably look like you."

"That's fucking twisted. What's wrong with your brain?"

"It's true. Just sayin'."

"Half my body is covered in scars. The ink just hides it. It's not there to be cool."

"Oh, boo-hoo." She waves her hand at me. "I think the only thing turning girls away is your shitty attitude."

I blow out an exasperated breath. "I have a realistic attitude."

"Call it what you want."

I look down at my boots and the mask near my feet, staring up at me. "I did sort of meet someone," I mumble.

She leans forward. "Okay. Now we're getting somewhere. And? Give me the details."

"She's sweet. And so fucking beautiful," I say wistfully. "She's fragile but tough. I like that about her. She's wicked honest." Just thinking about her is making me wish she was here with me in this hotel room with the jacuzzi tub in the corner and the view over the city. This was the wake-up call I needed, as twisted as it is. I don't ever want to touch or be with anyone but her.

"So what's the problem?"

"She was abused when she was young. Badly. I have a lot of pent-up fantasies, a shit ton of demons, and it's a big fucked-up mess in my head wondering how to handle her. To top it off, she's moving to New York soon, and I'll probably never see her again. She'll end up with some rich bohemian artist, and she'll forget all about me."

Tesla's mouth hangs open. "Wow. You had to go all out with the dysfunction, huh?"

I cross my arms over my chest. "You're not helping."

"All right, calm down. That's all okay, Ty. So you just go slow with her. See her on weekends. It's New York, not the moon. You can drive that in a few hours. What's the big deal? Everyone's messed up in some way or another."

How true.

"It's Holly Daniels," I say under my breath.

Her eyes go wide, and she sucks in a deep breath, exhaling slowly. "Oh fuck, Ty." Her fingers brush across her lips as she eyes the mask. "And that? That's the real problem, isn't it? You like it rough."

I nod, my hair falling down over my face. "Yeah."

She nods and licks her burgundy-stained lips that match the tips of her nails. "Lots of men have date rape fantasies," she says with a tinge of comfort and hope. "I've met a bunch of them."

"I don't have a rape fantasy, Tessie. I have a *reaction* fantasy. Fear being my top choice."

"So . . . you like them to be scared?"

"I like to make them feel the gamut. But fear is my major kink." I bury my face in my hands. "I can't talk about this. Not with you or anyone else," I mumble into my palms. She grabs my hands and pulls them away.

"I'm trying to help you. Can't you see that?"

"Yeah. I do. But it's a waste of time. Just leave. Please?" I plead. I don't want to deal with any of this anymore.

"No. I'm not going to leave. I don't care if we sit here all damn night. I have no better place to be. Do you?"

I don't answer.

She smirks. "I didn't think so."

She stands and crosses the room to the small refrigerator and takes out two bottles of water, sipping hers as she returns. I take the other from her and gulp half of it down. All this talking is making my voice even hoarser.

"You care about her, right?" she asks.

I wipe the back of my hand across my mouth. "Yeah. I fuckin' do."

"Then don't go screwing strangers. It's only going to make you feel worse. I'm going to guess she probably has feelings for you, too, and you're just in denial about it like you are with everything else."

I wish. "It's complicated. Right now we're just kinda friends."

She squeezes my shoulder. "That's the best place to start."

"Ya think?"

"I do." She plays with the cap of her water for a few moments. "This fear thing, it doesn't have to be a deal breaker, Ty. Everyone has fantasies, or fetishes, call them what you want. You might want to at least lose the mask, though. That's creepy as fuck."

"She was kidnapped, kept in a basement, starved, raped, and mentally fucked with, Tessie. I don't think she's gonna be up for role-playing just to feed my horny little dark side."

She doesn't even wince.

"Ya never know. One of the girls in this biz with me? She was molested when she was young and now she's really into wild stuff. I think it helps her cope, in a way. She'll fuck all damn day and night. Just the other day she—"

I put my hand up in disgust. "Okay, okay. Spare me the details."

She shrugs nonchalantly. "I'm just saying...just because Holly went through some really bad things doesn't mean she's some kind of prude or needs to be treated like glass. She probably just wants to be treated like a normal woman and not tiptoed around."

"I don't think she wants to be fear-fucked. And I don't want to do that to her. She's been through enough."

"Maybe let *her* decide what she wants? Don't think for her, Ty. Talk to her, take it slow. Feel her out. There's always a way to work through things if you want it bad enough."

I do want it. I want it really fucking bad.

"Well, thanks for your sexual expertise, Tessie. It's been quite enlightening, to say the least."

She rolls her eyes. "Just listen to me. Listen to *someone*, for once. Open up, trust someone. Get out of your own fucking way. That shit is getting tired."

I grin, feeling slightly better. "Not bad advice, little sis. I may even let you keep that two grand."

She kicks me playfully. "I'd rather you keep it and come visit me sometimes. And visit Mom. Can you do that? Stop punishing yourself, and the rest of us. We all miss you. We've all put the past behind us. What's done is done, Ty. You had an accident, you did some bad shit, and you let yourself fall into a really bad hole. It's not too late to climb out. God knows everyone in our family has tried to dig you out. You have to get your head together and do it yourself."

CHAPTER 21

Holly

He's different today, and I'm silently analyzing him from my wooden stool even though I know I'm not supposed to examine people. His hands shake as he picks out the tools he needs from the old red chest, and he's on his sixth cigarette since I got here.

"What's wrong?" I finally ask him, after almost an hour has gone by and he's barely said a word or even looked at me. It's been a week since our disastrous kiss, and up until today, I thought everything was okay between us. Now I'm not so sure.

"Nothing." He continues to hammer a piece of metal around a thin cylinder until I get up and grab the tool from his hand and lay it on the workbench.

"You're lying." I try to say it as unaccusingly as I can.

"I have work to do," he says gruffly.

"Why won't you look at me or talk to me today? Do you want me to leave?"

His eyes close for a long moment, and his hands grip the edge of the workbench. "No," he says under his breath. "Not at all."

"Then can you please tell me what's bothering you? You can tell me anything."

His head snaps up, and he looks at me with a strange, unnerving smile on his face. "Really? Anything?"

"Yes, of course."

"Fine." He picks up a rag and wipes his hands on it, then tosses it onto his tool chest. "I almost fucked my sister last night."

I take a step backward and wait for him to laugh or tell me he's kidding, but he just stands there.

"Oh," I say, blinking. "That's unexpected."

"You have no fucking idea. Last night was the first time I've seen her in years."

I close my mouth when I realize it's hanging open. "I'm a lot confused."

He touches my cheek with his thumb and then quickly pulls his hand away. "Join the club, sugar. I'm a lot fucked up." I love it when he calls me sugar, but my insides are all sorts of twisted up over him and his sister and how strange he's acting. Maybe he really is sick mentally, and it's taken this long for it to come to light.

"This is coming out all wrong," he says, reaching up to tie his hair back.

"I hope so."

"Let's go sit." He grabs my hand and leads me outside to the garden bench. Boomer and Poppy trail after us and look at us expectantly, waiting—just as I am—while he lights up another cigarette.

"Everything about you is driving me crazy. Your perfume, your voice, the shape of your lips, how you make me smile, how you look cute and innocent one minute, and all sexy as hell the next." He swallows and coughs. "I can't deal with this shit."

"Oh." I push my hair out of my face. I had no idea he felt this way. "I'm sorry."

"Don't be. I like it." He takes a long drag on his cigarette. "Too much."

I hang on to that space between him *liking it* and *too much*.

The contradiction confuses me. Boomer nudges my hand with his black leathery nose, and I pet his head while I try to make sense of what Ty is saying.

"Is it possible to like something too much?" I ask.

"Fuck yeah."

"I didn't know that."

He flicks the flame of his lighter on, then off, then on, then off.

"So last night...I met up with an escort."

I narrow my eyes at him, my confusion mounting. "An escort?" Have I seen those on TV? I can't remember.

"Upscale fuck-for-hire, basically. Like a high-class hooker."

"Oh." My vocabulary has greatly dwindled during this conversation.

"So I went to the hotel room, and the girl came in. And as soon as she started to talk, I recognized her voice."

The puzzle pieces instantly form a vivid picture in my mind, and my stomach turns. "The escort girl was your sister?"

Nodding, he leans back against the bench and stares up at the clouds. "Yup. Seriously fucking embarrassing. Just my luck, though."

Tears threaten to burst from my eyes, and my stomach roils. Intense jealousy, shock, fear, and sadness all clash inside me. Processing so many feelings at once is completely rattling. I swallow hard and let out a shaky breath. "Have you...been with an escort before?" If he says yes, my heart will shatter right here on this garden bench. The prince shouldn't be doing things like that.

"No," he replies. "Never."

My relief only lasts a few seconds. "Why this time?"

"You don't want to know, Holly."

"Yes, I do." *Do I?*

He smashes his cigarette out with his boot. "Because ever since I kissed you, I'm out of my friggin' head thinking about what your skin feels like. What you taste like, and how it would feel to have your thighs wrapped around my fucked-up head. Because I don't want you to move five fucking hours away from me. That's why."

My heart catapults up into my throat, and a tingly sensation spreads from my chest down to my toes. His admission creates a battle inside me, and I have no idea which side will win. The fear of a man touching me and hurting me again? Or the desire to be touched, loved, and wanted? "Oh," I breathe.

"Yeah," he says. "Oh."

I have to know more. "Then...why...why an escort?"

"Because I can't touch you."

Once again, my heart jumps, and I'm starting to worry this conversation is going to send me into cardiac arrest. "Why not?"

"I just can't."

I count to ten in my head. This is definitely one of those crazy real-life moments Dr. Reynolds told me I would eventually encounter. "Because of what happened to me?" I ask. "That's why you can't touch me?"

"That's part of it."

I've never felt more unwanted than I do right now. And that's saying a lot.

"What's the other part?"

He leans forward and rests his elbows on his knees. "Let's not do this, okay?"

"No. I think we should talk. Please..." I can't possibly let this conversation go. It will eat at me and eat at me, and I won't sleep for days, wondering about every little word and detail.

"Holly, look at me. Look at *you*. I look like someone beat me with a whole lotta ugly, sugar." He turns, but all I see is a beautiful man who finally trusts me enough to not hide behind hair hanging over half his face anymore.

"I don't see anything wrong with you. You're perfect."

"You're blind. I'm a fucking mess, inside and out. And you? You're gorgeous, and so sweet, but I think on the inside you're still a little bit messed up, too, and I'll only make you worse. We had proof of that a week ago. You deserve better. You *need* better."

"I don't. I need you."

He shakes his head. "It's just wrong for us. Trust me."

I wonder how long he's felt this way. I've been daydreaming about him more and more. Not to the graphic degree that he described, but in my own way. I've been hoping he would kiss me again, now that I know what to expect.

"Ty...do you think I don't want to be touched? Do you think I don't want *you* to touch me? Am I disgusting to you?" My voice rises in pitch. "Because of what happened to me? And because of how I reacted the other day?"

"No. None of that. I'm just not the right guy for you."

He says it right to my face, his beautiful blue eyes drilling into mine, but I don't think he believes his words any more than I do.

"Isn't that for me to decide?"

He gives me his lopsided grin. "I'm not the prince on the white horse, Holly. I'm just a fucked-up ugly loser on an old beat-up motorcycle."

"You're not any of those things," I say. "What if you *are* the right guy?"

His head shakes again. "I'm not. Not for you. Probably not for anyone."

Hearing him say that rips my heart apart, and tears spill down my cheeks as my entire body trembles. I start to sob uncontrollably. "Why not?" I beg. "What's wrong with me? Why do you think something's wrong with you?"

He stands and pulls me up with him. "Holly...I don't want

you getting this upset. Please...no more talking. Come on." He takes my hand again, and I follow him into the house, where he sets me on the couch, kneels in front of me, and takes off my shoes.

"Lie down," he whispers, and when I do, he pulls the blanket off the back of the couch and gently places it over me. "You're beautiful." His fingers trace the curve of my jaw. "And you're perfect. You deserve all the love in the world." His scratchy voice is soft, oddly soothing, caressing my soul and seeping into the deep cracks that threaten to break me. I wish he would let his walls down and let this sweet side show more often. I know in my heart this side is the man he was meant to be.

"I only want *your* love," I whisper.

"You have my love," he whispers back. "It's just not enough."

He's wrong. How could love not be enough?

"I want you to rest here with me, and we'll talk about all this later when you're calmer. I won't let you cry here, Holly. This is where we're safe, with the trees and the squirrels and the birds and Boomer and Poppy. Nobody hurts us here." He strokes my head, and his lips brush lightly across my cheek. I want to reach for him and pull him down under the blanket with me, feel his warm, strong body wrapped around mine, and stay here with him forever.

Instead, he sits on the floor, leaning his back against the front of the couch, his head near mine, and opens a book to read while I rest. Poppy has jumped onto the couch to curl up on my feet, and Boomer has squished himself into a ball on Ty's lap.

I have no idea what love is supposed to be like, but I can't imagine it can be any better than what we have right here. He just has to open his eyes and see it.

CHAPTER 22

Tyler

When I step out of the bathroom, she's awake, drinking a glass of water in the kitchen, staring out the window. I thought I'd take a shower while she was napping, and now I'm standing in this tiny space between the kitchen and the bathroom wearing nothing but a pair of jeans, shirtless, with my hair wet and slicked back.

All my scars on display.

She turns, and her eyes widen when she sees me standing there watching her. I can't tell from her expression if she's feeling fear of being so close to a half-naked man, or shock at all the scars from the burns and the glass, but there's no way for me to hide them now, because they're everywhere.

"I thought you were sleeping," I say. The conversation earlier has my thoughts all over the place. I ran from it all—everything she was saying and asking and everything I was feeling and fighting—because I'm scared of hurting her, and I'm scared of losing her.

Maybe you are the right guy.

I never expected her to react the way she did. I always thought she'd clam up and run if she knew what kind of thoughts ran through my head. I never thought she'd be open to any of it, or even remotely want it.

"I woke up when I heard the water running."

I take a deep breath. "This is what happens when you try to ride through a wall of glass windows in someone's house," I say, gesturing to my torso. Most of the time she acts like she doesn't see my scars at all. "This is also why drugs are bad."

Swallowing hard, she takes a step closer, clearly shaken. "That's horrible. You could have died..."

"I was in the hospital for a long time. I missed my dad's funeral."

Her eyes brim with tears. "I'm so sorry, Ty."

"I am too. I've done a lot of shitty things."

"Just remember you've done a lot of good things, too." Her voice is soft and sincere. "I'm proof of that." She touches her fingertips lightly to the scars that run down the side of my face.

I hold my breath, and I don't move. I don't want to do anything that will make her move away and take her soft touch with her.

"Is this...from the fire?" she breathes.

When I don't answer, she moves her hand away, but I capture it in my own and hold on to it, gently, between us, and rub my thumb along the top of her hand.

"The fire and the glass window. I could have more plastic surgery. It might make it look a little better. But I'm afraid to get all messed up on pills again." I shake my head to make my hair fall over my face, but she pushes it back away.

"Don't hide," she says softly. "Not from me."

With her free hand, she traces the other scars on my chest with her fingers, her eyes following as she explores each one. My chest heaves beneath her touch as I fight the urge to either hide myself from her or lean her into the kitchen counter and kiss her senseless. I lace our fingers together, and she squeezes my hand.

"I have scars, too," she whispers with a shaky voice.

Gently, I brush my knuckles across her cheek. "Show me," I whisper back.

Without breaking eye contact, she lets go of my hand, unbuttons the front of her sweater, and slides it off, letting it fall to the floor. A thin, cream-colored camisole barely covers her, its fabric stretching over her breasts. She steps toward the window, where the golden light of sunset casts just enough light over her for me to see her. She holds out her arms, showing me cigarette burns like the ones I've seen on Poppy's ears and stomach. She bites her lip as she lifts her camisole to show me her stomach and rib cage, and the long thin scars that slash across her, the memories of her torture etched into her flesh.

I hold my breath as her hands push the front of her jeans and panties down, and the gentleman in me wants to reach out and stop her, but it's too late—she's already pushed her clothes down to her mid-thigh. Rage, sadness, and a primal possessiveness rocket through me when I read the word carved into the delicate skin a few inches below her belly button, right above her pubic bone:

MINE

"This is the worst one." Her voice is weak, almost apologetic.

All of it is horrific, each scar the worst in its own right, because every one signifies a moment that a little girl was tortured, and no one should ever have to endure so much pain. Especially a child.

But the word...it *is* the worst. It's a brand. It's his sick mark on her that will never let her forget what he did to her and that he owned her.

Fuck you, motherfucker. She was never yours. She's mine.

"Shit, baby..." I choke on the dry ache in my throat and move to pull her clothes up before I gather her into my arms, holding her tight against me as she cries, her tears wetting my chest. "I'm so sorry," I whisper, kissing the top of her head.

Her arms slowly go around my waist, and she hugs me just as tight.

Lifting her chin up with my fingers, I gently coax her to meet my eyes again. "You're beautiful," I whisper. "Every part of you."

She bursts into more tears and buries her head back into my chest, hanging on to me like she's afraid I'm going to disappear.

I lower my head and press my lips to her bare shoulder, then turn my face into her neck, breathing her in before dragging my lips up to kiss her perfect tearstained cheek.

"You're not his," I say. "Your heart, your body, every part of you is yours. And *you* decide who gets to touch you from now on."

I hold her as she cries, letting her get it out, hoping it will break down more of the walls we've built around ourselves. This baring of souls and secrets and exposing our damages to each other is like an exorcism—expelling the demons.

When her sobs subside, without letting her go, I grab a napkin from the table and hand it to her to wipe her face.

She gazes up at me and touches my cheek, her finger caressing the grooved flesh.

"I want to be yours," she whispers. "Please let me be."

I can't resist or deny it anymore. I bend down and kiss her lips, softly at first, hoping she'll kiss me back. Her body and mouth stiffen at my touch, then slowly relax against me, and her lips part, opening against mine. I cup the back of her neck with my hand and hold her gently as my tongue delves into her mouth. I tangle my fingers in her hair and tug her closer, my pulse quickening when she gasps against my lips and then sighs into my mouth. My other hand grips her waist and slowly travels down to her hip, pulling her against my body.

She pulls away slightly and moves her hands to rest on my chest. "I have to tell you something..."

"Anything." I kiss the top of her head and gear myself up for another blow.

"I've never really been kissed before."

Relieved, I lift her chin so I can stare down into her eyes. "That's not true anymore."

A small adorable grin spreads across her face. "You're right." Her gaze lowers to my mouth, and I kiss her again, a little longer this time, until she pulls back.

"And...I'm a virgin. He raped me...but...not..." I capture her lips with mine, saving her from saying the words that she doesn't need to say and I don't need to hear.

When we slowly part, I hold her face in my hands. "We'll figure things out together," I say, then pick up her sweater and hold it for her to slip into.

Can I be good for her? I seriously don't know. The only thing I *do* know is I don't know how to let her go, how to not want more, especially when she's begging me to keep her.

CHAPTER 23

Tyler

The scent of spring is in the air, carried by the warm breeze. Perched high in this tree like a bird, I can see my house way in the distance, all the way down to the river. Other than that, I don't see much, except a few squirrels.

I'm feeling a lot, though.

Laid out in my lap is a folder filled with photocopies of Holly's file that my brother Toren got for me from a cop he's friends with. I know I'm not supposed to see any of this, but I need to know what happened to her, without her having to go through the agony of actually telling me.

I don't want to hear the words *rape*, *sodomy*, and *penetration* coming from her beautiful lips. Nor do I want to see the pain in her eyes as she describes starvation, psychological manipulation, and mutilation.

Our relationship is slowly becoming more intimate, sensual, and physical, and I want to be able to touch her, tease her, make her feel what I want her to feel, without setting off some trigger that will ruin the beauty of every moment. To help her move past horrible memories, I have to understand what she went through.

Holly is a mirage. From a distance, she is so beautiful and sweet and, at times, adorable and silly. Just a normal girl, almost unaffected. But behind that vision is a little girl with dark, sorrow-filled eyes, forever lost, waiting for the next strike, living in expectation of fear and pain. She hides it well. Like a prey animal.

In many ways, Holly walked herself right into the arms of another, much less dangerous, predator.

The lost, tearstained, melancholy girl is my biggest weakness, my truest fantasy. I can't resist her. When I was younger, I hid those feelings by dating someone like Wendy, a bubbly, popular, perpetually smiling cheerleader. We all saw where that got me.

Holly's mirage will always shimmer and fade and then surface again. No amount of time or therapy is going to fix the broken parts of her. Sad, but true. And even though I tried to brainwash myself into believing otherwise, most men won't know how to love her.

I do, though. I'm going to love all of her—the good and the bad, the smiles and the fears, the pretty and the dirty.

My phone beeps with a text, and I pull it out of my pocket to read it:

Toren

> I'm setting some meat in the food stations tonight.
> There's a missing terrier last seen in your area
> yesterday. Brown and white, about 20 lbs.
> Can you check traps in the a.m.?

> Sure

Toren

> Thanks. Text me with any sightings

> Always do

Toren

> How's the file?

> Depressing

Toren

I figured. I could stop by tonight after I fill the traps. If you want to talk.

> Nah, I'm good

Toren

You gonna be an asshole forever?

> Probably

Toren

Me and Asher are riding on Sunday. Come with us.

> I'll think about it

Toren

Don't be a dick. And make more bracelets, we sold out of the last ones.

> You got it.

Toren

Think about the ride. You owe me ;-)

I knew the file wouldn't come without a price, and it figures Tor would use it as leverage to try to get me to hang out with him. As much as I love to ride alone, I miss riding with my brothers every Sunday (weather permitting), which was a family ritual my dad started and I ended.

I go over the file more times than necessary, and by the time I'm ready to close it and burn it, I'm in a sick rage. All I want to do is dig that motherfucker up, take an ax to his rotting remains, piss on him, and set him on fire.

CHAPTER 24

Holly

I'm giddy as I pull into my parents' driveway. I have a driver's license. And a car. I feel a strange sense of freedom and maturity.

I wonder if this is what my parents didn't want me to feel.

I wouldn't have any of it without Tyler's help. He taught me to drive, set me up with a driver's education instructor, and helped me get the paperwork I needed. Then he surprised me with an actual *car*. I couldn't believe my eyes when he drove me to it and handed me the keys with that adorable grin on his face. Without even thinking, I threw my arms around his neck, and he spun me around in a circle and kissed me right there in the dark parking lot. Everything felt right and so very normal.

Zac's car is also in the driveway. I haven't seen him since the night we went to dinner, although we talk on the phone and text several times per week. I haven't seen my parents in over a month, and when I call, they are hardly ever home. Today is Saturday, and as I recall from our talks, Zac occasionally stops by for breakfast on Saturdays.

My brother stands to give me a hug as I enter the kitchen. "You look great," he says with a smile. "You want a bagel?"

I decline, too nervous to eat. My mother, who is sitting at the kitchen table with an elaborate spread of bagels, cream cheese, and butter, zeroes in on me, and without so much as a hello, she questions me. "Holly, how on earth did you get here? Please tell me those aren't car keys in your hand?"

It figures she would notice them before I have a chance to bring up this conversation on my own.

"Yes. I got my driver's license and a car," I answer excitedly. "It's in the driveway."

My mother practically slams her coffee cup down on the table, making Zac and me jump. "How many times have we talked about this and decided it was best for you to wait? How did you even manage to do all that without help? And how were you able to afford a car?"

"I..." I search for the right words that won't exacerbate my mother's annoyance.

"I helped her," Zac pipes up, his eyes meeting mine across the room, and I silently thank him for coming to my rescue.

My mom looks at him in disbelief. "You? Why would you do that? You know we wanted her to wait. She's not ready to be driving around. She could get lost—"

"She's old enough to drive, Mom. She's not a baby."

"She's not like other girls her age," she says, as if I'm not right there in the room. "She has to be more careful."

My brother glances at me, probably to make sure I'm okay, and then he confronts our mother. "She's fine, Mom. She should be able to drive herself around. Stop treating her like a prisoner, or like she's incompetent."

I love my brother.

"Mom, I'll be fine driving. It was costing a lot of money for me to use a taxi anytime I wanted to go somewhere, and I can't expect Feather to drive me around. I'm sorry for not going along with what you and Dad wanted, but this is what I wanted to do." I hold my own against her angry gaze, refusing to look away from her. "My therapist thinks it's a good idea for me to have some independence and start making my own decisions. She saw nothing wrong with me having a car and going for short drives."

"I guess what's done is done, then." Her voice is flippant.

"I was hoping you'd be happy for me, maybe proud of me," I say, not hiding the disappointment in my voice. "I'm just trying to live a normal life. I can visit you guys now, and go see Grandma, maybe even look for another part-time job."

She smiles weakly. "Of course I'm proud of you. I just think you should have waited. Your father would have bought you a nice, safe car."

"The car she has is fine, Mom," Zac says, even though he hasn't even seen it.

My initial excitement, which filled me during the drive here, has deflated. I had hoped my mother would be happy for me and see how much I've grown over the past few months. And I had stupidly hoped I could tell her how I felt about Tyler and have a real mom-and-daughter talk like I'd seen on *Gilmore Girls*, but that just isn't going to happen. I don't have a best friend relationship with my mother. I don't even have a mother-daughter relationship with her.

"Well, I just wanted to stop by and say hello. I was on my way to the bookstore," I lie.

"I'll call you during the week. I have to get ready to go to the salon." My mother stands and hugs me, still holding her coffee, and I'm afraid she's going to spill it all over me. "Maybe you can come for dinner one night."

I won't hold my breath for that. "Okay."

"Keep your car doors locked, even when you're driving. Someone could grab you at a red light. And stay off the highway; it's way too dangerous." I nod at her, making a mental list of everything she's saying. "And wear your seat belt. Don't touch your phone while you're driving."

"Jesus, Mom, she's not an accident magnet," Zac says. He moves toward me. "I'll walk you out." He touches my elbow and steers me out of the house and right to the front of my car.

"Okay, she can't hear us. Where did you really get the car from?"

I look down uneasily, unable to lie to my brother. "Thanks for covering for me. I really appreciate that."

"You're welcome," he says. "Mom doesn't need to know where it came from, but I do."

"Zac..."

"I'm on your side, Holly. I love you. But don't start shutting me out."

I straighten my shoulders and look my brother in the eye. "I got the car from Tyler."

He looks at me quizzically; then a flash of recognition lights up his face.

"Tyler *Grace*?" he asks.

I nod. "Yes."

"Is that where you've been spending your time?"

I nod again. "Yes. I help him in his workshop. And I told you Poppy lives there, so I get to see him."

He lets out a low whistle. "Holly..."

"He's my friend, Zac. He's good to me. He understands me."

"He's not right in the head, Hols. I know he saved you but—"

I refuse to listen to the "buts." "You're wrong. Those are just horrible rumors. He's smart, and sweet, and caring. He saves animals, and he bought me blankets. He taught me to drive and got me this car. We talk and text for hours, we read together, we go for walks, and drink bubble tea—"

"Oh shit, Holly. You sound like you're in love with him . . . Are you?"

His question rocks me. *Am I?* I know I can't wait to see him every day, and he makes me happier than I've ever felt, and I want to make him just as happy, if not more. I love it when he holds me and kisses me, and I'm seriously worried about possibly moving to New York and wondering how I'm going to cope with missing him so much.

"I don't know, Zac. I'm just trying to figure out who I am, and where I belong, and what I want. But I *do* know that, no matter what, I want him to be a part of it. I don't know how to label how I feel."

"I understand all that, but wouldn't it be better for you to be with someone who doesn't remind you of your past?"

"Tyler doesn't remind me of my past. He's helping me learn to deal with it. He makes me feel better."

"And how can he do that when he's not dealing with his own past? He won't even go out in public."

"I know that . . . but I think that will change in time. He's getting better, just like I am. We're helping each other. We do better together. Isn't that how it's supposed to be?"

Zac leans against the car. "I was hoping you'd have a fresh start in New York. What are you going to do about him?"

"I'm not sure yet. We can visit each other, right? He could come see me?"

"Well, yeah, but is he going to do that? I don't want to sound like Mom . . . but I really don't like the idea of you driving all the way here from New York to see him."

"I have no idea. We haven't really talked about it. I don't know how to think that far ahead."

His head hangs down as he absorbs all this; then he slowly

looks up. "Okay. It's your life," he finally says. "No matter what, I'm here for you. So is Anna. We want you to be happy and be with someone who will care for you, and love you. Just be careful. Tyler was a great guy when he was younger...but a lot's happened to him. He's got a lot of issues...I don't want you to end up with a broken heart."

♥ ♥ ♥

I text Tyler from the end of my street after I leave my parents' house.

> Can I come over to see Poppy?

Tyler
Of course. He was just telling me he misses you ;-)

> Tell him I miss him too

Tyler and the fuzzy duo are all sitting on the front steps when I pull into the dirt driveway, and it makes my heart clench. *This* feels like home. This is where I want home to be—with them.

He approaches the car as I'm getting out, and my heart jumps. I can't tell him, but he looks incredibly cute today. He's wearing a black baseball cap backward and a black T-shirt over a white thermal shirt with the sleeves pushed up, and I can't help but notice the taut muscles of his arms. His usual faded jeans hug his body perfectly, and today, instead of black motorcycle boots, he's wearing white sneakers. Ever since we've started kissing, my body has reacted differently to his, getting warm and tingly when he's near, my heart racing every time I think about him.

"Your first day of independence and you came here?" he teases.

"This is my favorite place to be."

He smiles and reaches for my hand, which has become a natural gesture of affection for us, and we walk to the edge of his yard to sit on the bench together, surrounded by flowers that have smiling faces that I love so much. Pansies, he called them, the first time I saw them here in his yard, and he plucked one and tucked it behind my ear. It's now hidden away with the cards he's given me, my own little smile from him, saved forever in the form of a flower.

"How was your first drive by yourself?"

"Very freeing."

"Good," he says. "That's what you need."

"You look different today," I say shyly. "I like it."

He winks at me, and my heart melts. He's been different since the kissing started, too, smiling more and saying sweet things to me. His attitude has diminished a lot since the first time I saw him, and his speech has improved. I hope I've had some part in that.

"I had a sort-of fight with my mom," I tell him.

"About?"

"The car. Zac was there, and he told her he helped me buy it."

"Your brother's a good guy."

"Yeah. He is. But he followed me outside when I left and made me tell him where I really got it, so I had to tell him the truth."

"And? How did he feel about it?"

I shrug. "He's worried about me getting into a relationship, especially with you. He's afraid you're a reminder of my past."

"Am I?"

"Not at all. I don't understand why I have such a hard time with my family. I love Zac and Anna, but I can't seem to form any kind of...relationship with my parents. They make me feel so *wrong*."

"You're not wrong, Holly. I think it's just a hard situation for all of you." His thumb moves gently across the top of my hand as he talks, and all my senses focus on that tiny touch. "Let's face it. You're all strangers. I know it's harsh. In time, things should get better."

"Do you miss your family?"

He answers without hesitation. "Every day."

"Then why don't you see them?"

"It's complicated. But ya know what? I think, like with your family, in time it'll get better. I want you to meet them."

"I hope so. Sometimes I feel so lost, Ty," I whisper, leaning into his side.

"You're not lost, baby," he says in his soft, scratchy tone. "I found you, and you're right where you belong."

His words make me sigh with contentment. "You always make me feel better," I murmur.

"Good." He kisses the top of my head. "Do you want to do something new today?"

I tighten my arms around his waist. "Yes. I love new things with you."

"Come inside with me." He grabs my hand again, and we go inside together, with Poppy and Boomer chasing after us with excitement.

"I wanted to bring you up in the loft," he says. "To watch the clouds through the skylight with you."

The usual apprehension washes over me as I peer over to the small stairway that leads to the loft, the one place in his house I've never been. Much like a basement, it's a space that is not easy to get out of. He waits patiently while I mull things over.

"You can go up first and look around," he suggests. "I can stay here, or outside."

I breathe air into my lungs. "No," I reply. "I want us to go up together."

His lips curl into his crooked smile. "Good answer."

Tyler's loft immediately becomes my favorite part of the house. It's small, with slightly slanted side walls with built-in shelves filled with books. The bed takes up almost the entire room, and it's covered with a dark gray down comforter with large black pillows and our special blanket. A narrow oak night table is on each side of the bed, one with a twisted metal lamp with a red light bulb. A two-foot dream catcher with rows of flowing beads, feathers, and tassels hangs on the wall over the center of the head-board. The floor is unpolished wood, with thick, colorful throw rugs.

"It's beautiful up here!" I exclaim.

"I knew you'd like it."

Directly over the bed is a window in the ceiling, exactly as he described, and I can't believe every bedroom doesn't have one of these amazing windows. He sits on the bed and takes off his shoes as I walk around and peruse the spines of his books and take in the details of all his wooden and resin statues. A large glass jar is on the floor in the corner, with a few coins on the bottom and several tiny folded pieces of paper thrown on top of the coins.

"What's this?" I ask.

His smile morphs into a frown. "Oh...that's a jar of failure and hope."

I blink at him. "It's what?"

He pushes his fingers through his long hair, and it falls back over his face. "The jar is a sort of family tradition. It started with my great-grandfather, I think. They would put coins in a jar when they were in their teens, I guess?" He clears his throat. "Then when they were ready to propose, they would use what was in the jar to buy an engagement ring." He shrugs. "I quit that idea a long time ago."

I swallow over the sadness that pushes through my good mood. "And the little papers?" They almost look like folded-up fortune cookie strips.

The muscles in his jaw twitch. "Every time you said, or texted, something nice to me, I wrote it down. And put it in there." His eyes shift to the jar with indifference. "It's stupid..."

I cross the small room and throw my arms around his neck. "It's not stupid," I whisper against his throat. "It's incredibly sweet."

He hugs me tight against him for a few minutes, then slowly releases me, his hands lingering on my waist. "Take your shoes off and lie on the bed with me."

Kicking off my shoes, I watch as he stretches out on his back, the material of his T-shirt stretching over his muscular chest and arms and riding up to reveal his hard stomach. My insides respond by swarming with that unfamiliar tingle.

I crawl onto the bed and settle into the spot next to him, and I join him in staring out the skylight at the blue sky and clouds above us.

"This is amazing," I say. "I need to have one of these in my own bedroom someday."

"Hopefully, someday you will. It's really cool at night when you can see the moon."

He turns on his side to face me, grabs my hand, and lifts it to his lips; then he moves his lips down to my wrist, then farther up my forearm. My breath catches as I watch his mouth move along my scars, kissing each one.

"Ty...," I whisper.

"Shh...I'm going to kiss them all."

I give myself over to him, relaxing into the softness of his comforter as he kneels over me and slowly removes my shirt, bending down to press kisses on each and every faded cut and burn, tiny versions of his own. His fingers brush against the silk fabric of my bra, causing my heart to race even faster, and he rubs his cheek against the swell of my breast.

"Your heart is like a little hummingbird," he breathes. "It was beating like this the day I found you..." He kisses the valley at the center of my chest, his tongue slowly sending a warm shiver up my spine. "I could feel it against my chest. It made me want to hold on to you forever."

I reach up to run my hands across his back, my mind growing fuzzy, drunk on his words and his touch.

"I've always wanted you to." My whispered words invite his mouth to mine, and he kisses me softly at first, then unapologetically rough and deep, pulling me further into a woozy haze. I move my hand up to the back of his neck, beneath his hair, and now I know why he tugs my hair when we kiss. The sensation of his hair moving between my fingers is addictive, and the deeper he kisses me, the more I want to tangle my hand in it.

He groans against my lips and rests the full length and weight of his body on top of mine, sending me into a frenzy of physical and emotional upheaval. We've never been this close, body to body.

His mouth comes down on mine again as his hand gently moves over my breast, pushing the fabric aside. His rough palm grazes over my nipple, and a small sound of surprise escapes me at the sensation jolting through my body from that tiny touch.

"I fuckin' love that sound...," he growls, and tugs the fabric up to expose my breasts, his mouth and tongue dragging over skin that's never been touched. Surprise and fear are chased away as he sucks a nipple into his mouth, his tongue flicking over the hard tip, and my entire body responds, craving more of this, more of him, more of everything that feels so incredibly good. For so long my life was filled with loneliness, fear, pain, and then an odd numbness. Ty is slowly obliterating those feelings and awakening an entirely new realm of physical and emotional experiences for me.

He looks wild when he sits up on top of me, his breathing heavy, eyes glazed, his hair messy around his face and shoulders. He pulls off his T-shirt and throws it onto the floor, and I can feel what he wants and needs radiating from him—the same thing I do.

Touch.

I run my hands from his stomach up to his shoulders, my fingers gliding over the damaged yet incredibly sexy mix of muscle, ink, and scars.

He leans down, his hair falling into my face. "Don't stop touching me...," he begs before his lips cover mine again.

I don't think I can.

We kiss until I feel I can no longer breathe, and then he moves farther down my body, kissing all the way down past my stomach to my most horrible scars. He holds me down, his hands pinning mine above my head when I try to squirm away, afraid he will be disgusted by me. But he keeps raining kisses across my skin, whispering how beautiful I am.

He releases my hands, and his fingers work the button and zipper of my jeans, pulling them down in a quick, determined motion and throwing them aside. He comes back up to caress my cheek and kiss my lips, so softly and lovingly in contrast to how wild he was a moment ago. I wrap my arms around him, trying to quell the voices in my head.

Pulling away, he brings his fingers to his lips, and I watch in fascination and curiosity as he licks them, then reaches down between us and slides his fingers between my legs.

I gasp at the sensation his slow circles bring and grip his shoulders tightly, which only makes him kiss me deeper with guttural moans against my mouth. He coaxes my thighs to spread farther apart, and his fingers caress me there, in the apex of soft wetness. This is new, so very new. Never was I touched there. The feeling is completely indescribable.

My mind begins to float, to a dreamy place, as his fingers stroke that special spot I didn't know existed. I kiss him like my life depends on it, like I might die if I stop, and after a few minutes of this exquisite torture, I explode into a wave of ecstasy. His other hand tangles up in my hair, pulling my head up to meet his fevered kisses, like he can't get enough of me either. I don't want him to stop. Ever. My entire body quivers and shakes, and he continues to kiss me as I cling to him, afraid of what this feeling is doing to me, that I may never recover. As the euphoria of that moment subsides, a shudder overcomes me, and I start to cry uncontrollably into his chest.

He tugs the magic blanket up over us and pulls me into an embrace. "It's okay," he soothes, kissing me whispery soft, stroking my cheek. "You're okay." He tilts my head up again to look into my eyes. "I'm right here with you. Everything's okay," he says softly, kissing my tears.

I continue to sob, without any comprehensible reason, and hang on to him for dear life. I'm petrified. I'm exhausted. I feel as if some massive energy just possessed me, stirred up every fear, every wish, every pain, every desire, every memory...and swept it all into a ball and forced me to swallow it, digest it, and then cough it out.

I feel reborn.

My body and mind sink into an utterly exhausted jelly-like mode, and I drift off to sleep, safe and comforted in his arms.

When I wake, he's asleep, his arms still around me. His body is warm against mine, and for maybe the hundredth time, I feel the deep pull of never wanting to leave him. I kiss his cheek, and he opens his eyes.

"Hey," he says, pulling me even closer.

"Hey."

"You okay, sugar?"

I nod and move my hand slowly across his chest, over the deep, healed gashes. "I'm sorry I cried...," I say, hoping I didn't ruin another moment between us. "I'm not sure..."

He moves his hand up to caress the back of my head. "Don't apologize. It's normal."

"It is?"

"Yup. I read about it. It's like a big release of feelings."

Yes. That's exactly what it felt like.

"Everything is good, Holly. I told you we'd get through everything together, and I meant it."

I lean up on my arm so I can see his face better. "I'm so lucky to have you," I say softly, loving how his eyes change color as I talk.

"I'm the lucky one." He pulls me down to meet his lips, and that special place between my thighs starts to quiver again.

Later, he makes us tea and toast, and then we take Boomer and Poppy for a walk to the river. We hold hands, and he stops every so often to pull me into his arms, backing me up against the nearest tree to kiss me.

"I've never seen you look so happy," I comment as we walk.

He takes a moment to reply, then glances at me sideways. "It's been a long time."

"I know the feeling."

He winks at me. "I know you do."

On our walk back to the house, my phone vibrates in my pocket, and I take it out to see a text from Feather.

Feather
Hi…where are you?

Walking with Tyler, Poppy, and Boomer

Feather
Steve and I are doing dinner and a movie tonight in town. You two want to come? I thought a double date would be fun and we could get to know Ty.

Ohhh I'm not sure

Feather
Come on! It will be fun. It's just us.

And everyone else in the restaurant. And the theater.

Let me ask him

I look up to find Ty leaning against a tree, smoking, looking all rough and sexy and so…just perfect.

"What's up?" he asks.

"It was a text from Feather."

He flicks some ashes onto the ground. "Everything okay?"

"She and her boyfriend are going to dinner and a movie tonight. She wants to know if we want to go, too."

He takes a long drag on his cigarette, holds it in his lungs for an extended amount of time, then exhales. His eyes, crystal blue a few minutes ago, darken as he stares off into the trees. He takes another aggressive drag on the cigarette. His mouth opens, but no words come. Instead he puts the cigarette to his mouth again and lets it hang from his lips, its smoke billowing up into his face as he hangs his head down, his hair falling over his face, perfectly trained to hide him.

I see the retreat, the abandoned smile, the door closing. His discomfort is palpable, and such a mirror to my own.

I wish Feather had suggested we all meet at our apartment, in private, instead.

"Holly..." He kicks at a rock with his shoe.

"I don't think I want to go out," I say, saving him from having to say it. I think we both see the same scenario in our heads: people staring, whispering, and asking questions. Feather and Steve being put in that same awkward space with us. A double date sounds like fun, but that doesn't seem like the best way for all of us to get to know each other first.

He comes closer and hesitantly touches my cheek. "Maybe...," he starts, and coughs.

I stare up into his eyes. "Maybe another time. Here... or at my apartment...," I finish for him.

He nods, and a faint smile touches his lips. "I can make us dinner tonight. We can watch a movie on my iPad. Just me and you."

"I would really like that," I answer softly, and pull out my phone to text Feather back that we won't be joining them this time. He holds my hand tightly as we walk back toward the house. "I'll make popcorn, too. It'll be even better than going out."

Maybe it will be, maybe it won't. But for now, his fingers linked through mine, his smile, and the lingering bliss of the morning we had has made me happier than I've ever been. I have no complaints or regrets.

CHAPTER 25

Holly

Our dinner and movie were cozy and perfect. We didn't miss anything not going with Feather and Steve. Everything we need and want is right here.

After the movie, Tyler lights a small fire in a pit in his backyard, and we roast marshmallows while sitting on a blanket, holding hands. His lips kiss my ear and linger there. "Stay," he whispers. I turn to him, and his lips find mine. "Stay here tonight," he says against my lips.

He watches me as I let his words sink in. His eyes darken, and his breathing deepens, and it hits me that I've seen this excited, lusty look in him before.

I nod slowly, agreeing, but also accepting. Some truths sink in slower than others. My hesitations...my surprise...my panic... my fear...my needs...my happiness...it ignites him. He feeds on it, like an emotional sponge.

And I have to admit, I like seeing him hungry for me.

"Okay," I reply softly. "I'll stay with you."

My head spins with the possibilities of what an entire night in bed with him could bring, but I count in my head and shut those worries down before they spiral out of control. I won't let any more moments with him get destroyed. Instead, I revel in the way his smile reaches right into me and flips a switch of happiness.

"We can watch the sky together through the ceiling window," he teases, poking at the fire. Then he throws in some sort of sand, which earlier he told me was fairy dust, that makes the flames a rainbow of colors. The fire becomes beautiful with its blue, green, and purple hues, and I wonder if the colors ease his memories.

"Does the fire bother you?" I ask with caution.

The flames reflect in his eyes as he ponders the question and his answer.

"Sometimes," he replies. "I guess I learned to respect it. It's like anything else. If you're not careful around things that can hurt you...they probably will."

I wonder if, someday, Tyler will hurt me. Maybe Zac is right and I might get my heart broken. I close my eyes, feel the heat of the flame against my cheeks, and try to picture life without Ty.

I can't.

"I saw someone go into a fire once," I say. "It was awful. It's one of the few things from my childhood I can actually remember clearly." I tighten my fingers around his. "It hurts my heart to think of you being in that kind of pain."

"The pain was horrific. It was everywhere—the searing pain. Even worse than going through the glass."

My stomach roils just thinking about it. "I wish I could have been there...to help you somehow. Or just to love you." The words slipped out so freely and naturally. I couldn't have stopped them if I tried.

His breathing completely stills, and I wonder how he'll react to my admission. The answer to that comes swiftly when he tilts my face to meet his. His thumb drags slowly across my bottom lip, and his eyes follow its trail, then drift up to captivate mine.

His mouth opens, and the words get trapped in his throat. But I don't need to hear him speak because I can see the depth of his feelings in his molten eyes. The space between us disappears, and he kisses me softer than he ever has, as if he's afraid he'll somehow break me or shatter our very existence.

I reach up and gently caress his cheek as we kiss, and he leans into my hand.

"I love you." The sweetest, ragged, whispered words drift from his lips to my ears, and I wish I could bottle them up and keep them forever.

Our lips part, but he keeps me in his embrace. We hold each other as we watch the colored flames lap the air, and I'm content and grateful in this special, private place with him, Poppy, and Boomer.

This truly has become my happy place, in every way.

His fingers slowly caress mine, and warmth floods me from my core to my thighs when I remember how they slid through my soft flesh, making me damp and quivering.

"Who was in the fire?" he suddenly asks, pulling me out of the delirium of my daydream.

"Huh?"

"You said you saw someone in a fire?"

I shake my head to clear it. "I don't know who he was." The day I was abducted is filled with horrible memories, but this one is the worst. "I just wanted someone to help me. Anyone. He may have died in that fire because of me. I have no idea."

He kisses my temple. "You're confusing me. How could it be because of you?"

"Because I was trying to get help."

"When?"

"The day I was taken."

"There were people around when he took you?"

"No . . . not at the park. But later that night, the man who took me was driving around with me in a car. He had me in the back seat with my hands tied behind my back. He pulled the car over and got out to talk to someone on a pay phone. I think they may have been arguing." I close my eyes, trying to picture the scene in my mind. "Through the tinted windows of the car, not too far away, I could see trees and a bonfire with people around it. I could hear them laughing. The bad man was really involved in his conversation and wasn't paying attention to me. I was able to get my hands free, and I bolted out of the car and ran for the fire." My heart pounds in unison with the little girl in my memory, remembering how her little legs ran as fast they could.

"Holly...you got away from him?" Tyler asks incredulously. "I never knew that."

"Almost," I say sadly. "I was so close. I ran up to two teenagers standing by the fire, a boy and a girl, and I grabbed the girl's hand and begged her to help me. But she laughed and pulled her hand away. I think she thought I was kidding." Ty rubs my hand in slow circles as I talk, listening intently. "So...I grabbed onto the boy's shirt, and when he turned and looked down at me, he was laughing, too, but when he realized I was crying, he knelt down and he held my hand and asked me if I was lost." I pause, remembering the glimmer of hope that flashed through me at the time. I thought I was safe. "But by then the bad man had caught up to me, and he grabbed my other arm, and he shoved the boy hard, and he fell into the fire. The man picked me up and ran with me back to the car, and he put me in the trunk and slammed the lid. Even from in there, I could hear the boy in the fire screaming. It was awful, and it was all my fault." I wipe at the tears streaming down my face. I can still hear those screams in my head.

Ty's hand has stopped rubbing mine, and he's staring off into the woods, his brow creasing.

"I just wanted someone to help me," I confess, knowing it doesn't change what happened. "I never meant to hurt anybody."

"No, sugar." His voice is strained. "You were just a little girl."

"I never saw another person again after that. He was the last person I ever saw, until you found me."

Letting go of my hand, Tyler stands abruptly. "I have to go," he says, popping a cigarette into his mouth.

I stand, too, and watch him pace in a small circle like a trapped animal. "Tyler... what's wrong?"

"I just remembered I have to be somewhere."

"Now?"

He nods and throws a pail of regular, non-fairy-dust sand over the fire to extinguish it. "Yeah." He points to my car. "Go. I'll call you."

"Go?" I repeat. My voice shakes, but he refuses to look at me. "I...I thought you wanted me to stay?"

"Please," he croaks. "Just leave. I'm begging you." His eyes are manic, flitting back and forth, and he sucks on the cigarette like a vacuum.

Stunned silent, I walk away from him, toward my car. Poppy tries to follow, but when Ty whistles sharply, Poppy turns and follows him, and Ty locks both pets in the house. I look back one more time before I get in my car, but now he's starting up his motorcycle, obviously leaving right now to go wherever it is he suddenly remembered he has to be. His bike tears out of his driveway and down the dirt road and, for a moment, I consider following him.

No. I won't do that. When girls do that on TV, they always see something they don't want to see, and I don't want to see Tyler doing anything that I'm going to wish I never saw. Not today, after our perfect day, which has suddenly become completely imperfect, without warning.

Maybe sitting by the fire brought on an episode, after all. Maybe he just needed to get away from it and didn't want me to see him scared. Maybe he doesn't know how to count, like I do. Maybe he remembered a lost dog needing to be found.

Whatever the reason, I do as he asks and I leave, my heart falling to pieces as I drive away. In my rearview mirror, I can still see tiny sparks of amber glowing where the fire was, and it fills me with sorrow.

CHAPTER 26

Tyler

My brother Tor told me—not too long ago, during one of our very rare talks—that karma is a demented bitch.

Oh, how right he was.

I fly down the mountain road, going double the speed limit, but I don't care. I should, though, because the last thing I need is to end up with my head through someone's living room wall again. But right now, all I care about is how fucked up and twisted the world is.

What is that theory about the six degrees of separation? That everyone is somehow connected in some way?

The slam of memories was too much to handle. I had to get away from her. And the fire. And the fucking sick twist of truth and regret.

I always had this weird feeling of déjà vu, in my gut, that I'd seen Holly's haunting eyes before, and I was right. They were the last thing I saw before I was almost burned alive.

And now I also remember *his* eyes. The moment he pushed me, and the moment I killed him.

Why didn't we do something that day? Why did Wendy laugh in her face? I don't even remember that. I must have been too drunk, which was rare for me at the time, but that night I tried a few shots of whiskey for the first time. I barely remember the little girl tugging on my shirt, or wondering what the hell a little kid was doing at a high school bonfire party, but now it's coming back to me in erratic, fragmented flashes.

By the time I was awake in the hospital room and barely coherent enough to form thoughts, I had completely forgotten about the little girl. I vaguely remember the nurses talking about the abduction, but I never made the connection. It never spurred a memory. As pieces of that night flash through my mind, I realize I must have assumed at the time the guy who pushed me was her father and she was one of those little kids who was constantly running off, like Tessie used to do. I force myself to think back as I roar through the winding roads on my bike, but I'm sure I never mentioned the little girl, or the man, to the police, the doctors, or my parents when they questioned me. I told them some drunk friend must have bumped into me. Holly was forgotten in the mess of my brain.

How the fuck do I tell her the twisted epilogue to her story?

Tonight, all I want is to forget about the little abducted girl who grew up to be a beautifully damaged woman looking for love in the worst of places. I'm going to forget about the love and happiness I felt, just an hour ago, before it all went up in a fiery inferno of twisted coincidence.

I need to forget everything.

My father. My future. My face. My family. Holly.

I'm going to forget that everything is my fault if it kills me.

Reaching behind me into my saddlebag, I pull out my mask and yank it over my face as I ride toward the warehouse. I need to fight. I need to hurt someone, and I need physical pain to take away the emotional agony I'm feeling. My opponent will hit me harder if he can't see my already scarred-up face. They always do. Maybe he'll fuck me up beyond recognition so no one will ever know who I am. *Not even me.*

I would welcome it.

CHAPTER 27

Holly

"I'm the only one you can rely on, little girl. I'm the only one who loves you enough to never leave."

Perhaps he was right. He was right about a lot of things, now that I think about it.

I don't want to go home and face Feather, but I have nowhere else to go. I certainly can't go to my parents, and I don't know how to get to Zac's house. I send Feather a text, telling her I won't be home. Now I understand the appeal of the text message to avoid having to talk to someone. Restless and confused, I drive around town listening to music.

So this is what it's like to have a car. You can drive all night and not go anywhere.

I turn the station to rock music, and the angsty music gets into my head, every song seeming to hold a hidden meaning into my life.

Making a careful U-turn, I drive back to Tyler's house. I don't care if he's not there and told me to go. He also told me I could come any time I want. He said it was my happy, safe place, and that's what I need right now.

Using the hidden key, I let myself into his tiny house, and Poppy and Boomer immediately run to me, tails wagging.

"Okay, guys. You have to be good," I whisper. "I'm going to hang out with you so we're not all alone."

I kick off my shoes and settle on the couch with the soft blanket over me. My heart hurts remembering how sweet Tyler was when he gave me the blankets and how he told me he loved me mere hours ago.

What happened? What went wrong?

The sound of his bike startles me awake, and I squint at the clock on the mantel: 2:00 a.m. Where could he have been this late at night? Did he go back and get an escort? Envy washes over me.

He wouldn't do that.

He loves me.

The front door swings open and he stumbles in. I sit up quickly and watch him maneuver through the tiny space.

"The hell you doing here?" His voice sounds worse than I've ever heard it, hoarse and garbled.

"I . . . I didn't want to go home. I wanted to be with Poppy. I was worried about you."

He steps farther into the room, and as my eyes adjust to the dark, I see the mask on his face, crooked, with blood seeping from beneath it. My heart leaps into my throat, my stomach sinking as I scoot back against the arm of the couch.

"Wh-what's going on?" I whisper.

"With?"

"You."

He falls into the chair across the room and puts his feet up on the old steam trunk he uses as a coffee table.

"Everything and nothing."

Swallowing hard, I say, "I don't understand."

"Neither do I, Holly."

"Are you bleeding?"

"Probably."

"Did you crash your bike again?" Panic seizes me when I realize he could be hurt.

"No. I was in a fight."

"What? With who? Why?"

He yanks the mask off, and tiny blue sparks of static electricity
light up his head.

"A paid fight."

My confusion and frustration mount. "I don't know what
that is."

He sighs and leans his head back in the chair, staring at the
ceiling. "It's when people get paid to beat the shit out of each
other. Like boxing, only dirtier."

"When did you start doing that?"

"Years ago. I told you this once before."

Yes, he did. But I didn't think it was like this—leaving him
bloody.

"But...why?"

He shrugs. "I only do it now when I need it."

"When you need money? I'll give you money; I have a bunch
saved up. I don't want you getting punched...or hurt..."

"No," he croaks loudly. "Fuck. Not money."

I stare at him, completely lost as to what's going on here.

"Just stop, Holly."

Ignoring him, I go to the kitchen and wet a paper towel. When
I turn on the floor lamp next to him, I gasp at the blood dripping
from his nose, some dried at the edge. Leaning over him, I gently
wipe his face, and I smell alcohol on his breath.

"Isn't this dangerous for your face?" I ask. "To get punched
after all the skin grafts and surgery you've had? What about your
throat? What if you got hit there?"

Without warning, he grabs my arm and pulls me onto his lap. "Stop fussing over my fucking face."

"Have you been drinking?"

"A little."

"Ty..." I'm confused and disappointed, and not at all sure what to say.

"You shouldn't be here. I'm in a real bad fucking mood."

"Then go to bed. I'll stay down here." I gently push his hair off his face. "I don't understand what happened," I say, resting my hand on his shoulder. "We were having such a nice date. I thought we were happy."

His hand slowly slides down the outside of my thigh, the warmth of it seeping right through the fabric of my jeans.

"Because that's what happens." He swallows. "Nothing good ever lasts for me."

"But it didn't have to happen. We're fine," I protest as his hand grips my leg.

Snaking his arm around me, he pulls me down on him until I'm lying against his chest, my head on his shoulder, my face against his neck. I don't move, unsure of his motive and equally unsure how I feel about being so close to him when he's acting so strange.

"You have no idea how bad I wanted this," he says, and I can't deny how sexy his voice can be when his raspiness touches the right words at the right time. My thighs tighten in response, warmth radiating from within.

"I want you to be happy. Tell me what's wrong," I whisper.

His arm tightens around me. "You make me happy."

I relax into him after hearing his words and close my eyes as his hand lightly trails up and down my arm, over the uneven texture of my scars, without hesitation.

Yes. Bring the happiness back. Please.

"You really don't know, do you?" he finally says.

"Know what?"

"I was there," he finally says.

"Where?"

"The boy you grabbed for help. The one he pushed into the fire. It was me."

A jolt of pain slices through me, almost blinding me in its ferocity.

I sit up, nearly falling off his lap, but he catches me and holds me against his chest. "What?" That can't be true. We couldn't have been in the same place at the same time so many times. That's the kind of thing that happens on TV, and even I know that doesn't happen in real life. "I don't believe you."

"Holly, it's true. You described the entire night exactly how it happened. It was me. Look at me. Think back."

The blue eyes...the shaggy blond hair...

I shake my head. "No..." I don't want it to be him. I don't want the horrible screams I heard to belong to the man who's become my best friend, taken care of my dog, and given me special blankets and a dream catcher.

The man I love.

"I could've saved you. I was drunk, and I forgot you afterward. I never told anyone. Maybe if I had..." He gulps and coughs, and I close my eyes, hating his pain and struggle. "I could have described him to the police. I looked right at him. They could have drawn one of those pictures. He was a teacher. Someone would have recognized the photo in this small town. I fucked up, Holly. I fucked up so bad. I'm so fucking sorry."

My heart is breaking inside, cracking and shattering, its tiny pieces coursing through my veins. "That's not how I see it," I say tearfully. "Not at all."

He turns his face toward mine. "Really? How the hell do you see it?"

"If I hadn't grabbed you, he never would have pushed you. You never would have gotten burned. You never would have—"

He never would have been in pain. He never would have been on drugs. He never would have fought with his father. He never would have crashed his bike. The moment I touched him, I destroyed him.

His lips come down hard on mine, silencing me as I ramp up into hysterics.

"Shh...," he whispers. "Are you crazy? You were just a little girl looking for help. I fucked up. You didn't do anything wrong at all."

He's wrong. So very, very wrong. "I'm so sorry, Tyler," I cry. "If I had just not done that...I ruined your whole life..."

"No," he says vehemently. "*He* ruined our lives. *Him*. That sick monster."

I pull away from him and stand, feeling trapped and panicked. I think I need my pills. "I should go...," I say, looking around for my backpack. "Where is my backpack?"

He jumps up from the chair. "You're not leaving like this." He puts his hands on my shoulders and forces me to look at him. "I'm all twisted up, Holly. But I'm not letting you run out of here when you're this upset. You're staying here with me."

One...two...three...four...

I swipe my hand across my wet nose. "I'm all twisted up, too. Where the hell is my backpack?"

"You're not leaving. And I don't think you brought it today. Stop looking for it."

I run my hands through my hair. How could I leave the house without my backpack and books? Is that why all this bad stuff is happening? "I feel sick." I try to pull away from him, but he holds on to me.

"You're okay," he says softly. "I think you're having an anxiety attack."

My heart races rapidly as I stare back into his eyes. "I'm so glad you killed him, Tyler," I whisper. "I know I shouldn't say that... but I hate him so much...even more now than I ever did. I hate him! I hate him!" I scream.

He pulls me into a hug and holds me tight, stroking my back, hushing me.

I hate the bad man. I hate myself. I hate my parents. I've never felt so much sheer anger in my life. I feel like it's ripping me apart from the inside out. "I'm scared," I sob. "I don't want this to be true."

"I know. Neither do I."

We hold on to each other in the dim room, the shroud of reality enveloping us. We can't escape this. No matter what, this is us. We're tied together by this awful course of events, unknowingly walking the same path.

What's next? Where do we go from here?

I look up at him, searching his eyes, but all I can see is the hue of the purple and blue bruising around his eye and cheek and blood trickling from his nose. All evidence of his need to self-punish because of *me*.

"Maybe we just need some time," he says a little too hopefully. "To let it sink in. It's all fucked up."

Time. Everything in life comes down to time.

His eyes lock onto mine, endless pools of blue sucking me in. "I meant what I said earlier."

"I did too," I whisper.

Nothing could ever change that.

"Then that's what we have to focus on, right?"

I want to believe him...but his entire life has been built around

focusing on the bad things that have happened to him. It's why
he hides out here, ostracizing himself from his friends and family.
How is he going to move past that awful night, now that we both
know what happened? How will I?

I wait on the couch while he showers. I accept that I'm going to
need to talk to Dr. Reynolds first thing next week to discuss all
this. I've always felt regret over the boy being pushed into the
fire, but now that I know it was Tyler, it adds a whole new level
of insurmountable guilt. I'll probably be in therapy for the rest of
my life trying to come to terms with this, but no matter what, I
won't let it come between us.

"What are you thinking about?" Tyler asks when he comes
back to the living room in a pair of black gym shorts. I'm relieved
to see him without blood all over his face, not to mention that
terrible mask.

"Everything…how so many bad things happened to you in
your life because of that one moment…I want to go back and undo
it. I want to somehow change all of it for both of us." I shake my
head and try to fight back tears. "What did we do to deserve this?"

"I wish I knew. I just stood in that shower 'til the water turned
ice cold trying to get my head around this…because if I don't, I'm
afraid I'm going to lose my mind. And you. I won't let that happen." He stares at the floor for a few moments, chewing the inside
of his cheek nervously before he continues. "If those things hadn't
happened, I wouldn't have been living out here. I never would
have found you in that hole." He sits on the couch next to me,
our legs touching. "It happened the way it had to happen. I guess
I was given a second chance to save you, and I didn't fuck it up
this time. It was worth it. You're safe. And we found each other."

I shake my head, still filled with so much guilt I feel nauseous. I can't stand the fact that anything I did, accidental or not, has caused so much pain in his life.

"I don't know, Ty," I reply with tears spilling onto my cheeks. "I would rather have never been found than have you ever get hurt."

A deep sigh pushes his chest up and down. "And I would fall into that fire a thousand times to be able to save you."

An ache soars from my heart and lodges in my chest. "In my books, love doesn't come with such awful repercussions. It makes everyone happy."

He flips his damp hair out of his face and turns to me, his eyes filled with determination. "I think you have to let those books go, sugar. This...what we're dealing with right here is reality. It's ugly and it fucking hurts like hell, but it's real. Life ain't no fairy tale. If we want this to work, we have to accept that."

"I need my books..." My voice is childlike, even to me. Maybe I was better off locked in the basement with nothing but books, TV, and Poppy. Maybe real life is just too hard for me.

"You don't, Holly. You're free now. You can let the books go. Those stories are over now." He grabs my hand in his and lifts it to his lips, closing his eyes as he kisses it. "We have each other, right? We have our own story."

I nod. "Yes, we do." *I hope.*

"Then we'll be okay. Nothing else matters."

I can see right through him, trying to be strong for me. But I know deep down, he's petrified, and so fragile with guilt and self-hatred he could crack at any moment.

We hold each other, kissing softly, until our hearts and minds calm down. We whisper promises to each other under our blanket, and as his clock ticks away the night on his mantel, I start to believe that he's right. We'll be okay.

Suddenly, Boomer's and Poppy's heads both shoot up from their sleeping positions, their ears twisting around like little antennas. A car door slams in the driveway.

"Is someone here?" I ask. "It's four a.m."

Ty kisses my forehead before rising from the couch. "Stay here." I pull the blanket over my lap as he crosses the small room and opens the front door, and a man steps inside, his heavy boots clomping against the wooden floor.

"What the hell are you doing here?" Ty asks. "Do you know what time it is?"

"Lighten up, scarface. I had a huge fucking fight with Darcy. I had to leave."

"She kicked you out?"

"Not really. It was just better for me to give her some space." He finally notices me. "Shit, I didn't know you had company, man."

Ty runs his hand through his hair and looks from me to the man. "Tanner, this is my girlfriend, Holly." I smile at the term *girlfriend*. "Holly, this is my brother Tanner."

A brother! I never would have guessed this person was a relative. They look nothing alike.

"Sorry to barge in," he says, fingering his beard. "Nice to meet you, though."

"It's okay," I reply, wondering if I should leave them alone since Tanner is clearly going through something. Ty's brother is a bear of a man, a few inches taller than Ty, and even more muscular. He's wide like a wrestler, taking up a huge amount of space in the tiny room. His brown hair is shaved on the sides, but the center part is braided and hangs well past his inked shoulders. He reminds me of a Viking I saw on TV.

He's dark and intimidating in comparison to Tyler's light hair and eyes, and boyish smile.

"I should go...," I say. "So you two can talk."

"No," Tyler barks. "You're staying."

Tanner puts his hands up. "I'm gonna go, man. I'm sorry... you're always alone, so I thought I could crash here."

Ty grabs his arm. "Fuck you. And you're not leaving either." He coughs. "Do you need to talk or do you just need somewhere to sleep?"

His brother picks up Boomer and throws him over his shoulder like a ragdoll, stroking his hand down his back. Boomer starts to chew on his hair. "I don't wanna talk, Ty, but I gotta say it's good to hear you talking so much. My brain's just too exhausted right now. I need to sleep, and I'll be out of here tomorrow."

"All right. We were just about to go up to the loft, anyway." Our eyes meet across the room and I nod as my heart does a little trot. "You can try to squeeze your ass on the couch."

Tanner shrugs. "I've slept in much worse places than this."

I stand and shyly offer him the blanket. "If you sleep with this, you'll feel better. It's magic."

Smiling with charm I didn't think such a towering, brooding man could have, he takes the blanket from me. "Thanks, sweetheart. I need all the help I can get right now."

Don't we all?

CHAPTER 28

Tyler

She cries in her sleep, and her body twitches as if it hurts. I watch her, wondering what's happening in her mind right now—what she's seeing and feeling. I worry about what demons could be brainwashing her.

I lie on my side and watch her sleep, taking in every delicate detail of her face, the length of her eyelashes and how they rest on her cheeks like little feathers, the way her lips part as she breathes. I want her in my bed like this every day, with the sun shining down on her golden hair like a halo.

Earlier, I teetered on the edge of letting guilt and regret consume me. First my father and now this...this insane fucking regret that's eating me like a virus. The night of the fire is still a haze in my memories, but I keep going back there, replaying every moment. If Wendy wasn't such a self-centered bitch, she probably wouldn't have laughed and ignored a terrified little girl. If I had been sober, I probably wouldn't have fallen when he pushed me. If I had just remembered everything when they questioned me at the hospital, maybe they would have found Holly right away.

So many fucking ifs.

The escape of drugs is so tempting. To go back to that place where nothing hurts, where I don't have to face all these unfair twists and turns of life, to go down that rabbit hole of numbness would be a great vacation right now.

But if I put myself in that place again, I'll let Holly down. I'll lose her, and all the happiness and hope that comes with her. I'll drag her happiness down with me. If I don't hide how much the guilt is killing me inside, it will tear her apart.

For her, I'll stay sober and straight.

For her, I'll put on the strong and happy mask.

For whatever crazy reason, she loves and trusts me. She sees past all my fuck-ups and ugliness and *bad shit*. Is she so lost in her fairy tale that she's blind to it all? Or does she honestly love me enough to accept it?

I don't even care. As long as she's here, in my life and in my arms.

She's everything. My past. My present. My future. My twin flame—the one who shares the path of my soul.

Tanner's already gone by the time we go downstairs for breakfast, and now she's staring at her food, lifting the pancakes with her fork, flipping them over. She catches me watching her from across the small table and quickly puts her fork down.

"I wasn't doing that," she says. "I was just looking at them."

I raise my brows at her. "You think I would drug you? Or try to bribe you?"

She looks down at her plate in guilt. "I can't help it. I just do it."

"I know, sugar. I just want you to be able to eat without being afraid of it."

"I do, too."

She slowly cuts up her food into tiny pieces and takes a cautious bite from her fork.

"Can I ask you something?" she asks in between bites.

"Of course."

"If I asked you to, would you stop doing the fighting?"

That's the last thing I expected her to ask me. "Maybe. Why?"

"Because I love your face. I don't want it getting hurt anymore."

You skeeve me out.

Her words rock me, right into my soul. She doesn't know how much her words mean to me, but I know she's the only person I'll ever meet who has the true capacity to understand. We're kinda made of the same ripped-up cloth.

I chew my pancake and swallow it, not able to get my voice to come out. Instead I stand, walk around the table, grab her face in my hands, and kiss her until she's breathless and clutching my shoulders. I fist her long hair at the back of her neck and lift her up off the chair, not breaking our kiss as I back her up against the table, pushing our plates to the other side. Fuck breakfast.

"Okay...," I whisper against her lips. "I'll quit fighting. For you."

That gets a big smile out of her. "You mean it? You won't fight anymore?"

"I won't...if you do something for me." I lift her up and set her on the table, moving to stand between her thighs, my hands circling her waist.

"What?" she asks curiously.

I lean in and nip at her neck, eliciting a faint squeal. "Leave your books home." I drag my tongue up the side of her throat. "Trust us to make our own story."

Her head falls to the side as I ravish her neck, and her throat hums. "Okay," she says. "I'll try."

"Don't try." I move my lips to her ear. "Just do."

Her hands slowly glide up my back, her nails leaving a trail of shivers up my spine. I lift the hem of her shirt and let my fingers skim across her stomach, feeling her twitch in response. I dive into her mouth, kissing her deeply, leaving her lips just long enough to get her shirt up over her head. My fingers hook in the straps of her bra and slowly lower them as I move down to kiss her neck, my tongue leaving a trail of dampness straight to her peaked nipple. She gasps when I suck it gently into my mouth, and her hands squeeze my shoulders. I cup her breast with one hand, while my other hand slowly travels down over the curve of her waist to the band of her sweatpants.

My *sweatpants. I have a beautiful girl wearing my clothes, kissing me on my kitchen table, even with my fucked-up face and our messed-up pasts.*

She lifts her body slightly as I slowly pull off her pants and panties, a subtle green light. I visit her mouth, and this time, her tongue meets mine, and her legs wrap tighter around me as we kiss until we're both moaning and frantically pulling each other closer, pressing our bodies together, seeking more. I cup her breasts in my hands, teasing the tips with my thumbs as I leave the sweetness of her mouth to bend down and kiss her stomach, my tongue lapping over the scars, erasing the intention of the word sliced into her. Her arms wrap around my head, hugging me to her, and she bows down and kisses the top of my head as I show her what *mine* really means.

Kneeling, I gently push her back with my palm until she's leaning back on the small table next to the sticky bottle of maple syrup. Her legs tremble as I caress her thighs. I drink in the sight of her before I touch my lips to her, so warm and wet, waiting for me. Her hips rise, and her hands grip the edge of the table when I run my tongue through her folds, slowly tantalizing her. I skim my hands up her inner thighs, and when they reach my mouth,

I gently part her with my thumbs and delve my tongue into her, licking her untouched walls. Her legs tighten around my shoulders, and her hand clutches the back of my head, gently tugging my hair as she squirms beneath me and sighs my name.

Witnessing her desire, and the trust she's put in me to share it with her, is the most beautiful experience of my life. It placates all my deepest needs and wants. The pleasure and love in her eyes is a much bigger turn-on than seeing fear.

My mouth finds her clit, pulsing with need, and I suck it into my mouth as I gently push my thumb into her. Her faint sighs and whimpers fill the room. My cock throbs as I fuck her with my thumb and my tongue, aching to sink into her wet pussy.

I will not fuck an abused virgin on my kitchen table.

No matter how bad I want to.

Standing, I move my lips up her body, sucking and nipping a trail up to her mouth. She kisses me hungrily as I lay my body over hers, and I lean my crotch against my hand, letting the weight of my body push my thumb into her, then slowly out, then in again, showing her what it's like to have a man's body between her legs, pumping into her. She tightens around my finger, her hands sliding from my shoulders to my neck, holding me and kissing me like I'm her lifeline. When she starts to shudder beneath me, I pull my mouth from hers so I can watch her eyes flutter closed, watch the shape of her lips as she comes, see the pulse in her neck throb.

As she comes down, I kiss her softly. My lips linger over hers as I gently pull my hand from between her legs and press my hard cock against her, feeling the warm wetness of her through my shorts.

I pull her up into my arms and carry her into the living room, settling down on the couch with her straddling me. She smells of syrup and lust, and I want to devour her.

"I love you," she murmurs dreamily against my lips. "The way you make me feel...I don't even know what to say."

"You said everything I need to hear."

She sits up on me, her long hair flowing down over her breasts. I grip her waist tighter, not wanting her to move. Every inch of my body is screaming for a part of her, even an innocent wiggle on my lap.

She fingers a lock of my hair absently and peeks at me shyly from beneath her bangs.

"I know what to do," she says softly. "For you..."

My eyes narrow at her in confusion as she stands, giving me a gorgeous view of her naked body. She kneels on the floor between my feet. I instantly snap out of my haze when she reaches for my waistband, and I grab her hands in mine.

"Holly..." My voice catches in my throat.

"I want to." Her gray eyes lock onto mine as she pulls my shorts down, and I'm powerless under her sweet, sultry gaze, and the sudden warmth of her mouth descending on my rock-hard cock.

All the way down.

My eyes literally roll back in my head as she expertly deep throats me, her lips touching my balls as she takes the full length of my shaft.

Oh, fuck. Nothing has ever felt so amazing.

Her tongue swirls around my tip, sucking hard, so perfectly... my cock and brain battle over the euphoria, and then the rage... Women aren't born knowing how to suck dick this way. This was taught. Practiced. *Perfected.*

Forced.

I grab her head in my hands and gently pull her off me. "Baby, you don't have to do this."

Her eyes shimmer, her lips still puckered and damp. "You don't want me?"

"I do, but..." Not if she's forcing herself out of some trained habit.

"Please let me be normal," she pleads with her hands gripping my thighs, on the verge of tears. "Let me forget. Let us both forget and just *be us*. I want you... only you... in every way. *You* are my choice. Let me show you. Let me love you. Please..."

Her wet lips sliding down my dick rob me of any defense, and I succumb to her, because I need her, and I love her, and I want all of her, and everything she makes me feel. No matter how hard it might be sometimes.

I guess we're perfect together because her demons are strong enough to wrangle with mine.

CHAPTER 29

Holly

Two months later

Time, something that once stood still for me, is now looming all around me. Choices need to be made, and no amount of talking to Feather and Dr. Reynolds has made it easier for me. Because I never had choices before.

Zac and Anna are moving soon, and their invitation to accompany them to New York is still a very intriguing option for me. A new start, away from this town, its memories, and its people who know every single thing that happened to me, feels like a good choice. I've wondered if that means I'm running away...but I don't think it does. I just want to be Holly, not the Girl in the Hole. But if I stay in this tiny town, that's who I'm always going to be. There has only been one time in the past year that I have gone out to the store, or to the cafe, or to the ice cream shop, where someone hasn't stared at me, whispered about me, or approached me. *One time.*

Soon I'm going to have a niece. A tiny little person who will only know me as Aunt Holly. I can watch her grow up, experience new things with her, and celebrate all the milestones that I missed in my own life and in my siblings' lives. She'll never have to know that once I was stolen. She'll never look at me with odd, fearful fascination like Lizzie does, still wondering how her dead sister is walking around. I blame my parents for that, and I've slowly accepted the growing distance between us. As Ty said, maybe in time that will get better, but for now, I have to make *me* better.

But going to New York means leaving Tyler. Not breaking up, but leaving our routine and trying to build a new one. He says he'll visit every weekend, but I know he won't. He's not ready to take that step yet. It's that time thing again—he needs it to gain his confidence back. I'm not sure how happy we'll be only seeing each other once or twice a month after we've been spending almost every day together. We both love our walks, our snuggles on his couch, our hanging out in his workshop, our long talks on his garden bench while Poppy and Boomer play around us. I'm afraid I'll miss him so much I might be miserable living so far away. Zac suggested that Tyler move to New York, too, so we can both have a new start, together. But Tyler loves the woods too much. He would go insane in the city, with no forest to walk in, and no mountains to explore on his motorcycle. He would be like a caged animal. He can't live in a place where he will be so totally out of his comfort zone, and I would never want him to. And he could never bring a fox to live in the city. Rehoming Boomer is not an option.

I cross my bedroom and pick up the letter that came last week. I hold it and read it again, for the tenth time perhaps. I almost threw the envelope out when it came, thinking it was junk mail, but at the last minute I tore it open. My mouth dropped when I realized it was from a publisher who wants me to write my story so they can publish it. Zac, Anna, and I had a conference call with them a few days ago, and they assured me it could be written by me, with the help of an editor, and they promised not to change my story or words in any way. They even offered me an advance for a surprising amount of money. All I have to do is sign the contract.

Do I want to write my story for the world to read? I'm not sure. I'm trying to get away from everyone knowing who I am, and what happened to me. Publishing a book about it puts me right back in that place I don't want to be in. And if I'm in a relationship with Ty, it puts him in that place with me, because I can't write my story without including him. What I really want to write is children's fairy tales, like the ones that filled my days with hopes and dreams. That's what the world needs to read, not stories about little girls getting kidnapped. Anna suggested I approach the publisher with that idea, and I just might, once I get my thoughts together about it.

Another choice to make, on top of all the others.

I pull one of my old books out of my backpack and thumb through the worn, dirty, faded pages. In these stories, there aren't any hard choices. Everything somehow magically works out. I turn to the last page, where the couple is walking happily in the distance together, and I touch them with my finger. Maybe the happily-ever-after just doesn't happen, after all.

CHAPTER 30

Tyler

I inhale more smoke and turn the small ring over in my fingers. She'll never see it or wear it. But I feel a strange sense of comfort knowing it exists. It took me weeks to make, melting down the coins from my jar and fabricating a band of thin, intertwining branches. The tiny carved copper bird's nest, filled with three miniature blue gem eggs, took the longest. A tiny piece of forest that would have sat on her finger. A weirdly good engagement ring that will stay in my drawer for the rest of my life.

What am I doing?

She's home packing right now, getting ready to move to a big city and start an actual new life. She has so many possibilities: She could be a model, write a book, go to college, make new friends. The sky she loves so much is truly the limit. I promised her everything would be okay, that nothing will change. Every word a sword through my heart and an utter lie.

I don't want her to go. She's my heart, my love, my best friend, my sensual angel with broken wings. We've only just started our journey, and I know we could go so far, all the way to forever...

But if I love her, I'm supposed to set her free. Isn't that what we're told? She's choosing to go, and I can't stand in her way. What can I possibly offer her? A life of hiding in my bubble?

This, I tell myself, is the way it's supposed to be. Because I'm a mess and she's a mess, and together we'll probably be an even bigger fucking mess because my life has been, and probably always will be, one disaster after another and I refuse to do that to her, or to us.

She's leaving.

I know my role in this story: I'm supposed to let her go. She's supposed to be the one that got away, the one I'll dream about, fantasize about, and wonder about for the rest of my life. I've known that all along. I may be the hero, but I'm not the happily-ever-after.

I can't let her be like the fox, afraid to go out and live, trapped with me in a little place of nothingness in the woods where time barely moves. She deserves so much more. She deserves to see the world that was taken from her and experience all the wonderful and beautiful things that life has to offer her. Being with me will only hold her back.

I'm going to let her go and watch her fly. I'll watch her from afar. I'll catch her if she falls. Every time. Any time. But I'll step back into the shadows and let her be free to have endless choices without me and my issues holding her back.

And me? I'll be happy knowing *she's* happy. I'll hang on to every moment, every memory, every touch, every kiss. I'll remember how it felt to be so unconditionally wanted, loved, and accepted.

CHAPTER 31

Tyler

"What's got you looking more fucked up than usual?" Tanner asks, punching my arm as he walks past me at my workbench and sits on the stool on the other side.

Holly's stool.

"Nothin'. Just working."

He cocks his head at me. "Don't bullshit me, Ty. You've been moping for days."

"Shouldn't you be at the shop? Or at your own house?"

"I took a few days off." He pulls a knife from his ankle sheath and starts to clean his nails with the tip. "Darcy won't answer my calls or texts. She doesn't want me in the house."

Frowning, I glance up from the belt buckle I'm polishing, and he's got a dead-serious look on his face. Tanner has been with his wife forever, and I've never seen them fight, or even raise their voices at each other. I guess while I've been hiding, a lot has changed.

"What happened?" I ask.

"I fucked up. Bad. And I have no idea how I'm going to fix it."

"I'm sure you'll work it out. She loves you."

He scrapes the knife along his nail. "I don't deserve her love right now." He blows out a deep breath. "I don't want to talk about it. You havin' a problem with that little cutie with the blanket? She's a fuckin' doll, Ty."

I shoot him a warning glare and he grins back at me. "I know who she is, Ty. I wasn't born yesterday. I think it's cool. Maybe now you'll get your head out of your ass."

"It ain't gonna last. She's moving."

"Moving? To where?"

"To New York with her brother and his girl."

He grimaces. "Why the hell would she want to live in New York?"

"To get away from everyone in this town who knows what happened to her. She goes through the same shit I do. Assholes staring and asking questions. She wants to go somewhere where nobody recognizes her. Her parents treat her like crap."

"That's a lame reason to move, isn't it?"

"You don't know what it's like, Tanner. It sucks."

"How do you feel about her moving?"

"How do you think I feel? I love her. I don't want her to move. But I'm not gonna ask her to stay here just for me."

He flips his knife up into the air and catches the handle. Someday, I know he's going to slice his fingers off doing that. "Did you tell her you don't want her to go?"

I sigh. "Not exactly."

"Why the hell not? You're gonna let some beautiful chick that believes in magic blankets just walk out of your life?"

I shake my head at him, growing annoyed with this conversation. "Because I want her to be free to make her own choices. Because for eleven years she had no choices at all. That's why. It's the right thing to do. We haven't even been together that long. I have no right to ask her to stay, no matter how I feel about her."

"Has it occurred to your dumb ass that maybe her choice is you, and she just wants you to man up and tell her what you want? Maybe she needs to hear it. Did you forget that Mom and Pop got hitched just a month after they met? So don't give me that time bullshit."

"This is different."

"It's not. Trust me on this; women want to hear what you want. They want to be swept off their feet a little. I learned that the hard way. She doesn't have to move all the way to New fucking York to get away from this town, Ty. As Pop used to say, use your head. And for the love of fuck, tell her how you feel." He shoves his knife back into its sheath and stands up. "I'm gonna go crash on your couch. Don't screw this up, Ty. You finally have a chance to be happy."

As he walks out, Poppy comes running in and sits at my feet, wagging his tail expectantly.

"All right, all right," I mutter.

I spend the next week putting a plan together with Tanner's help. He seemed to need the distraction just as much as I needed the help.

By some miracle, the first part of my plan falls into place with incredible ease, as if it was meant to be. Now I just need the second part to come together. I text Lukas, my tattoo artist, who's the king of all things artistic:

> Hey—you interested in doing a custom illustration for me?

Lukas
> Hey man :-) A tat, or...?

> An illustration on paper. A few of them.

Lukas

> I'm always up for that. Whatever you need,
> stop by tomorrow night and we'll go over it.
> Come late like you usually do.

> I'll need it fast. Within a week
> if possible. I'll pay ya extra.

Lukas

> I can do that. Does this have something to do with
> the girl you told me about at your last session?

> Yeah. It's something special
> I want to do for her.

Lukas

> No charge then. Consider it a gift from me
> and Ivy. But bring her with you for your
> next ink. I'd like to meet her.

> You got it. Thanks, bro.

Boomer jumps into my lap, knocking my cell phone out of my hand. I pet him as I stare out the window, thinking about how lucky I am that even though I've pushed people away and acted like an asshole to most of them, they're still there for me, waiting for me to come around. Pop was right that awful night we fought. I can still have the life I want.

CHAPTER 32

Holly

My apartment looks incredibly lonely with my and Feather's things all packed up and piled in the living room. Tomorrow she's moving in with Steve—she's packed twelve boxes of stuff—and I'm waiting for Zac to pick me up in his rented truck and take me to New York to begin the next phase of my life.

I have three boxes and two bags of clothes on hangers. As I examine our piles of belongings, it feels very depressing that my entire life, everything I own, fits into just three cardboard boxes.

I'm nervous about the move. Anna has raved endlessly about New York, sending me links and pictures of all the things we can do and see, like museums, aquariums, and art shows. New York looks fascinating, busy, and noisy—easy to get lost in. I guess, in some ways, I want to be lost just as much as I don't want to be. I want to blend, to not stick out. To not be noticed.

People don't understand when they ask me what I want in life and I answer that I just want to feel safe, warm, and loved. To see the sky every day. I don't want money. I don't want things. I don't want fancy clothes or cars.

I want my prince, with his beautiful blue eyes and his crooked smile and his messy hair and his scarred-up inked arms, his crazy grinning fox, my fuzzy white dog, long walks in the forest, Christmas trees, and kisses that take my breath away.

Most of all, I want him to ask me to stay, to live in the woods with him in a storybook house surrounded by pretty flowers and wildlife. I want to watch him work and see his smile every day and drink bubble tea. I want to lie in the grass with him, and hear his beautiful raspy voice tell me what all his tattoos mean. But no matter how hard I hoped, he didn't ask me to stay.

A knock on the door startles me, and I assume it's probably one of the other residents coming to say goodbye, or maybe Dr. Reynolds. I cross the room and open the door; no one is there—but there's a large rectangular box on the ground. I look toward the other apartments and across the parking lot, but I don't see anyone. I pick up the box, close the door behind me, and carry it over to the kitchen counter. I don't have a knife, so I have to rip it open with my fingers. Inside is another white satin box with the dried flowers with the smiling faces sprinkled on top of it. Cocking my head with curiosity, and with a fast-beating heart, I open the lid, push aside purple tissue paper, and find a brand-new leather-bound fairy-tale book with a beautiful illustration on the cover of a two-story cottage, dotted with velvety moss and flowery vines, surrounded by a thick forest, flowers, and hovering hummingbirds. In the distance is a small white bridge over a river.

It's titled *The Story of Us* in gold flourishing script and has gold metal embellishments on the corners.

It's breathtaking.

I turn the page, and there are no words, just a colored illustration of a blond girl walking through the trees with a little white dog at her feet.

Tears spring to my eyes, and I cover my mouth with my hand as I look over to the next page, which has a man with long blond hair, also walking alone in the woods, with a red fox running in the distance.

Oh my. It's *us*.

I turn the page, and now the couple is walking together, holding hands, and on the next page, they are sitting on a blanket, having a picnic. I turn to the next page, and it's a winter scene, with snow falling over a decorated Christmas tree in the woods and a white dog and red fox playing with a red bow. Swallowing over the lump forming in my throat, I turn to the next page. Here, the couple is lying in the grass, with puffy white clouds in the sky. On the adjacent page, the girl is sitting in a field of flowers, and the man is watching her from the side. I turn to the last page, and the man is on one knee, proposing, and the girl is smiling down at him.

And on the very last page, they are on a motorcycle, and she's wearing a white wedding gown, the veil trailing behind them in the wind as they head down a winding mountain road toward the little cottage pictured on the front cover. The white dog and fox are waiting for them on the porch. Five words are typed above them in the clouds, in ornate script: *Believe in your fairy tale.*

Tears fall down my cheeks as I hold the fairy-tale book made of us. My heart hurts as I turn the last page over and find a hand-written note:

Holly,

I'm not a prince. I don't have a white horse. But I have a bike. And a ring. And a new house in the woods, in a town where nobody knows us. I'll start to go out. With you. I promise. I have Poppy and Boomer. I'm a good weird.

I have all the love in the world for you.

We can fill in the words together.

Meet me outside, and I'll take you to our happily-ever-after.

Love always,

Ty

I can't move. I have to force myself to breathe.

Is this real?

I blink several times, but the book is still in my hands. I close my eyes and count to ten, then open them. It's still here. I read the note again. The words are the same.

Holding the book against my chest, I slowly walk to my front door and swing it open. And there he is...leaning against the seat of his motorcycle. He smiles when he sees me, a real smile, the one I live to see every day, and he slowly swaggers over to me.

My heart gallops in my chest like a wild pony at the sight of him. *My prince.*

"Tyler, I—" He grabs my face and kisses me, long and slow, dizzying me, making me forget my own name and everything I wanted to say. I wrap my free arm around his neck and hold on to him tight. I don't know much about life and love, and how it's all supposed to work. I still have so much to learn and experience. But I do know that I want to do it all with this man, and no one else.

When we finally part, he takes a deep breath, reaches into his pocket, and pulls out a tiny box.

"I love you," he says with throaty emotion. "I don't want you to go. Ever. I thought letting you go was the right thing to do...but I can't. I don't want to lose you, or not be with you every day. And I really don't think you want to go. We'll go slow. Or fast. Whatever you want. I found us a perfect house. We can start new together. Away from the assholes of this town. I even had a ceiling window put in the bedroom."

I smile and burst into happy tears. I've never heard him talk so fast and excited. "Ty...I love you so much..."

He flips open the box and pulls out a small ring. "Poppy wants to know if you'll marry me...when you're ready?" Taking my hand in his, his eyes meet mine as he waits for my answer.

"Yes," I whisper, smiling ear to ear. "That's all I want."

He gently slides the ring onto my finger and lifts my hand to his lips. "Now you're my princess." His crystal-blue eyes sparkle with promise. "I'm here forever. No matter what life throws at us. We'll never be lost or alone again."

My heart feels like it's going to burst when I see the beautiful little bird's nest on my hand. Before I can ask, he answers me. "I made it from my coins. There wasn't enough to buy a ring. I screwed up the tradition."

I laugh and circle my arms around his waist, resting my head against his chest, right over his heart. "You didn't mess up anything. It's so perfect. I love it."

He strokes my head and hugs me with his other arm. "I've been texting with Zac for weeks. He's not coming. He was pretty sure you would say yes."

"Weren't *you* sure?"

"I was hoping."

"So was I...you have no idea." I hug him tighter.

Touching my chin, he coaxes me to look up at him. "I have a really good idea what hoping feels like." He bends down to kiss the tip of my nose. "I can't wait to show you our new house. Poppy, Boomer, and my bed are already there. We'll do the rest together. I've been texting with Feather, too. There's a guest room with her name on it." He takes a deep breath and takes my hands in his. "I have to stop hiding. I need to fix things with my family. I hope you're okay with this...but Feather set up a housewarming party. Next week. Zac and Anna are coming, and your grandma. Feather and Steve. And my family. Your parents haven't answered yet...but hopefully they'll come around..."

I nod, letting my excitement about bringing our families into our life push the disappointment about my parents to the side. "Oh wow...I would really love that."

"You're gonna love the house, it's even better than mine."

"Can we go there now?" I ask excitedly. I can't wait to step inside the beautiful little house pictured in the book.

He flashes me his adorable smirk. "That was my plan, sugar."

This time, I'm not nervous at all when I get on the back of the bike with him. I wrap my arms and my legs tight around him, my body pressed against his. He reaches down and squeezes my hand on his waist, and we ride off into the blue horizon, way up into the beautiful White Mountains, past farms with cows grazing and sparkling waterfalls, to the most perfect cottage nestled at the edge of the forest. As we pull into the stone driveway, I'm so giddy to get closer that I almost jump off the bike before Ty pulls in front of the walkway leading to the front door.

When we're safely off the motorcycle, he grabs my hand and stands beside me as I breathlessly take it all in. I'm overwhelmed by the perfect sense of *home* that overcomes me. The cottage is nothing short of whimsical, with a tin roof, arched wooden door, stone siding, and a small balcony on the second floor. I'm delighted to see there's also a small barn a few hundred feet away, which I am sure will be Ty's workshop. The property is blanketed in lush grass, huge trees offering lots of shade, flowers in rainbows of color (even my smiling flowers!), wooden birdhouses, and birdbaths...and the old garden bench from Ty's yard. The fact that he moved the bench where we spent hours sharing all our hopes, dreams, and sorrows with each other brings tears to my eyes. This seemingly simple act shows me he values our memories and our journey just as much as I do.

"Ty . . ." I shake my head slowly, still in disbelief. "It's beautiful."

"It's old, but it's solid as a rock. The plumbing and electric are new. The kitchen and bathrooms have been updated, but they kept its charm. You ready to go in? Do you want to go in alone first? There's a basement in this one. But it's empty except for some old bottles and tools, and there's a doorway to get out."

I wait for the flash of fear to come, bracing myself for the cold chill that will creep up my spine and spider out to my limbs . . . but it doesn't come. I feel nothing but peace and comfort here, surrounded by all the things I wished were real as a little girl . . . and now *are* real.

"No," I say as my thumb lightly runs over the band of my engagement ring. Its smoothness grounds me, becoming my new security blanket—my own symbol of love, safety, and belonging with a person and place. "I want us to go in together." My stomach does a quick flip-flop when he turns and winks at me, and we approach the front door to our home together, side by side.

"What about your little house?" I ask as he digs in his pocket and pulls out a key. Knowing how much his house means to him, I'm worried he will miss it if he leaves just to get this new home for us.

"We'll keep it. Tanner is going to stay there while he figures things out. I'd like to keep it in our family. Who knows, we might want a place to escape to on weekends if we have kids someday."

Oh my . . . he's talking children . . . A vision of little shaggy-haired, blue-eyed blond toddlers running through the grass with Poppy and Boomer stamps itself on my internal wish list for life.

His hand hesitates on the doorknob as he eyes me from behind the shock of hair that's fallen across his face. "You okay with a kid or two? With someone like me?"

"Only with you," I whisper, afraid if I say the words too loud, some evil life force will hear and come snatch it all away from me as punishment for escaping the bad man.

A wistful glint sparkles in his eye. "I'm gonna hold you to that." The key clicks in the lock, and he pushes the door open, motioning for me to enter first. As I do, Poppy and Boomer come running to us, their nails clicking on the slate floor like little tap dancers.

I kneel down and let them jump on me for cheek kisses. "Do you guys love your new home?" I ask. Boomer does his crazy fox squeal and wiggle, and Poppy wags his tail wildly with approval.

"I think they like it," I say, standing to gaze around the small foyer we're standing in.

"We can go furniture shopping tomorrow and pick up your things." He leads me to a living room with windows overlooking the front yard and a stone fireplace on the far wall, similar to the one at his house. I nod, unable to muster up words to describe the happiness I feel. We tour the small dining room and kitchen, and a room that could be a bedroom or office, with glass doors leading to the back patio. Everything about the cottage is so incredibly charming with its earth-tone paint and wood and stone accents that Ty informs me were harvested from the property. I can feel the love that was put into years of making such a unique home, and I vow to continue to love it just as much for the rest of my life. As we walk through each room, I can't imagine ever living anywhere else.

The very best part of this house, though, is the second floor, which has a bathroom, a small guest bedroom, and a master bedroom that Tyler has turned into the most romantic room imaginable with his bed perfectly positioned under the new skylight so we can watch the clouds and stars while we snuggle beneath it. Above the bed he's hung an elaborate dream catcher to capture our bad dreams and cherish the good ones. Photos of his Christmas trees, Poppy, and Boomer are hanging on the walls in vintage wooden frames. An entire wall is an actual bookshelf... waiting to be filled with books and statues. Scented wax warmers are placed on the nightstands, glowing with dim light and permeating the air with the sweet scent of vanilla. And finally, the very best part that steals my breath, dried smiling flowers sprinkled on and around the bed and our folded magic blanket. He watches me nervously, waiting for me to react, but I'm suspended in disbelief, unable to find words, because none of them come close to describing the extreme love and gratitude coursing through me.

Ty understands me. Cares for me. We share the same pain and hope. I've witnessed him go from a man of no words or smiles, who yawned at my arrival, to a man who has healed me with patience, words, and caresses. He blesses me with the most handsome, sexy smile ever, and has now given us a home that promises a lifetime of special memories.

After moments of silence that really isn't silence at all, but a space of time filled with a deep exchange of emotions that are better felt than spoken, he pulls me into his arms and covers my mouth with his, once again pulling me into that mesmerizing place where I can't think but can only feel. As his mouth possesses mine, and his hand slips to the back of my neck to clench a handful of my hair, tugging gently as his kisses deepen, I feel *so* much. I slide my hands up the back of his shirt, needing to feel his skin, the warmth and solidity of him. A faint moan sounds in my throat when his tongue sweeps fervently over mine, and his hand roves down over the curve of my hip to cup my ass, pulling my body hard against his, letting me feel him pressing against me through our clothes. The hardness of him ignites an army of electric tingles that flow from the center of my thighs and disperse in all directions—to my breasts, to the tips of my fingers, to my toes—every cell aching for more of him and the sensual static he creates.

So this is desire... feeling I may just die if we can't possess every inch of each other.

He cradles my face in his hands, and our kisses subside to barely-there, feathery touches. His eyes are as deep and alluring as a midnight ocean, locked onto mine as he continues to render me powerless with his lips. Weak and wobbly, I lean my body further into his.

"I love you...," he whispers against my lips.

"I love you...I love this house." I let out a dreamy sigh. "I love us."

He tilts my head back and kisses my throat, sucking lightly before moving his lips up to brush his nose across my ear. "I'm fuckin' wild for you. I'll build you a castle up in the clouds to make you happy."

"No...I never want to leave here." I turn my head to catch his lips, and he kisses me hungrily, backing me up until my legs hit the edge of the bed. Gently, he pushes me back onto the bed, among the dried flowers that I'll gather up later and put in a box with the notes he's given me. I want to save every souvenir of our life together that I possibly can.

I circle my arms around his neck as he gently falls on top of me, and I welcome the careful weight of him. His thick hardness between my legs sends quivers through my thighs, and when he grinds himself against me, my insides scream, *Yes, more.*

Feather told me, during one of our late-night ice cream chats on the couch, that someday my mind, body, and heart would all come together with the right guy, and I'd want him like crazy in every way possible—regardless of the things that had been done to me. And, boy, was she right.

I lift his shirt and he quickly pulls it off. His skin is like sizzling velvet under my tentative touch. He dives into my neck, devouring the sensitive spot near my collarbone. His hair falls across my face and neck—soft and smelling of coconut and tobacco, the sweet, masculine scents tangled together in such a perfect representation of him.

He slowly removes my shirt and bra, his lips and fingertips trailing up and down my arms, then down between my breasts, teeth grazing here, tongue caressing there, coaxing each inch out of its coma of sensation. My body awakens under his patient, sensual touch as numbness recedes into the shadows of the past, and a deep yearning takes its place, here to stay.

He stands and removes my boots, then reaches for the button of my jeans, glancing up the length of my body until his gaze rests on my face, searching my expression for a sign of consent, and I smile softly.

Yes.

My jeans and panties are slowly pulled off, and he kneels at the end of the bed, his hand still holding my foot, and he plants a ring of kisses around my ankle, following the faded rope scar from so long ago. Mistakenly, I thought it had healed, but I realize it hadn't, not really, until this man I love put his hands on me and freed me. He moves up my body like a lion, slow and sure, dragging his tongue up my inner thigh, sending goose bumps across the surface of my skin. I reach for him, my hands just barely touching his tousled hair, but he resists my urging. Instead, his lips halt right below my belly button. He traces the lettered scars with his lips, lavishing kisses across each one, his hands capturing mine at my sides. As I close my eyes, a single tear slides down my cheek. Maybe it's for the little girl who was sliced for crying too much for her mommy. Maybe it's for the man who's always going to punish himself. Or maybe it's for us, for being so twisted and tied with guilt and love.

A twin teardrop falls upon my chest as he crawls up the bed, and my heart clenches with overwhelming love for him. He kisses my lips, then pulls away slightly. "We're going to be weirdly good together," his raspy voice whispers. "I promise."

I smile against his lips as they come down on mine again, harder this time, sealing his statement. *I know we will.*

His hand slides languidly down between our bodies as we kiss, his fingers expertly working their magic, his thumb flicking my clit into a frenzy while his finger gently pushes into me.

I reach up and push his hair back from his face and move my lips across his cheek, kissing across his scars, until I reach his ear. "I want you," I whisper.

His breathing deepens as I slide my hands down his muscled back until I reach the band of his jeans, skimming my fingers to the front to unbutton them. He leans up a bit and watches me with lustful eyes as I pull the zipper down. Noticing the tremble of my fingers, he covers my hand with his and kisses me long and deep, his warm breath mingling with mine, before standing to kick off his boots and step out of his jeans. I'm unable to take my eyes off him, my cheeks burning as I take in his muscular, tattoo-decorated body. The scars might be there, but I don't see them. All I see is a whole lot of hotness that even my virgin body is undeniably craving. Call it chemistry or instinct, lust or love. It's all those things and more...and I'm damp between the thighs, my pulse quickening, reveling in all his hard, commanding nakedness.

As I lie there thanking whatever God may be listening for the love and devotion of this beautiful man, a flicker of confusion distracts me when he pulls his wallet out of his jeans pocket, but understanding slowly settles in when I realize what he's doing. *Protection.*

My eyes widen as he saunters back to the bed.

"You are so. Fucking. Beautiful." He cups my breast in his hand, lowering his head to swirl his tongue over the peaked nipple before pulling it into the warmth of his mouth, the graze of his teeth making me gasp.

Grasping his cock, he rubs the tip slowly up and down my opening, and my entire body quivers and clenches at the sensation. I grip his arms, biting my lip.

His mouth meets mine again, and a groan sounds in his throat when I press myself up against him and wrap my leg around his. I'm a puppet to the mounting passion, succumbing to the strings of desire.

"Tell me you want me again," he begs, his voice deeper and growlier than ever, and it melts me like warm chocolate.

"I want you." I kiss his lips softly and stare up into his fiery blue eyes. "All of you. Always."

He slides into me, hot and throbbing, showering me with never-ending kisses as he moves in and out of my depths, my body stretching to take him in.

If it hurts, I don't feel it. That part of me was taught to shut off long ago.

What I *do* feel is an exquisite ecstasy that builds with each thrust and an intense craving to ride against his hard body and bury my face into his neck as he shudders and moans my name. Within seconds I'm chasing him to that same place, my body quivering uncontrollably, my heart pounding in perfect unison with his.

Touching my cheek, he brings my face to his and kisses me so softly...so lovingly...and for so long that I think my heart will finally burst into a million pieces just so I can love him even more.

He grabs the magic blanket and pulls it up over us, turning us onto our sides together, wrapping me in his embrace under our ceiling window. Just as we slip into a blissful nap, Poppy and Boomer jump on the end of the bed and snuggle at our feet.

I'm not lost anymore. I'm finally home, where I'll be safe, warm, and loved by this beautiful man fate handed to me...and I'm going to make him smile every day for the rest of our lives.

Fairy tales *do* come true. You just have to believe.

They lived happily ever after.

BONUS SCENE

Tyler

I find her in the kitchen staring into the open silverware drawer. Hugging her from behind, I rest my chin on her shoulder, closing my eyes for a moment to breathe in the light cherry scent of her perfume. She relaxes back against me, but I sensed the anxiousness in her before she did.

I brush my lips across her ear. "What's going on with the forks and spoons, Sugar?"

Her chest rises and falls with a deep breath. "We only have four of each."

My eyes scan the drawer as I nod. "Yeah, that's how the set comes."

"But when we have company, there won't be enough. When your mother and my gram come…and if my parents come, we won't have enough, and then—"

I turn her in my arms and brush her hair from her face. Worry fills her beautiful eyes.

"We'll get another set." My version of soft voice still comes out raspy. "I'll go online and order the exact ones we have, so they'll all match."

She swallows. "But what if my parents don't come, then we'll have too many."

Ah, the real problem—the real *worry* is etched in her words.

She's afraid her parents aren't going to come to the little house-warming party my mother arranged. It was Mom's idea to have a small private dinner—just her, Holly's grandmother, and parents. A new start, she called it. I agreed it was time for me to be part of my family again, and I agreed even more that Holly's parents needed to get their heads out of their asses and start treating her like a daughter and not a stranger.

But it's been over a week since my mother emailed, then called, Mrs. Daniels and all messages have gone ignored.

A lone tear slides down my fiancée's face, and I capture it with my thumb, cupping her cheek and pulling her to me for a kiss.

"Don't worry," I whisper. "They'll be here, and we'll have more than enough knives and forks."

Nodding, she gives me a sad little smile that cracks my heart before she winds her arms around me and rests her cheek against my chest.

My soul starts to rage.

Fuck those douchebags.

I promised Holly I'd never let anyone hurt her again, and her asshole parents are about to find out I meant it.

It's just after noon when my motorcycle rumbles onto the black asphalt of the parking lot. I pull into a spot defined by perfect yellow stripes, kill the engine, and step off my bike.

Staring up at the six-story, mostly glass building, I light up a smoke. I wonder how many poor birds fly into this monstrosity.

The chains on my motorcycle boots clank on the stone walkway as I approach the—you guessed it—double glass doors. I snuff out my cigarette on the bottom of my shoe and shove it in my pocket before entering the building. Classical piano music is playing from hidden speakers in the marble-floored reception area. Two men in suits are sitting in black leather chairs, engrossed in a talk about file transfers. The walls are stark white, decorated with abstract paintings in grays, blacks, and glimpses of red. It's cold and sterile. I'd lose whatever's left of my mind if I had to work in a place like this all day.

I saunter to the reception desk, where a young woman who matches the decor leers at me suspiciously. Porcelain skin. Jet-black bobbed hair. Red lipstick. A thin silver headset sits on her head like some kind of administrative tiara.

"Deliveries are at the back of the building, you'll see the loading dock," she says.

"I'm not delivering, I'm visiting."

My raspy voice grabs her attention. "Who are you visiting?"

I lean against the curved partition she's perched behind like some rare animal. "I'm here to see Cynthia Daniels."

One of her eyebrows arches up. "Do you have an appointment?"

I shake my hair out of my eyes. "Don't need one."

Her dark eyes flash over the scars on my face. "Actually, you do."

"Actually, I don't. Press whatever little buttons you have to, and tell her she has a visitor."

"And who shall I say is visiting?"

Smirking, I say, "Tell her that her son is here."

Her throat bobs as she swallows and presses numbers on a keypad.

"Your son is here to see you," she says softly into her headset. "Yes, your son. Okay. I'll let him know." Her eyes shift back to me. "She says she'll be right down."

"Good."

I stroll around the lobby, ignoring glances from the two men in the leather chairs, and pop a stick of gum into my mouth.

When the elevator dings, I turn to see the silver doors slide open. Cynthia scans the room, forehead creased, until her gaze lands on me.

The expression on her face is priceless.

Her eyes widen. The smile on her lips drops to a thin line. Her complexion pales to almost the same stark white as the walls.

Grinning, I meet her at the center of the lobby under a large chandelier, which, from the look on her face, she's hoping will fall on my head.

"What are you doing here?" she seethes.

"Apparently you didn't get the invitation to your daughter's housewarming party, so I thought I'd deliver it in person."

Her nostrils flare. "I don't have time for this right now. I have meetings—"

"No problem. I can wait." I pull off my old leather jacket. Wearing only a faded black T-shirt, my muscular but very scarred, tattooed arms are on full display. Cynthia watches in horror as I flop onto a small leather couch and put my boots up on the glass table.

"Get your filthy feet off that table and get the hell out of here," she practically growls.

The receptionist's mouth falls open as she peeks at us from behind her computer screen.

"Careful, Cynthia," I say, chewing my gum. "Your mask is slipping."

Straightening, she plasters a fake smile on her face. "Why don't you come up to my office where we can speak privately?"

"I thought you'd never ask." I stand and follow her to the elevator.

"You've got a lot of nerve coming to my office," she says after the doors have closed.

"You've got a lot of nerve ignoring my mother's calls and

emails. And treating your beautiful daughter like shit." I step closer to her, and she backs up until her spine hits the wall. "Let's get something straight, Cynthia. Nobody treats the people I love like dirt. I'll train you like a fucking feral dog until you start acting right."

Fear flashes in her blue eyes.

"Like it or not, I'm here to stay. I'm marrying Holly. You can make this easy, or you can make it hard." I pop my gum in her face. "And guess what? Hard is gonna be a helluva lot of fun for me and pure torture for you."

The doors slide open on the fifth floor and I follow her down a long hallway, ignoring the curious faces peeking at me from gray cubicles. How can people sit in little boxes all day?

"What exactly do you want, Mr. Grace?" Cynthia asks as she leads me into her office, featuring a wall of windows. She closes the door behind us, then walks around her large desk and sits, gesturing to one of the two chairs on the opposite side like we're in a job interview.

Sitting, I say, "Come on, Cynthia, I'm gonna be your son-in-law. Call me Tyler."

Not looking at me, she begins typing on her keyboard, eyes riveted on the slim monitor in front of her. "I'm losing patience with you, Tyler. In case you haven't noticed, this is a place of business, and I have a lot of important work to do—"

I grab the power cord from her monitor and yank it out.

Her shocked gaze flies to me. "Put that back," she demands through clenched teeth.

"I'm going to shove it up your ass if you don't pay attention to me. You have a really hard time treating people you think are below you like humans, don't you?"

The quiver of her bottom lip tells me I struck a nerve.

"What's wrong with you?" I ask her. "Your daughter is beautiful. Smart. Sweet. Caring. Classy. She wakes up happy every day. She's a true survivor. Which is a miracle considering what she went through. But you treat her like she's damaged goods, or like she's a derelict stranger."

"She *is* a stranger to me. She's not my little girl—"

I shake my head in disbelief. "She is. Why can't you see that? Isn't she everything you'd want her to grow up to be?"

Her eyes water. "What that man did to her, it's…" She shakes her head. "It's disgusting. Unthinkable and deprived—"

"Exactly. What *he* did to *her*. To a defenseless child. He's the fucking pig, not her."

"You don't understand. It's all I see when I look at her."

Blood boiling, I lean forward. "Then look a-fucking-gain. Holly isn't what he did to her. Holly is a loving, innocent woman. She put her life back together. She put all that behind her. She's taking writing classes, she has a beautiful home, she's getting married—"

She scoffs. "To *you*."

"Damn fucking right to me. The one who saved her life and killed that asshole who took her. The one who loves her unconditionally, treats her like a queen, and gives her anything and everything to make her feel safe and happy. Including trying to talk some sense into her cunt of a mother."

Her head snaps back, her lip curling in revulsion. "I want no part of my daughter marrying a vulgar animal like you."

"And I want no part of having a judgmental bitch for a mother-in-law, but here we are."

"I think it's time for you to go."

I bark out a laugh. "I'll decide when this meeting is over. You might want to clear your calendar for the day."

"What's it going to take to get you to leave?"

"I want you to reply to my mother's email and tell her you'll be delighted to come to our housewarming party. Tell her you'll bring something yummy, like cream puffs. Then I want you and that spineless dick you call your husband to come to your daughter's beautiful home and act like you're happy for her." I let my gaze settle on her. "You look like a woman who's used to faking it, so that shouldn't be a problem for you."

A muscle in her cheek spasms. "Anything else?"

I rise from the chair. "Yeah, you can plan on coming to our wedding because for some crazy reason, your daughter wants you celebrating with her. If I have to shove you two assholes bound and gagged into the back of my truck to get you there, I will. I'll stop at nothing to give Holly what she needs to be happy."

Her expression softens slightly. "I'm beginning to see that."

"She deserves it." I spit my gum into her trashcan. "Thanks for the chitchat. I'll see you Saturday. Don't worry about Grandma, I'll be picking her up the day before so she can spend the night. She and Holly love spending time together."

I head for the door and pause with my hand on the knob. "Ya know what's really twisted, Cynthia? Holly is more hurt by how you and your husband treat her than she is about what that scumbag did to her. Maybe you should think about that."

She's sitting on the swing on the front porch when I pull into the driveway. Boomer and Poppy are lying together on the top step, tails wagging. My heart aches seeing my little world, wondering how the hell I got so lucky.

Even though our horrible pasts brought us together, I thank the universe every day for putting Holly in my life.

She meets me on the walkway, eyes sparkling, blond hair

blowing, a wool shawl wrapped around her shoulders. The beauty to my beast.

"How's my sunshine?" I ask, leaning down to kiss her.

"Great." She smiles up at me and grabs my hand. "Where did you go?"

"I had to take care of a little problem."

She glances up at me as we climb the porch stairs. "A lost dog?"

"Yeah. I don't think it's lost anymore."

"Good. Are you hungry? I made us vegetable soup."

Kicking the kitchen door shut behind us, I pull her into my arms.

"Starving..." I dip down to kiss her neck, my mouth traveling over her warm skin to her collarbone. "But soup can wait."

"It definitely can," she whispers, caressing my cheek.

Smiling, I effortlessly pick her up and carry her to our bedroom.

Holly

From the living room window I see their car slowly coming down our long gravel driveway.

My heart immediately kicks into rapid beats.

"They're here." My voice is soft, but filled with surprise. "I can't believe they actually came."

Tyler comes up behind me, peering over my shoulder. He rests his hand gently on my waist. "I can."

I feel like my feet are rooted to the floor as we watch them park in front of the house, climb out of the car, and approach the front porch. I know I'm supposed to greet them at the door but anxiety has me frozen. What if their faces are filled with fake smiles and judgment over our little house? What if they cringe away from adorable Poppy and Boomer, who expect everyone to pet them? What if they're rude to Tyler? It's one thing for them to act a certain way in their own home, but I can't allow them to be rude in *our* home—a place Tyler and I have vowed to never allow negativity. This is our sanctuary.

Tyler guides me to the front door with his arm around my waist and swings it open. My parents are on the doorstep—smiling nervously but without a trace of cringe. My mother is holding two white boxes that are tied closed with red-and-white-striped string that doesn't stop the scent of bakery goods from escaping.

"Come on in," Tyler says, closing the door behind them before extending his hand to my father to shake. I realize I can't remember if they've ever met in person before. "We're glad you came."

"Thanks for having us," my father replies. "This property is beautiful. How many acres do you have?"

"Ten," Tyler answers.

My father's brows rise with what I first think is surprise, but is actually praise. "Wow."

I still haven't uttered a word. I've leaned into their hello kisses, but I'm not sure of the right thing to say.

"This is my mother, Tammy Grace," Tyler says as Tammy joins us in the foyer. "Mom, this is Cynthia and Steve Daniels."

"We're so happy you were able to come," Tammy says.

"We are too," my mother says, glancing at Ty. "Tyler made sure we got the messages you sent me. I apologize for not responding."

"Let's go into the living room where it's comfortable," I finally say. "Gram is waiting for us in there."

Ty hugs me and presses a reassuring kiss to my temple as we all move into the other room. "I'll get us some drinks and snacks," I offer.

"I'll help." My mother follows me into the kitchen, where I start putting cheese and crackers on a wooden board Ty ordered when he bought more silverware.

"Holly, your house is beautiful," my mother says as she puts the bakery boxes in the refrigerator. "Everything is so unique and cozy."

The compliment is so unexpected that words catch in my throat for a few moments. "Thank you. Ty made most of the wood furniture...like the dining room table, the coffee table, the corner shelving unit...if I show him a picture of something I like, he just magically makes it for me."

"I had no idea he was so talented. You're lucky. I can't even get your father to fix the loose door on our closet." She laughs a little, and I do, too. I'm wary of this new, friendlier version of her, but it seems sincere. "I can tell how much he loves you."

Hesitantly, I ask, "Do you want to see the rest of the house? I have an office."

"I'd love to."

Poppy and Boomer follow us excitedly as we head down the hall. "I can't believe you have a fox living in your house. He doesn't make a mess, or get into things?" she asks with curiosity.

I smile down at Boomer, who's circling our feet. "Sometimes he has accidents in the house, and if we're not careful, he'll steal our food, but he's usually well-behaved. Ty's had him since he was just a little baby. Unfortunately, he got so used to being a pet that he couldn't be released. Tyler tried, but he just kept coming back. He's free to run around outside and in the woods, but he always stays right with us."

"That's fascinating. Lizzie would love him, and the little white dog, too. She's such an animal lover."

We enter my office, which is my favorite room after the bedroom, as it has lots of windows overlooking the flower garden, and I can see the barn—Ty's workshop—from the windows as well.

I lick my lips nervously. "Maybe, if it's okay, you could bring Lizzie here for lunch one day? I'd love to see her. She can play with the pets. They're very gentle; they won't hurt her. And I promise not to scare her. I won't mention anything about my past."

Her face falls, and she lets out a long sigh that carries a slight waver. "Holly, I'm so sorry for how I've acted. I know it's no excuse, but I had such a hard time getting over everything that happened. I realize it made me act like a horrible person and mother. I've made so many mistakes, but I'd like to start over, if you're willing to give me a chance?"

I blink at her. Even not knowing her very well, I know how hard that was for her to say. "Of course I am," I say with a hopeful smile. "I don't dwell on the past. I only believe in now, and the future."

She returns the smile. "I'd love to bring Lizzie here to visit you. She always asks about you."

"I'd really like that. You can come any time. We're home every day. This is where I work," I say, pointing to my desk where a stack of notebooks sits next to my computer. "But I do sit outside and write a lot, too."

Gazing out the window, she says, "I don't blame you. Your yard is just as beautiful as your house."

"We have a lot of birds and butterflies. And rabbits, deer, and squirrels. They inspire my stories."

"It's nice to see you so happy. Your father and I were initially worried about you moving way up here in the woods, being so secluded, but just being here . . . I can feel it myself. It has a kind of magical, peaceful quality to it, doesn't it?"

"It does. We really are happy here. We go for walks. We sit outside and watch the wildlife. And the stars at night are so bright. We cuddle and talk under my favorite blankets. It's like living in a postcard." Ty knew exactly what I needed to feel safe and happy, and he found the perfect space and home for us to build a forever together. We vowed to leave our horrible pasts behind us that day he asked me to marry him. Filled with love, faith, and hope, I happily got on the back of his motorcycle to come here, and I've never wanted to leave.

💜 💜 💜

After dinner, Gram disappears into the guest room for a few minutes and then returns, beckoning for Ty and I to join her on the love seat. Glancing curiously at each other, we sit with her.

"I have something special I'd like you two to have. Let's call it a wedding gift."

My stomach flutters at the word *wedding*. Our small ceremony is planned for just two months from today, right here in our yard. Every morning, Ty wakes me with a kiss and tells me how many days are left until I'll be his wife.

Gram hands me a tiny green velvet box. It's soft and worn in places, as if it's been touched often.

"Open it," she urges.

I do, and a small gasp escapes me when I see the two wedding bands inside, each engraved with an antique filigree design. The smaller, thinner ring has embedded tiny diamonds.

"These were mine and your grandfather's wedding bands. I'd love for you to have them and wear them with as much love and devotion as your grandfather and I did."

Tears well up in my eyes. "Oh, Gram...they're so beautiful." I touch the beautiful rings, remembering them on their hands. It still amazes me that sometimes my very young childhood memories unexpectedly sift back into my mind. I always consider them little gifts.

"We'd be honored to wear them," Ty says, his voice low and scratchy with emotion. "You're sure? These are special—"

The light in her eyes when she smiles makes my heart feel like it's bursting. "That's exactly why I want you two to have them."

"I love them, Gramma," I say tearfully. "You have no idea how much this means to me—to us. I promise we'll wear them every day with love and will never take them off." I hug her, gentle but tight. I can't wait to wear her wedding band nestled against the engagement ring Ty made for me, and to see my grandfather's ring on my husband's finger.

♥ ♥ ♥

Later, Ty and I stand on the front porch together and wave as my parents and Gram drive off. When their car has disappeared into the night, he pulls me into his arms and encircles my waist.

"You okay, baby?" he asks softly.

I nod. "Today went so much better than I thought it would. My parents were so nice, like I remember them from before."

His lips twitch into a small smile. "I noticed. I think they finally let go of the past."

"It seems like it. My mom is going to bring Lizzie over for lunch. I can't wait to see her."

He kisses the tip of my nose. "I'm glad."

"I really like your mom. When you were showing her your workshop, she was beaming. She loves you so much, Ty. I think we should spend more time with her, and the rest of your family."

Hugging me tighter, he says, "We will. And with yours, too. I like the idea of your Gram spending a weekend a month here with us."

"I do, too. She was excited when we suggested it. She's going to teach me how to cook something every time she comes."

He releases my waist to cup my face in his hands. "I love seeing you happy, and being loved the way you deserve to be loved. Nothing makes me happier."

I cover his hands with mine and stare up into his eyes. "I feel the same way. I want everyone to see you and love you the way I do."

"I only care about how you see me and love me."

My chest aches a little with love for him. "That's sweet... but I still want everyone to see how amazing you are."

We go inside and share the last of the cream puffs that my mother brought with her. Laughing, we kiss powdered sugar off each other's lips. We walk through the house with Poppy and Boomer chasing us, joining us for our nightly ritual of turning off the lights and drawing the blinds. Upstairs, we silently undress each other, and crawl under our soft magic blanket. The pets settle at our feet. I curl into Ty's arms with my face pressed against his chest, as close to his heart as I can get. He gently weaves his fingers through my hair, making my scalp tingle, until we drift off to sleep, completely content.

I used to sleep on a concrete floor, shivering in the cold. I used to eat stale bread. I used to fear the opening of a door and human touch. I used to think that smiles, family, and love were things I'd never have. But I never stopped wishing for them.

Believe in the fairy tale you see in your heart, no matter how out of reach it might seem.

EPILOGUE

IN LOVING MEMORY OF TYLER AND HOLLY GRACE

Tyler Grace, 85, and his beloved wife, Holly Grace, 73, passed away peacefully, within one week of each other, in their home on December 17 and December 24, 2070, following a mutual five-year battle with cancer. The loving couple had been married for "never long enough" as they often said. In the words of their daughter, they lived together, laughed together, battled sickness together, and passed together, just as they wanted to.

The couple is survived by their daughter, Talia, and her husband, Jake, as well as their son, Thomas, and his wife, Marli. They are loved by eight grandchildren.

Tyler was a metal wizard, crafting jewelry, accessories, and lawn statues in his home-based workshop. He had an extensive horror mask collection and a passion for vintage motorcycles and Christmas trees. His wife was his biggest love, and their children will fondly remember them as being the embarrassing couple that never stopped kissing and touching each other.

Holly is the bestselling author of ten children's books, most notably an illustrated series featuring their dog, Poppy, and pet fox, Boomerang, with whom they shared their life for many years.

The couple ran a nonprofit animal sanctuary with their children, giving a safe forever home to abandoned and terminally ill pets and wildlife.

They will be forever missed and forever loved by their family and friends.

IN CASE YOU MISSED IT,
READ TOREN'S STORY IN
THE PREVIOUS
ALL TORN UP NOVEL

"Well-written tension and forbidden longing. The angst in this was incredible! Loved every second!"
—Penelope Douglas, *New York Times* bestselling author of *Birthday Girl*

ACKNOWLEDGMENTS

This book was hard to write. I struggled, I cried, I screamed, I pounded the delete key. When I finally got my head back together, and the characters trusted me enough to write their story, I was very lucky to have some very special friends help me in more ways than I can count.

I don't like to publish names for privacy reasons. But I think... and I hope...that those special gals know how very much they mean to me, and how grateful I am to have them with me on my writing journey. Some have been with me since the beginning, and some are new, but each of them means the world to me and I wouldn't be able to write my characters without them. Honestly, I wouldn't be able to get through most days without their patience as I ramble and rant. Thank you for believing in me.

Never underestimate how much the simple act of just listening, or just saying hi, or just *being* there can impact another person's life.

Thank you to all my readers and the amazing people in my Facebook group! You guys make me smile every day.

Heartfelt thanks to all of you—whether you read my books, chatted with me, left a review, blogged, beta read, edited, proofed, promoted, commented, liked, attended a take-over, posted hot pictures of guys or cute pets in my group, or just listened to me—thank you! I love you!

As always, thank you to my love, Eddie Eddie Eddie, for being so patient with me, for all the little gifts to make me smile, and for talking to me for hours on end about my characters. I love you. ♥

ABOUT THE AUTHOR

Carian Cole has a passion for the bad boys, those covered in tattoos, sexy smirks, ripped jeans, fast cars, motorcycles, and of course, the sweet girls who try to tame them and win their hearts.

Born and raised a Jersey girl, Carian now resides in beautiful New Hampshire with her husband and their multitude of furry pets. She spends most of her time writing, reading, and vacuuming.

Carian loves to hear from readers and interacts daily on her social media accounts. To find out more or subscribe to Carian Cole's newsletter, visit:

CarianColeWrites.com

Facebook.com/CarianColeAuthor

Instagram @CarianCole_Author

X @CarianCole

TikTok @CarianCole.Author